A PLACE TO CALL HOME

www.**penguin**.co.uk

Also by Val Wood

THE HUNGRY TIDE
ANNIE
CHILDREN OF THE TIDE
THE GYPSY GIRL
EMILY
GOING HOME
ROSA'S ISLAND
THE DOORSTEP GIRLS
FAR FROM HOME
THE KITCHEN MAID
THE SONGBIRD
NOBODY'S CHILD
FALLEN ANGELS
THE LONG WALK HOME
RICH GIRL, POOR GIRL
HOMECOMING GIRLS
THE HARBOUR GIRL
THE INNKEEPER'S DAUGHTER
HIS BROTHER'S WIFE
EVERY MOTHER'S SON
LITTLE GIRL LOST
NO PLACE FOR A WOMAN
A MOTHER'S CHOICE

For more information on Val Wood and her books,
see her website at www.valeriewood.co.uk

A PLACE TO CALL HOME

Val Wood

BANTAM PRESS

LONDON · NEW YORK · TORONTO · SYDNEY · AUCKLAND

TRANSWORLD PUBLISHERS
61–63 Uxbridge Road, London W5 5SA
www.penguin.co.uk

Transworld is part of the Penguin Random House group of companies
whose addresses can be found at global.penguinrandomhouse.com

Penguin
Random House
UK

First published in Great Britain in 2018 by Bantam Press
an imprint of Transworld Publishers

Copyright © Val Wood 2018

Val Wood has asserted her right under the Copyright,
Designs and Patents Act 1988 to be identified as the author of this work.

A CIP catalogue record for this book is available from the British Library.

ISBN 9780593078495

Typeset in 11.25/14 pt New Baskerville ITC Pro
by Integra Software Services Pvt. Ltd, Pondicherry

Printed and bound in Great Britain by Clays Ltd, Elcograf S.p.A.

Penguin Random House is committed to a sustainable future for
our business, our readers and our planet. This book is made
from Forest Stewardship Council® certified paper.

For my family with love, and for Peter as always.

PREFACE

There were some who arrived in the town hungry and weary, with muddy cracked boots and threadbare clothing, having travelled on foot from other towns that were not so industrious as this one was. Or so it was said, for many of these travellers were unable to read, and had made the journey on the basis of rumours passed on by their fellow unemployed workers that this town had work to offer in industry and commerce.

Others were loyal agricultural labourers who, not having taken heed of the uprising in the countryside a decade earlier when angry young men took fiery revenge on their masters for poor wages, stayed faithful to their employers only to be dismissed because of the falling price of grain. They too set out to find work on the hard town streets rather than sleep under hedges while they starved in the countryside they loved, which had failed them so badly.

Then there were some who had travelled from afar, from Russia, Poland and Prussia, by foot and rail and ship, to find safety, but this town was not to be their final destination; they rested in the accommodation that had been prepared for them, bathed and ate, then shouldered their bags and crossed the station concourse to board a train to Liverpool. From there they embarked on vessels that took them away to another, larger country, where, so they had heard, there were even richer opportunities.

1

And then there were those who washed themselves and their clothes, ate the food that was offered them, slept peacefully, gave thanks for the kindness offered in friendship and then moved on to other burgeoning northern towns, such as Leeds and Manchester, in the hope of finding friends or relatives who had made the same journey and advised them of the prospects that were attainable.

But some, traumatized by their fear of what might have happened if they had remained in homelands that had rejected them, exhausted by their flight and their travel into the unknown, decided to stay in this town that had welcomed them to its shores, and put down roots of their own.

CHAPTER ONE

1854

It was a late afternoon in August. The sun was losing its heat, but it was still warm enough for Ellen to put her face up to the golden rays and know that her nose would freckle. She had made her monthly visit to her mother and father in Holmpton and shared Sunday dinner with them and her brother Billy, and was on her way to call on her friend Polly, one of six sisters, before she returned to the large farmstead a few miles away where she worked as a general maid.

She was humming softly to herself and gently swinging the basket containing a cake from her mother when she turned in at the Randells' gate and there was Harry, Polly's older brother, with a foot on a spade, digging over a patch of earth. She stopped and he looked up.

He had always lived in this remote part of Holderness close to the sea, as she had too until starting work for Mrs Hodges. She'd often seen him when she was growing up, for this was a small population of less than one hundred souls and everyone knew everyone else, but they'd never had a proper conversation; just a quick nod and a greeting, which was the usual thing for the lads in the village, who were mainly tongue-tied in front of girls. Since he had started work as a farm labourer she had seen less of him, but she recognized him at once.

'Hello,' she said. 'Is Polly at home?'

He'd taken his foot off the spade to look at her and with a quickened breath she thought that she hadn't realized how fair he was, his long hair bleached blond by the summer sun and tied at the back of his neck by a bootlace, and his eyes as blue as the sky.

'Erm, yeh, I think so.' He cleared his throat. 'Just go on in.' He indicated the house door, which was wide open. 'I think they're all there.' He chuckled and she saw how his eyes danced. 'Sometimes I lose count.' He came towards her, carrying the spade. 'I know you,' he said hesitantly, and with what she thought was a shy smile, 'but I forget your name.'

'Ellen,' she said. 'Ellen Snowden.'

'Not Billy Snowden's little sister? No, you can't be – not that young bairn!'

She wasn't sure whether or not he was teasing, or if he had her mixed up with one of her sisters. She had often been with Billy when he and Harry had hailed each other, or met at harvest time when the whole village turned out to bring it home, the girls and women wearing their bonnets to keep the sun off their heads, and the men with their shirt sleeves rolled up to their elbows.

She fingered the end of the thick brown braid which hung over one shoulder, and told him, 'I'm not a bairn any more. I was fifteen in May. I finished school in July and work at 'Hodges' farm.'

He continued to gaze at her and then suddenly blinked. 'Fifteen, eh? Well, good luck with your life, Ellen. The Hodges're good folk. So, are you planning on staying wi' them? Not spreading your wings and going to fly from 'village, are you?'

Ellen looked back at him and moistened her lips with the tip of her tongue. Not now I'm not, she reflected thoughtfully, although I might have done before. She shook her head, and as she walked towards the door she heard him begin to whistle a tune that was vaguely familiar. She'd heard it on a penny whistle; Irish, she thought it was, though she couldn't put a name to it.

Harry had seen her soft brown eyes, her chestnut-coloured hair. The old song sprang immediately to mind. 'Fifteen, eh?' he'd said, tongue-tied himself for once. Fifteen, the same age as his youngest sister Polly, and sister of his best friend Billy. He'd seen the shyness and the signs of burgeoning womanhood. He'd wait.

He was four years older than her, the same age as Billy, and he'd waited until she was old enough before he asked if they could walk out together; she'd just turned seventeen and she'd said shyly that he must ask her father and Mrs Hodges, and wondered if he had been counting the years. Mrs Hodges said that Ellen was a good worker and she'd be sorry to lose her, and that Cook was particularly put out, for she had said Ellen had good cool hands for bread-making. She guessed though that her parents would be relieved to have the last of their daughters courting, for she was one of eight girls and two boys.

'Summat in 'water,' her father had mumbled. 'This village is awash wi' daughters.'

They had begun their courtship along the quiet lanes of Holmpton on Sundays when they both had time off, and on one of those days he'd turned up early, driving a two-seat trap pulled by a sturdy mare that his employer Mr Oswald had lent him.

Her father had watched from their cottage window and asked Billy if she would be safe with him. Billy had looked out and nodded. 'Every hair on her head, Da.'

They'd driven down the long road to the peninsula of Spurn Point, where the sea lashed against the prominent finger of land and the estuary surged on the other side, and here it was that Harry told her about the tune he had whistled on that first day and again on this.

'It's an Irish folk song, I think,' he said, when she asked him. 'At least, I first heard it sung by a gang of Irish labourers who came to help with 'harvest one year.'

He'd taken hold of her hand as they stood watching the seabirds soaring above them, the first physical contact they had had. 'It's a song about a girl with nut-brown hair.'

'Nut-brown hair?' She turned towards him.

He nodded. 'The colour of a chestnut,' he'd said softly, and put her hand to his lips. 'Just like yours.'

5

She'd seen the love in his eyes and she gently moved her hand and reached on tiptoe to kiss him on the mouth. It was the first time she had kissed a boy and she knew she would kiss no other.

They married the following spring, walking in procession to Hollym, for Holmpton church, as ancient as the nearby crumbling cliffs, was unfit for weddings or funerals in case its medieval walls collapsed on the congregation. All of her sisters and Harry's were attendants, dressed in their Sunday best with flowers in their hair, and Billy was best man.

Mr Oswald had offered them a tied cottage on his land near the hamlet of Rysome and said that when the present foreman retired Harry would take his place. 'It's a job for life, Harry,' he'd told him. 'You're a good lad. I wish I'd had a son like you.'

He had no sons at all, but three squabbling daughters and a mean-spirited wife, which didn't seem right for such a generous and kind man.

'So there you are, my lovely,' Harry said, coming in on a cold March afternoon. 'Why aren't you working your fingers to 'bone instead of sitting there with your feet up all comfy by a warm fire?'

'Because,' she said, lifting her cheek to take his kiss, 'I'm feeding your daughter who won't wait a second when she's hungry.'

With a gentle finger he stroked her breast and bent and kissed the top of the baby's head. 'What's she having?'

'Yesterday's roast beef and Yorkshire pudding,' she said, laughing, and patted her daughter's cheek as she gave her father a milky toothless smile.

'Shall I burp her?' Harry asked, and she lifted Sarah, named after Ellen's mother, into his arms.

'Where are you off to?' Ellen fastened her blouse. 'Have you time for a cup of tea?'

'Mm, no,' he said, putting Sarah to his shoulder and gently rubbing her back until she gave a satisfying belch. 'I was passing on my way to 'farrier so thought I'd just check up on you both, see what mischief you were up to. I'm just getting this hoss shod,

6

and when I've tekken him back to 'farm I'll be home. Be glad to get indoors; 'weather's worsening.'

He handed the baby back to her. 'I'll be about an hour, but don't rush to get a meal ready; I'll have leftovers if it's easier. Just like Sarah.'

'Get away with you,' she said, and walked to the door with him, looking in satisfaction at the cotton nappies blowing in the east wind and thinking she'd bring them in before it began to rain, and then stood watching him as he walked the carthorse away down the track.

But he didn't come home in an hour as he'd said, and it was another hour after that before she heard his tread and then the scrape of his boots on the iron bar fixed to the wall and the rattle of the latch as he pushed the door open. She did not hear the usual cheery greeting and she paused in what she was doing, sensing that something wasn't right as he came into the room.

'It's Ozzie,' he said, with a break in his voice. 'He's dead. I found him in 'yard when I got back from 'farrier. Cold he was; no chance of saving him. When I hammered on 'door his wife and daughters were all in 'parlour singing hymns, while Ozzie was lying out there on his own. I went to fetch 'doctor but it was too late.' Tears flooded his eyes. 'Best man I ever knew,' he said. 'Better even than my own da; would allus listen to what anybody had to say.'

He swallowed hard and shook his head. 'They've took it bad,' he said. 'All wailin' and weepin' and cryin' what'll they do now without a man in 'house. It's not lookin' good, Ellen. I've got a bad feeling about this, as well as being devastated over his going so quick and unexpected. Not good at all.'

7

CHAPTER TWO

During the following eighteen months, as Harry helped the foreman to run the farm for Mrs Oswald, Ellen gave birth to another
daughter whom they named Maria, but everyone called Mary.
It had been a good farming year: the dairy cattle had yielded
more milk than usual, and they sold the glut to local cheesemak-
ers; they'd traded some of the young bullocks at a profit; and
the harvest had been brought in on time and fetched a reasonable price. Although he hadn't previously had any experience of
keeping accounts, Harry had helped Mrs Oswald as much as he
could.

Then one of the Oswald daughters, Dora, began courting a
man from Hedon and he had a different way of doing things; he
began looking after the books, and although Harry was relieved
to relinquish what he thought of as a chore he was also rather
suspicious of the man's motives, especially when he and Dora
announced their wedding date, in what in Harry's opinion was
undue haste.

Another twelve months went by and Dora's new husband,
Andrew Charlesworth, gave up his work as an accountant's clerk
and took over the running of the farm for Mrs Oswald and her
daughters. He gave the foreman, Aaron Jackson, his notice to
quit, and told Harry that in future he would be answerable to
him.

'Know about farming matters, do you, Mr Charlesworth?' Harry
asked him. 'About growing grain and fattening up bullocks?'

8

'I've read up about it,' he countered, 'I know how to read,' and looked at Harry as if implying that he didn't. 'I've also read that American wheat is far superior to English and that it's hardly worth our while growing it. I'm going to rethink our options.'

'We don't grow a lot of wheat,' Harry told him. 'Though we've got good land for arable crops, barley, rape, oats and rye, and root crops o' course; and Mr Oswald allus did well wi' cattle and pigs. We've allus been a mixed farm, a safer option if one crop fails. But we can't leave that amount of acreage fallow, so what would we grow in its place? More barley mebbe?'

'That's up to me to decide, not you,' Charlesworth answered sharply. 'We've no sheep, so I might diversify.'

'Sheep!' Harry looked askance. 'But our land here isn't suitable for sheep rearing. Up on 'Wolds with all their grassland, that's sheep country. Dairy, mebbe; I've often thought we could sell more milk to Hull dairies for mekkin' cheese.'

It wasn't like Harry to argue, but as he said to Ellen later, he couldn't bear to think that Ozzie's farm, which had been in his family for generations, could be swept away by sheer ignorance and arrogance.

'But surely Mrs Oswald should have some idea?' Ellen protested. 'She's been a farmer's wife; she would know about such things. I do, and I was onny a farm labourer's daughter.'

'She's not a countrywoman; Ozzie told me that some years ago,' Harry said. 'He said he was attracted by her pretty ankles!'

Ellen rolled her eyes. 'Men!' she exclaimed. 'I thought it was because of their cooking – or the colour of their hair,' she added mischievously.

Harry grabbed her round the waist and nuzzled into her neck until she shrieked for him to put her down and told him that she was expecting again. 'So you'd better treat me carefully.'

He kissed her and said he thought he did, and that she'd better provide a son this time to help him earn some money, for he didn't think that Mr Charlesworth would give him an increase. Charlesworth didn't, and he told Harry a few days later that he was going to breed sheep as he'd previously said. 'My wife fancies seeing lambs frolicking in the fields,' he smirked, and

9

then glanced suspiciously at Harry, who asked mildly if they'd be breeding them for their fleece or the meat.

'For the fleece, of course. She wouldn't want to have them slaughtered.'

Harry sighed as he told Ellen about their conversation. 'I'm going to have to look for another farm,' he said. 'At least, I'm going to ask around.' He took a breath. 'I won't be hasty, but I can't think that this job will last; it's not the job for life that Ozzie predicted.'

Charlesworth bought the sheep himself at a local market and bought twice as many rams as ewes; Harry reckoned that he couldn't tell the difference. Neither did he know anything about dipping, and had no ready pool or stream for them. The farm workers, used to harvesting grain and root crops and unused to sheep, went elsewhere, but loyal Harry, not wanting to leave the farm where he'd worked since leaving school, hung on.

Then, late the following summer, came the final blow. Charlesworth gave them notice to quit the tied cottage and told Harry he was taking on a Dales man who knew about sheep and would be bringing his family. He was going to make him foreman and told Harry he could stay on as a labourer if he wished.

'I'm contracted until November Hirings,' Harry said stubbornly. 'Or you can pay me up to then and I'll leave next week. Them's the rules, Mr Charlesworth, as you'll know, being a legal man.'

Charlesworth blustered and said he'd think about it and Harry hoped he hadn't been too hasty. They'd have nowhere to live and they now had three children to consider. As he'd asked, Ellen had dutifully produced a boy, whom they'd named Thomas.

'I can ask my ma if I can bring 'bairns and stay with them till you find another farm. Mebbe you can stay with your ma and da? They've both got more space since all our sisters have married.'

Harry wasn't happy about that either, but realized they wouldn't have any other option. But then Charlesworth changed his mind and agreed that they could stay until November. It seemed as if he had taken advice, and as he had no legitimate reason to sack

Harry it wouldn't look good in the farming community; word would get round and farmhands would be unwilling to work for him.

'We've time to pack everything,' Ellen said, trying to keep cheerful. 'You'll soon get another farm.'

But he didn't, even though he put out the word that he was looking for another position. There were seasonal labouring jobs, but Harry wanted something more permanent, something he could settle into.

'If we had the money,' he pondered one evening, 'I could settle for working for myself. Just a small plot, just enough to keep us.'

Ellen had shaken her head. 'No, you couldn't,' she said. 'You like 'security of working on big farms, you enjoy having a lot of acreage to look after, and, be honest, you like looking after large herds of animals too.' She paused. 'And 'camaraderie of working with other men.'

'Camaraderie,' he joked. 'My wife, the reader of big words.'

'Well, what would you have called it?' she challenged him.

He thought about it and then said, 'Aye, you're right. Companionship. Friendship. I do. I've known most of 'lads round here since I was just a nipper. I wouldn't really want to work on my own.'

He wouldn't, she thought. He was such an easygoing, friendly man. Everybody liked him. Everybody trusted him, and that was all very well, but if there were no jobs going . . . She sighed and thought that she might ask her mother if she'd be willing to look after the children for a couple of days a week, and ask around to see if there were any washing or ironing jobs in some of the big houses. Or she could ask Mrs Hodges if she could help out there.

When Ellen visited her mother she agreed that she would have the children for one day a week, but said she couldn't manage more. She was already looking after Frances's little girl and Julia's son for two days.

'I'm not as young as I was,' she said. Sarah had the bones of a sparrow and was stick thin in spite of having given birth to ten children. 'You girls forget.'

11

'You're not old either, Ma, but you're right, we should try to manage just as you used to,' Ellen agreed. 'It's not fair of us to expect you to help out.'

'It's not that I don't like having 'em here,' Sarah said. 'I do, but when they're all together they run rings round me.'

She looked at Ellen's three children and they gazed solemnly back at her. 'Especially you, young peazan,' she said fondly to Thomas, who was sitting angelically on his mother's lap chewing on his wet fist, with his round cheeks rosy from teething. He dropped his fist and struggled to slide down on to the floor, where he crawled rapidly to his grandmother's feet. Heaving himself up by her skirts, he pummelled her knees until she picked him up and nuzzled her nose into his neck, making him squeal. 'I love 'smell o' young bairns,' she murmured, and Ellen was reminded that her mother really wasn't old. She had spent her youthful years of marriage giving birth to her children. Ten children should be enough for any woman to bring up into adulthood, she considered. Ma was one of only a few women of their acquaintance who hadn't lost a child in infancy.

Three were enough for her and Harry, she thought, but no doubt they would have more; how could you avoid a pregnancy when you had a loving marriage? Impossible, no matter how careful you might be.

'What 'you doing, Ma?' she asked as her mother put Thomas on the floor to crawl, and picked Mary up on to her knee. Sarah was pressing her fingers to Mary's throat and behind her ears.

'I just thought she seemed a bit quiet; a bit, you know, wearisome.'

'She's been quiet all day,' Ellen said. 'And she said her throat was hurting. I hope she's not going down with something.'

'She feels hot. When you get home, sponge her down wi' cool water and let her chew on a strip o' willow bark. Then put her to bed and see if she'll sleep. She should settle.'

The toddler put her head against her grandmother's chest and closed her eyes. Sarah kissed the child's forehead. 'She's not well,' she murmured.

12

When baby Sarah was born, Harry had made a wooden cradle and Ellen had made a pretty cover for it; then, as Sarah grew and became too heavy for Ellen to carry when she was pregnant with Mary, he'd fashioned a wooden box on wheels with a long wooden shaft for a handle. Ellen had padded the box with an old cotton sheet stuffed with feathers, as she had done for the cradle, and used it as a perambulator, for they were not able to afford that modern luxury; such things were not for them. She could at least pull or push the cart as far as her mother's house and home again.

Now, with little Sarah walking alongside her, she put both Mary and Thomas in the cart and set out for home. The cart was heavy with both children in it and by the time they arrived home she was tired; she lifted a sleepy Thomas into her arms and then patted Mary's cheek to rouse her. 'Come on, m'darling, let's have you inside and mek you a drink.'

But Mary was lethargic and grizzly and couldn't summon the energy to climb out of the box. 'Open 'door for me, Sarah,' Ellen asked. 'Can you lift 'latch?'

But Sarah wasn't tall enough to reach the latch, so with Thomas in her arms Ellen hurried up the stony path, opened the door and placed the baby in a chair, where he immediately awoke and began to wail. Ellen ran back to Mary, who was slumped in the cart as limp as a rag. She picked her up and put her to her shoulder. The child was burning hot and Ellen rushed inside, unfastening the buttons on her daughter's coat and removing her bonnet as she went. Mary's hair was wet with sweat.

Ellen set her down in a chair and undid the fastenings on her dress, then quickly reached for the enamel bowl in the sink, which she had scrubbed out that morning with carbolic soap. She poured water into the bowl from the kettle, which fortunately had been standing in the hearth and not on the kettle hook so was not very hot, then removed all Mary's clothing, stood her in the bowl and rinsed her down with a flannel.

Sarah began to giggle and undo her shoes, and Ellen saw that she thought they were playing a game and wanted to join in;

then Thomas turned himself round and began sliding out of the chair she had settled him in. He landed with a bump on the floor and began to scream.

Mary could barely stand, her arms and legs were so feeble, but Ellen kept her arm round her and continued to sponge her, trying to cool her down.

Sarah had given up on the buttons on her shoes and was trying to climb into the bowl with Mary. 'No, Sarah, you must wait,' Ellen said. 'Please go and play with Thomas so that he doesn't cry.' Then the door opened and Harry came in.

'What's going on? I can hear Thomas shrieking from outside.' He bent down and picked up his son. 'Stop that now, Thomas. Ellen, he's got blood on his mouth. He's cut himself.'

'He fell out of the chair.' Now that Harry was home, Ellen turned her full attention to Mary. 'Mary's sick.'

She wrapped the child in a blanket, for she was now shivering. 'Put some water in 'kettle, Harry,' she said, 'but don't overfill it.' She tried to recall what her mother had said. Willow bark, that was it. She kept some in a tin; it was a cure-all for childish ailments and headaches too, but Mary needed to drink. 'Put it over 'fire,' she said, her voice trembling, and Harry put Thomas down and took Mary from her, cradling her in his arms.

'I'll hold her. You get whatever you need; you know where everything is,' he said, sitting with Mary on his knee and Thomas squashed at his side so that he couldn't escape.

He looked down at the little girl and lightly stroked her cheek with his finger. He took a breath; she was shaking, and her breathing was laboured, and he lifted her so that she was leaning into him and gently he rubbed her back. Ellen brought a cup of tepid water, but instead of lifting it to Mary's lips he asked Ellen to bring a spoon and dribbled a spot of water on to them, and when she opened her mouth he trickled in a drop more.

'Sit down, Ellen,' he said quietly, and she gazed at him with wide and frightened eyes and did as he asked.

14

Carefully, he stood up and placed Mary in her arms. 'Just hold her,' he said and knelt beside her, drawing Sarah and Thomas towards them; his eyes filled with tears and his voice choked as he murmured a prayer, and added, 'I'm going to run for 'doctor. Keep her safe.'

CHAPTER THREE

It was fortunate that the doctor lived in Holmpton village and had come home for his midday meal before beginning his district rounds; his housekeeper answered Harry's urgent hammering on the door and the doctor saddled up his horse and set off immediately as Harry ran back home.

Harry raced across meadows and through a thin copse to shorten his journey and heard the children as he ran down the path to the cottage. He pushed open the door and saw Ellen trying to pacify Thomas, who now had a very swollen lip, and Sarah splashing her hands in the bowl of water, while Mary was lying on her mother's knee and rasping as if she wanted to cough.

'Doctor's on his way,' he said breathlessly and picked up Thomas to quieten him. 'He said there's measles in Holmpton.'

'Oh, no, please. Not measles,' Ellen moaned. 'There's no cure for that. But she hasn't got spots, so—'

'He's here.' Harry had heard the horse's tread outside. 'Come on, Thomas, let's go and look at 'doctor's hoss.'

He opened the door and took hold of the horse's snaffle as the doctor dismounted. 'Inside, sir. I'll mek 'hoss fast.'

He hooked the reins over an iron peg and let Thomas stroke the mare's neck and then followed the doctor into the house.

The doctor was a youngish man, new to the district after the previous physician's retirement, and he was already kneeling by Ellen's side with his left hand against Mary's forehead and the other fumbling to open a small black box.

16

'Can I help you, sir?' Harry put Thomas down.

'No, thank you.' The doctor removed his hand from Mary to open the box, which contained a glass thermometer wrapped in a piece of flannel that smelled strongly of antiseptic. 'It's rather precious. I wouldn't like to drop it.' He shook the instrument vigorously and asked Ellen to lift Mary's dress, then placed the thermometer beneath the child's armpit and waited.

'Is that a thermometer, doctor?' Harry asked. 'I've never seen one so small.'

The doctor nodded, and after a few moments removed the instrument and looked at it steadily. 'Medium fever,' he murmured, and then sat back on his haunches. 'Has she complained of a sore throat, or earache?' he asked Ellen.

'A sore throat, yes, but not earache.' Ellen found she was trembling. 'Though she was rubbing the back of her neck. And she didn't want to eat or drink anything.'

The doctor looked down Mary's throat. 'She perhaps found it painful to swallow,' he said. 'Her throat is inflamed.' He patted the little girl's arm and looked up at Harry. 'Yes, it is a thermometer. A much smaller and more convenient one than we've had previously.' He wrapped the instrument in the piece of flannel and put it back in the box. 'It tells me that your little girl does not have a high fever, so I don't think she has measles, but if she comes out in spots' – he turned to Ellen – 'you must send for me immediately, and keep the other children away from her as it's very contagious.'

He thought for a moment before going on, 'At worst it might be quinsy. At best, tonsillitis. If she has difficulty swallowing, don't worry about her not eating, but give her sips of cool boiled water. Just continue what you've been doing.' He glanced at the bowl of water. 'Bathe her to bring down her temperature, but don't let her get cold either.'

'Thank you, doctor,' Ellen said tearfully. 'We're very grateful.'

He nodded. 'Keep the other children away, if you can. One sick child is enough to deal with.'

17

When Harry had seen the doctor out, he turned to Ellen. 'I'll tek Sarah and Thomas to my ma and ask if she'll look after them for a day or two, just until Mary's got over 'fever.'

Ellen knew Harry well enough to know he was still worried about Mary; she had seen it in his face when he said he was going to fetch the doctor. She shook her head. 'Not Thomas,' she said. 'He's too much for her. Besides, I have to feed him. Just tek Sarah. She's no bother.'

Sarah was weaned but Mary and Thomas were not; he was a greedy and demanding child and would scream if he was hungry and her milk wasn't readily available.

'But Mary needs feeding too. Isn't it a risk?'

'I'll bathe with carbolic,' she said briskly. Women understood these things; she wouldn't risk passing on infection between her children. 'And I'll wean Mary on to a bottle.'

Harry dressed Sarah in her coat and bonnet and told her they were going to see Granny Randell and she went with him quite happily. He returned in half an hour to say that his sister Meg had just weaned her latest child and had said she would wet-nurse Thomas if Ellen agreed.

Ellen raised her eyebrows and thought Meg might regret the offer, as Thomas could bite with his sharp little teeth, but she was too grateful to demur. It meant she could now concentrate solely on Mary, who coughed and wheezed and was still very lethargic and sleepy in her arms.

When Harry came back after delivering Thomas to his willing aunt he found both Ellen and Mary fast asleep, at least he hoped Mary was only asleep. He put his fingers near to her mouth to feel if she was still breathing; she stirred slightly and gave a little cough but didn't wake.

He tiptoed to the fire and shook the kettle to make sure there was water in it before placing it over the coals, then sat down in the other fireside chair and gazed at Ellen and Mary. He should have been at work; he had only come home because he wanted to ask Ellen something, and had found her in the middle of a crisis, with a sick child and a screaming toddler. Now she was fast asleep, strands of hair escaping from the bonnet that she hadn't had time to take off.

18

The kettle began to steam. Quietly, he opened a cupboard to take out two cups and a teapot and made tea. Ellen began to stir, and he tiptoed out of the room to fetch a jug of milk from the scullery. When he returned, Ellen was awake and looked at him sleepily.

'Goodness,' she murmured. 'What am I doing sleeping during the day?'

'A lady of leisure, you are,' he joked softly, so as not to waken Mary. 'A manservant making you a pot of tea! Whatever is 'world coming to?'

'It's not the right order of things, is it? Especially for a man who was spoiled by all his sisters.'

'No indeed,' he said, pouring the tea. 'My ma would have a seizure if she should see me.'

'Don't tell her then, will you?' Ellen gave him a grateful smile as she took the cup from him. 'Will Sarah be all right with her?'

'She's had a few children of her own, hasn't she? I think she'll manage! How do you think Mary is faring?'

Ellen shook her head, glancing down at the sleeping child. 'I don't know,' she said quietly. 'She's not so hot now. I think 'willow bark helped. I might never have thought of it if my mother hadn't said.'

'These mothers know a thing or two.' He sat down opposite her. 'You'll be 'same when you've got a few more years on your back.'

'Why did you come home?' she asked suddenly. 'Although I'm glad that you did. I don't know what I'd have done if you hadn't walked in the door.'

'A knight in shining armour,' he said. 'Well, 'fact is . . .' He hesitated. 'I came to tell you something, and to ask you something as well. But it can wait. I ought to be getting back or Charlesworth will have something to say about me slacking.' He rose to his feet. 'We'll discuss it later.'

Ellen sat up, disturbing, but not waking, Mary. 'Put her in 'bed for me, will you? She might sleep now.'

Harry took Mary from her arms and Ellen opened the door into the bedroom where he put her down on the bed and covered

19

her with a blanket. Mary turned over and put her thumb in her mouth.

They both smiled, and Harry took Ellen's hand as they tiptoed out. 'I think she'll be all right now,' he whispered. 'That's a proper sleep she's having.'

Ellen wiped away a tear. 'I was so worried. What would we do if we lost any of them?'

'Hush,' he said, wrapping his arms round her and dropping a kiss on her forehead. 'Don't think of it.'

'So what were you going to tell me?' she said. 'Just so that I can think about it until you come home.'

He gazed at her. 'It's onny a thought. An idea. Nothing might come of it. It's just summat one of 'farm lads, Josh, mentioned. Charlesworth has given him 'sack.'

She drew in a breath. 'Why? What's he done?'

'He's done nowt. Charlesworth just said he didn't need him any more.'

Ellen licked her lips. 'So – what did he say?'

'He said he was going to try for work in Hull.'

'But he's a farmhand. What can he do in Hull?'

'Plenty of jobs in factories if you're willing to work, and he's a strong lad, so why not?'

'And your question to me was . . . ?'

Harry looked down at his boots; there were wisps of straw still clinging to the soles even though he'd scraped them before he came in. Then he looked up. 'I was going to ask you – how would you feel about going to live in Hull?'

20

CHAPTER FOUR

Ellen said nothing. She couldn't think of anything to say. She felt that the breath had been sucked out of her. The worst thing that had ever happened was Mary becoming ill, but now the thought of leaving all she had ever known, her parents and family, and travelling to an unknown place, somewhere she had never been, added to her distress. She felt dizzy and abruptly sat down.

'Don't worry about it.' Harry's voice seemed to come from far away. 'It was onny a thought. I've upset you, haven't I? I'm sorry, I shouldn't have said, not on top of 'worry you've had wi' Mary.'

She opened and closed her mouth but no words came out.

'We'll talk about it later,' Harry said hastily. 'I'll have to go. Charlesworth'll be looking for me.'

She nodded. 'Go,' she said huskily. 'Go on. We'll talk when you get home.'

He hesitated as he reached the door. 'Don't worry, will you? Just mek sure that 'bairn is all right.'

'I will,' she whispered, but her brown eyes were large with anxiety as he opened the door and gave her an apprehensive glance.

Harry had always looked after her, kept any anxieties away from her, but now, she realized as she sat in the quiet of the room, she must share the worries, must not let him take all the responsibilities on his shoulders. Decisions on their future must be taken together. They'd talk over their prospects, and if moving away was what they had to do, then so be it; it would be as

21

difficult for Harry as it would be for her. Harder, in fact, for farming was all he had ever known.

Later that evening, Mary seemed a little better, though she was fractious and had difficulty swallowing. Ellen trickled honey and cool water down her throat and that seemed to ease her discomfort; she gave her more willow bark and by the time Harry came home she had fallen asleep again and was curled up back in her bed.

Ellen had made a casserole of pork and vegetables which she and Harry ate together and he remarked how quiet it was without the children.

'Well, they would've been in bed by now,' Ellen reminded him. He agreed that they would have been, but said that knowing they were in the next room was always comforting. He had gone in to check on Mary and was relieved to see that she seemed to be sleeping evenly and that her breathing was easier.

'So tell me,' Ellen went on. 'What was this about going to Hull?'

Harry sighed. 'It's two things. This morning when I looked at 'last field of corn I thought it looked almost perfect. Another two days of sun and it would be ready. Ozzie would have been ecstatic. I'd been waiting for Charlesworth to give me 'go-ahead for harvesting; it would have been for 'very last time, so I said to him we ought to be getting extra men in; and he said, no we shouldn't. I've sold the crop; *we* don't need to do anything, it'll be harvested and cleared by the buyer. I just stood and stared at him. I couldn't believe what he was saying, and then he said, when it's done we'll be sowing grass for more sheep.

'Then Josh came to tell me he'd be finishing at 'end of week and I asked him where he was going. He said he was going to try Hull; that he was onny forty and couldn't afford to finish work, and he'd heard there were plenty of labouring jobs in town.'

'But you're not a labourer,' Ellen reminded him. 'You're an experienced farmhand.'

'And soon I'll be an out-of-work farmhand; there are few good jobs available in farming and those in work are hanging on by their fingertips. Machines are tekking 'place of labourers.' His expression was grim. 'To be honest, I'd wait until Hirings, but

22

I hate 'notion of standing in line waiting for somebody to look me over; that's why I've put 'word about that I'm looking for another position. Ozzie had a good reputation and the fact that I've worked for him since I was a lad should be recommendation enough, but there's been *nothing*. Nobody has come forward to enquire, and I reckon' – he clenched his fists – 'I reckon that Charlesworth will become a laughing stock afore long and I don't want to be associated with him. I don't want my name being tarnished by his.'

'I can understand that,' Ellen murmured. 'But what kind of labouring work would it be in town?'

'Josh said he was going to 'timber docks first, then mebbe 'railway dock. They'll want lads wi' muscles there. There are several docks in Hull; there's Queen's Dock, where shipping and trade comes in, then Humber Dock, and Junction Dock, and there are plans to extend Victoria Dock.' He paused. 'And there are plenty of mills, oil mills and seed-crushing mills, and I know about seed and grain.'

'So you do,' she whispered, watching his face. 'So – mebbe it will be all right.'

'Do you think so, Ellen?' He looked earnestly at her. 'Cos I wouldn't want to do anything if you weren't happy about it.'

She reached to grasp his hand on the table; his fingers were tightly clenched and she eased them until they began to unfold. 'I know you wouldn't tek a chance if 'odds were against us,' she murmured. 'But where would we live, Harry? We onny pay a peppercorn rent here, but even so we haven't much money. Would we struggle to get by?'

'We'd struggle on a farmhand's wages anyway. We've been lucky wi' having this cottage, Ellen.' He shook his head. 'Even if we stop in Holderness, money's going to be short.'

Ellen was silent. It was true. Her parents had managed because her father had always had regular work, but now she wondered just how they had coped with so many children. Everyone she knew grew their own vegetables and kept chickens or a pig if they had the space. Could they do that in town? Would they even have a patch of soil to grow what they needed? No use asking

23

Harry, he knew as little as she did about the town of Hull. He had never been there either.

The doctor called the following morning to enquire after Mary. He looked down her throat again and said the inflammation had gone down. 'Tonsillitis,' he said. 'Not quinsy as I feared. She should be well again in a day or two, but keep giving her the willow bark, and if you take her out and there's a cold wind make sure that she wears a warm scarf round her neck.'

He smiled at the little girl, who hid her face against her mother's shoulder.

'Thank you, doctor,' Ellen said. 'I'm very grateful. What do we owe you?' She hoped it wouldn't be too much.

'Nothing.' He shook his head. 'I don't charge a fee for children. Besides,' he added, 'I haven't prescribed anything. You were doing the right thing, using your common sense. Don't hesitate if you should need me again.'

'Thank you,' she said gratefully. 'But – we might be moving from 'village into Hull.'

'Oh?'

Ellen nodded. 'My husband is going to seek work. His former employer, Mr Oswald, died and 'new farm owner is making some changes, and there's no place for Harry in his plans.'

'Would that be Mr Charlesworth?' When Ellen said yes, he went on, 'I'd heard he's bought sheep. I understood that Holderness was more of a pig-breeding area, but then I'm not a countryman. Well, if you do decide to go to Hull I can give you the name of a good doctor.'

He opened his black bag, brought out a pencil and notepad, and began writing. 'Dr Lucan; he was a Holderness man originally, but he's been in Hull for some time. Very well thought of and very experienced.' He passed her the details. 'He's good with children, too, and has several of his own.' He put on his top hat and touched it. 'Good luck, Mrs Randell. I hope all goes well with your husband's work prospects.'

She repeated what he'd said when Harry came home, but Harry was distracted and gave only a vague reply before saying,

24

'The Dales man has come and is harassing Charlesworth over 'accommodation for his family; Charlesworth in turn is harassing me and I'm sick of it, Ellen. I loved this job. I would get up every morning and plan my day, knowing that Ozzie trusted me to do what was necessary, but now . . .' He got up from the table and walked to the window. 'Now, 'heart has gone out of it. I don't want to be working there any more.'

'Then give Charlesworth notice and tek a day off to go to Hull and seek work,' Ellen said determinedly. 'If you've given notice he can't sack you. Mebbe he'll knock off a day's pay, but that can't be helped. And I'll start packing.'

She looked round the room. It wouldn't take long. Most of the fittings had been supplied by Mr Oswald; they'd get everything that was theirs into a small wagon. She'd ask one of her sisters to help her pack the linen and crockery, and her brother Billy would help Harry with their few pieces of furniture. That was one advantage of having a large family.

Harry turned towards her. 'Are you sure?'

'Yes,' she said firmly. 'We've no other option, and we'll . . .' Her lip trembled, but she went on bravely. 'We'll think of it as a turning point in our lives.'

Harry took her in his arms. 'I allus knew you were 'right girl for me,' he murmured, kissing her lips. 'That first day I saw you, do you remember? You came to our house to see . . . who was it, our Janey? I knew then that I'd wait for you to grow up.'

'Polly.' She smiled. 'And you asked me if I'd be stretching my wings and leaving 'village; and until then I'd thought that I might if my da would allow it.'

He leaned back, holding her at arms' length. 'Really? Where had you thought of going?'

She laughed. 'I had an idea that I might like to work in a town, so when Mrs Hodges offered me a job I thought that when I'd had some experience in cooking and baking I might go to Hull; but on the day we met I decided to stay for a while and see what happened next.'

'And what did happen next?' he teased.

25

She rubbed her cheek against his and closed her eyes. 'I fell in love,' she said softly. 'With someone who loved me, and I knew I couldn't leave unless he came with me.' She opened her eyes. 'And that's what's going to happen next,' she said tenderly, 'onny we'll have a few little people with us.'

'We'll be all right, won't we?' he said, and she nodded. 'You know that I'll work my fingers to 'bone for you and our bairns.'

She kissed him. 'I know that,' she said. 'We'll manage fine.'

Harry did as Ellen had proposed. He was pleased that she had made the choice, as he hadn't wanted to pressure her into agreeing, and it had surprised him to know that even when she had been so young she had thought that she might go to live and work in a large town like Hull.

He gave notice to Charlesworth. He had found his original contract with Oswald, which had never been changed, not even when Charlesworth had taken over, and so in theory he could stay on until 11 November, Martinmas, the traditional hiring day. As they were still in September, he had plenty of time to seek work.

The carrier called at Patrington and Hedon on Tuesdays and Fridays, returning on the same days, and the Tuesday after giving in his notice Harry rose early to walk to the Patrington road and catch the carrier on his way into Hull. He hoped to find work immediately, otherwise he would have to stay in a hostelry until Friday to come home again. There was the option of the railway train, but he didn't want to spend the money. The carrier was much cheaper.

Ellen had packed him beef and cheese and several slices of bread, and he had put them on top of a small bag of money tucked into the bottom of a knapsack.

'Be careful, won't you?' she said, as he opened the door to leave.

He smiled. 'I'm not going to 'ends of the earth, Ellen,' he joked, though unsteadily. 'It onny feels like it.'

Ellen turned back into her kitchen; though the cottage was small, just one room, a scullery and a bedroom, it had been

26

theirs. A good fire burned in the range, and the kettle hung on the hook above it. She felt sad to be leaving, but it had to be. She would begin her packing later, but now she would visit Harry's mother in Holmpton and tell her of their proposed plans, and then she would call on her own mother and do the same there.

CHAPTER FIVE

Harry had mixed feelings as he strode out towards the main road along which the carrier made stops at some of the villages between Patrington and Hedon – Ottringham and Keyingham were two, he knew – before heading into Hull itself.

He had never been out of Holderness. There had never been any need; everything he wanted was there. His family had always worked on the land, his father and grandfather and great-grandfather before him. As had Ellen's, as far as he knew.

But now was the time for change, and it wasn't only the fact that Charlesworth was taking over the farm. Had Mr Oswald lived he would perhaps always have employed him, but there were many farmhands moving into towns to try for a better living than they could make in the countryside; and besides, Harry thought, acres of land were being lost to the sea, which meant that farms were shrinking and cottagers' homes were disappearing over the edge into the coastal waters.

Perhaps that's why Charlesworth has brought the sheep to the inland fields, not just to please his wife. He'll know more about money matters than I do, Harry mused. I onny know about money in my pocket. Perhaps Ozzie was working at a loss. He looked up as he heard the rattle of wheels and saw the carrier coming towards him; he began to run, his pack bumping on his back. He's early, he thought as he put out his hand to hail the driver.

28

'Just in time,' the driver said as he climbed up beside him. 'Another minute and you'd have missed me.'

'Our clock must be wrong,' Harry said. 'I thought I'd timed it perfectly.'

'Nah!' the driver admitted. 'I've made good time; nobody waiting at Patrington. Will you want a lift back?'

'Not sure,' Harry said. 'Depends if all goes well.'

'Lookin' fer work, are you?'

'Aye, and I don't know if I'll be successful today, so I might have to stop over. I'll be looking for accommodation for my family as well.'

The driver grunted. 'Well, good luck wi' that. Just watch what you're doing, and keep your money bag safe. Where 'you looking, oil mills, grain mills?'

'Mebbe,' Harry told him. 'Wherever I can, oil or seed, or on 'docks. I can't afford to be choosy.'

'Try Wincomlee, Wilmington or Sculcoates,' the driver said. 'There're plenty o' mills to choose from, though I wouldn't advise you to live down there. Housing won't be what you're used to.'

Harry nodded his thanks, but hid a small smile. Their present cottage was cosy, but it wasn't lavish by any means. He'd surely find something of the same standard.

'Aye up.' The driver spotted a figure holding out his thumb further up the road. 'Seems like all of Holderness is on 'move, seeking work. There'll be nobody left in 'countryside at this rate.'

'In that case I'll come back,' Harry sighed. 'I'm not moving through choice.'

'You married, then?' the driver asked as he reined in. 'Got a family of your own?'

'Yeh, a wife and three bairns, so I've got to earn enough to feed and clothe them.'

That was also the new passenger's mission, except that he was newly married with a wife who would work until she bore children. 'I'd be happy if she didn't have any just yet,' he said morosely, 'but I expect she will. You know what women are like.'

29

Harry and the driver exchanged glances. 'Nowt to do wi' you, I suppose?' the cabby grunted.

The passenger shook his head. 'I've telled her I don't want any yet, but I don't think she was listening. That's why I'm going into Hull; mebbe my job prospects will be better there. I might try for shipping, or mebbe loading on 'docks.'

They pulled into the market town of Hedon to drop off supplies, and picked up a woman passenger. Harry had had enough of the gloomy young man so he gave up his seat at the front and sat in the back with the crates. The young man got out, saying he needed the privy, and shot off to the nearest hostelry. The driver waited for five minutes and then set off again.

'I'm not hanging about,' he muttered. 'I'm not here for 'good of my health; my time means money,' and he cracked the whip and moved off at a spanking trot out of Hedon, along the wide road which had once been marshland alongside the Humber estuary, past the docks and the tops of cranes and the tall masts of schooners and ships prepared to sail to every country and seaboard known to mankind, until they crossed the bridge over the River Hull and turned right, and the driver lifted his whip in salutation to the King Billy statue – or was it, Harry wondered as he scanned the town, in acknowledgement of the hostelry of the same name – as they reached the edge of Market Place, where the carrier stopped.

Harry helped the woman down before turning to pay the driver, who shook his head when Harry offered his fare.

'No need to pay me until you return,' he said.

'It might not be today,' Harry reminded him, 'so I'd rather give it you now. I don't like owing money.'

The driver gave an appreciative nod. 'Good lad,' he said. 'Hope you get on all right.' He told Harry to cross the town and come out on the eastern side. 'Look for North Bridge over 'river,' he said, 'and then turn left, and that'll bring you into 'industrial area wi' mills and factories and what not. You're sure to find summat to your liking.'

Harry thanked him and walked on, lingering a little to look at the market stalls that were clustered around the great church in

30

the centre of town, and then continued towards another equally ancient church, St Mary's, which bounded narrow and dark cobbled entries; Scale Lane, Bishop Lane, Chapel Lane, the space between the buildings only just wide enough to take a cart or small carriage. He was curious enough to wonder what was at the other end of these lanes, for they were busy with people and handcarts and some of the men were wearing clogs which clattered on the cobbles, so he followed them.

At the bottom another narrow road ran crosswise, and on the other side even narrower entries led to the waterway, which they'd crossed further up before entering the town. He was intrigued to see that, narrow though it was, the road was lined with some very grand buildings, and he stopped a man who was carrying a sack over his shoulders to enquire its name.

'High Street,' the workman answered. 'This was once 'main street of 'town afore new building started and 'town began to spread. All of 'bigwigs used to live down here in these houses, but they didn't like 'stink o' blubber when whaling reigned and they moved out into 'country. So 'rest of us live here now. Down yonder' – he nodded to the smaller alleyways and seemed happy to talk – 'we call 'em staithes; they belong to 'shipping merchants who use these buildings as offices cos they've got Old Harbour right on their doorstep for loading barges. We've got a ring o' docks now, and 'road leads on to Wincomlee and other villages, except they're not villages any more. You a stranger here?'

'I am,' Harry said, confused by all the information. 'I'm looking for work. Somebody said I should go to Wincomlee.'

'Aye, it's not far.' The man told him to retrace his steps, look for the New Dock and then head for North Bridge. 'Plenty o' work if you're prepared for hard graft, but don't expect to mek your fortune, cos you won't.' He shouldered the sack up higher. 'Believe me, I know. If you can mek ends meet you'll be doing well.'

He lifted his hand and departed; Harry was tempted to walk down the staithes to look at the river, and even though he heard a church clock strike and reminded himself why he was there, he slipped down to look over into the busy waterway. It

31

was low tide and the harbour was packed with barges, tugs and other workboats with barely a finger space between them; men were swarming over them, jumping from one to another, loading and unloading, and bustling in and out of the tall warehouses on either side of the narrow river. Harry about-turned and started on his way to find North Bridge and hopefully employment.

As a countryman he had always lived in open spaces with clean fresh air scented by spring blossom, summer's heady golden corn, freshly scythed hay meadows and the salty aroma of the German ocean. Never in his entire life had he been engulfed by towering chimneys blasting out thick black smoke, nor deafened by the dull thump and grind of heavy machinery, a thousand times louder than the ring of the blacksmith's anvil; nor had he ever hidden his nose and mouth beneath his hand to escape the choking dust-filled air that not only reeked, in this area by the River Hull, of corn or rape or linseed, or whatever product was presently being crushed, but also carried an acrid, pungent, overpowering stench of paint, whiting and glue that made him baulk.

Can I work in such a place, he thought, as he continued past lofty red-brick warehousing where seed was delivered by barge into large yards and shunted into hoppers and seed bags, and glanced in at old windmills now being converted to steam. But what choice have I, he answered himself bleakly, thinking that no one needed to know about corn to work here; he wouldn't need to check the grain with his fingers to feel the quality, nor to let it stream through his fingers to test the strength or see the colour.

There was no use for sentiment here; the golden bloom of rape, the blue linseed flower, or flax as it was sometimes called, which produced the seed would be crushed and processed into foodstuffs, oil or cattle cake; paint and soap and tallow would be produced to feed the industry which in turn fed the people, giving them work and money to survive.

When he reached Wincomlee he tried the first factory he came to, climbing up a flight of steps towards a wooden structure

32

that served as an office and reading a notice pinned to the door which proclaimed bluntly *No Vacancies.*

At the second mill the notice simply read *Out.* Harry didn't know if it meant callers should leave or the owner or foreman was not at his desk, but it didn't really matter: the reasoning was clear enough.

He passed by several other buildings, noting that many were dilapidated and the yards strewn with old machinery, and he decided that if he should be successful in his application the first thing he would do would be to clear up and get rid of the rubbish. He paused at another, which had *R. Tannerson and Son* painted on the outside wall, and through the bump and grind of machinery he heard the sound of laughter. He went in and strode across the yard, patted an old horse who had his nose in a hay bag, and climbed another set of stairs to an office where the door was open.

A man in his forties with an unlit pipe in his mouth was sitting in a chair with his booted feet on a desk and reading from a sheaf of papers. Harry knocked on the door and the man called, 'Come in, the door's open,' and then, looking up, crashed his feet to the floor.

'Beats me,' he muttered and threw the papers on the desk. 'What's a man to do?'

Harry was sure that it wasn't a question aimed at him, so he said nothing as the man continued.

'What would you think was the best thing to do, buy local and pay twice the price or buy from America at a better rate?'

'What would you be buying, sir?' he asked.

'Why, grain of course; rape, flax, the usual thing.'

'Then buy local,' Harry said firmly. 'Stay loyal to 'local farmer so that he can hold on to his farm and farmhands, and keep our economy strong.'

'And what about people like me and the folk I employ?' The man put his elbows on the desk and stared at Harry. 'What about when Mr and Mrs England can't afford to pay for the foodstuffs, soap and clothing that your local farmer produces, so he grows less than he did, and then because I can't afford to pay his high

33

prices I have to sack my men when there's no work for them so they can't feed their families or keep a roof over their heads? What then?'

Harry was stumped. He'd felt angry towards people like Charlesworth who had dropped nicely into a well-run farm, but he hadn't given a thought to men who had plunged money into other businesses which also served the population. He rubbed his hand over his neat beard, which he'd trimmed especially to look for work.

'Not sure, sir,' he said, choosing his words carefully. 'I think there has to be a compromise somewhere.'

'You're damned right, there has!' The man thumped the desk. 'Now then,' he went on. 'Who are you exactly?'

'I'm a former farmhand, sir, Harry Randell, looking for work cos there's none in 'country.' Harry gave a weak grin. 'Is it *fait accompli*?'

'Had a good education, have you? Speak another lingo?'

'No sir, I've never used that expression afore, but I know what it means.'

'Which is?' The man drew his dark eyebrows together.

'It means that it's out of our hands. American wheat is already coming into Britain. Agreement has been struck.'

'So we've to make the best of it, is what you're saying?'

'Aye, I reckon so,' Harry nodded. 'But I'm no businessman. I suppose it's a question of looking for 'best deal you can strike.'

'Right, Mr Harry Randell. I like a man who can think. When can you start?'

CHAPTER SIX

'Straight away, sir,' Harry told Roland Tannerson. 'Except that I've to find accommodation for my wife and children first and bring them down from Holderness – would Monday be suitable? Start of next week? Erm, what sort of work will I be doing, sir, and what about wages?'

Tannerson gave a dry laugh. 'I wondered when you might get round to asking.' He told Harry what to expect in wages, which was six shillings a week. It was roughly what he earned at the farm, but he would now have to pay rent out of it.

Tannerson must have noticed his drooping expression, even though Harry had nodded in agreement. 'Not as much as you expected?'

Harry decided to be honest and tell him what he earned now. 'It's just that I onny pay a peppercorn rent, sir, and we keep our own hens and grow vegetables and suchlike; I doubt we can do that in town.'

Tannerson considered. 'Right, I'll give you an extra shilling a week towards your rent; I know what it's like to be without money. How old are your children?' When Harry told him, he said, 'Can't be easy, I know, and your wife can't work either, with young children, though some have to when they're desperate. Well, we'll see how you shape up in your first month; if you work well there'll be a rise in wages. I believe in being fair. Now then, watch out where you look for accommodation. There are some

35

hovels round here that you wouldn't keep pigs in. Don't go down the Groves, because that's where the Irish live.'

'I've nowt against Irish, sir,' Harry said.

'Nor have I.' Tannerson grinned as he agreed. 'But they tend to keep to themselves and some of them live in dire conditions. No fault of theirs,' he hastened to add. 'Some of them share a room with several other families and their landlords do nothing to make their lives bearable but charge exorbitant rents for the privilege of living without running water or their own privy.'

'Thank you, sir. I appreciate your advice and your job offer. You won't regret it. I'm not a shirker; you'll get your money's worth out of me.' Harry touched his forehead. 'Six o'clock sharp on Monday morning.'

He set off down unknown streets. Some were full of warehouses and workshops and no housing, others had small terraced houses set in the midst of industry, but Harry didn't enquire about any of them. He couldn't bring Ellen and the children to live in a noisy dusty atmosphere such as this, and after walking about for half an hour or so he was beginning to despair of finding anything suitable; he worried too that he might miss the carrier to take him home.

He was hungry and thirsty, and slipped into a hostelry. There weren't many customers, just a group of four old men wearing cloth caps with mufflers tied at their necks, sitting at a table by a low fire, drinking beer as they concentrated on their rows of dominoes. Two of them looked up and nodded at Harry, the other two were absorbed in their next move. He tapped on the bar counter and a middle-aged man came out from a back room. 'What can I get you?' he asked, and Harry asked for a pint of stout.

'Haven't see you in here afore,' the landlord commented as he pulled the pint to a creamy head and placed it on the counter.

Harry licked his lips; it looked like a good pint. 'No, I'm not from round here. I've come job-hunting.'

'Aye? Any luck?' The landlord picked up the glass and lifted it to examine it, topped it up, and then handed it to Harry, who took a satisfying gulp.

36

'That's good,' he said. 'Yeh, wi' Tannerson, if I can find my way back again.'

'Ah, he's a good boss, I hear. Everybody speaks well of him. But he expects a day's work out of everybody.'

'Fair enough,' Harry said, and spying a slice of pork pie sitting on the counter under a glass cover he asked, 'Is that pie goin' beggin'?'

'Here, have it and welcome,' the landlord said. 'It's 'last slice.'

Harry was beginning to think that living and working in Hull was going to be all right after all. The landlord seemed happy to talk so he asked him if he knew of anywhere he could find decent accommodation.

'You'll want somewhere near to work, will you?' the man asked. 'If you're working in Wincomlee you could try Trippett or Church Street, or mebbe Wilmington, it depends how choosy you are.' His lips turned down. 'There're some slums you wouldn't want to bring your bairns to in spite of 'cheap rent.'

Harry was getting worn down by the picture painted of poor housing; he thought there must be some decent places somewhere. He finished off the pie and the pint, thanked the landlord, said he'd see him again and left to do his own searching for a suitable house to live in.

He soon got lost in the midst of crowded courts and short streets that finished at brick walls, with no way out except to go back the way he had come. Many of these places were without drains or gutters and the courtyards or streets were awash with mud and debris.

Harry backed away; where would the children play? Ellen wouldn't allow them out of the house into such an area. He walked on and saw a man in a shabby coat and bowler hat with a bag strapped across his shoulders come out of a nearby court. Rent man, he thought. He'll know.

'Excuse me, sir,' he shouted, and the man stopped as if frozen in his tracks. Warily, he turned round, putting his hand on his bag.

'I'm not carrying money,' he grunted. 'Nobody's paid me owt today.'

37

Harry's mouth opened and closed. Did the man think he was a thief? He stopped and held up both his hands to show he had nothing in them. 'Sorry,' he called out. 'I didn't mean to startle you. I'm looking for a place to live, somewhere decent to bring my wife and bairns.'

The man pushed his hat up his forehead; as Harry came nearer he saw the headgear was several times too big for him. 'Sorry,' he said again. 'You are a rent man?'

'Might be,' the fellow said. 'What's it to you?'

'I just said. I'm lookin' for a place to rent.'

The agent looked Harry up and down. 'Where 'you living now?'

'Holmpton,' Harry said, knowing that no one would have heard of Rysome. 'It's in Holderness. Near Withernsea.'

The agent's face suddenly lightened. He'd obviously heard of Withernsea, though Harry couldn't understand why. Withernsea was only a small village on the coast, although bigger than Holmpton.

'Oh, aye. I knew somebody once went on a train to Withernsea. It's going to be a seaside place, isn't it?'

Harry gave a little frown. 'Erm, yes.' He wondered how such a man could be trusted to collect rent. 'Withernsea is a seaside place already,' he explained. 'It's a village near to 'sea. Trains have been running there for a few years.'

'Yeh, I know. Where do you want to rent?'

'Somewhere decent, wi' a small garden if possible.'

The man's face split into a grin. 'Hah! Made o' money, are you? There's nowhere wi' gardens round 'ere. If you want a garden you'll have to go further out, Beverley Road or somewhere like that . . . and there's a park.'

'Look, do you have anything?' Harry was becoming impatient. 'If you haven't I don't want to waste time, yours or mine.'

'I've got a couple; don't know if they'll suit. Come wi' me.'

Harry followed him back to the court the man had just left. It was very narrow, with four two-storey houses on each side of a grimy footpath. The agent selected a key from a ring of others and strode up three steps to a front door and put the key in the

38

lock, indicating to Harry to follow. Harry noticed that to the side of the steps a cellar window showed below the path, and pondered that although it might be rather dark it would be a useful area for storage.

The agent showed him into an empty room facing the street. 'It's just one room,' he was told. 'Other room is upstairs, but that's already let. Privy's at 'top of 'court – to share.'

'Share wi' how many?'

'Just eight houses; 'folk at 'other side have their own privy.'

'What do you mean?' Harry frowned. 'Other side of where?'

The agent looked at Harry as if he were a halfwit. 'Other side o' court. They're back to back.'

Harry shook his head. 'I don't know what you're talking about.'

'Just come from 'country, haven't you?' the man commented. 'There's another court at 'back of these. Houses are joined together. Come on, I'll show you.'

He suddenly seemed galvanized into action, and led Harry out of the house. Locking the door behind him, he trotted down the steps and along the street for a few yards before turning left into a narrow alley, where he turned left again into another very small court with identical two-storey housing.

Except, Harry fingered his beard, it wasn't. These were, in fact, three-storey houses with one level below ground. Three steps led up to the doors and below the steps were small windows to let in a minimum of light.

'Can I have a look?' he asked, curiosity getting the better of him, even though he had no intention of renting one.

'I've onny got a basement room left; I didn't think you'd want it,' the rent man told him but opened the door anyway and led the way in and down another short flight of stairs at the bottom of which he unlocked a second door.

Harry wrinkled his nose; it was dark, and smelt of damp and sewage and stale air. There were two small windows, one facing the back court, the other facing the street they had just left, and he wondered how anyone could possibly live in such a place and survive.

'No, thanks,' he said. 'It's not suitable.'

39

'Nah.' The agent turned away. 'You wouldn't keep a dog, Irish or Jews in here, would you?' He considered for a moment. 'I've got just one more that might do. It's a bit further up 'riverbank towards Church Street. Where is it you're working?'

'Tannerson's mill.'

'Right, come on then. I'll show you, then I'll have to be off afore my boss comes lookin' for me, thinking I've run off wi' his rent money.'

'I thought you said you hadn't collected any?' Harry grinned.

'I haven't, but he doesn't know that, does he? Not that it's worth 'effort of running off wi' pittance I collect. It doesn't even cover my wages.'

'Well, if you can find me somewhere liveable, you can be sure I'll pay what we owe every rent day.'

His companion nodded and sighed. 'Aye, that's what everybody says, but I'll tek your word for it.' He marched out of the court, and down the street, taking several turnings before they arrived at the end of another long street of two-storey houses.

'This one's 'whole of bottom floor,' the agent said, stopping outside the last house in the row, which had a space alongside leading presumably to the rear; this terrace, it appeared, was a single row of houses, not back to back. 'Two rooms and a yard wi' a privy, so 'rent is more than 'others. Former tenants were in arrears so they've had to move out; not that my boss'd want them to stop anyway. He doesn't like Jews. I've given them till today so they should have left.'

Harry frowned at his comment, but followed him inside. The tenants were still there, a man and woman with their three young children, one about the same age as Thomas sitting in a cardboard box wearing only a nappy and crying, the adults collecting up pieces of crockery. On a wooden chair were several grubby sheets and a pillow; what he could see seemed to Harry to be all their worldly possessions, for there was nothing else in the room.

'We are leaving,' the woman said, looking first at the agent and then at Harry with large dark red-rimmed eyes. 'Sorry, but our child not well.'

40

Harry felt sorry for them and bent down to speak to the wailing infant. 'Hey,' he said softly. 'What's up, then?' He wondered if the child was hungry, and taking off his knapsack felt around until he located the bread and cheese that Ellen had wrapped carefully in a cotton cloth. The toddler stopped crying and the other two children drew closer. He looked at the mother for permission before breaking off a piece of bread and giving it to the toddler, who grabbed it and began to chew. Harry broke the cheese and gave a piece each to the other two children. One, a little girl, looked at the food and then at her mother, who nodded and murmured, 'Eat.'

Harry wondered if it was the first time she had eaten cheese. He had caught a slight accent as the mother spoke and wondered where they had come from.

'Thank you. Thank you,' the husband said fervently. 'You are kind.' He was tall and broad-set with handsome dark eyes, thick eyebrows and short dark stubble.

'We are ready,' the woman said, wrapping a blanket round the child in the box and lifting him out. 'Where can we go? You have another room?'

The agent shook his head. 'No. You must go to 'parish and ask for help.'

'Do you have work?' Harry asked the man.

He shook his head but said nothing, and taking the baby from his wife he turned for the door. The woman ushered the older children in front of her, and Harry followed them out. He hadn't much money, but he knew he had more than this family. He put his hand in his pocket. He'd been promised an extra shilling a week in his wages and thought the first one would be well spent if he gave it away.

'Try for work at 'mills,' he said, handing over a shilling. 'In Wincomlee.'

'Thank you. You work there?' the man asked him, taking the money. 'You give me job? I am good worker. Very strong. Engineer.'

Harry lifted his hands. 'No. I came looking for work too.' He wasn't sure if he had been understood, but the man sighed, thanked him again and turned away.

41

The agent was standing with his hands in his pocket when Harry went back inside. 'If you want this place I'll need a shilling for 'first week's rent and you can move in straight away,' he said.

The two rooms had originally been one; there was a fireplace and a thin dividing wall with a doorway but no door, beyond which was a small scullery with a sink and a door leading outside. Harry looked out of the back window; he could see a small yard with a box-like structure which he thought would be the privy. 'What's outside of 'yard?'

The agent shrugged. 'Just an area and 'river. Do you want it or not?'

'Yeh!' Harry made an instant decision. I'm not in a position to be choosy, he thought, and if the new job is all right we can look for something better when we have some money. 'I'll leave a shilling as a deposit and it'll cover next week's rent, and I'll need a receipt. We'll move in on Saturday.'

The agent nodded and took out a receipt book and wrote in it, asking, 'What's your name? Right, I'll see you here at ten o'clock on Saturday morning, Mr Randell, to hand over 'keys. My name's Dennison.'

'Thanks.' Harry handed over the shilling. 'I'll need a rent book with 'amount paid entered in it.'

'You'll lose it if you get in arrears,' he was warned. 'So be sure to pay on time. Now if you'll excuse me, I'll try to catch up wi' that family. I've remembered I might have another place for them.'

'They've no money,' Harry frowned.

'You gave 'em summat, didn't you?'

Harry stared at him. A shilling. He'd intended it for food for the children. What a dilemma. Now the parents would have to decide whether the children would eat or have a place to lay their heads. He was angry. There'd be some landlord having a good dinner tonight and not even thinking of the plight of the tenants who were paying for it.

42

CHAPTER SEVEN

The rent agent scuttled off to catch up with the former tenants and Harry hoped that he had something better to offer them than the room below ground. He thought it was appalling that people should have to live in such conditions, but then reflected that it would mean the workhouse otherwise and no one wanted that, particularly people with children.

The sun came out in a cloudy sky and he stepped away from the house and strode down the side of it to see what was behind the yard. The gate was locked from the inside and he regarded that as satisfactory. It would mean that the children would be able to play outside without Ellen being anxious about them wandering off.

Beyond was a rough area of scrubland with a broken-down boundary fence boasting many gaps. Harry squeezed through one of them and came to a wide muddy bank leading down towards the River Hull. In the distance he saw tall factory chimneys and many industrial buildings; beyond those were church steeples and what he thought were oil mills and kilns. The water reached halfway up to the top of the bank and he mused that although the river was narrow here a young child could easily drown in its depths, yet there were children playing about on the water's edge, boys of perhaps eight or ten, and older youths sitting on the opposite bank with fishing rods.

He called across to two of them. 'Have you caught owt yet, lads?'

One of them looked up and shook his head. 'Not yet. Missed 'early morning tench, but there'll mebbe be roach later.'

Harry nodded. That was encouraging: food for free. He had an old fishing rod in a shed at home; he'd search it out and bring it with him. He strolled nearer the edge, to where the young lads were larking about. One of them, already barefoot, was taking off his shirt and breeches.

'Is 'water warm?' Harry called to him.

The boy crouched to make his way down the bank. 'Yeh. It'll save me having to get a bath on Friday.'

Harry laughed. 'Did you bring soap?'

'Nah.' The lad slipped and slithered his way down. 'I'm not that mucky.' He looked back at Harry. 'You're not a school-teacher, are you?'

'No. Why? Should you be at school?'

'Yeh, but I'm leaving at Christmas so it don't matter.'

Harry put his hands in his pockets. 'Have you got a job to go to?'

'Nah, that's why I'm muckin' about here. If I'd got a job I wouldn't be here, would I?'

He stood up, naked and straight, and put both arms out in front of him, his hands and fingers pointing forward. He took a deep breath and the other young lads stopped what they were doing to watch him. 'Don't forget you can't swim, Stan,' one of them shouted.

The swimmer let out the breath. 'I know! I'm just going to learn. Now will you shurrup!'

With that he took another breath, lifted up on to his toes and dived in.

Harry moved closer and he too held his breath. Young varmint. He was about to take off his own boots when the lad surfaced, spluttering, and began a doggy paddle towards the bank. 'Telled you, didn't I?' he shouted, breathless but triumphant. 'Telled you I could swim!'

Harry grinned and turned away. The boy was a survivor.

He hurried now, as time was getting short and he wanted to get home tonight, but could he find his way back to Market

44

Place in time to catch the carrier? He had to ask directions more than once and finally resorted to running, reaching Market Place just as the carrier was moving off. Harry called out for him to wait.

'I'd given you up,' the driver remonstrated. 'Thought you were stopping!'

Harry climbed up beside him. 'No,' he panted. 'I think I might have come back 'long way round. I'd no idea Hull was so big. Oh!' He took a breath. 'Some of 'housing . . .' He shook his head despondently. 'Anyway, I've got a job and somewhere reasonable for us to live. I start at one of 'mills on Monday morning, so we've got from now until Saturday to pack up and arrange 'hire of a wagon to come back in again.'

The carrier nodded his head and pursed his lips. 'I know somebody in Patrington who hires out carts and wagons. I'll give you his address, and you can drop him a postcard if you want him.'

Harry thanked him, but privately thought that he would ask around Holmpton first and try to get some help with loading their few items of furniture. Ellen's brother Billy might be agreeable, or maybe a labourer willing to earn a copper or two. Charity begins at home, he believed, and there were many local farm workers who were struggling.

'You can drop me here, thanks,' Harry said, reaching into his pocket for the return fare as they approached Holmpton. 'We live at 'Rysome end so I'll cut through Three Foot Lane.'

'Rysome? Nowt much there now, is there? Allus was a pretty hamlet, though. Nice woodland. I used to go rabbiting there when I was a lad. Had many a one for 'pot. My ma used to make 'best rabbit pie I've ever tasted.' He shook a finger. 'But don't tell my missus.'

'Oh, aye.' Harry grinned as he jumped down. 'I won't! Thanks for 'ride.'

'You're welcome. Good luck wi' new job and don't forget us out in Holderness when you're mekkin' a fortune in Hull.'

Harry lifted a hand in farewell and thought that Holderness pigs might fly before he made his fortune. He was about to

45

become a mill labourer, no longer with the prestige of running a farm on behalf of a well-respected farmer; no longer working out in the fields, scything or threshing with the sun on his back, or breathing in the aroma of a golden harvest. Nor would he feel the drenching rain refreshing the earth. From now on he would be just another cog in the wheel that turned to crush the selfsame grain that he might once have gathered. He breathed out a great sigh. It would be a different life, and one that he would have to conquer, or fail and fall on fallow ground.

After Harry had left that morning, Ellen fed and dressed the children and was pleased to see that Mary had some colour back in her cheeks; she still had a husky voice and Ellen put a spoonful of honey in a cup with a few drops of warm water for her to sip. Mary licked her lips and then lifted the cup high so that Thomas couldn't grab at it. Ellen then gave the same to him and Sarah, knowing that it could only do them good.

'When we've finished tidying up,' she told them, 'and prepared dinner for Dada when he comes home, we'll get ready and visit Granny Snowden and Granny Randell. How would you like that?'

Sarah clapped her hands together, and Mary and Thomas followed suit. Sarah went to fetch their coats and hats and tried to dress Thomas in his, but he refused to let her and attempted to do it himself, screaming and kicking his feet when he failed.

'Thomas, stop that or I won't take you; you are such a handful sometimes,' Ellen scolded. The child looked up at her and then at his hands, and Ellen hid a smile; he knew what she was saying all right.

It was fortunate that both grandmothers lived fairly close to each other, Harry's mother at one end of Holmpton village and hers at the other. Sarah and Mary walked by her side, holding hands, and Thomas, wrapped in a blanket to keep him snug and stop him struggling, was tucked on to her hip.

She wondered how Harry was getting on in his quest for work and somewhere for them to live and knew she would miss living

46

in Holderness. She had known nowhere else; her parents, and grandparents too, though she could barely remember them, were Holderness people, as were Harry's.

She called first of all on Harry's mother to tell her of their plans; Harry's sister Meg was also visiting and soon retrieved Thomas from her arms.

'Now then, you young peazan.' She held him up in the air and he chortled and squealed in delight. 'Let's have a look at those sharp little teeth.' She put her finger to his bottom lip and he obligingly opened his mouth. 'My, but they're sharp.' She gave him a smacking kiss on his cheek and then sat down with him on her knee. Her own child, Joe, ran towards her and smacked Thomas on the head and then ran away. 'I'm pregnant again,' she told Ellen cheerfully. 'I must have got caught even before I stopped feeding Joe. I hope I get a girl this time. Four boys are enough for anybody.' She jiggled Thomas to stop him from crying.

'Oh, goodness,' Ellen said. 'However do you manage?'

'She doesn't,' Mrs Randell said, handing Ellen a cup of tea. 'She's higgledy-piggledy, but she loves her babbies. She'll soon have as many as I did.' She too sat down and smiled at Ellen. 'Now then, what's happening with our Harry?'

Ellen took a sip of tea and looked down, at Sarah and Mary, who were playing on the floor with a jumble of toy bricks. 'Harry went to Hull this morning to look for work.'

Mrs Randell frowned. 'So it's true. Somebody told his da that he'd seen him getting on to 'carrier's cart this morning.' She shook her head. 'He's mistaken. There're no farms in Hull to 'best of my knowledge.'

'There are not,' Ellen agreed. 'He's looking at labouring work, in mills or factories.'

'He's no miller either.'

'Not a flour miller, Ma,' Meg butted in. 'There are different kinds of mills – seed-crushing mills, oil mills, that kind of thing. He's adaptable is our Harry. He'll find something.'

'It's a long way to travel every day; will he have to buy a hoss and cart?' Mrs Randell frowned.

47

'No,' Ellen said softly. 'We haven't got that kind of money. We have to move off 'farm; we'll have to live in Hull.'

'Live in Hull! How can he do that?' Mrs Randell seemed shocked and her voice rose. 'He's my onny son. I'll be left wi' onny my daughters.'

'You've got plenty of sons-in-law, Ma,' Meg said quietly. 'And you've still got our da, don't forget, and I expect Harry will come regularly to see you.' Ellen glanced at Meg, whose manner remained impassive. She smiled at her mother. 'It'll be all right, Ma,' she said. 'You don't have to worry.'

Mrs Randell was failing, Ellen realized as she walked back through the village to her own parents' cottage. It hadn't been apparent to her previously. Was it the shock of hearing the news of Harry's leaving the district that had brought on her distress? But as she had left the house, Meg had murmured, 'No need to tell Harry about Ma. He needn't feel anxious about going; he has to earn a living and there isn't one here. There're plenty of us to tek it in turn to visit her, and Da is capable. He'll tell us if she needs any extra help.'

Her own mother was more encouraging when Ellen told her about their plans. 'We'll miss you not popping in, and we'll miss 'bairns as well. It's a shame when families break up, but you have to go where 'work is. That's 'way it is.' She was silent for a moment, and then said, 'Course, what you're doing is going back to your roots. Your roots, I mean, not Harry's. His family has allus lived in Holderness.'

'But so has ours,' Ellen protested. 'Your parents were born here and I thought theirs were too.'

'They were,' her mother agreed, 'but afore that our fore-bears lived in Hull. Whaling folk they were, and 'first to come to Holderness after an accident at sea was a man called William Foster. I don't know how or why he upped sticks and came out into 'country, but come he did, he and his wife and bairns. Another bairn was born here, further up 'coast, out Aldbrough way, and she – Sarah, she was called – did well for herself, marrying into 'gentry, so I understand. My owd granny used to spin me tales about Sarah Foster who married a Mr Rayner and produced

48

this big family. There were a lot of 'em, seemingly, millers and farmers, and shipowners too, and they're still scattered throughout Holderness, though some of them lost land to 'erosion and had to move inland.'

'Really?' Ellen was astonished. 'So is that why you were named Sarah? And I've named my Sarah after you; and then there's Billy – he's a William, and so is our Maria's second child, William!'

'Aye, I expect so. And William Foster's wife was called Maria, seemingly. But there again,' Sarah went on, 'we all tend to use 'same names as our relations; it gets confusing at times.'

The subject was changed, and Ellen's mother, who was a practical woman, asked when they would be moving. Ellen had to say she didn't know until Harry arrived home to say if he had managed to find work.

'You'll need to borrow a hoss and cart,' Sarah said. 'Our Billy'll know somebody and I expect he'll give Harry a hand wi' handling furniture, though you'll not have much.'

'We haven't,' Ellen agreed. 'But we have enough. We'll manage, I expect.'

Sarah got to her feet and patted her shoulder. 'You will,' she said quietly. 'You're a practical young woman.' She stood for a moment, and then added, 'That's not to say we won't miss you being near, cos we will.'

Her mother was obviously sad to think they would be moving out of reach, and as Ellen walked home later she thought that she must write regularly and tell her parents how they were coping with living in a large and busy town. It will certainly be different, she thought as she crossed the yard to her own front door, the hens scattering around her feet. Here it was quiet and peaceful; they had no neighbours, just a vista of cornfields and copses, green hedgerows hiding blackbirds' nests, birdsong every morning and the trumpeting cry of pheasants, and she thought regretfully that she wouldn't be making bramble and apple jam; nor would the children collect conkers from the chestnut trees as she did when she was a child.

49

She pushed open her door and ushered Sarah and Mary inside to the warm and welcoming kitchen. Perhaps, she thought, one day, if we make enough money, we'll be able to afford to rent a house with a garden where the children can play. For she had no illusions: she was certain they were going to a place with hard pavements, factory chimneys, smoke and grime, and she would not know a single person there.

CHAPTER EIGHT

Harry arrived home about an hour later, just after she had fed the children. He came through the door and wrapped his arms around her. Then he held her at arms' length with a smile in his eyes. 'Well, Mrs Randell, are you ready for our next adventure?'

She nodded. 'I think so,' she said in a small voice.

He kissed her cheek. 'That's my brave girl. I've found work at a mill, a decent employer I think, and a house. Well, it's 'ground floor of a house and a yard at 'back where 'bairns can play safely once I've cleared it of rubbish and scrubbed it out.'

'What do you mean 'ground floor?' she frowned. 'Don't we get the whole house?'

He shook his head. 'I've found accommodation near to 'mill and it seems that all 'houses in that area are divided up into rooms by landlords so they get rent for each one.' He gave a deep sigh. 'Believe me, Ellen, some of them are rat holes; local corporation should get them cleaned up cos they're not fit for folk to live in. This was 'best I could find for 'money we could afford.'

Ellen turned away to put the kettle on the fire to make him a drink and return a dish of stew to the oven, and thought that although she and her parents and siblings had lived together in a small cottage, it wasn't the same as living cheek by jowl with strangers.

Then Harry told her of the couple who had to move out of the house because they couldn't afford the rent. 'They were still

51

there when 'rent man took me to see it,' he said. 'Foreign, they were, with bairns about 'same age as ours. They had no money; 'rent man said they should try 'parish.'

Ellen put her hands to her mouth in dismay. '*No*,' she breathed. 'That means 'workhouse. That's a last resort. What kind of place have they come from to end up somewhere like that?'

'Worse than where they are now, I imagine, poor souls,' Harry said. 'He was looking for work; he said he was an engineer, but I don't fancy his chances when there are so many local folk looking too; the rent man said that his boss wouldn't be bothered whether they took his rooms or not, as he didn't like Jews.'

'What a dreadful thing to say,' Ellen protested. 'I hope you gave them a copper or two, Harry. I can't bear to think that their children will go hungry.'

He smiled. He knew she would say that there were always some worse off than they were. And it was true.

They ate after they had put the children to bed and Harry told her they'd be moving on Saturday ready for him to start work on the Monday. Ellen was startled by the swiftness of it and began thinking of what to pack first. She told Harry what her mother had said about Billy giving them a hand and he decided he'd go over after they'd finished eating and make arrangements. Billy was still single and knew a lot of people. Harry was fairly sure that he would know somebody who would loan him a horse and cart.

'I don't suppose Mr Charlesworth would lend you their wagon?' Ellen said,

'I wouldn't even ask him,' Harry said, and Ellen remarked that he was cutting off his nose to spite his face.

'Aye, mebbe I am, but I have my pride, and we'll see if he meks any offer. He might even be peeved that I'm leaving before I said I would, but 'new foreman will be pleased to have 'cottage, I expect.'

Ellen looked round at the cosy room with the flickering firelight and the warm welcoming glow of the lamp. 'Anybody would be,' she said with a catch in her voice. 'They'd be fools not to.'

52

As soon as Harry had gone out to see Billy, she opened the cupboard doors and took out her few pans. She took out her cutlery too, but on second thoughts she put that back again. They had to eat and therefore needed knives and forks. She could manage with one pan for three days. She began to think that perhaps she should prepare and cook food to take with them, for she didn't know what facilities there would be; she'd forgotten to ask Harry if there was a fireplace or a range for cooking.

When she and Harry had come here after their wedding they had had nothing except what they had been given. Harry's mother had provided them with a pair of sheets and pillow covers, and then her mother did the same, and offered two chairs that she no longer needed. Ellen had made curtains from material she had found in her mother's cupboard, and she looked at them now. They were heavy and still serviceable and kept out draughts, and she thought that she would take them, along with everything else they possessed. It still wouldn't fill a cart, and the new family who were coming here would undoubtedly bring their own goods and chattels.

By the time Harry arrived home again she had sorted everything from the downstairs cupboards into piles ready to pack. Harry said that he and Billy had been loaned a small wagon for free and that Billy would drive it to Hull and back for them.

The next morning they were both up earlier than usual; Harry to tell Charlesworth they would be gone by Saturday morning, and also to finish off a few jobs around the farm. What he was really doing was taking his leave of the workplace where he had spent so many happy years; but it had changed since Ozzie had died and the heart had gone out of it for him.

He walked through a small woodland that he had played in as a lad and kept in good order since he started work for Ozzie, pruning trees and bushes, and cutting back brambles, nettles and thistles from the paths, but leaving some clumps and patches for the birds, bees and butterflies to feed on or collect the pollen from. He thought that on their last day he and Ellen should bring the children to the woodland. Thomas would be

53

too young to remember, but perhaps a vestige of memory might be retained by Sarah and Mary.

'They'll build memories of their own,' he said to Ellen, and she agreed that they would, but not of here, of their new home in Hull.

'Let's take them to look at the sea as well,' she said, 'for who knows when we'll come back?'

'But we will,' he assured her. 'We'll come to visit our folks, won't we? We shan't desert them for ever. This'll allus be our home.'

And so that is what they did. Friday morning was sharp and bright, the summer sun losing its heat; there was a smell of burning stubble and blackberries, sloe berries and rosehips were palely changing colour on the hedgerow, wild crab apple was dressed in wispy spiders' webs, and everywhere shades of burnished russet brown and gold shone amongst the leaves as the trees slowly changed into their autumn robes.

Sarah and Mary danced down the woodland paths and Thomas too struggled to get down from his father's arms to join them. He was walking well and Harry and Ellen each took a hand and he kicked out his legs and chortled at the crunching of fallen leaves.

Then, with Thomas back in Harry's arms and Sarah and Mary holding hands, they turned towards the path that led to the cliff top, and although they were getting anxious that they still had things to pack and must say goodbye to their families, they didn't want to miss this last walk. It was special to both of them and Harry whistled the tune of 'The Girl With The Nut Brown Hair' as they walked. *She looked so sweet from her two bare feet to the sheen of her nut-brown hair.*

'Do you know how long I've loved you?' he asked her.

She smiled. 'Since I was fifteen.'

'And do you know how long I will love you?'

'For ever,' she said, putting up her face for his kiss.

The sea lashed below the cliffs and Ellen kept tight hold of her daughters' hands. 'My ma said that our forebears came to Holderness from Hull,' she told him. 'First one to come had been a whaling man.'

54

'That must have been a hard life. I wonder why he came out here,' Harry said curiously. 'Unless he chose Holderness so that he could still see 'ocean. They say that seafarers get salt water in their veins.'

Ellen nodded. It was history, she thought. We all have a story to tell over time. 'Come on,' she said softly. 'We've said our good-byes. Now we need to say hello to a new life.'

CHAPTER NINE

The children were excited to be climbing into the wagon to travel to their new home, each clutching a cloth bag containing their favourite things. Sarah had a rag doll that one of her aunts had made for her; Mary had her building bricks; whilst Thomas had the much-washed blanket that he liked to hold until he went to sleep.

Ellen had explained to Sarah and Mary that they were going to live in a big town, but as neither had been anywhere but her own village they didn't know what that meant.

'It might feel like a prison to them,' Harry muttered to Billy as they drove away. Neither he nor Ellen looked back at their former home. 'There's no garden where bairns can play, onny a yard where Ellen can hang out 'washing. Nowhere to grow our own vegetables or a few flowers.'

'You can grow taties and carrots in a sack,' Billy said practically. 'Granted, not now cos it's too late, but you could plant for next year, if you're still there. And,' he added, 'you can beg a wooden box from 'grocer or somebody and Ellen can fill it wi' soil and scatter some flower seeds in it if she has a mind, though I tend to think it's a waste o' time growing summat you can't eat.'

Ellen leaned forward to listen. 'What's a waste o' time?'

'Growing flowers,' Billy grinned.

'It's good for the soul,' she responded, 'especially if there aren't any flowers or trees to look at.' She suppressed a sigh. 'Mebbe there's a park near to where we're going.'

56

'Dennison mentioned there was one, but he didn't say where, and I didn't see one,' Harry said. 'We went into Hull this way, through Hedon and back out up Holderness Road. Top end of Holderness Road leading out of town is pleasant enough, but a bit swampy in parts, so we shan't be visiting you in winter, Billy, in case we get bogged down. There's a place midway called Summergangs where 'road runs through some fields. We'll be able to walk there on a Sunday.'

'It'll be too far to walk to Holderness,' Ellen remarked from the back of the wagon as she pointed out the tall ships' masts to the children as they passed the dockyards. 'And we won't have 'luxury of a wagon to ride in.'

Harry shook his head. They wouldn't, that was for sure, and he began to feel anxious over Ellen's feelings when she saw where they were going to live. He'd given her little information about the house, and she hadn't asked; it was as if she didn't want to know. He'd gathered up a sack of sticks to make a fire when they got there, so that the room would look cosier.

After an hour they stopped to let the children run about and stretch their legs, and then they sat by the roadside and ate bread and cheese before they set off again.

It began to drizzle as they approached Hull and crossed the town through Market Place and then over the River Hull's North Bridge; Harry hoped that the rent agent would be there so that they didn't have to hang about waiting for him with the keys, and he thought too that if it had been a bright sunny day the area would have looked more cheerful, but the sky was grey and a thin dark cloud hung ominously over them as if it were about to open into a deluge.

Billy looked up; it was as if he had been reading Harry's thoughts. 'It's nowt much,' he muttered. 'It'll clear up later; onny a slight depression.'

Harry eased out a breath. It was that all right, and he hoped that it wouldn't last.

Dark, soot-smeared bricks, a grimy wooden front door and dirty windows. Ellen gazed at the terraced house where Billy had pulled up the wagon at Harry's instructions.

57

Wherever have you brought us to, Harry, was her first thought, but she didn't speak it; she knew he hadn't had any choice or he wouldn't have brought them here. The street was dank and dreary, long and narrow with tall chimneys and what looked like a mill tower in the distance. A young boy in cut-down trousers leaned on a wall on the opposite side of the street and watched them with interest.

He crossed over and spoke to Billy. 'Are you lot coming to live here?' He looked at the two little girls and the child in Ellen's arms. 'Have you got any older bairns? Cos there's nobody to play wi' round here.'

Billy solemnly shook his head. 'Sorry, mate, not me. I'm onny the driver.'

'Ah!' The boy wiped his nose on a jumper sleeve and moved away. 'I can't play wi' lasses.' He turned back and shouted, 'There were foreigners living here afore. They wouldn't play either. Not tag or owt.'

Harry took Thomas from Ellen and helped her down. 'I'm sorry,' he began, but she interrupted him and gave a small, though wavering, smile.

'Hush. First thing I'm going to do is clean that window, inside and out.'

Harry nodded. If anyone could make the best of a situation it was Ellen.

'Is this your rent man?' Billy asked. 'They all look 'same, don't they? Shifty, and wearing cast-off clothing.'

'I don't know,' Harry said. 'We've never had one. Ozzie allus took 'rent out of my wages at 'year end.'

Ellen gave a grim laugh. Billy didn't have a rent man either; he still lived at home with their parents and paid board and lodgings to their mother, so he couldn't know, but nevertheless the man coming towards them matched his description perfectly.

'Good morning, Mr Randell.' Dennison tipped his battered bowler to Ellen. 'Mrs Randell. In good time, I'm happy to see.' He fished about in his case. 'The keys!' He offered them to Ellen with a flourish.

58

'You can open 'door for us.' Ellen smiled sweetly. 'I suppose it's been left in good order? Clean and tidy? Though I notice that 'window glass needs cleaning.'

'Ah, yes, I'm afraid that's a hazard due to 'conditions in this area, Mrs Randell; nothing much can be done about that.' He unlocked the front door, led her into the small hallway and pushed open the door to the downstairs room.

'No lock on this door?' she commented and looked up the narrow stairway. 'Who lives upstairs?'

'Another family,' he said. 'Very respectable.'

'I'll need a key for this door,' she said firmly. 'You'll send a locksmith to fit one today, please; we can't move in without that assurance. We might not have much but what we have is precious.'

Dennison looked at her in amazement; he had evidently never had demands made on him before.

Ellen looked at Harry. 'Otherwise we'll have to ask for our deposit back, isn't that right, Harry?'

'Aye, it is.' Harry called to Billy through the front door. 'Don't unload yet, Billy, we might have to move somewhere else.'

'Oh, but . . .' Dennison stammered, before recovering a little. 'By all means; I'll organize that. You have my word.'

'Today!' Ellen said. 'It's only just ten o'clock. You'll easily be able to get someone here before midday.' She looked at him questioningly.

'Yes,' Dennison sighed. 'Masters. Jack Masters. He does work on some other houses belonging to Mr Benstead. I'll send him round afore dinner.'

'Thank you.' She looked round the room and went through into the scullery, too bare with only a sink, a draining board and one cupboard to be called a kitchen. 'And he can put a chain on 'back door as well whilst he's about it. We can't be too careful with young children about.'

She decided not to make further demands; he would, she was sure, baulk at doing much more, but she was satisfied that he'd realized that neither would she accept anything substandard, however inferior and far from what she had expected this place might be.

59

Harry and Billy began bringing in the furniture and their belongings, and gathering up a group of very young children who stood by the wagon watching them, including the boy who had spoken to them earlier. Sarah and Mary solemnly observed them from the window and each held Thomas by a hand to stop him going out of the door, whilst Ellen lit a fire in the grate. She stood up as the twigs and the wood caught hold and began to draw. At least the chimney must be clean, she thought. It was one of the questions she had thought of asking Dennison.

She picked Thomas up, and when Harry brought in a chair she sat down to feed him and hoped that he would fall asleep, freeing her to begin unpacking and wash out the cupboard before stacking it with crockery.

Billy carried a box of pans into the scullery. 'We've got a wooden cupboard in 'shed at home, Ellen,' he said when he came out again. 'There's nowt much in it. I'll borrow the wagon again next week and bring it and one or two other things.'

'Like what, Billy? We haven't any space for anything else.'

'Like whitewash and a brush,' he said. 'I'll paint 'scullery for you. It'll look cleaner and brighten it up.'

'Oh, would you? Thank you, Billy. Harry's going to clean 'yard so that 'children can play outside, and fix up a washing line, though it's going to take ages to boil a kettle on this small fire to do any washing. I'll have to ask if there's a wash house nearby.' A sob caught in her chest and she stifled it. How would she cook anything that wouldn't take all day?

Thomas fell asleep and she placed him on one of the easy chairs and covered him with his blanket. The men hadn't yet brought in their bed or the small one for the children. She looked round the room, wondering where they could put them, and decided that the only possible place was on the opposite side to the fire, alongside the inner wall of the room, where they could borrow heat from the next door house, if there was any.

Harry went outside to look at the yard and came back with a smile on his face. 'Come and look here, Ellen,' he said, and the two girls followed her to explore.

60

'What is it?' she asked as she stood on the outside step. Harry was examining a waist-high brick structure with a space beneath it and a wooden lid on top. 'It's a wash tub!' she exclaimed when Harry stepped back. 'Oh, wonderful! We can have hot water for washing and baths every weekend. Except we didn't bring our bath tub! I forgot about it. It's still hanging on 'wall by the back door.'

'Don't worry, Ellen,' Billy said. 'I'll pick it up when I go home, and if 'new folk have moved in, which I doubt, I'll say we didn't have room for it on 'wagon.'

Ellen gave a big smile. 'Everything's going to be all right,' she said, and put her arms round Billy and gave him a squeeze, and then did the same to Harry, who dropped a kiss on her nose. 'We're going to be all right.'

Billy folded his arms. 'I hope you realize,' he said gruffly to Harry, his long-time friend, 'just how lucky you are being married to my little sister.'

61

CHAPTER TEN

The room began to look more homely once the furniture was in place, even though there was hardly room to move with the two beds against the wall, a chair on each side of the fire and the kitchen table and a bench against the scullery wall. Ellen had swept the floor and mopped it and washed the inside of the window and surrounding frame. There was a lot of dust and soot but essentially the place was reasonably clean. She thought that it would be a full-time occupation keeping dirt and grime at bay, considering the area they were in; it was coming in through the ill-fitting windows and under the doors of this old housing.

She wondered about the people who had lived here previously; how difficult it must be for them, especially if they didn't speak the language well. They will be so vulnerable, she thought; open to the trickeries of every conniving fraudster who might take advantage of them.

Harry had cleaned the wash tub, half filled it with water from a tap in the yard and lit a fire beneath it with the remains of the wood they had brought. They were used to getting washed in cold water, but providing the fire stayed in long enough to get the water very hot it should still be warm by the next morning, and what a luxury that would be, he reflected, to wash in warm water.

'I've had a thought,' Billy said. 'I don't think Jack Rogers will mind if I keep 'wagon over tomorrow, so I'll come back in 'morning rather than next weekend with what you need.' He looked round the yard. 'If I bring two large brushes we could paint 'walls out here as well as 'scullery. What do you think?'

'We could. They'll not stay white for long, but yeh, that would be great, Billy. Thanks.'

Billy left shortly afterwards, saying he'd be back early the next morning. Harry cleaned the outside windows, front and back, and Ellen put together the food she had prepared before they left. The children were getting tired with all the excitement of the day and she had decided to feed them early and put them to bed; she wondered if they would sleep, as they were used to being in a separate bedroom, whereas now they were all in one room for living and sleeping.

She had put out the girls' food and was about to feed Thomas with a little warmed broth and bread when there was a knock on their door; Harry went to answer it and Ellen heard him giving brief answers, then finally saying, 'Sorry if we've bothered you.'

She looked at him questioningly. 'Woman from upstairs,' he said. 'She wanted to know how many children we had and hoped they were well behaved, as she has a sick mother living with her who shouldn't be disturbed.'

'What kind of sickness?' Ellen was alarmed. 'I hope it isn't anything catching.'

'She didn't say,' he replied, and then grinned. 'She was trying to look over my shoulder to see inside the room, but I blocked her.'

'That's not a good start, is it? Not very welcoming for someone who is sharing 'same house.'

'Don't let it bother you,' he said. 'Besides, 'bairns aren't noisy.'

'I might go up and introduce myself tomorrow,' Ellen said. 'I suppose it must be worrying when new neighbours come in, especially if she has a sick mother.' She sighed, and thought that the woman might have waited a day or two before issuing her warning.

The next morning, Harry suggested that after breakfast they might take a short walk around the neighbourhood to acquaint themselves with the district, find local grocers' shops and possibly a baker's where Ellen could buy fresh bread, for there was no oven in the house, but she reminded him that Billy was coming to paint the yard and scullery.

'Ten or fifteen minutes, then?' he asked. 'He won't be this early and I'd rather we explored together than you wander about on your own. Just to begin with,' he added. 'I'm sure you'll soon get your bearings.'

He was aware that it would all seem strange to her; like him she had lived all her life around Holmpton and played hide and seek in the woods at Rysome. There had been no danger except for falling over the cliffs into the sea, and all the children of Holderness were aware of the erosion and took extra care not to go too near the cracked and crumbling edge, although some of the more adventurous boys, like Harry himself, had dared each other to get close.

Ellen dressed the children and was relieved that the morning was sunny and dry. They took the keys, for Dennison had been true to his word and sent the locksmith to fix a lock on the hall door and a chain in the scullery as she had requested, and Harry suggested that they went round to the back of the terrace to look at the river where he had seen the lads fishing on his previous visit.

There were more fishermen there that morning and some already had catches in their trugs. 'Will 'water be clean?' Ellen asked. 'I was thinking of all 'industry round here.'

'It must be if 'fish are swimming in it,' Harry said. 'I forgot to look for my old rod; what do you think? Should I fish? It's food for free.'

'My da used to have a rod,' she said, 'and a trug. He used to fish from the beach when I was little. We'll ask Billy to ask Da if you can have it.'

They stayed out for ten minutes and Harry pointed out the various seed-crushing mills, sand and lime works and tanneries. Ellen had thought it might be nice to bring the children to run around on the grassy area during the spring or summer, but now she had seen the industry on their doorstep she worried over the noxious air that sprang from the tall chimneys and kilns and what it might do to them.

64

A chill wind had got up and grey clouds scudded overhead. 'It's not very warm, Harry,' she said. 'Shall we go back in? We'll tek a walk on another Sunday.'

As they walked back to the front of the terrace, they saw Billy driving the wagon towards them. With him was Ellen's mother.

'Good heavens,' Ellen said. 'They must have been up at 'crack of dawn.' As she spoke she felt her eyes prickle. She was so pleased to see her mother, for she had wondered how long it would be before they could travel back home again to see everyone. Home, she thought tearfully. No; this is my home now, and love it or hate it I must make the best of it. I will try to love it, but right now I'm finding it very hard.

Harry helped his mother-in-law down from the cart, while she asked him to bring in a large basket and a box containing eggs, and warned him not to drop it. Ellen put out her arms to hug her mother and said how happy she was that she'd come, and the children tugged on their grandmother's skirts, delighted to see her again so soon.

'Come in, come in, Ma,' Ellen said when the greetings were over, trying to sound cheerful. 'Welcome to Hull.'

'Hmm!' Mrs Snowden glanced about her, and with pursed lips looked up at the house before stepping inside.

'I know, it's not what we're used to, Ma,' Ellen began, 'but—'

Her mother wagged a finger. 'Needs must when 'devil drives. Circumstance has forced you here, so you must put up wi' it till your fortune turns.'

Ellen nodded and sniffed. 'Yes, I know, but I do miss everybody already, and . . . and I don't know anybody here.'

'You soon will.' Her mother looked about the room and then headed for the scullery. 'For goodness' sake, you onny arrived yesterday. Get settled in and then go out walking wi' 'bairns, and folk'll soon talk to you.'

'You're right, I know. It was a shock, that's all. I'm glad that you're here, Ma. I feel better already.'

Her mother turned and smiled. 'You'll feel even better when you see what I've brought.'

65

She picked up the basket that Harry had carried in and took a clean cloth from the top of it, then took out a cooked chicken, a basin of stuffing ready for cooking, and a turnip already chopped into cubes for boiling. From the box she brought out a dozen eggs that she said the hens had laid that morning, and a freshly baked loaf.

Ellen exclaimed at how early she must have got out of bed that morning, but her mother simply said, 'I proved 'bread last night and baked it this morning. It's still slightly warm; and I see that you've no oven so you'll have to fry 'stuffing over the fire, but it'll taste just as good. So there's your dinner almost ready for you. Best put 'turnip on now if you've a pan handy, for it takes for ever to cook.'

Her mother was so thrifty and practical, Ellen thought; that was through bringing up so many children without much money. I must learn to be the same if we're to survive, for there's no doubt that money will be tight.

Billy distempered the scullery walls, splattering much of it over himself and the children, who wanted to help. Then Harry, who was a much neater, cleaner worker, began on the outside walls and soon the yard and the scullery looked much brighter than they had done. Next spring, Ellen thought as she gazed at the transformation, she would beg a wooden box from a grocer and plant some flower seeds.

Ellen's mother and brother had a pot of tea but neither would eat any of the food that had been brought, although Ellen was sure Billy wouldn't have refused had his mother not been there. She brought out a cake tin and offered him a slice of fruit cake, which he accepted.

'In return for your hard work, Billy,' Ellen said. 'We want you to come again but you won't if we don't offer you any victuals.'

He grinned. 'I won't come again until 'walls need another coat o' paint.'

Harry smiled grimly. 'I hope we'll be out of here afore then. And to something better.'

Ellen looked round the room. It all looked very comfortable: the fire was glowing, the two girls were playing on the clipped

66

rug she had brought from Rysome and Thomas was lying on his stomach on one of the beds, playing some game of his own; perhaps when we do leave for somewhere else, she thought, we might be sorry to go, but at least we'll be leaving it in a better condition than when we arrived.

At dinner time, Billy and his mother waved goodbye as they set off back to Holderness. 'I'll write,' Ellen promised as Billy lightly tapped the whip on the horse's back. 'Take care, Billy. Give our love to everybody, Ma, and to Harry's ma too.'

She felt choked as she and Harry stood on the step and watched the wagon drive away. He put his arm around her. 'Come on, love. Shall I scrub some taties and put them in 'fire to bake? Turnip should be nearly cooked by now, and we'll have a splendid feast wi' that chicken, eh?'

Ellen took a deep breath. 'Yes,' she said. 'Let's do that. We'll celebrate being in our new home.'

He gently squeezed her. 'That's my girl.'

CHAPTER ELEVEN

The next morning Harry was up at five o'clock to be sure of being early into work. Ellen built up the fire and fried him eggs for breakfast, and packed him up some slices of chicken, crusty bread and a bottle of tea. He was only ten minutes from the mill and regarded that as a bonus. He gave her a kiss but didn't disturb the children, as they were still sleeping, Sarah and Mary in one bed and Thomas in theirs. They had all slept well.

Ellen waved him off from the door and saw that there were crowds of people, men and women, tramping down the street on their way to work, but it was the children she noticed most. They were so thin and puny-looking, Ellen was convinced some of them had never had a decent meal in their lives. Young girls huddled beneath thin shawls with their bare feet in wooden clogs; the boys wore flat caps and had their collars turned up and their hands tucked into the pockets of cut-down threadbare coats. One child stood in the doorway opposite and watched everyone going by. She thought he might be too young to work yet, and as she watched him she realized it was the boy who had spoken to them on the day they'd arrived. Perhaps his mother works, she thought, and so he comes out for company. Returning her attention to the older children, she remembered how when she had started work her mother had made sure she had a hearty breakfast of porridge or eggs before setting off for the farm. Once she had proved herself and Mrs Hodges had decided she would keep her on, she lived in, but Mr and Mrs Hodges had always been generous with their victuals, knowing that their farm workers and house staff worked better with good food inside them.

Going back indoors, she built up the fire again and stirred the porridge, hoping they wouldn't run out of wood and wondering if they could afford a bucket of coal. Perhaps we might take a walk later and collect some kindling, she thought; we must build up a stock for when winter comes. She recalled stepping out of the cottage in Rysome, where there was always a ready supply of twigs or branches that she could trail back to the woodpile for when it was needed.

She unlocked the back door, and taking a clean bucket went into the yard to test if the water in the copper was still warm. The fire had burned out, but when she lifted the wooden lid and tested the water it was just about right for the children to wash in. She plunged the bucket in and half filled it, then replaced the lid and carried the bucket inside. She scrubbed out the stone sink and decided that it was about the right size for Thomas to sit in whilst she washed him down.

After about fifteen minutes she saw through the window that the throng of workers had dwindled; now there were groups of young men passing by, many of them in neat trousers, jackets and caps but some in large bowlers that came down over their ears. Perhaps they were messenger boys, errand lads or office clerks. She had never seen so many people together and was fascinated by the idea of who they might be and where they could be going. The young boy had vanished.

The girls began to stir. First Sarah sat up and then Mary turned over and put her nose above the blanket, and Ellen sat on their bed and gave them both a kiss. 'Good morning, sleepyheads,' she murmured, and smiled. 'How are you this morning?'

'Very well, fank you,' Sarah piped, but Mary just closed her eyes and snuggled down again. 'Where are we, Mama?' Sarah looked round the small room. 'Is this our new house?'

Ellen felt a lump in her throat; however would she keep them entertained all day without a garden to play in? Even in winter she used to dress Sarah in warm clothes and let her run around the garden to discover such treasures as winter snowdrops or

69

aconites, or build a snowman, or even chase – but never catch – a rabbit.

'It is,' she said, 'and a little later we'll dress up warm and go out for a walk to see where we are.'

'I know where I am,' Sarah said, throwing back the blanket. 'I'm in bed, but I'd like to go home now, please.' She climbed out of bed and went towards her clothes, which were neatly folded on a chair.

'First we wash, don't we?' Ellen said. 'Come along, Sarah, you can be first. I've got some warm water for you to wash in.'

She moved the child's clothes on to the bed and took the chair into the scullery for Sarah to stand on, then poured some of the warm water into the sink.

'I'm not dirty,' Sarah told her. 'I've been in bed.'

'I know, but you'll feel fresh and clean after a wash. Come, climb on the chair and wash your hands and face.'

Sarah was a dutiful child and did as she was bid, but Ellen believed that when she was older she would mull over suggestions or instructions and make up her own mind whether or not to follow them. Ellen was happy with that. She liked to see independence in a child; when she and her sisters had been little, they had been encouraged by their mother to think for themselves.

Sarah said she could dress herself, so Ellen roused Mary, who was still snuggled down, and told her to come and wash whilst the water was still warm because there was porridge waiting for them. 'I'm sure you're hungry after that long sleep,' she said, smiling.

'Don't want porridge,' Mary said. 'I'll have bread.'

'Porridge first,' Ellen insisted, 'and then bread, and then we must go and find a baker to buy a fresh loaf, and you can have 'crust if you like.'

By now Thomas was waking and climbing out of bed. He clambered into his mother's arms, and Mary insisted she could wash herself just as Sarah had done, so Ellen let her, and thought that wiping up the overspill afterwards was a small price to pay in order to get them all washed and dressed.

70

Thomas sat in the sink whilst she washed him down and then she wrapped him in a towel and blanket and sat by the fire to feed him, deciding that now was probably the time when she would begin to wean him in earnest. He was old enough, he had all his teeth, and as she had done with Sarah and Mary she would give him bread and milk, *pobs* as it was called, until after a few months he was eating the same food as the adults.

They were ready: washed, fed and dressed, but it seemed to have taken much longer than usual. Ellen asked Sarah and Mary to take Thomas's hands whilst she locked up and then shepherded them out of the front door. She picked him up to carry him, for it would be quicker than letting him walk; he struggled to get down but she promised he could walk on the way back.

They headed the way that the workers had gone and she hoped that there would be a baker's somewhere near. If I were a baker I'd have my shop where people were passing by and the enticing aroma of freshly baked bread would draw them in. It was a very long street of terraced housing, but there were no shops as yet; at the bottom of the street she saw only the tops of tall chimneys and the towers of seed-crushing mills.

Thomas was heavy and he wriggled constantly to get down and walk beside his sisters, so before long her resolution failed and she allowed him, but instead of toddling forward he turned to look back the way they had come and pointed. Ellen sighed and took his hand. 'Come along, Thomas; you wanted to walk.' But he pointed back again and Ellen turned to see a tall woman and her children hurrying towards them, the woman signalling for her to wait. Ellen noticed how striking she was, her eyes and the hair showing beneath her shawl a very dark brown, much darker brown than Ellen's.

'I think you live in house where we lived. I saw you come out.'

Ellen nodded and pointed up the street. 'Yes? We moved in on Saturday.'

'Your husband gave us money, and bread for children.'

71

'Did he?' Harry had said he'd given them something. He didn't mention giving them his bread. 'I'm sorry if we took your house,' Ellen added as an apology.

The woman shook her head. 'The rent man – he say we had to leave. We have no more money to pay.'

'I'm sorry,' Ellen said again, but an answer swiftly came back.

'Not your fault. We are not from here. We are from Poland. We have all papers but my husband cannot get work.'

'Where are you living now?'

'We have room. It is a – what you call – a *piwnica*, a cellar, under ground.'

Ellen stared, her lips parted. 'Under 'ground?'

She nodded. '*Tak*! Yes. It is, erm – odour, stink. Wet?'

'Damp?' Ellen asked.

'*Tak* – yes. Your husband give us money and the man – he take the money and let us have this room.'

Ellen gave a soft exclamation. Harry had said that he was worried the family would have to make the choice between food or rent. Perhaps someone gave them food; the parish, maybe?

'Would you like to come back with me for a cup of tea?' she asked. 'But first I must buy bread; as you know, there isn't an oven in the room for me to make any. Is there a baker's shop anywhere near here?'

The woman nodded. 'Come, I will show you.'

Ellen and the children walked by the woman's side and the children all gazed shyly at each other. There was a girl and a boy about the same age as Sarah and Mary, and a boy roughly Thomas's age being carried by his mother.

'I'm Ellen,' she said after a moment. 'What's your name?'

'Anna Bosco.' She pointed a hand at her children. 'Zofia,' she said of the eldest girl, 'and Jakub, and this,' she jiggled the littlest, 'is Aron. My husband is Filip.'

Soon the older children were giggling at each other, although not speaking, and Ellen wondered if Zofia and Jakub spoke English. 'When did you come to England?' she asked.

'One month ago. We came on ship from Rotterdam. We stay near railway station and are given food, but then we leave so

72

Filip can find work. Some friends, they go to Liverpool and then America but we want to stay in England; we look for our . . .' She struggled to find the words. 'Erm – Filip's *cowsuns?*'

Ellen looked at her. 'Cousins?'

'Yes! But we cannot find them. Perhaps they leave to go somewhere else, we think.'

They had left the street and cut down another and now they were led on by the tantalizing smell of freshly baked bread. All the children eagerly looked up, even though Sarah and Mary had eaten breakfast.

'It is someone's house,' Anna said. 'It is good bread. Made with water, not milk.'

'You've tried it?'

'Yes.' Anna's face fell and Ellen suspected she had no money to buy more. She was aware that she didn't have much money either, not until Harry collected his wages on Saturday, but she thought she had enough to buy an extra loaf.

'In Poland I make good bread,' Anna said. 'Rye bread; you like it?'

'Yes,' Ellen said. She baked with wheat and rye flour, but preferred wheat.

'I also make matzos.' Anna looked questioningly at Ellen, who shook her head.

'I don't know what that is,' she said. 'Is it Polish?'

Anna hesitated. 'It is Jewish; for the Passover.'

'Oh, I see,' Ellen said. 'That's why I haven't heard of it. I don't think I know any Jewish people.'

'We are Jews,' Anna said simply. 'Is that all right for you?'

Ellen frowned. What kind of question was that? 'Yes,' she said. 'Why not?'

In Holderness some residents attended chapel, others went to church. Ellen generally chose church because her parents did, though she didn't go every week, and when she was a child she had often gone to chapel in Hollym if her friends were going. But she didn't rigidly prefer one over the other.

'I don't always go to church,' she confessed, 'but sometimes I pray at home. When Mary was ill, I prayed then.' She considered.

73

'I think it is a personal matter that everyone should decide for themselves.'

'Not for Jews, it is not. We are born into Jewish faith and often we are punished for it.' Anna took a deep breath. 'Here is baker's shop.'

Ellen blinked, thinking this was not a conversation for a baker's shop, but she was intrigued. She smiled at Anna. 'Thank you,' she said as she stepped inside and opened her purse.

CHAPTER TWELVE

It was only a small shop with a queue of women waiting to be served. Anna stayed outside with her children; Thomas, who had been standing by Ellen's knee, put his nose up to the tantalizing aroma and raised his arms for Ellen to lift him. Leaning forward, he pointed at the bread on the shelf behind the counter and began to jiggle impatiently, clapping his hands.

The other women turned and smiled at him. 'A hungry boy, is he?' one of them asked, and Ellen replied that he was, always.

The baker who was serving looked hot and flustered; she finished attending to one customer and muttering 'Excuse me a minute' hurried to a back room, where they heard the bang of an oven door and the crash of a baking tray on to a table.

'Sorry,' she said on her return. 'I'm trying to be in a dozen places at 'same time.'

'Is Ginny not here this morning?' someone in the queue asked. 'Slept in again, has she?'

The baker nodded and turned to serve the next woman. She took the money and put it in the till and hurried into the back room again, returning with a wooden tray of freshly baked bread.

Thomas started to yell, stretching out his hand for the bread, and Ellen hushed him. 'In a minute, in a minute,' she said. The baker looked up, and as she served the next customer she also picked up a misshapen, one-legged gingerbread man and gave it to Thomas with a ghost of a smile on her face.

75

'Thank you,' Ellen said gratefully as she stood at the counter. She was the last in the queue at the moment but guessed she wouldn't be the last to buy, as the baker asked if she'd excuse her for a moment to take more bread out of the oven. She had a good trade, Ellen thought, but she seemed very harassed; when she came back she wiped her forehead with a cloth.

'Sorry to keep you,' she said. 'It's been such a busy morning. What can I get you?'

Ellen had noticed that there were two loaves on a bottom shelf and wondered if it might be yesterday's bread, and therefore cheaper. 'How much is your bread, please?'

The woman emitted a disgruntled sigh. 'Do you want brown bread, household bread, wheaten or oat? Large? Two pounders? Tuppence for today's household loaf. Bread cakes thruppence a dozen, or I've got yesterday's loaves a penny each . . .' She reeled through prices, weights and sizes.

Ellen reckoned up, deciding on the most economical way of spending what little money she had. 'I'll have those two from yesterday, one of today's two pounder households, and six bread cakes, please,' she said, handing over a silver sixpence and receiving a ha'penny change.

Whilst she waited for the bread to be put in brown paper bags Ellen glanced round; the shop was very clean, as was the woman's apron under the dusting of flour.

'Do you do all your own baking?' she asked.

'I do. I used to bake customers' own, but so few have facilities for making dough, let alone baking the bread, that I gave up on that option. Are you new around here?'

'Yes. We only arrived on Saturday, so I don't know my way about yet.' She indicated over her shoulder to Anna waiting outside. 'You were recommended. She said you had good bread.'

'Did she?' The woman looked towards the door. 'Are all those children hers?'

Ellen smiled. 'Two of them are mine.' Sarah and Mary had gone outside to wait with Anna's children. 'So you do everything yourself?'

76

'Aye, at 'minute I do. The girl I had doesn't always turn up. I'm going to have to look for someone else.'

'To make and bake? Or to serve?'

The woman humphed. 'They'd have to bake as well as I do, but not everybody wants to get up so early; they've got to be here by five. That's why Ginny doesn't always turn up. But today is 'last straw.'

'I'll ask about,' Ellen said. 'I know somebody who can bake bread.'

The woman nodded but didn't appear to be convinced. Then she said, 'My husband was our baker; he died last year, so now I do it. You've got to have stamina for this job.'

She nodded, and excused herself again. She had to put in another batch, she said, ready for her dinnertime customers.

Ellen handed yesterday's loaves to Anna and said she'd share the bread cakes when they got back home. 'She's looking for help in 'bakery,' she added.

Anna thanked her effusively for the bread. 'But Filip cannot bake!'

'But *you* can,' Ellen said. 'Or that's what you said.'

'How can I work when I have children?'

'I'll look after them.'

Anna stopped. 'You don't know me. Would you? How? A baker starts very early. And there's Aron – how would I feed him?'

They continued up the street. 'You'd have to wean him,' Ellen said. 'How old is he?'

'Nearly two years.' Anna was silent for a moment and then said, 'How would we do this?'

'Let's go back home and have a cup of tea. The children can have some bread and jam, and we'll discuss it.' Ellen looked at her. 'It might not be for long. When your husband gets work you could stop.'

They walked slowly back and Ellen hoped she hadn't bitten off more than she could chew. Looking after six children wouldn't be easy, but then her own mother had had more children than that and seemed to manage. Except, of course, we used to play outside, she thought, we weren't under her feet all

77

day, and besides, the older girls looked after the younger ones. She glanced at Sarah and Anna's Zophia; they were not yet old enough to look after themselves, let alone their younger siblings.

She unlocked the front door and then her own and then put her head up. Had she heard someone shout?

'What was that?' Anna said. 'There is someone else in house?'

'Yes, upstairs; a woman and her mother. I haven't met them. The daughter came to our door and asked Harry how many children we had. She didn't want any noise, I think; she said her mother was ill.'

'I remember now,' said Anna. 'We never saw them.'

They both looked up the bare staircase. 'I ought to go up,' Ellen said. 'Perhaps the old lady has fallen.'

They went into the room and deposited the bread on the table. Ellen filled the kettle and put it on the fire. 'Would you slice 'bread cakes? And there's some jam in 'cupboard.'

'Jam? What is jam?'

Ellen laughed and took the jar out of the cupboard to show her.

Anna took it from her and then she laughed too. '*Dżem*. It is the same. And what are bread cakes, please?'

Ellen opened up the paper bag and took out the rounds of bread. 'These are bread cakes. Some people call them rolls, but these aren't rolls.'

'They are shape of cake, yes, I understand, but are made of bread. That is good. Now you go upstairs, and I will feed children. Yes?'

'Yes,' Ellen said, thinking that although her children had eaten breakfast, perhaps Anna's children hadn't.

There was just one door on the top landing and Ellen knocked. 'Is anyone there?'

A groan came from inside. 'Door is open,' a woman's voice answered, so Ellen cautiously pushed it and put her head round. 'Hello?'

There were two chairs, a double bed and a small bedside table with a jug and a cup on it, and a very small fire in the grate. 'Hello?' she said again. 'Where are you?'

78

'I am on the floor,' a quavering voice answered her. 'I fell out of bed.'

Ellen went inside. At first she couldn't see anyone, but then she saw that what she had thought was a heap of clothes was an elderly woman propped up against the far side of the bed. She was shivering, even though she had a blanket wrapped round her that she must have pulled from the bed.

'What happened to you?' Ellen knelt beside her. 'I'm Ellen Randell, your new neighbour from downstairs.'

'I am so glad to see you, my dear.' The woman clutched Ellen's hand. 'I am Mrs Johnson. I have been sitting here for long time. I reach for cup, but could not grasp it and overstretched. The table was not near enough.'

'Do you think you've broken anything? Your leg, or your arm?' Ellen wondered how she could lift her back into bed. 'Where is your daughter?'

'At work. She work at Flax and Cotton Mill. She will not be home for long time. What time is it?'

'I'm not sure. Nearly midday, I think.'

'I am so thirsty. Could you pass me some water, please?' Mrs Johnson put up a thin blue-veined hand.

'Of course.' Ellen poured water into the cup and handed it to her. 'Would you like a cup of tea if I bring one? I have a friend staying with me. I'll ask her to help me lift you back into bed.'

'Tea would be very nice, but I am a nuisance.'

'You're not a nuisance.' Ellen took a pillow off the bed and put it behind the old lady's back, and then wrapped another blanket round her. 'I'll make some tea and bring it up and think how we can get you back into bed. Are you able to walk at all? Usually, I mean?'

'I can stand if someone steadies me, but I shall be all right now that I know that someone knows I am here; and please, tea without milk.'

Ellen ran down the stairs and found that Anna had sat the older children at the table, had made jam sandwiches and cut them into six pieces, put some more wood on the fire and hung the kettle over the flames. Ellen took a large teapot from the

79

cupboard and made tea whilst she explained what had happened upstairs.

'If we take Thomas and Aron up with us, the others will be all right for five minutes.' Ellen glanced round the room. The fireguard was in front of the fire and the front and back doors were locked, and in any case the children would be busy eating. But first she'd take Mrs Johnson a cup of tea as she'd promised; a good strong cup with a teaspoon of sugar in it.

'We're just going to help the lady upstairs,' she told Sarah and Mary when she came down again. 'Can you two be in charge and look after Zophia and Jakub? We'll take Thomas and Aron up with us, so we're trusting you to be very, very good and eat up your bread and jam.' Anna translated for Zophia and Jakub, who both nodded just as Sarah and Mary had done, picked up Aron, and followed Ellen and Thomas upstairs.

The old lady exclaimed and smiled when she saw the two children, who sat on the floor whilst their mothers, each with an arm under her, heaved her on to her feet and deposited her back into bed. Ellen plumped up her pillow and straightened her sheets and blankets, and said she'd bring her another cup of tea if she'd like one. She refused. 'Perhaps not, I think,' she said, 'but thank you very much, both of you lovely ladies.' She looked at Anna. 'You are very beautiful,' she said. 'Not from these parts, I think?'

'No,' Anna answered. 'I am from Poland.'

'Ah.' Mrs Johnson's expression changed, and she murmured, 'Not a happy country just now.'

'No, not for some,' Anna said quietly.

The old lady reached out and took her hand. 'You will be safe here,' she said. 'I know this.'

Ellen was surprised to see what she thought was a flash of understanding between them. Did she think Anna and Filip hadn't been safe at home? Mrs Johnson, it seemed, wasn't just a poor bedridden old lady. She knows more than I do, Ellen mused.

Downstairs again, she poured tea for herself and Anna and told the children how good they had been. They all had jam

80

spread across their faces and she suspected that they had helped themselves out of the jar.

'May we get down now, please?' Sarah asked. 'We'd like to play.'

'Would you like some paper and pencils to draw pictures?' Ellen asked.

'Yes, please.' Mary slid down from her chair. 'I'm going to draw a picture for Dada to show him when he comes home.'

When the children were occupied and Ellen had brought out a large saucepan and two wooden spoons for the two youngest to bang on it, Anna opened her purse and took out two pennies to pay for her loaves. She put the bread to her nose and breathed in the aroma. 'It is very good,' she said. 'For old bread. Good bread keeps well.'

'Anna,' Ellen said cautiously. 'What did Mrs Johnson mean,' she pointed up to the ceiling to indicate their neighbour, 'when she said you'd be safe here?'

CHAPTER THIRTEEN

'I told you we are Jews,' Anna replied. 'It is a long story why we come here; not everyone welcomes us. I will tell you about it at some other time, yes?'

'All right,' Ellen said. 'Let's talk about bread.'

'I could do it.' Anna was hesitant. 'But I must speak to Filip first. He is a very proud man and thinks he alone must provide for his family.'

Ellen nodded in agreement. Harry would be the same. 'If you tell him that it might help you out for the moment,' she suggested. 'And that maybe you could get out of 'rathole where you're living now.'

Anna gasped. 'There are rats? Have you seen them?'

'No, no,' Ellen reassured her. I must remember that Anna doesn't understand our expressions, she thought, although there probably are rats; we're very near the river and their room is in the basement. 'I only meant that the place where you are living doesn't sound a very nice place to be.'

'Ah, yes, of course. Do you think I should ask the baker first if I could work for her? She might not want me.'

'Well, let's see how we could manage if she did,' Ellen said positively. 'She told me that she starts at five o'clock, so that would mean bringing 'children early. But if your husband is at home he could bring them here before he goes out to look for work.'

'And what would I pay you?'

'Oh.' Ellen hadn't thought of that, but Anna's children would need feeding whilst they were staying with her and she couldn't afford to pay out for extra mouths. 'With food,' she said. 'We could share 'cost of vegetables, and meat if we could afford it, and mebbe you could bring home day-old bread if there is any? But perhaps you should ask Filip before we plan.'

Harry had chanced upon Filip as he set off for work that morning, when Filip caught up and walked alongside him. They recognized each other; they were bound to. Harry remembered Filip's dark hair and beard and his height; Filip would have recognized Harry's fair, almost blond hair, stocky build and blue eyes even had he not seen him come out of the house where the Boscos had lived. He told Harry he was getting desperate. They were receiving money from the parish coffers but it was very little, and only because they had a family. He said Anna was becoming thinner by the day, and that none of them had enough food; most of what there was was given to the children.

'There might be soup kitchens in 'town,' Harry said. 'I'll ask some of 'men at work when I get to know them. This is my first day, so I don't know anybody yet.'

'It is difficult; we eat kosher food. The Jewish community have helped us. Where you work? Maybe I ask them for a job?'

'Why not? The owner I met seems decent,' Harry said. 'It's just along here; look up on 'wall. *R. Tannerson and Son.* Give them a try. They can say no, but they might say yes. This is new to me,' he said, as they approached the gates. 'I'm a countryman; thought I'd be in farming for all of my life.' He shook his head. 'I don't even know what job I'll be given.'

He hadn't been told by Tannerson and he hadn't asked; he just needed work. He didn't know why he recommended that Filip should try, except that he had taken a chance himself and was certain that his new acquaintance would take anything that was on offer.

'I know about milling and seed crushing,' Filip murmured. 'At least about the machines that does – do the milling. I am engineer.' He repeated what he had already told Harry. 'Every

83

country in the world needs engineers. But not always foreign ones.'

That was true, Harry thought. We all like to use our own folk first. But then he remembered a school friend who had left the district and set off for Australia. His father had boasted that he'd travelled inland – upcountry, he'd called it – and was now running his own sheep farm. He was welcomed, but Harry supposed the difference was that Australia needed fresh labour for their vast country. But surely we all move on at some time, otherwise why am I here, a countryman in the middle of an industrial town?

Filip was looking at all the women and children walking down the street, dozens of them, many of them in clogs, others in old boots. 'Where do they go?' he asked Harry. 'It does not seem right that children should work when they are just out of school. It is the same in my country.'

'I don't know,' Harry answered, glancing over his shoulder. A woman was walking close behind them with her eyes firmly fixed on the ground. She looked up and her eyes locked with Harry's.

'G'morning,' he said, recognizing her. It was the woman from upstairs who had knocked on their door to ask about the children and explain about her sick mother. She muttered something in return and Filip moved to one side so that she could get past. He put a finger to his peaked cap in greeting, saying something in a language Harry didn't understand.

She glanced at him and muttered something, but Harry didn't catch what it was.

'How do you know her?' Filip asked him, staring after the woman as she walked swiftly on.

'I don't; she lives upstairs in 'top room. She came down to say that her mother was sick; she was bothered about 'children mekking a noise, I think.'

'How is it that I don't know this?' Filip had a puzzled frown on his forehead. 'We live in same house for four weeks.'

Harry shook his head. 'Mebbe they just lived quietly.' He shuffled up to join the men at the gates. 'Are you coming in?'

Filip still had his eyes on the woman in front. 'Later, I think. I wait until the machines are running. I will try elsewhere first.'

84

'Right!' Harry said. 'Good luck, then.' He wondered what it was that was preoccupying Filip, who had begun to stride out in the direction the woman was taking. 'Mebbe see you later?'

Filip lifted a hand in response, but didn't answer.

Harry walked across a large yard that was littered with steel bins, sleds and two-wheeled handcarts, canvas sacks and wooden boxes and reported to the foreman, whose name he discovered was Ellison; Ellison sent him through wide double doors and he saw Mr Tannerson in discussion with a group of men standing by belt-driven rollers. The owner looked up as Harry approached. 'Yes?' he said. 'Can I help you?'

'I, erm, you said I should start work today, Mr Tannerson. Where would you like me to begin?'

'Did I? Ah yes, so I did. Well . . . what was your name again?'

'Harry Randell, sir.' Harry began to sweat in spite of the cold air coming off the river. I hope he hasn't changed his mind.

'Ah, yes,' he said again. 'The countryman. Kirkwood,' he called over to someone. 'Can you come over and find a job for our new recruit? I'll sort out what he can do later.'

It all seemed very casual, Harry thought. Not what he'd expected at all, but he supposed that if Tannerson was in the middle of a works meeting it was not surprising he'd forgotten him.

Kirkwood came across to him. 'How do?' he said. 'What trade 'you in?'

'I was a farmhand,' Harry said, 'but there's no work in 'country so I've come to town.'

'Ah, well, there's plenty of work in oil and seed crushing if you're prepared for hard graft. We're waiting on a delivery coming upriver, and once 'barges get here it'll be all hands on deck. Are you used to manhandling stuff?'

'Certainly am,' Harry grinned. 'There's no harder work than being out in 'fields ploughing or handling sacks o' corn.'

'Is that right?' Kirkwood raised bushy grey eyebrows. 'Well, we'll see, won't we?' He paused for a moment and rubbed his chin. 'Until 'delivery arrives I'm a bit flummoxed as to what I can

85

give you to do, but mebbe you could mek some space in 'yard. Shift some of 'barrows and carts.'

'Yep, I can do that, owt that's useful,' Harry replied, anxious not to be seen as a spare part, and he'd noticed the assortment of equipment scattered about in what seemed to be a haphazard manner. 'Is there somewhere I can put my things?'

Kirkwood pointed to a room off the loading bay where there were wall hooks and a couple of wooden chairs. Harry deposited his coat and the knapsack containing his *lowance*, as countrymen called it – his dinner of bread and cheese – and went back out into the yard to find himself a job.

Filip hurried after the woman, who was walking very fast, scurrying in fact as if she wanted to get away from something or someone. When he was only a few yards behind her he called, 'Excuse me!'

She barely hesitated before putting her head down and hurrying along even faster. He lengthened his stride. '*Shalom,*' he said quietly, but clearly enough for her to hear.

She reduced her speed and slowly turned her head. '*Shalom,*' she greeted him in barely a whisper. 'What do you want from me?'

'Nothing.' He smiled. 'I am Filip Bosco. I am from Poland – and you?'

'It does not matter where I am from.' She turned her face away from his gaze. 'I am Edith Johnson.' She pronounced the letter J as a Y.

'Johnson?' he said, pronouncing it correctly. 'Edyta Jablonski?'

'Edith Johnson,' she repeated. 'I must go. If I'm late, I lose my job.'

'I'm sorry,' he said. 'I'm going to the cotton mill to look for work. Perhaps I can walk with you?'

'No,' she said frostily. 'You can't. There will be gossip.'

'*Do widzenia.*' Goodbye. He didn't detain her but let her walk on alone; he was disappointed that she didn't want to talk, but no doubt she had her reasons. They all did, the passengers on the boats and trains that they had travelled on; all had their

86

reasons for leaving their homeland, and not only the Polish. Germans and Russians too were moving on, and particularly the Jews, always the Jews; and all were cautious, unable to trust anyone completely until they had proved their friendship.

On impulse he walked on, turning into Cumberland Street where someone had told him the new cotton and flax mill was, but not intentionally following Edyta Jablonski; the last thing he wanted was to make an enemy. That was why he had left his homeland and come to England. He wanted peace and harmony for himself and his family, not strife as he had experienced it in Poland.

He saw the wide double doors through which the women and girls were entering but he walked past them, going further round the building and walking with purpose as if he knew where he was going, which he didn't. However, he guessed that most mills and factories, as in Poland, would have the offices set apart from the working area, and he was right. He turned a corner and saw several young men and a few older ones, presumably clerks, heading through an open single door behind which stairs led to an upper floor.

Filip followed them up to the first floor, nodding to those who greeted him, and asked an older man if he could direct him to the office manager.

'Well, that'll be me.' The man, a short stocky figure, lifted his head to look up at him. 'I'm 'office manager. What is it you're after?'

Filip took off his cap. 'I am Filip Bosco. I am engineer,' he said. 'I wish to enquire after employment.'

'An engineer? Ah, well, you need to speak to Jarvis, he's 'works manager. Come on, I'll tek you. It's a warren of a place if you don't know it and you'll never find him.' He called to one of the young men. 'Get started on 'wages, will you, and when Hargreayes gets in tell him I want 'invoices finishing afore dinner.'

'Yes, Mr Marshall,' the clerk said and scurried away.

'Come wi' me,' Marshall said, and led the way back downstairs again. Filip smiled. Better this way, he thought. Better to be taken to the man in charge by someone who knew him, rather than wandering around asking all and sundry.

87

He was led into the mill where the machines were already in motion, humming and rattling, and he was saddened, as he always was, to see very young girls as well as women gearing up to their regular work instead of being allowed their childhood.

'Jarvis!' Marshall called across a row of looms to where a man was speaking to one of the women. He waved a hand to him. 'Have you got a minute? You're wanted.'

Filip saw the woman bob her knee to Jarvis, who turned away and came towards them. 'Yes?' he said brusquely.

'This is Mr Bosco,' Marshall said. 'He's an engineer.' He nodded to Filip. 'Good day to you, Mr Bosco,' he said, and turned to go back where he'd come from.

'Yes, sir?' Jarvis said. 'What can I do for you?'

CHAPTER FOURTEEN

Harry came home from work that evening as pleased as punch. He gave Ellen a big squeeze and kissed her; then he looked down at all the children who were fast asleep in bed.

He rubbed his chin. 'I'd swear we onny had three bairns when I went out this morning; what have you been up to since I left? Where have these others come from?'

Ellen laughed and explained about meeting Anna and the children on the way to the baker's. 'We formed an instant friendship, isn't that strange? I've known all of my other friends since I was a child, but Anna and I seemed to have such a lot in common, so I asked her back here and we got talking and now she's gone back to their room to mek a fire before her husband Filip comes home. Bairns were very tired by then so I popped 'youngest into bed and they were asleep in minutes, and then the others climbed in with them.'

'She must have thought you very trustworthy to leave 'children with you when you'd onny just met!' he said incredulously.

'I know,' Ellen agreed, and then went on to explain that Anna was going to apply to the baker for work, if Filip agreed. 'And I said that I would look after their children if she was taken on. She will pay me in food and bread from the bakery.'

Harry was smiling. 'You won't believe this, but I met him on my way out this morning. He was looking for work.' He stretched out in one of the fireside chairs, where a fire burned merrily in the grate. 'I liked him,' he said, and then looked round the

89

room, his gaze falling on the sleeping children in their bed. 'I have to say, Ellen, you've made it look very cosy, but have you thought about where *we're* going to sleep?'

'Anna'll come back to collect 'children when Filip gets home.' But she looked at them all sleeping so well and wondered if she could bear to disturb them. 'So tell me, how did you get on, Harry?'

'Well, I've been gofer today,' he grinned.

'Gofer? What does that mean?'

'It means you're asked to go for this and that and fetch t'other. I cleared up 'yard, which was full of old boxes and bits of machinery, and storage bins and sacks that 'last lot o' grain came in, so we're ready for tomorrow when 'next shipment of grain arrives. Oh aye, and that reminds me, I brought some wood home to burn on 'fire.' He got up from the chair and headed for the back door. 'I've left it outside 'yard gate so I'll fetch it in now afore it disappears into somebody else's fireplace.'

As Ellen was about to dish up the soup she had made, Filip and Anna came to collect the children. Anna was introduced again to Harry, and Filip to Ellen. Filip was bursting to tell Harry the news that he had worked on one of the idle looms at the cotton mill and managed to fix it.

'They say they can give me regular work, but not every day,' he explained. 'So, for now . . . how do you say, we can keep wolf from house, for they pay me immediately, and I thought if I can visit other factories and say I am available, then perhaps they might do the same.'

'They might,' Harry agreed. 'You might like to try Tannerson's, where I am, cos there was a problem this morning with one of 'dryers.'

Filip said he would go in in the morning, and then, seeing they were about to eat, he said they would leave.

Ellen asked if they would like to stay and eat with them as she had made a large pan of soup; she knew Harry would be hungry after a long day, but she said there was plenty for all of them and of course there was bread.

'Excuse me, Ellen,' Anna said. 'but is there meat in the soup?'

Ellen shook her head. 'No, sorry, it's onny vegetable. We finished all of 'chicken that my mother brought, but I boiled up 'carcass for stock. We can't afford to waste anything.'

'No, no, vegetable is good . . . I meant—'

Filip interrupted. 'Anna is saying that we don't eat pork. Chicken is good and we will be happy to eat soup with you if there is enough, and next time you will eat with us.' He looked round the room. 'Though our room is not so nice as this one. You are home-maker, Ellen.'

'So what can you eat?' Ellen asked rather anxiously.

Filip gave a very hearty laugh. 'It depends how hungry we are! Anna will only cook kosher food; some food is forbidden, like pork and ham and shellfish, but I confess I might not be so strict if my belly was empty.'

Harry groaned. 'So you can't have bacon and eggs for breakfast?'

Pulling a miserable expression, Filip shook his head, and then grinned. 'Eggs yes, but not bacon, and the smell is so – tantalizing!'

'There's only potatoes, onions, carrots, lentils and chicken stock in my soup,' Ellen said earnestly. 'And I always wash my hands.'

Over their simple meal they discussed Anna's options for employment, with Ellen looking after the children.

'I was a teacher before I had my children,' Anna said. 'And one day, when they are older and when my English is better, perhaps I will teach again. This is a reason why we leave Poland: so we have better opportunities. We have so many, erm, restrictions in our own country.' Her eyes filled with tears. 'We leave behind our parents, our sisters and brothers, our friends. They say that one day it will get better, that we must live in hope. But I fear for them and we worry for our children.'

Filip took her hand and Ellen and Harry looked on in dismay. They had thought it a hardship to leave their home, but they had travelled only a few short miles. They hadn't had to leave their homeland and families behind.

91

'For a thousand years Poland was a haven for Jews, but now it is ruled by the Russian empire; it has been for many decades,' Filip explained. 'It is true there have always been anti-Jewish riots, but it was our country. We even had our own Parliament, but slowly over the years many communities have fled, and now we cannot call Poland our own.' He shook his head. 'Russia does not like Jews; it doesn't like Roman Catholics very much either; and now they have partitioned our country. We Jews are controlled as to where we can live and what we can and cannot do. We cannot hold our own land, and we are restricted in professions. Our situation gets worse and worse.' His eyes gleamed like fire. 'And one day, I say *Enough!* If we cannot live a free life in our own country then we will find another where we can.'

'I didn't know – I had no idea it was so bad,' Harry murmured. 'I've been blind and deaf to what has been happening in other countries. We onny worry about our own lives.' There was silence for a moment and a piece of wood on the fire suddenly sparked and cracked and made them all jump. 'Well, my friends,' he went on, 'you are very welcome here.'

Anna wiped away her tears, and so did Ellen, who had been very affected by what Filip had said.

He was speaking again. 'But let me tell you something. Some people still look over their shoulder. Even here in this town.' They all looked at him. 'This morning I tried to talk to the woman who lives above you. She works at cotton mill.'

Ellen glanced at Anna; neither of them had mentioned Mrs Johnson upstairs who had fallen out of bed.

'I spoke to her,' Filip went on, 'but she didn't want to talk to me. She said there would be gossip. She is still afraid.'

'What? You think she is from your country?' Ellen asked.

'Her mother is foreign,' Anna interrupted. 'Not Polish, but she is Jewish.'

'She is,' Filip agreed.

The two women then went on to explain what had happened in the room above that morning, and as they talked they heard the front door open and close and the sound of footsteps going upstairs.

*

92

Ellen suggested that Anna should take Aron home as he would need her in the morning, and leave Jakub and Zophia with them if she was going to apply for work at the baker's shop; if she went early she could come straight back to see them and reassure them that she hadn't abandoned them. Anna looked questioningly at Filip for his approval and he nodded.

'I will look after Aron while you see this baking woman,' he told Anna. Then, turning to Ellen, he said, 'We must pay you, of course, if you take care of our children. You cannot do this without payment.'

She didn't argue with him; it was a matter of pride, she could see, and even though she had originally told Anna she would look after the children for food only she realized Filip wouldn't approve of that. So she agreed, and the extra money would be gladly received.

Filip picked up a still sleeping Aron and wrapped him in the blanket they had brought; he shook hands with Harry and kissed Ellen. 'You have saved our lives,' he said. 'You are good people.'

Anna too kissed Ellen and looked down at the other sleeping children, Sarah, Mary and Thomas at one end, Zophia and Jakub at the other. Sarah had her cheek laid on one hand, and Mary's thumb was touching her bottom lip. 'I would trust no one else with my family, but I trust you, Ellen.'

'Don't worry,' Ellen said. 'They'll be safe and warm here, and you will see them early in the morning before they realize you haven't been here with them all night.'

'My poor babies,' Anna murmured. 'We have brought them through so much.'

'And they won't remember any of it,' Ellen said, 'because you have made them feel safe.'

When Anna and Filip had left, Harry sat by the fire to take off his socks. The lamp had puttered and popped, so Harry turned it off to save the oil, leaving only the light from the fire. He sat back in the chair and briefly closed his eyes and Ellen began to undress. She wasn't shy of undressing in front of Harry but was always discreet, beginning with her garters and stockings and

93

removing her dress or woollen skirt and top, then slipping on her nightgown and taking off her undershift beneath it.

He had opened his eyes and watched her, smiling a little, and as she sat on the edge of the narrow empty bed and began to unpin her plaits, which were fastened on top of her head, he rose from the chair and went towards her. He put out his hand and said softly, 'Let me do that,' and sat beside her.

Gently he unfastened the metal clips to let loose the braids, and kissed the back of her neck. 'She looked so sweet from her two bare feet,' he whispered the words from the old song, and slowly began to undo the plaits, 'to the sheen of her nut-brown hair.'

She closed her eyes as he nuzzled into the smooth concave beneath her throat with the tip of his tongue and he felt the throb of her pulse as he explored her skin, her cheek, her eyelids, her earlobes.

Ellen's lips parted as she lifted her face to take his kiss and he murmured, 'You know how much I love you?'

She nodded and said softly, 'As much as I love you?'

Thomas, squashed between his sisters, mumbled something and turned over, but didn't waken, and as Harry began to undress Ellen slipped into the bed which tonight only she and Harry would share.

CHAPTER FIFTEEN

Anna was taken on as an assistant at the baker's and after a few days, once she had proved that she could bake good bread, she was offered regular employment. Then word got around that she was Polish and the baker, Mrs Brownlee, asked her to make rye bread and pinned up a notice in her window to say it was available to order. Soon other immigrants were arriving and not only giving a weekly order for bread, but introducing themselves to Anna who then found that she was mixing with people who understood her language or spoke Yiddish and could give her advice about living in the town.

'But always I will speak English,' she said to Ellen. 'This is now my country.'

Filip obtained work at Tannerson's mill and was then recommended to another factory. 'You are a good man,' he told Harry. 'It was meant that we should meet. That day when you gave me shilling, you gave me hope.'

During October Ellen wrote to her mother and to Harry's sister Meg to ask how everyone was and to say how sorry they were that they wouldn't see them at Christmas.

It's too far to come, she wrote, *especially if the weather is bad. Neither do I think the carrier would bring us all.*

A postcard from Ellen's mother came back immediately to say that Billy would come the following weekend with a live chicken and a bag of corn so she could feed it up ready for Christmas, and that she had also made a plum pudding and a Christmas cake, knowing that Ellen didn't have an oven.

Oh, Ma, Ellen thought. She would hate to kill the hen, as she always had, but the cake and the pudding would keep in tins and would be a welcome addition to their Christmas dinner.

'Perhaps we could invite Filip and Anna and their bairns to eat with us,' she said blithely to Harry when he returned home after work. 'It won't be very homely for them in that one room.'

'I think perhaps they might not want to,' he said as he kissed her cheek and tousled Thomas's curls. Zophia, Jakub and Aron had been collected by Anna when she finished work at midday. 'Their religion!'

Ellen stared blankly at him for a second. 'Oh!' she said. 'Of course. I'd forgotten. But they could have some meat from the bird and eat it whenever they wanted.'

'They might have other plans,' he said, sitting down to take off his boots. 'I saw Filip this morning and he's going to look at another house.'

Ellen was pleased that they might be moving from the cellar room, but she hoped they wouldn't be too far away. When she said this to Harry, he said that he hoped they too could look forward to moving further away from the factory smells and the poor air.

'There won't be time yet,' Harry said, 'but if we can survive here until after Christmas is over, Ellen, I think we could start looking elsewhere. Tannerson seems to be pleased with what I do, and although I'm only labouring at 'minute, at least we have a regular wage coming in.'

Ellen looked round the room; how quickly they had adapted to what they had, but it was true that the air they breathed was filled with the stench of smoke and oil of all kinds, fish manure and chemicals, paint and cattle cake, and the dust that was constantly with them. All the children coughed, and especially Mary, whose chest and back Ellen rubbed with camphor every morning, placing a patch of flannel beneath her vest.

96

She had looked out from the doorway this morning as Harry left for work; it was still dark as it was not yet six o'clock, but she had seen a silver sliver of breaking dawn. The children were still sleeping, so she looked out again five minutes later, ignoring the heavy tread of boots and clogs as the workers of the factories and mills made their way down the street and gazing towards the horizon.

The shard of light had widened, and although she couldn't help comparing the dawn of the town with the ones in the wide skies of Holderness, there was a beauty ascending this morning, heralding a fine day. The silver light was a curtain, rising to show the break of day as the sun's rays spread beyond the house tops, highlighting the dark windmills and the tall factory chimneys and filling the confined span of sky with a fusion of cobalt blue, amber and rose.

It's the same sky, she had thought. My family and friends in Holderness will be looking at the same view, except they have more of it. Her throat had tightened as she'd thought of her old home, but she knew she must accept their new life. I will make it a happy one, she decided, even though we might always be poor. I will make a home that my husband and children will be glad to come back to, and I'll make friends; there are good people living here and I'll seek them out. This will be our town.

She turned now to Harry as he finished speaking. 'You're quite right, Harry,' she said. 'Once you're earning more money, we'll look for somewhere else, with a separate bedroom and mebbe a patch of garden.' She smiled. 'And there will be someone who'll be glad to take this one and make it their own.'

Billy came on the Sunday, bringing a basket of victuals as promised, a young hen, a bag of corn, some pieces of wood, nails and a hammer to knock together a box to keep her in, and a sack of straw to line it with.

The children were delighted with the hen and chased her round and round the yard wanting to stroke her. Ellen groaned, knowing that they would cry and refuse to eat her if she wrung her neck.

'Tell a lie and say she escaped,' Billy grinned, watching Harry sawing the wood for the box. 'Or that a fox got her.'

'I don't think there'll be many foxes round here. She's a very pretty hen,' Ellen added. 'And a young one. Are you sure you haven't brought 'wrong one? Ma said it had gone off 'lay.'

Billy shrugged. 'That's 'one she pointed to; mark you, one hen looks like any other to me. They're not like pigs or cattle, which do look different. And they all scattered when I tried to catch her.'

Ellen went inside to make a pot of tea and rustle up something to eat for Billy as he said he wanted to get home before dark. He followed her into the house.

'Ma said would I tell you to tell Harry that his ma isn't too well and suggest he comes over when he can to see her.'

'Oh!' Ellen stopped slicing the loaf. 'Yes, I'll tell him. Meg said not to worry him, but he'll want to know.'

Harry, coming in through the door and shooing the children before him, heard her. 'Who'll want to know what?'

'Your ma isn't well, Harry,' she explained. 'Meg said before we came here not to tell you that she was failing; she said there were enough of them to help out.'

He stood still. 'What's 'matter with her? Is she sick?'

Ellen shook her head. 'She's tired, I think. She's had a hard life. Time now for her to sit back and let others do for her.'

'But I'm *here*, aren't I? Her only son.' He pondered for a minute, clearly worried. 'But how do I get there and back? It would mean taking time off work to catch 'carrier, an' I'll lose pay.'

Billy spoke up. 'Your ma wouldn't want that, and I reckon there'll be nowt much you can do if you are there,' he said. 'It's women who tek care of bairns and owd folk when they're sick. But leave it for a week, say, and I'll borrow 'wagon again and come and pick you up after work on Sat'day and fetch you back on Sunday. How'd that be?'

Harry clapped him on the shoulder. 'Great,' he said. 'You're a mate, Billy. You always were.' He turned to Ellen. 'You'll be all right for one night on your own, won't you?'

'Yes, fine,' she said, thinking that it would be the first time Harry wouldn't be there since the day they were married.

The weather was beginning to turn and rain fell almost every day of the following week, and when it wasn't raining the lowering clouds were dark and gloomy, blotting out much of the light. Harry brought home pieces of timber from the yard and walked by the river bank to collect kindling and fallen branches to burn on the fire; some of it was damp and didn't burn but gave off a smouldering choking smoke and the children coughed even more.

On the Friday, Mary coughed and coughed until her eyes streamed and said that her chest was sore in spite of the vapour rub and the honey and hot water. Ellen sat with her on her knee during the night and rubbed her back. 'I think I'd better look up the doctor Dr Selby recommended and ask if he can call,' she said. 'I don't know if he lives round here. I should have asked about that before.'

'I've got another idea.' Harry took Mary from her and walked about with her, gently patting her back. 'Why don't I tek her to your ma's tomorrow when Billy comes? Good country air, and your ma allus has a good fire so she'll be right as rain in no time.'

Ellen's face was consumed with misery. 'I can't even look after my own child,' she muttered, almost in tears.

'Now, don't tek on,' Harry said calmly. 'It's very damp here by 'river and she had a chesty cough when we first came. It's not anybody's fault, except mebbe mine for bringing you here in 'first place.'

So then Ellen protested that he had had no option and conceded that a day or two of country air would benefit Mary, and her mother would be pleased to have her. She was an easy child, not one to get into mischief, and she wouldn't be a bother at all.

Saturday afternoon, Billy arrived promptly, and without stopping even to have a cup of tea he said they should be off. Ellen dressed Mary in her warmest clothes with a woolly hat and a blanket to wrap round her; she sat on her father's knee next to Billy as he took the reins and waved to Sarah and Thomas,

99

who tried to clamber in after her, and put her face towards her mother for a kiss.

'Be a good girl for Granny, Mary, and we'll see you soon.' Ellen was choked as she waved goodbye, and as tears ran down her cheeks she wasn't consoled in the least by the fact that Mary seemed quite cheerful as they pulled away.

She put more wood on the fire and placed a pan of soup on it to cook for the evening meal, and then sat down to mend a hole in Harry's thick work socks. Thomas climbed up on to one of the beds and then slid on to the other one, happy with a game of his own devising, and Sarah came and wrapped her arm round her mother's neck.

'Are you sad?' she murmured. 'Is Mary coming back?'

'Yes, of course she is. She's only going to be away for a few days.' But even as she spoke, Ellen knew that if Harry didn't bring her back with him the following day there was no saying when they would see her again. It wasn't fair to keep imposing on Billy; he was a good-hearted man, always had been, but it wasn't right to keep asking favours of him.

'I'm missing her,' Sarah said, and then pressed her little hand on her mother's abdomen and bent down to put her ear on it.

Ellen laughed. 'What are you doing?'

'I'm listening to the new baby,' she said. 'When he comes, can we call him William?'

CHAPTER SIXTEEN

Ellen gazed at her. How could she possibly tell? She wasn't completely sure herself; nor had she yet told Harry, as she didn't want to put more pressure on him just yet. Sarah was guessing, of course. She knew where babies came from, and puppies and kittens too. Ellen smiled; she probably thought there was a cupboard full of babies tucked inside her, and as for its being a boy, well! She was a very imaginative child, a little girl with old wisdom in her eyes.

'When I next have a baby,' she compromised, 'and if it's a boy, we might call him William, like Uncle Billy.'

'Oh!' Sarah said. 'Is Uncle Billy called William?'

'He is; sometimes people who are really called William get called Billy instead.'

Sarah considered this carefully and then said, 'Not like the other William. He was called Will.'

Ellen decided not to consider this remark. Sarah often went off on imaginary flights and she never knew if the child had been listening to adults' conversation or just making up stories. Her mother had had a brother called William who died before Ellen was born and he it was for whom Billy was named, but Sarah couldn't possibly know about him.

She sighed. It was going to be a long twenty-four hours before Harry came home and she could have adult conversation.

Mid-afternoon she decided she'd take the children out for a walk by the river bank, taking a sack to gather up kindling and

101

small branches. A change of air will freshen us all and we might see people to talk to. She missed conversation such as she had had with locals in Holmpton. Her days here seemed to follow the same pattern, day in, day out, week in, week out.

Filip was looking after the Bosco children today and Anna was working, so they wouldn't be calling in, and she remembered that Harry had said Filip was going to look for another room.

As they stepped out of the front door Ellen saw her neighbour, Mrs Johnson's daughter, hurrying up the street carrying shopping. She waited, holding the door open for her.

'Good afternoon,' she said brightly. 'Have you finished work for the day?'

The woman looked startled. 'Yes,' she said briefly.

'How is your mother? Is she well?'

The woman's eyes darted about. 'You know my mother?'

She had an accent, but not as strong as her mother's; Ellen thought that was probably because she was mixing with other workers whereas her mother seemed to spend all day alone in their room.

'Yes, did she not say? She had fallen out of bed. My friend and I helped her back in again.'

Miss Johnson stared at Ellen as if confused. 'No,' she said. 'She didn't say. Thank you,' she added as an afterthought. 'You are very kind.'

'Not at all,' Ellen said. 'Just being neighbourly. I was pleased to help.'

Her neighbour gave a brief nod. 'We must not be a nuisance.'

Ellen laughed. 'That's what your mother said, and she wasn't a nuisance; it would have been dreadful if she'd been on 'floor all day until you came home.'

Miss Johnson seemed to consider this, and nodded again. 'Thank you,' she repeated and put her hand on the door. 'Good day.'

What a strange woman, Ellen thought. Filip had said that she didn't want to talk to him, which was all very well; he was a man and a stranger to her, after all. But I'm a neighbour and her poor mother is stuck up in that room all day with no one to talk to and

102

no one to help her if she should need it; and she felt quite cross that the younger woman should appear so unfeeling. Unless, she considered, she had some special reason for being the way she was.

As she walked the children round the corner towards the river she reflected that she was getting to know more diverse people than she had ever known in Holderness. And, she thought, they're folk who have been daring enough to have travelled from afar. They have taken their lives into their own hands and finished up here. What tales they must have to tell.

Edith Johnson, as she was now known, locked the front door behind her and slowly climbed the stairs. Why had her mother not told her that the young woman from downstairs had been up to their room? Had she hurt herself when she had fallen out of bed?

Her mother was sitting in the chair by a low fire. Edith sighed; it was no kind of life in this small cold room with a washbasin meant only for handwashing but also used for preparing vegetables. For her mother's convenience there was a bucket with a lid, which Edith emptied into the outside privy every evening; and she never forgot that they could have had a better life if she had been a more obedient woman.

She put down her shopping; when they had first arrived here she had traipsed a long way to find kosher food and had discovered a Jewish butcher whose wife had agreed to supply her with a cooked chicken once a week, for she had no means of cooking except over the fire in the small grate.

'We will eat well today, *Mutter*,' she said. 'I will prepare the vegetables now and they might be ready by this evening. The fire is so slow.' She was aware that she was repeating herself. It was what she always said, and her mother always nodded.

Mrs Johnson lifted her head. 'You deserve more than this, Edyta,' she murmured. 'You are not happy.' She gazed at her daughter. 'Tomorrow your brother comes and he will ask the same question.'

Edyta took a deep breath and sat down opposite her; the vegetables must wait. 'And it will be the same answer. I do not wish to leave Hull and live with him and his family.'

103

'But I do, Edyta.' Her mother's face was pale. She had not been out of the room for three years. 'We cannot live here any longer. It is a prison. I hear the children downstairs and think that that is what you must have.'

Her daughter began to protest, but her mother interrupted. 'You are still young enough to bear children, and if I leave to live with Ezra and his family you will be free.'

Edyta put her hands to her face. '*Mutter*,' she said after a moment. 'You know that I only want to marry one man and Ezra won't agree to it. I cannot make that decision; it is too hard.'

'It pains me to say it, Edyta, but you must. I give you the choice,' her mother said softly. 'Do not waste your life because of me. I will go with Ezra.'

'He won't let me visit you.' Edyta began to cry. 'I might never see you again.' She left her chair and knelt by her mother's feet. 'We have been through so much together. I can't let you leave . . .' She smothered a sob. 'If only I had never met Karl we wouldn't have this dilemma.'

'But you did meet him.' Her mother stroked her smooth dark hair. 'It was fate that he should be on the same ship, looking for a new life just as we were.' She paused. 'And he is a good man. He will look after you.'

Edyta couldn't speak for a moment, but then said softly, 'Yes, he would, but I'm not sure that I can take that step and leave the culture I have known.'

She dried her eyes and stood up, and began to gather the vegetables to chop and cook to eat with the cold chicken. 'Why are you saying this now? We have discussed this problem so often.'

Her mother paused, and then said, 'I didn't tell you before, but I fell out of bed and couldn't get up. Then I heard the family come in downstairs and called. The young woman, not much more than a girl herself, came up and was so kind; she said she had a friend with her and would ask her to help pick me up. Her friend was Jewish, Polish she said. They brought their youngest children upstairs because they were too young to leave alone, and I saw that the women were friends and the *Kinder* were too;

they sat on the floor together as their mothers lifted me and made me comfortable.'

'What are you saying, *Mutter*?'

'I am saying that it is all right to have friends who are not of our faith or our culture. That we should be able to live together in harmony. That is why we left our homeland, is it not? It was what your father wanted, for us to be settled, to live without harassment; to be no longer constantly moving on. The wandering Jew will settle here. In this country we will finally find the peace we are looking for.'

'But that is not the same as marrying someone from another faith, *Mutter*; not when my own brother would ostracize me and stop me from ever seeing you again.' Edyta's eyes again filled with tears.

'I will talk to your brother,' her mother said softly. 'He will listen to his Jewish mother and respect her wishes. We will not be parted, Edyta. Only by a few miles, and never in our hearts. I will promise you this.'

The afternoon brightened as Ellen and the children walked by the river bank picking up twigs, but the wind was cold, blowing upriver from the east. Herring gulls flew overhead, screeching and diving on to the rooftops where they appeared to be surveying the landscape. If they had come inland to escape the weather at sea, Ellen worried that it would be colder on the flat plain of Holderness than it was here in Hull in the shelter of the buildings and wondered if she had done right in letting Harry take Mary with him.

Thomas held up his cold red hand; he'd lost a mitten and Sarah found it on the ground, wet and soggy. Ellen took it from her and put it in her pocket, and picking up Thomas she decided they would go back home, make some soup, and at least have the warmth of the fire, low though it was.

As they turned the corner into the street, she saw Filip and the children coming towards them; he was carrying Aron on his shoulders and lifted a hand in greeting. Zophia and Jakub began to run towards them.

105

'Please to come to your house?' Zophia begged, clutching Ellen's shawl.

'Ellen, I am so sorry,' Filip said. 'We are for ever in your debt. The room I have looked at is no good, but I have heard of another. We must leave this one we have, I am so afraid for the children; the walls are running with water and there is a stench from the privy. It is not fit to live in.'

'Leave it now,' she said impulsively. 'Don't stay and don't pay the rent! Bring your blankets and your warm clothing, bring everything you have, and we'll share the cost of coal. It isn't fair,' she exclaimed. 'How can anyone charge money for such a terrible place?'

The children raced to the door and Filip took Thomas from her as she fumbled for her key. 'Come in. Come in,' she said as she opened the door to the room and the children tumbled in, heading towards the fire.

'We've gathered up some twigs,' she said, 'but not many. I think everybody else has already been out collecting kindling before us.'

Filip took the sack from her. 'I will get some now,' he said, 'and bring them back. Then I see about new room; is that all right?'

'Of course.' Ellen bent to put the kettle over the flame and adjusted the fire guard to make it safe. 'Do whatever you must.' She was mentally preparing. She would make the children cocoa. There was no milk, but the Bosco children didn't drink milk, so that was all right, and she'd put a spot of sugar in it to make it sweeter. That would warm them up, for they all had red runny noses.

She made the cocoa and gave a cup each to Sarah, Zophia and Jakub, who sat on the rug in front of the fire whilst she sat on one of the beds with Thomas and Aron on either side of her, giving them sips from their cups alternately.

Filip came back with a sack full of wood and twigs and smiled when he saw all the children sitting contentedly, their mouths rimmed with cocoa. He put more wood on the fire, and turning to Ellen asked, 'Did you mean it? Your offer?'

106

'Of course. Now go and tell Anna she is to come straight here when the bakery closes, and then collect your things.'

He nodded. 'I am so sorry.' His voice was choked.

'No need to be,' she said softly. 'It's onny a room. What kind of life would it be if we couldn't share a room with our friends?'

He gave a harsh laugh. 'I could tell you what it would be like, Ellen, but I won't. We have, I hope, put that kind of life behind us.'

CHAPTER SEVENTEEN

When Ellen opened her eyes the next morning, her first thought was that she must be dreaming. She was squashed into her bed with Sarah and Thomas either side of her and at the bottom of the bed was Zophia. In the other bed lay Anna with Aron beside her and Jakub at the bottom, and on the floor beneath them on a thin mattress covered by a blanket was Filip.

When Harry had left the previous day with Billy and Mary, she had thought she would be lonely, but not a bit of it. Anna had arrived at her house late in the afternoon, bringing fresh bread and vegetables, and the two women had set about peeling potatoes and chopping onions up small to make a stew on a fire that had burned quite brightly, for Filip had brought back not only more wood, but a small bag of coal he had bought from a passing coal wagon.

He had also visited the synagogue and found someone who had directed him to a different landlord, who promised him better rooms than the one they had been living in. They could view the next day and move in immediately if they liked them.

'We are rich!' Filip had exclaimed. 'And dining with friends, except Harry is not here. Where is he?'

Ellen explained that he had gone to visit his mother and taken Mary with him, and Anna asked if he would object if they stayed with her overnight.

'He won't mind. He'll be pleased to help you, and besides,' Ellen had commented, 'he'll be glad that there was someone in 'house with me whilst he was away.'

108

Filip had nodded and given a merry grin. 'He worries that his young wife would be nervous without him, yes?'

Ellen blushed. 'Perhaps.' She lowered her eyes. 'I'm alone during 'day when he's at work, apart from 'children I mean; but I've never stayed alone at night since we married.'

Now, as she listened to the gentle breathing of Sarah and Thomas, the occasional soft snore from Filip and the shifting of ash in the grate, she thought how lucky she and Harry were, for although conditions were not good in this room in comparison with the Holderness cottage, they were secure; they had a roof over their heads that didn't leak, a fire to warm them and food to sustain them. We are so blessed, and life will get better.

She slid quietly out of bed, removing her day clothes from beneath her pillow where she had stowed them to keep warm, and in her nightgown and woollen stockings that she had worn all night padded silently across the floor to the scullery where she hastily dressed, wrapped her warmest shawl around her shoulders, buttoned up her boots and eased back the door bolt to step outside to visit the privy.

It was still dark, with only a glimmer of silver light in the east, but even so, she saw the first gleam of frost on the rooftops and the yard wall, felt the slight crunch of frost beneath her boots and sensed the sharpness of cold air in her nostrils as she breathed in. Not winter yet, she silently pleaded. We're only just in October.

When she came out of the privy and had washed her hands in the sink, she decided that she would ask Filip to light a low fire beneath the outside wash tub so that they could draw off warm water to fill a jug and have a warm wash in the kitchen sink rather than a cold one.

She added twigs to the still glowing ash in the grate; when they had caught she added more kindling and then small coals and sat back on her heels to watch in pleasure as the flames licked and grew bigger and she could feel the warmth.

'A primitive pleasure.' Filip's throaty voice made her turn. He was leaning up with his elbow on the floor, his dark hair standing

109

on end as he looked towards the fire. 'It's where we gather, isn't it, as we share friendship, trust and stories.'

Ellen stood up, feeling rather embarrassed at seeing him on the mattress, even though his chest was covered by a flannel shirt.

'Yes,' she murmured. 'A fire has allus been an essential part of life. Mekkin' food and keeping warm are amongst 'most important things we do, but Harry says that mekkin' fires is a job for men.' She smiled, her cheeks dimpling. 'So I'm going to ask if you'll mek one under 'wash boiler so we can have some hot water.'

'Does it work?' He threw off the blanket and stood up. He was wearing a pair of thin cord trousers. 'We never used it when we lived here.'

'Yes!' she said. 'It works well if there's enough wood or coal to light 'fire, and today there is.' She pondered for a moment. 'I've just had a thought. I suppose we could even boil a ham in there – or vegetables. They take for ever on this fire.'

She was speaking without thinking and it wasn't until she saw the whimsical grin and the raised eyebrows that she realized what she'd said.

'Oh! Sorry! I'm so sorry, I didn't think! How stupid of me—'

'Don't apologize, Ellen,' he said, and added wryly, 'if it is only a slice of ham that separates your tradition from ours, then we have little to worry about.' He turned to the bed where Anna was just waking, tapped the side of his nose and lowered his voice. 'But don't tell my wife I said so.'

Ellen smiled and went to fill the kettle to put over the fire. She liked this man; he was open and honest, and she was sure he was a good Jewish man who followed tradition as far as he could, but wouldn't hesitate to give help to anyone of a different faith, or ask for it in return.

The children were waking and Ellen took cups from the cupboard to make more cocoa to warm and nourish them. They could all have bread and jam for breakfast. She gave a deep sigh. Harry, and she hoped Mary too, would be home today, and perhaps there would be some better news about his mother's health.

110

After breakfast Filip lit the fire under the boiler outside and offered to take the children for a walk to collect more firewood. The weather was still cold but it was dry, and there was a ripe smell of old apples and bonfires on the air. Anna said that Aron shouldn't go out because he had snuffles, and Ellen was uncertain of letting Thomas go either as he was inclined to run off.

'Not with Filip, he will not,' Anna assured her. 'He's good with children. You needn't be concerned; they always behave themselves with him.'

So she let Thomas go and the two women tidied the room, washed the dishes and made the beds, prepared the vegetables for soup and then sat down together, Anna with a cup of coffee and Ellen with tea.

'Tell me about yourself, Ellen,' Anna said. 'You are very young to have three children already.'

Ellen gave a little shrug. 'I was married at eighteen,' she said, 'and the babies came along.' She stretched a hand flat to her stomach and raised her eyebrows. 'And keep coming.' She raised a finger to her lips. 'Harry doesn't know yet. But what about you? Tell me about your travels. That must have been difficult, especially with 'children.'

Anna gazed into the fire and nodded. 'It was,' she said softly. 'Very hard. At first we had good life. We live in Warsaw, where there was a large Jewish community, for we tend to group in towns and cities rather than in the countryside. But over the years many Polish people came to see Jews as a threat because of our numbers.'

She shook her head. 'When I first meet Filip he was full of idealism and was not afraid to speak out against injustice. He had qualified as engineer, but he could only work in Jewish factories, not for anyone else, because many Polish politicians saw us as competitors taking the work from Polish people. But *we* were Polish,' she said vehemently, banging her chest with a tight fist. '*We* were born there, but we were no longer welcome. And then,' she went on angrily, 'some of our people began to move away to Prussia, where they thought they would have more freedom.'

111

Her mouth trembled. 'Filip was marked out as a troublemaker by the Russians and I was afraid for him and our children; he was *not* a troublemaker, but he would not stand by without protest if he thought something was wrong.'

'I'm so sorry,' Ellen began, but again Anna shook her head, and then took a deep breath.

'At first Filip said we must stay; it was our right to live in peace in our own country, but then,' her voice dropped, 'there was to be a demonstration and Filip was going to join it, and we were warned by someone that Filip's name was on a list and that he might be arrested for – I think you call it – causing disturbance?'

Ellen didn't know either, and thought that she knew little of what was happening in her own country, let alone other countries. 'But if it hadn't already happened and he hadn't done anything wrong?'

'It was to stop him in case he did,' Anna explained. 'But it was – what you say, the final straw?'

'How terrible,' Ellen murmured, comprehension sinking in that she had led a privileged life. 'Surely having an opinion wasn't against the law?'

Anna gazed into the flames of the fire. 'It was. It is,' she muttered. 'And so we left immediately. We pack only essentials and left our home, our parents, our friends, and caught a train; we travel all night and all the following day, changing trains and sleeping on benches on station platforms. I was pregnant with Aron and was often sick.'

'So where did you settle?'

'We rested for few days, and then caught a train into East Prussia. You see,' she explained, 'Poland is occupied by Russia, Prussia and Austria, and Filip thought that if we tried to register to live in Austria they would want to know why we had left our home, and he was afraid the authorities would send us back. The children were tired and I wanted to stay, but Filip was uneasy, so we set off again and headed for Berlin and that took a very long time and by then I was nearing my time of giving birth.'

112

Ellen reached out and placed the kettle over the fire. This was proving to be a very long story, and she wondered, if she had been in Anna's position, whether she would have survived.

Anna was almost talking to herself; it was as if she had bottled up their story for so long that once she began the telling of it, she could barely stop. Ellen made tea and handed her a cup which she took and sipped without a word, and then she began again, telling of moving on to a district near Berlin where other Jews had settled and they were given shelter and food and a room was found for them.

She looked up at Ellen as if breaking out of a reverie. 'We are so lucky,' she murmured. 'Just as when we met you and you invited us in, fellow Jews saved us, as you and Harry did. Filip was given work, so he earned money, and I gave birth to Aron and we stayed for a while; we felt we were amongst friends. And then Filip met a man who told him he was going to travel to America. He was a single man and said there was plenty of work and that Jews were welcome.' She sighed. 'And Filip, he began to plan that when I was fit to travel and Aron was thriving then we would travel to America too.'

'Goodness,' Ellen said, astonished. 'You are a very patient wife.'

Anna shrugged. 'What else can I do? Filip is my husband; I must do what he thinks best. He has ambition and wishes to work to keep us in bread and by a warm fire. So we set off again. We left our new friends and travelled to Hamburg, and from there we make our way to Rotterdam and take a ship to England, to Hull.'

'And so here you are; and are you now resting before the next journey?' Ellen heard the rattle of the front door and the sound of the children's excited chattering as they tumbled into the hall and Filip's booming voice telling them to take off their dirty boots.

Anna's face lit up into a smile. 'No! Now I feel that England is home. We are at the end of our journey. After meeting you and your family, I see now that although it will be difficult for a time to earn money, we can settle here. We are not threatened,

113

we are welcomed. I have told Filip that I do not want to travel to America as many of our fellow passengers on the ship did. I want my children to be brought up in England, to speak English.' She shrugged. 'Maybe we live in Hull, or maybe we move somewhere else; it is small country, we do not have to travel for weeks to get from one end to other. England is an island.' She gave a huge smile. 'Now I tell my husband what I want, and he say yes. So we will be English family now.'

CHAPTER EIGHTEEN

Harry didn't arrive home until early afternoon. He had worried throughout the journey, which was wet, cold and uncomfortable, about Ellen's reaction when she saw that he hadn't brought Mary back with him. He knew she hadn't really wanted to let her go, and had only agreed because a day or two in the country would do the little girl good; she hadn't bargained on not knowing when she would see her daughter again.

'You'll be for it!' Billy had grinned as Mary had tearfully waved them goodbye from the small window at her grandmother's cottage. 'Our Ellen won't be happy to be missing one of her bairns.'

'I know,' Harry had sighed. 'But I did it for 'best. Mary's not well and I'm hoping that being away from 'smoke and being warm and dry will help her.'

'Aye,' Billy agreed. 'Ma allus has a good fire and broth constantly on 'simmer.'

'I can't believe 'difference between town and country,' Harry muttered. 'I know there's plenty o' folk in poverty in 'countryside, probably as many as in town, but it doesn't seem as obvious – and, well, my da was allus in work while we were growing up even though he didn't earn much and we too allus had a good fire to come home to.'

Billy shook his head. 'There are plenty o' countryfolk in poverty, but we don't allus see them; they're camping out under hedges or in an open barn, or trudging towards 'nearest village or town. Trouble is, Harry, you were lucky to work for Ozzie and

115

you'd have eventually been foreman if he hadn't upped and died, and if Charlesworth hadn't tekken over then sooner or later you'd mebbe have had your own patch o' land to grow what you needed to keep your family. I reckon Charlesworth looked at 'accounts and saw that things weren't as good as they seemed; there's fruit and flowers coming in from Holland and wheat from America and Canada and it's all a lot cheaper than we can produce and grow cos transportation to bring it here is getting cheaper.'

Harry looked in astonishment at his brother-in-law. They'd been pals since they were five-year-olds, and Billy was the one who always acted on instinct; Harry had never put him down as a thinker. Have I been living with my eyes closed, never noticing what's been going on around me?

'Why do you think I haven't married?' Billy continued. 'I could have done, any time.' He grinned again. 'And I'm not boasting. But 'fact is, I live at home and pay my board 'n' lodgings and save a bit, and one day I'll have enough to pay my passage to Canada, cos 'time will come when there'll be no work here on 'land and I don't want to work in industry. I like to breathe clean air. If I had a wife she might not share my ideas about leaving 'country.'

'So – when are you planning this new life?' Harry was almost lost for words. 'And why Canada? Why not America? Folks are flocking there, or so I've heard!' He was thinking of the Bosco family who had considered it; he knew no one else.

'That's 'reason I'm not going. Canada is a big country and there are plenty of jobs there if you're prepared to work, and I am. Not yet, I've not saved enough, but soon.' He looked at Harry. 'You could come wi' me, you and our Ellen and your bairns; we could fill Canada wi' Yorkshire folk.'

Harry laughed. 'It felt as if we were coming to 'ends of earth coming to Hull,' he said. 'I don't think I could cope wi' leaving England.'

Sarah looked up from her drawing when she heard the rattle of the cart outside and lifted the net curtain. 'It's our da,' she squealed, 'and Uncle Billy,' and made a dash for the door. The

116

other children looked up but didn't get up from the rug, not even Thomas, who was absorbed in crayoning squiggles on a sheet of paper.

Ellen drew back the bolt and put her head out of the door to greet them; she was still hoping that Mary would have come back with them, but as Harry and Billy walked towards her her smile disappeared.

'No Mary? Is she worse?'

Harry bent to kiss her cheek. 'I let her stay,' he murmured. 'I thought it for 'best; she was still coughing this morning. Your ma has rubbed her chest wi' camphor and put a piece of red flannel under her frock. Your Lizzie said she'll ask 'doctor to call if she doesn't improve.'

'Lizzie,' Ellen breathed. Lizzie who hadn't any children even though she had been married longer than Ellen. She had had a miscarriage in her second year of marriage but nothing since. She can't have my child, Ellen thought. But Lizzie would make a good mother; she was caring and kind and loved all of her sisters' children very much. Oh, I'm being silly, and I know it's for the best. Harry did right. But he must fetch her back the minute she's better.

'Well!' Billy folded his arms as he saw the Bosco children and Thomas on the rug in front of the fire and Aron sleeping on one of the beds. 'Surely there are more than there were yesterday?'

'The Bosco children,' Ellen murmured. 'Filip and Anna have gone to look at this other house they've been offered.' She was still thinking about Mary. 'I said I'd keep 'children here. They'll be back soon.' She turned to Harry. 'How was your ma?'

He gave a little shrug. 'She didn't speak to me. I thought she was ignoring me because we've come to live in Hull, but Meg said that's 'way she is now; she's nowt to say to anybody, not even to Da and he can't understand why, when she's usually had so much to say. She's happy to see all of 'grand-bairns, though, so the girls tek it in turns to drop in and chat to her.' He pressed his lips together and said in a choked voice, 'She doesn't know which is which or who belongs to who.'

117

'Well, that doesn't matter,' Ellen said gently. 'The children won't mind. She's still their gran.' Someone knocked on the front door. 'That'll be Filip and Anna. Will you let them in, Harry?'

But it wasn't them. It was a short man with a dark beard and wearing a wide-brimmed black hat and a black coat, asking for Mrs Johnson. As Harry turned to speak to Ellen, the upstairs door was opened and the younger woman came hurrying down. As she greeted the visitor and he stepped inside, Filip and Anna arrived on the doorstep and there was a flurry of people all looking at each other.

'*Shalom*,' the newcomer said to Filip, and lifted his hat to Anna. On his head he wore a black skullcap.

Harry stood back and turned to Ellen with a question in his eyes; she motioned him to come inside and they partly closed the door, but Zophia and Jakub heard their parents' voices and ran out into the hall.

'They're speaking Yiddish, I think,' she whispered.

Presently Anna knocked and came in with the children, followed by Filip. 'I am so sorry,' Anna said. 'That was rude of us, but what a strange thing to happen.'

'It was. Especially as the young woman didn't want to speak to me when I last met her,' Filip said.

'And still doesn't,' Anna added wryly.

'Is the man a relation of hers?' Ellen asked.

'Her brother,' Filip said. 'It is their mother who lives upstairs. Did you not help her one day?'

Ellen nodded. 'She fell out of bed, poor lady. I go up to see her often and take her a cup of tea or coffee. She loves to see Sarah and Thomas.'

'And I bring her rye bread from the bakery,' Anna said.

'She's well looked after, then,' Harry commented. 'Billy, these are our friends Filip and Anna Bosco from Poland. This is Billy, Ellen's brother and my long-time friend.'

Filip and Billy shook hands and Anna nodded. Billy remarked, 'Poland! You've come a long way. It seems that 'whole world's moving. Are you stopping in Hull?'

118

'For the present time, yes,' Filip said, and looked at his wife who had sat on the edge of a bed and was smiling down at a just awakening Aron, and then at Ellen. 'We have taken the rooms, Ellen, so you will not be – erm – disturbed with us any longer.'

'I'm not at all disturbed by you,' Ellen answered. 'And I hope you'll still come and visit us?' She would miss seeing them and the children.

'Of course we will.' Anna got up and put her arms about Ellen. 'You are my very good English friend, and you must come and see us in our new house – not a whole house,' she added. 'Just half a house, further up from here, in Church Street, and with a fire and a sink – and,' she clenched her fists in joy, 'with a fire in yard as you have so we can make hot water to do our washing.'

'Oh, I'm so pleased for you,' Ellen said. 'You must of course have your own place, but leave the children here until you have made it warm and comfortable. Do you have beds and furniture?'

Anna shook her head and glanced at Filip. 'Not yet. We have been promised beds and bedding,' he said. 'The people I met at the synagogue, they are collecting things for us.'

He stopped speaking and stood beside his wife, putting his arm around her. When he spoke again, this tall, broad-shouldered, bearded man, who had seemed afraid of nothing, had a catch in his voice. 'We have received only kindness since we came here. God has been good to us in directing us towards you special people.'

Anna put her hand over his. 'It is true,' she said softly.

Ellen brushed away a tear. 'Well, in that case I'll put 'kettle on and we'll celebrate wi' cups of tea and coffee,' she said. She lifted the nearly full kettle from the hearth and placed it on the flames, and went into the scullery to count out the cups and take down the teapot from a shelf whilst she composed herself.

Billy followed her. 'I'm going to get straight off home, Ellen,' he said. 'Weather's worsening in Holderness and 'road'll get boggy. Ma's sent another chicken, cooked early this morning and ready to eat.'

119

'Oh! Thank her, Billy, won't you. She's an angel. Thank you for coming, trailing up and down that long road home. Tek care, won't you? It's getting dark already.'

'Don't worry, I will.' He kissed the top of her forehead. 'You're a good lass, our Ellen. Keep brave. Your fortune'll change, be sure of it.'

She nodded. 'I'm happy enough, Billy, though I'll be happier when Mary comes back.'

'Ma will look after her,' he assured her. 'She's got a good fire to keep her warm and she'll onny let her outside if 'weather's all right.'

'I know.' She was choked. 'I know.' She took a breath. 'We're lucky, aren't we, wi' a family to support us?'

'Aye, we are.' He decided that this wasn't the time to tell her of his own future plans, and he hoped that Harry wouldn't tell her either.

The Boscos ate with them; they shared the chicken, which they ate with potatoes cooked over the coals, and Filip said humbly, 'One day we will return the great favours you have given us. One day if I make my fortune you will be the first to share it.'

Ellen smiled and wondered if this was the fortune that Billy had said she would one day gain; but I have good fortune now, she thought.

As they sat at the table they could hear raised voices upstairs in Mrs Johnson's room. One a male voice, undoubtedly, and another which could only have been Mrs Johnson's daughter, and both were speaking in anger.

Filip lifted his head, listening. 'She is refusing to do something,' he murmured, 'and her brother is insisting. *Tch.* That is not good when private conversations are shared by others.'

'Mebbe we should sing – loudly,' Harry said mischievously. 'Come on, Sarah, Zophia, Jakub, lah lah, lah la la!'

The children began to sing in high excited voices, with Thomas and Aron banging on the table with spoons, until the grown-ups hushed them.

120

'We're carol singing.' Sarah bounced up and down on her seat. 'Can we do that, Da? Can we go carol singing at Christmas? Zophia, will you come as well?'

'Yes, yes!' Zophia squealed and asked her mother something incomprehensible to everyone but her parents, but they both smiled and shook their heads and Filip gently patted her cheek.

'It's too soon,' Ellen told her daughter, and got up from the table. 'It's not Christmas yet for *ages*. Come on now, children, it's almost bedtime. Let's see who can be 'first into bed, and whoever is can choose a bedtime story.'

Sarah and Zophia quickly began to undo their buttons and take off their socks and dresses; Jakub dived into a bed with all of his clothes on and covered himself with a blanket. Thomas climbed in after him, followed by Aron, and soon they were all hidden beneath the blanket and giggling.

The adults laughed, and then Filip said quietly, 'Well done, Ellen. No religious dissension in this household.'

'No,' Ellen responded. 'And I hope there never will be.'

CHAPTER NINETEEN

Anna and Filip left the children overnight and went to prepare their new rooms, unpack their few belongings and light a fire.

'It is much better than the other place, but we can still not call it home. But', Filip added more cheerfully the next morning when Ellen handed him a cup of coffee, 'this morning I went – erm – to get wood from the river bank?'

She smiled. 'We called it twigging out in 'country; it's when you pick up all the small, broken bits of tree branches: twigs. If they're dry it makes good kindling to start a fire.'

He nodded his head. 'Twigs. That is what I call it now. It is good word. So, we are to leave you, Ellen – except that we are not. We thank God that we met you; that I met Harry, and Anna met you. It was meant to be: our paths crossed and we shall remain friends always, yes?'

'Yes,' she said. 'I hope so. Can I do anything for you now?'

'No. You have set us on our way to a new life.' He turned to Anna, who was dressing their children in their coats and scarves. 'Are we ready, *kochanie*?'

Co-hanya, Ellen heard; was it a term of endearment? Anna had nodded and smiled so sweetly at him, her face relaxed, that Ellen was sure that it was. They must both be feeling such relief that they had found a place where they could settle for a while, even if they decided to move on at some later point. They could now pause and collect themselves for the next part of their lives.

122

Filip was working with more companies, all by recommendation, and at last he was earning enough money to pay the rent and buy food. Ellen had offered to carry on looking after the children if Anna wanted to continue working at the bakery, and Anna had said she would like to, perhaps part time, when they were settled in their new rooms.

When they had all left, and Ellen had promised that she would bring the children to visit them, she prepared soup and put it over the fire to cook, then dressed Sarah and Thomas in their warmest clothes to take a short walk by the river even though there was a strong thick and cloying smell, which she couldn't identify. She decided they would walk in the opposite direction from the mills and she would try to identify where they might be able to live once Harry was making enough money for them to move.

There were ducks and grebes and gulls on the river and Thomas chuckled and pointed to them; a little grebe, disturbed by their presence, dived into the water, briefly exposing its fluffy rear before disappearing completely for several seconds and bobbing up again further along the river.

Sarah picked up twigs to carry home for the fire and Thomas, finding a long stick too whippy and green to burn, trailed it behind him or happily splashed it in pools of water, stirring up the mud.

'Just a little further,' Ellen said to Sarah, 'and then we'll turn round and walk home again.'

'It's not home,' Sarah piped up. 'We only live here. Soon we'll go back home again and see Gran and Grandda and Auntie Lizzie and Grammy and Grandpa and Auntie Meg and Auntie Polly' – she heaved a big breath – 'and *everybody*. We'll go for Christmas dinner!'

'No, we can't do that, Sarah,' Ellen explained. 'This is where we live now.'

'Yes, I know,' the little girl said fervently. 'But we'll go for Christmas *dinner.*'

Ellen didn't enlighten her further, but as she about-turned the children to walk back the way they had come she was thinking, I wonder? Would it be possible?

123

Her mother had always cooked roast beef for a special treat at Christmas, or sometimes a leg of pork or a bird if Ellen's father had been given one by his employer, for he still worked as a casual labourer. She also cooked Yorkshire pudding to make the meat go further, and during autumn prepared and steamed a plum pudding with a polished coin hidden inside it. Since she served the pudding, she could make sure that the coin was found by one of her many grandchildren on Christmas Day.

Ellen sighed. The faithful little hen that her mother had sent with Billy was still alive and clucking, but she had given up laying now the weather was colder, and Ellen had reluctantly decided that her time was up; she was destined for the pot. But suppose they did go to Holderness? Would it be possible? It would only be for Christmas Day, for Harry would probably have to work on Boxing Day; she didn't know what happened in town. In their former home Harry had always gone out to check the farm animals on Christmas Day and Boxing Day, never trusting anyone else to look after them as well as he did; but then he would come home to enjoy the rest of the day with his family.

No, she thought as they tramped back. It was too far. They must enjoy Christmas here in Hull; but then, what about Mary? She couldn't possibly have Christmas without her younger daughter.

'In you go.' She ushered the children inside their door. 'What about a nice cup of cocoa to warm us up?'

She checked the soup; it was nowhere near ready. The vegetables were still hard. The children would have to eat bread and jam for their midday meal. She'd give them it now, she thought, and they could have it with the cocoa, but she'd have to take the soup off the flames to boil the kettle. She sighed as she added small pieces of coal to the fire and put the kettle back on top. How she missed her kitchen range, for its warmth as much as for the cooking artefacts: the kettle hook, the spit rack for roasting meat, and the side oven. She hadn't realized just how lucky she had been.

When the kettle had boiled she made the children's cocoa and gave them a thick slice of bread with jam, and when they had eaten she encouraged Thomas into bed, wrapped in a blanket

124

to keep warm. She gave him the building bricks that Harry had made for him, smoothing the edges so that he didn't get splinters in his fingers, and he played happily with them until, tired after the walk or just bored with his game, he put his head on the pillow and went to sleep.

Sarah played with her rag doll, tucking it up in bed next to Thomas and talking to it in a quiet voice. She was just telling it to be good and it would be rewarded with something nice when Ellen, knitting vests by the fire, heard a gentle tapping.

She put down her needles and wool and opened the door. It was Edith Johnson.

'Hello,' Ellen greeted her, noticing that the woman's face was flushed and her eyes were red. She wondered why she wasn't at work. Perhaps she was ill; she didn't look well.

'Won't you come in?' she said. 'The heat . . .' indicating that it was escaping through the open door.

'Sorry. I'm so sorry.' Miss Johnson hovered at the edge of the door. 'I wondered if your friend was still here.'

'Please come in,' Ellen insisted. 'It's very cold.'

'Sorry,' Edith said again, stepping inside. 'It is warm in here, warmer than in our room.'

'Yes. Please come and sit by the fire. Yours is a small grate.'

Edith sat gingerly on the edge of the chair. 'I'm sorry to bother you. Your friend . . .'

'Anna Bosco.' Ellen helped her out. 'They moved to another house only this morning.'

'Oh!' The woman seemed distressed. 'I was hoping to talk to her – to ask her opinion.'

'I can tell you where they've gone to live.'

'Her husband will be at home, perhaps?'

'I don't know. Yes, mebbe. They're making 'house comfortable.'

'Of course!' Miss Johnson stared into the fire, which was now burning merrily. 'It's just that I have a – predicament and I don't know what to do.' She stifled a sob and put her hands to her face. 'I am at the end of my wits.'

She's older than me, Ellen thought. I don't suppose I can help her. Though perhaps I can.

125

'Is there anything I can do for you?' she asked. 'Is it your mother? She's not ill, is she?' It would be awful if she were, Ellen thought. Nobody would want to be trapped in a cold upstairs room when feeling ill. 'Are you not at work today? Is it because of your mother?'

'My *Mutter* is the best in the world,' she answered. 'And if she is ill, it is I who has made her so.' Her accent, normally slight, was now strong and guttural. 'It is because of me she is sitting in a cold room when she could be sitting in comfort in my brother's house.'

Ellen stared at her. 'Would you like to tell me about it?' she said softly. 'I can't promise that I can help you, but perhaps talking about your problem might enable you to see a solution.'

Miss Johnson stared back at her. 'You are so young,' she murmured. 'And you have a husband and children.' She glanced towards the bed where Thomas was fast asleep and Sarah had picked up her dolly again and was rocking it gently, talking to it and wrapping it up in one of Ellen's shawls.

'I was married at eighteen,' Ellen told her, thinking that everyone regarded her as young. 'We didn't want to wait, though we could have done.'

'I don't mean to pry.' Miss Johnson gave a small smile, which Sarah thought lightened her features entirely.

'Does your mother not want to live with your brother?' Ellen asked.

'She would live with him and his wife and children,' Miss Johnson looked down into her lap, 'if I would go too.'

Ellen was shocked. 'And have you not been invited?'

'Oh, yes, I would be made very welcome; my brother will gladly give me a home, but I don't want to live with him and his family. I won't.' Tears flooded her eyes. 'I don't care for his wife, nor she for me, but that is not the reason; it is challenging, but not insurmountable. She is a good Jewish woman. No, it is my fault entirely. My difficulty is that my brother wants me to marry a friend of his; it would be a good match between our families. We have come far together. The trouble, you see, is that I love a man who is not of our faith. He is not a Jew.'

126

Ellen gazed at her. She remembered an incident in their village when a young woman whose parents were churchgoers and a young man whose family were Methodists wanted to marry, and both families objected. The couple were both too young to wed without permission, so they ran away together. She recalled the whispers that spread through the village, when *living in sin* was whispered behind cupped hands, and schoolgirls such as herself wondered what it meant.

She had seen the couple years later, laughing together and holding hands, married with two children, and had wondered what all the fuss had been about. But Edyta was surely old enough to make a decision for herself, or were there family ties and traditions that forbade it?

'Are you not old enough to decide for yourself?' she asked. 'Or must you rely on your brother to keep you until you marry?'

Edith Johnson stared at her. 'My brother pays the rent for our room, which is in his name. I work to buy food and coal. Everyone must work in this new country, as we did in Prussia.'

She hesitated for a moment, and then went on. 'I met Karl on the journey from Hamburg. For him there is no difficulty. He is Prussian, but unlike many of his fellow countrymen he does not hate our race. He has left his country because he does not like their politics; he thinks that all people should choose their own destiny, their own religion.'

Ellen nodded. And why not? It's called freedom, she thought, but did not say. 'And do you believe that?' she asked.

Edith hesitated. Then she answered in a mere whisper. 'No one has ever asked my opinion. When I told my brother I loved Karl and he had asked me to marry him he was angry with me; he said that they would disown me and that I'd never see my mother again.' She cleared her throat. 'But my mother says that isn't true, that I will always have a place in her heart, but now she says I must decide; she is getting old and tired.'

She leaned forward, her head cupped in her hands. 'She is imprisoned in that upstairs room. She hasn't been outside for so long; she has only breathed stale air and I am afraid for her. I am afraid that I will be the cause of her death.'

127

Ellen lifted the kettle on to the fire. 'Then you must decide,' she said resolutely. 'Does your mother object to your marriage to Karl?'

'She wants me to be happy; to have children.' She cast a glance across to the bed, where Sarah, tired and bored without Mary, was now lying next to Thomas, her rag doll abandoned. Her arm was across her brother, and she was almost asleep. 'I have heard your children playing and I know that is what I want too.'

'The Bosco children have stayed here with us,' Ellen told her. 'They all play well together. There is no division between them in spite of the different language and culture.'

She wondered what Filip Bosco would think about the situation. Would he, as a Jew, be on the side of her brother, or after he and Anna had shared in their family life would he have another opinion?

'Is there not?' Edith Johnson's eyes were still on the sleeping children.

Ellen smiled. 'Sarah asked if Zophia could sing Christmas carols with us, but I don't think that will happen.' The kettle began to steam and she rose from her chair. 'Will you have a cup of tea or coffee?' she asked.

'Thank you, coffee please. You are very kind.'

'No milk?' said Ellen.

Edith Johnson looked across at her and laughed. 'No milk.'

128

CHAPTER TWENTY

'I met Karl as we travelled by train on our journey towards Hamburg. People were nervous, wondering if we would be turned back.' Edyta hunched into herself as she remembered. 'He was not escaping, as we Jews were; he was travelling legitimately. His paperwork was in order. He was looking for a chance to see the world; he had carpentry skills and intended to use them to pay for his travels. Then we met again when we caught a ship to travel down the River Elbe. Our intention then was to take another ship from Hamburg across the German Ocean to England.

'My father became very ill before we reached Hamburg and Karl was very helpful; Father said he was a good friend to us. He was there when my father died and Ezra was grateful to him for he swiftly found suitable accommodation so that we could make the necessary arrangements for the burial. He did not interfere in any way, but was there to do what he could. We were all devastated by Father's sudden death; he had taken a chill which quickly caused pneumonia.'

She sat silently, her hands clutching the cup, her gaze vacant as if she were reliving the day. Coal shifted in the grate but she appeared unaware of anything in the present, though Ellen wondered about her mother sitting alone in the cold upstairs room.

'On the ship he and I spent more time together,' she murmured. 'We became drawn to each other and both forgot that

129

we were from different cultures and had different beliefs, and only felt the attraction.'

Ellen understood that sensation, recalling it from first kissing Harry and realizing that there could be no one else in her life, despite being only just out of childhood herself.

'Destiny,' she said softly, and Edyta looked across at her and blinked, as if realizing she wasn't alone.

'Yes,' she whispered. 'And he is still here, waiting for me to make a decision. He has abandoned his dream of travel unless I will go with him. But he has also said that he will live wherever I want to be; as man and wife, not only as a friend.'

'Then he's a good man,' Ellen suggested. 'Is it your religion that keeps you apart?'

Edyta shook her head. 'I can still pray in my heart, as anyone can. It is my heritage, my tradition and culture, that parts us.'

'Then you're the onny one that can make the decision,' Ellen maintained. 'You don't have to obey your brother, do you?' She thought that although she might have taken advice from her older brothers, she would have made up her own mind in matters of the heart.

'He is head of our family,' Edyta murmured, 'but,' she lifted her head and contemplated, 'I would obey my mother first.'

They were both startled by the knocking on the ceiling, and Edyta jumped up, slopping the remains of her coffee down her skirt. '*Mutter!* I told her I wouldn't be long.'

'Bring her down,' Ellen said impulsively. 'Bring her down! Let her sit here by the fire. Talk to her where it is warm and comfortable. I won't listen, I promise.'

'It won't matter if you do listen.' Edyta permitted herself a smile. 'Do you speak German – or Yiddish?' She stared at Ellen as if she were grasping a lifeline.

'Hah! No!' Ellen gave a small laugh. 'Come on, I'll help you.' She glanced at the children. They were both still sleeping, Thomas emitting snuffly snores, and she thought that when he woke she would give him some honey and hot water in case he was harbouring a cold.

130

She put a few more pieces of coal on the fire and then waited on the upstairs landing whilst Edyta went inside their room to speak to her mother.

She came out in a few seconds. 'She will come,' she said. 'Though she says we must not be a nuisance.'

'How will we get her down?' Ellen decided she would ignore the declaration; it was Mrs Johnson's constant guilty refrain. What was important was getting her safely down the stairs.

In the end, Edyta stood by her mother's side with her arm about her waist, and Mrs Johnson put her hands on Ellen's shoulder and step by step they reached the bottom of the stairs.

'That was easier than I expected,' Ellen said, opening the door to her room.

'I am just a sack of old bones,' Mrs Johnson wheezed and followed her in, pausing for a moment when she saw the sleeping children and whispering something.

'Come and sit by 'fire.' Ellen plumped up a cushion and held a blanket to put over Mrs Johnson's knees as she sat down.

The elderly lady sighed. 'You are a good woman,' she murmured. 'A true friend in need.'

'No,' Ellen demurred. 'I'm onny doing what any decent folk would do. Shall I put 'kettle on again? Though 'coffee might be weak as there's not much left. Our Polish friends like coffee and have said they'll top up 'supplies when they next call to see us.'

'We have coffee,' Mrs Johnson began. 'Edyta . . .' But Edyta was already on her way upstairs, and came down a few minutes later, bringing a tin of coffee grains which she handed to Ellen before disappearing upstairs again. When she reappeared she was carrying a bucket of coal and several pieces of wood.

Ellen watched as the other woman replenished the fire and stacked the wood at the side of the hearth. It's good wood, Ellen thought. Almost too good to burn; it's not kindling. And then she remembered that Edyta had said that Karl, her would-be husband, was a carpenter and guessed that he had supplied it. So she still sees him, she thought, and he must be aware of where and how she lives. Does he bring the coal? Edyta couldn't carry it far herself and I haven't seen a coal wagon outside.

131

The practicalities of living in an upstairs room filled her head. He, Karl, is still a contender for Edyta's heart, she thought. She's not simply using him as a supplier of the necessities of life, for he would have worked that out for himself by now and left. He comes because he has hope.

Ellen told Edyta and her mother that if they wished, Mrs Johnson could stay by her fire if Edyta wanted to go to work; she had missed the morning shift and would lose wages but would be paid for the afternoon if she went in now.

Edyta considered it. 'I can be home again by six o'clock; would that be all right? You may keep the coal and the wood. We are very grateful for your – kindness,' she added in a low voice.

With the extra coal and wood I could build up the fire, Ellen thought, so the soup will be cooked by the time Harry comes home. How lovely for him to come back to a warm room and a hot meal. Keeping warm and providing food were such an essential part of life; they were both necessities and luxuries.

She realized too that it had taken a huge effort on Edyta's part to ask for help, not only from a stranger but from someone with different beliefs; well, she thought, if she is to take the next step to achieve what she really desires then she has surmounted the first challenge. I hope she finds that the next isn't as difficult as she fears.

'It is no trouble to me,' she was saying, when there was a loud knocking on the outer door to the street.

The three women looked at each other. Ellen wasn't expecting anyone. The Boscos wouldn't have knocked so hard, but she saw the anxious glance that passed between Edyta and Mrs Johnson and guessed that it was someone for them.

'I'll go,' Ellen said. 'It might be my brother,' though she knew that it wouldn't be, not at this time and on a weekday. Closing her door behind her she crossed the small hall and opened the front door.

The man standing there was Edyta's brother Ezra. He lifted his hat. 'I beg your pardon. I have called to visit my mother, Mrs Johnson. She lives upstairs.' He pointed with his finger as if to prove his cognisance.

132

'I know,' Ellen said. 'But she is in my house right now.' She opened the door wider. 'Won't you come in?'

He looked startled and she heard a small hiss of in-taken breath, but he followed her through her door and she closed it behind him.

'Would you like a cup of tea or coffee, Mr Johnson?' she asked. 'Kettle's still hot.'

He glanced at her and then back to his mother, sitting so comfortably by the fire with a cup of coffee in her hand, and then at his sister, who had risen as he had entered the room and was gazing defiantly back at him.

'No; thank you,' he said. 'I think perhaps my sister and I need to have a conversation upstairs.'

'Mrs Randell doesn't speak or understand our language, Ezra,' Edyta answered him in English. 'We can speak here; it is much warmer than upstairs.'

He replied in a harsh guttural voice that was easy enough for Ellen to understand even though she didn't know the foreign words. He was not going to have an argument in front of a stranger, warm fire or not.

Edyta shrugged and turned to go out of the room, then stopped. 'Thank you for your kindness, Mrs Randell.' She was about to say something else when Sarah sat up in bed and said huskily, 'Mama!'

Ellen smiled at her. 'What a lovely sleep you've had.'

Sarah slid off the bed and went towards the fire, standing by Mrs Johnson's chair. 'That's a big fire,' she said, holding out her hands to warm them.

'Hello, Sarah,' Mrs Johnson murmured. 'Would you like to sit on my knee to be nearer the fire?'

'Yes, please,' Sarah answered croakily. 'It's warmer here than in your room, isn't it?' She climbed up on to the elderly lady's knee while Ezra looked on in amazement. 'In our other house at home we had a *big* fire to warm us and to cook our dinner.'

Mrs Johnson didn't answer, but turned her gaze on to her son and daughter. She spoke to them in her own language, but again

133

Ellen understood. She was telling them to go upstairs and settle their differences once and for all.

In the upper room, Ezra closed the door and turned furiously to his sister. 'What are you thinking of? You do not know these people and yet you sit by their fire, drinking their coffee.'

'It is *our* coffee, if truth be known,' Edyta answered defiantly. 'Mrs Randell was kind enough to invite our mother to sit by her hearth, in which incidentally,' her voice shook, 'was burning coal that *I* supplied. That young woman goes out every day to collect firewood to keep her children warm and cook soup for her family; the least I can do is give her coal and wood which will not burn in our small fireplace. Think of *that* when you next sit comfortably by your own fire, and know that *we* are being neighbourly.'

'*Mutter* could sit by it also, as could you if you were not so stubborn.' The colour rose in his cheeks as he spoke angrily. 'If you did not choose only to suit yourself.'

'Instead of obeying you,' she shot back. 'Do you not think, Ezra, that I would like my own hearth and home and not share yours and your wife's?'

'Which you could have if you married Paul Kline.'

'I do not want to marry Paul Kline! I know who I want to marry and who wants to marry me.'

'Then marry him and know that you will not see your mother again.'

'What have you got against Karl apart from the fact that he is not of our race?' A sob cracked in her throat. 'Do you not see that he is a good man? He will allow me to bring our children up, God willing that we should have any, to follow Judaism.'

Ezra sank into the chair that was set against the small fire and put his hands to his forehead, covering his eyes. 'I'm weary of this, Edyta,' he burst out. 'I know he's a good man, but I am only doing what I think is for the best; what I think our father would have done.' He lifted his head to look at her and she saw tears in his dark eyes. 'Don't you see, I am trying to be both father and brother to you?'

134

With a jolt, she understood. He was missing his father. He had been thrown into the role of head of the household, both spiritual and domestic, before he was ready, and he was too proud to admit it.

'Our *Vater* is gone, Ezra,' she said softly. 'You must speak to our *Mutter*; ask her advice as a son, and she will enlighten you. And then you can be my loving young brother again, as once you were.'

CHAPTER TWENTY-ONE

Ellen had not yet told Harry that she was expecting another child, but the time had now come, for the nausea that she had experienced with her other three pregnancies was beginning to become apparent. Fortunately, so far the queasiness was light and only occurred after Harry had set out for work. She wondered, though, just what his reaction would be to hearing of another addition to their family when they were already stretched to pay for rent, food, coal and clothing.

One evening, after they had eaten supper and Sarah and Thomas were tucked up in bed, she placed another small and precious piece of coal on the fire and turned down the lamp. She sat in the chair opposite him and he stretched out his sock-clad feet towards her, placing them down on top of her slippered ones. He gazed at her and gave a lazy smile.

'Confession time?' he murmured.

'What?' She caught his gaze and blinked.

'It's a ritual.' His eyes held hers. 'You've always done it; whenever there's something important to discuss, you build up 'fire and turn down 'lamp.'

'Do I?' She was astonished, never having realized that she was so predictable.

He leaned forward and reached for her hands and pulled her gently towards him to sit on his lap. As he nuzzled her ear and cheek and nosed her hair, he breathed in her warm aroma of homely smells, of soap and woodsmoke and the glycerine she used every night to soothe her sore chapped hands, and began as he often did to undo her braid. She leaned her head back, captivated, and closed her eyes as he unfastened the plait and ran his fingers through the strands, teasing them apart then stroking them smooth into a shining cape that covered her shoulders down to her waist.

'Don't ever cut your hair,' he breathed, and she gently shook her head.

'I won't,' she murmured. 'Unless we become really poor, and then I'll sell it.'

'We'll never get to that state,' he began, but she stopped him by turning her head and kissing his mouth.

'Don't you want to hear what I have to tell you?' she murmured.

He gave a little chuckle. 'Let me guess; you're expecting another child.'

She sat up straight. 'How did you know?' she demanded.

He looked at her and ran a finger down her cheek. 'It's a certain look on your face,' he whispered. 'Your eyes melt, your lips are fuller, and it's as if you're holding a secret.'

'I thought I was holding a secret,' she confessed, 'but even Sarah asked me if I had a boy would we call him William.'

'You told Sarah!' Harry was astonished.

'No, of course not. It's far too soon. But you know her funny little ways; she has an old head on her shoulders and comes out with all kinds of odd remarks.'

'Why William?' he asked.

'I'm not sure,' she mused. 'She said something about *other* William, and I wondered if she'd heard my mother mention an earlier William – not our Billy, but one of our forebears who once lived in Hull before he went to live in Holderness.'

He smiled. 'Come on,' he said, easing her off his knee. 'She's a child, full of dreams and imagination. It's onny coincidence, nowt more.' He took her hand. 'Let's go to bed.'

He murmured to her that night that he knew she was unhappy about Mary's still being in Holderness and that he missed her too, and had asked Roland Tannerson if next weekend he might borrow a horse and wagon to fetch her home.

137

'Which means that our little Mary will be back with us well before Christmas.' He gently kissed her. 'How's that for an early Christmas present?'

'The best ever,' she said, her voice tearful. 'I do love you, Harry. More than I can ever say.'

'Would you love me even more if I suggested that you and 'bairns came wi' me, wrapped up warm in blankets and straw?' he teased. 'Could you manage that, do you think?'

'Oh, yes!' She squeezed him tight. 'And we can see both our families.' She sat up in bed, leaning on her elbow, and began planning. 'I'll bring 'little hen's box inside and leave her seed and scraps so that she's not hungry while we're away.'

Harry raised his eyebrows in the darkness. 'This is 'little hen you're planning on us having for Christmas dinner?' he asked.

'Yes,' she said seriously. 'We don't want her dying of cold whilst we're away.'

He nodded. 'Spoken like a true countrywoman.'

Laughing, he repeated this story to Mr Tannerson at midday on Saturday as he put the horse he was to borrow into the traces. 'So she's fattening 'fowl up ready to make into soup on Christmas Day.'

Tannerson laughed too, and then said, 'Soup? Not a roast?'

'We've lived off soup since we first came to Hull,' Harry explained. 'My wife works miracles on that small fire; we've no proper oven, you see, but after Christmas I'll use my Saturday afternoons to try and find somewhere better to live.' He patted the mare, and then checked her hooves for the journey.

'You didn't know that I always give my workers a bird or a joint of beef for Christmas?' Tannerson said.

Harry looked up. 'No sir, I didn't, but it will be very much appreciated.' He grinned. 'We can joint it and put it in a big pan for stew and if we shift Christmas Day three days along it might be ready to eat!'

'Are you joking?' Tannerson asked.

'No sir, I'm not,' Harry said grimly. 'It's what Ellen has to do to put food on 'table. When we were living out in 'country she made her own bread and scones and cakes just as her ma had taught her; it was 'best way of stretching out my wages. Pay wasn't as good as here, but we had 'advantage of being able to bag a rabbit or mebbe a duck sometimes, so there was allus summat simmering on 'range.

'But we're better off than 'folks upstairs,' he went on. 'Poor old lass stops in bed to keep warm cos 'hearth isn't big enough to build up a fire. Or at least she did,' he added thoughtfully. 'She now spends a good deal of time in front of our fire since Ellen found out. Still, it's better than in 'countryside where you'd sleep in 'hedge bottom if you were out of work and couldn't afford 'rent; or being chased out of your home country cos of your religion like some other folk I know.'

Harry realized that he was talking too much. 'I'd better get off. I'm keeping you from hearth and home, sir. Thanks very much for 'lend of hoss 'n' cart. Hoss'll be fed and 'wagon looked after.'

Roland Tannerson had been listening to him with his arms crossed over his chest. 'Yes,' he said, nodding thoughtfully. 'I'm confident of that.' He handed Harry the keys to the main gate. 'Bring her in to the stable when you get back on Sunday night,' he said. 'You can drop your family off at home and then make sure the horse is bedded down with the others.' He gave a sudden grin. 'You'll know how to do that, I expect.'

'I reckon I haven't forgotten,' Harry answered, taking the keys from him, pleased that he was to be trusted with them. 'Much obliged, sir. Thank you. My wife is cock o' hoop that we can fetch our little Mary home.'

Tannerson nodded, and with his arms folded across his chest again watched the progress of the horse as she pulled the wagon at a spanking pace down Wincomlee. Before it disappeared from sight, he thought he heard Harry whistling a tune he had heard a time or two from his Irish granny.

Ellen had dressed the children in layers of warm clothing, with shawls and blankets to sit on and keep them warm, and tucked them into little nests of straw that Harry had brought in the wagon along with a tarpaulin in case of rain.

139

Sarah was very excited and played with her peg dolls in her *little house*, as she called it, and Thomas snuggled down with his favourite knitted blanket. Ellen had also brought along a picnic of jam and bread, cheese, a cake that she had bought from the baker and a metal jug that she had filled with hot milky tea and tucked inside the straw to keep warm.

The sun was sinking behind them, leaving a fiery red and golden-streaked sky in its wake as they reached the periphery of Holmpton. Harry emitted a relieved sigh as he drove into familiar terrain. The mare picked her way carefully between muddy potholes as if trying to keep her feathered fetlocks dry, and he resolved to wash and trim them before driving back to Hull again. She was a dependable beast, who had plodded on at a steady speed causing him no anxiety, and she deserved a little special attention.

'Here we are,' Ellen breathed as they entered the village.

'Home again,' Harry said, but she answered quietly, 'No. Onny visiting. Our home is in Hull now.'

'Aye, I suppose so,' he murmured, and she knew that he still missed his former home. She did too, but she had accepted the inevitable change in their fortunes and wondered how long it would be before he too settled.

She had sent off postcards to her mother and her sister-in-law Meg to tell them they were coming but would only stay for the one night. Harry was to sleep at his parents' house and she and the children would stay with hers.

To her delight, Mary was watching from the window for their arrival and waved eagerly from beneath the lace curtain she had lifted to drape around her shoulders before disappearing to emerge at the door, weepy with happiness. Ellen wrapped her arms about her and hugged her tight, and then it was Sarah's turn to embrace her sister. Both jumped up and down exuberantly until Mrs Snowden urged them all to come in and keep the draught out.

'Is there no hug for your dada?' Harry said to Mary, opening his arms. Mary jumped up so that he could swing her round in the confined space of the warm kitchen, which suddenly seemed to be much smaller than Ellen remembered. She wondered how her mother had ever managed in it in her younger days.

She took off her coat, bonnet and shawls and then relieved Sarah and Thomas of theirs. 'It's good to see you, Ma,' she said. 'Where're Da and Billy?'

'They've been up in 'woodland near Rysome since after dinner, and now they're loading up a couple o' sacks of logs and firewood for you to tek back wi' you,' her mother said. 'Some big branches came down over 'lane one night and nobody else seemed to want 'em so your da sawed them up for you. He said you'd probably have to buy wood for a fire in 'town, but here it's free for collecting.'

'Oh, bless them,' Ellen said gratefully. 'You wouldn't think how important a fire can be until you're without one.'

Her mother nodded. 'Aye, it's one of man's basic needs, that and food and shelter. If you've got those three you can survive.'

'Some money to pay 'rent helps too.' Harry grinned as he patted her shoulder affectionately. He had learned many years before that his mother-in-law rarely accepted any other form of fondness except from her many grandchildren, when it was gladly returned.

She didn't immediately acknowledge his comment but looked towards Mary and lowered her voice. 'She should be all right now that her chest has cleared, but I've packed up a bag of flannel and embrocation to put on her chest if 'weather turns colder. Whatever you do, keep her off arsenic and cocaine, cos that's a road to ruin.'

'It's 'dust and grime that's 'problem, Ma,' Ellen said. 'We're living in 'heart of industrial area.'

'Then get out when you can towards 'estuary,' her mother advised. 'Get 'bairns to tek deep breaths of 'salty air that's coming in from 'sea. Let 'em have a good cough and a spit to get rid of congestion.'

Ellen and Harry exchanged a covert glance. Thomas would enjoy learning to spit, but they'd have to teach the young varmint not to do it in front of anyone else.

141

'Has Ellen told you what she's been up to since going to live in Hull, Ma Snowden?' Harry asked.

'Been up to? Why, whatever do you mean? She was allus a quiet little lass, not one for busybodying or interfering.'

Ellen too lifted a questioning eyebrow. What had she done? Nothing untoward, surely?

Harry gave one of his teasing grins. 'She's an international ambassador, committed to helping others. That's what.'

'What 'you talking about, Harry?' Ellen asked, and her mother muttered that he was a joker in the pack.

'It's true,' he said, putting an arm about her. 'My wife is a dedicated unpaid assistant to anyone who needs a helping hand; particularly to anybody coming to this country requiring a roof over their head or a place to warm themselves. I'm very proud of her.'

Mrs Snowden scowled. 'Come on, you peazan. What do you mean?'

'I mean that Ellen, single-handedly, is overcoming prejudice and bigotry by simply being herself and treating everybody she meets as equal, whatever their nationality or religion or owt else for that matter.'

'Well, I'm sure I don't know what you mean,' Ellen's mother humphed. 'We don't know any such people save Mrs Coggin in 'village, who's a Catholic.'

'Oh, but . . .' Ellen began, 'I'm not . . . I don't . . . what I mean is, if you're thinking of the Boscos or Mrs Johnson and her daughter, then they're just 'same as us. There's no difference between us, Harry, as you very well know.'

'Well,' Mrs Snowden said, when all had been explained, 'I've nivver met them, but I don't suppose they've got two heads, and I dare say they're pretty much 'same as us when it comes to wanting somewhere to rest their weary bones and earn an honest living. So you do right, our Ellen, to offer them sanctuary; nowt special about that.' She glared at Harry. 'So don't you be giving her a swollen head by thinking that there is when it's onny human decency to do so.'

Harry opened and closed his mouth. He had wanted to praise his wife but somehow he had ended up at odds with his

142

mother-in-law, and possibly his wife too, though he thought he had caught sight of a twitch of Ellen's lips as she glanced at him. He sighed. It seems I can't do right for doing wrong. He decided to go outside and look at the stars and leave the women to sort out the world's difficulties without him.

CHAPTER TWENTY-TWO

Ellen's mother had cooked a shank of ham, and when Ellen's father and Billy came home they ate it cold for supper, with potatoes baked in their skins in the oven and red cabbage cooked with sliced spiced apple. She had also made a nutmeg-flavoured rice pudding with a brown skin on top which Ellen cut up into pieces for the children and Harry, who all loved it.

When they had finished eating and cleared away, Harry said he'd better be getting off to his mother's house where he was to spend the night. He would stable and feed the horse there.

'I hear your ma's not all that well,' Ellen's mother murmured. 'Give her our best wishes.'

'Thank you, I will,' Harry replied. 'She didn't remember who I was when I last saw her. I'm hoping that Meg has reminded her I'm coming to see her.'

Mrs Randell nodded, and Ellen's father got up and said he'd drive down with Harry to his parents' cottage and then walk back to stretch his legs. Billy said he'd go too, and Ellen smiled, knowing the two of them would call in at the nearest hostelry on the way home. Harry kissed Ellen goodnight and murmured that he'd see her in the morning.

Upstairs, the three children climbed on to the bed in the room under the eaves where Mary had been sleeping, the two girls chattering together but Thomas already falling asleep as Ellen undressed him and tucked him between the sheets.

144

'Can we have a story, please?' Mary asked. 'It's ages since you read to me.'

'I know,' Ellen said, giving her a hug, 'and when we get home we can read every night just as we always did, but now you must close your eyes,' and she thought how important it was that the children could look forward to a bedtime story before falling asleep.

When she came down again her mother lifted the steaming kettle off the fire to make them a night-time drink. 'Now then, our Ellen. You'll have cocoa, will you, and not tea?' She looked across at her daughter. 'You've summat to tell me, I shouldn't wonder?'

Ellen smiled. Trust her mother to notice. 'I expect you've guessed, have you, Ma?'

'I reckon so. I've had enough of my own and seen all my daughters in 'same condition, so aye, I could tell there'll be another grand-bairn afore long.'

'I've onny just told Harry,' Ellen said, thinking that it was just as well that she had, since her mother was so acute as to guess.

'Aye, well, they don't need to know till you're sure, but you'd best find midwife when needed, for it's too far for me to travel when it's your time, and your sisters are tied up wi' their own bairns, all but our Lizzie, who has difficulties of her own at 'minute wi' a sick husband.'

Lizzie's husband had been unwell for several months. It had started with pleurisy, and Dr Selby had told him to take time off work, but how was that possible when there was rent to be paid? Lizzie had been travelling to work in Withernsea in a grocer's shop, but had had to give it up to look after Albert.

That reminded Ellen that Dr Selby had given her the name of a Hull doctor, but she couldn't remember where she had put the slip of paper with the name on it. I must make that a priority when I get back, not only in case the children are ill, but for Harry and me too. Later, as she made up her bed on the palliasse next to the children's bed, she thought that she must send Lizzie a letter and wish her husband a swift recovery.

145

It was only a short visit, but Ellen was pleased that she had made it to bring Mary home again. She hadn't seen any of her sisters, nor her eldest brother Gilbert and his family, but the next morning she gave Billy strict instructions to tell them that she hoped to see them in the spring, when they would come again if at all possible.

'Harry's going to look for another house,' she told Billy as he began loading the sacks of wood into the wagon. 'We can't stay in the present one for much longer. We need a separate bedroom, and it would be nice to have an oven to bake my own bread.'

Billy nodded as he listened, and although Ellen didn't say, and he wouldn't dream of broaching the subject either, he thought how difficult it would be for a woman to give birth in a one-roomed house without any privacy.

'I caught a couple of codling off 'beach yesterday,' he told her. 'Ma's got them in 'larder if you'd like to tek them back wi' you. They'll mek two nice dinners.'

'Oh, that would be lovely, if Ma doesn't want them.'

'I'll catch more,' he said. 'They're practically jumping out of 'sea into 'fish basket.'

'Oh, well then!' She smiled. 'But be careful down 'cliff, won't you, Billy? They'll be crumbling fast seeing as it's been so wet.'

'Are you telling me summat I don't know, Ellen?' He laughed. 'You're as bad as Ma. I've been scaling these cliffs and fishing these waters since I was a seven-year-old.'

'I know,' she said sheepishly. 'But still . . .'

He pulled on the single plait that was hanging down her back. 'Go on wi' you, talk to Ma, and I'll finish loading up this fire-wood. There's mainly ash here, which will burn well, and I've put some apple wood in as well. If you cook 'fish on this it'll give them a nice flavour – and give your neighbour upstairs less to complain about.'

Ellen chuckled. She hadn't thought of that when accepting the fish. Perhaps if she invited Edyta and her mother for a fish supper they wouldn't notice the smell quite so much.

Harry had been quiet when he returned from staying with his parents and murmured to Ellen that his mother hadn't known

146

him, and wanted to know why he was staying in their house. He'd stayed up late talking to his father and his sister Meg, who was spending most of her time with her mother and felt she was neglecting her own family. Not that they grumbled, she was quick to say, and she always brought her two youngest children, who were not yet at school, so that her mother could chat to them.

'I don't know what I can do,' he told Ellen. 'Not now that we're so far away. It's all falling on Meg, though it seems 'rest of my sisters are planning a rota to tek it in turns to be wi' Ma whilst Da is at work.'

'It's a blessing we're both from large families,' Ellen said. 'What do you think, Ma? What do you think is 'best solution?'

'I reckon it's best as Harry's sisters are planning; they need to tek it in turns to be there so that she doesn't wander off. And neighbours will watch out for her; I will for one. If any of yon lasses aren't able to come over to stop wi' her then she can come to my house if somebody will fetch her. She'll be happy to sit by my fire, or mebbe peel a few taties, and we can mix and bake a few scones together. She'll feel useful then.'

'Would you, Mrs Snowden?' Harry's face lightened.

'Course I will. What were we saying last night about human decency?' She didn't speak for a moment, and then said in a tight voice, 'Besides, she and I were girls together and we can mebbe talk about old times.'

'She's lost a lot of her memory,' Harry reminded her.

Mrs Snowden shook her head. 'Not for 'past she won't have; onny for 'present. I'll tell our Billy to ask Meg to call on me and we'll work summat out between us.'

Harry had done as he'd promised himself whilst in Holderness and washed and trimmed the mare's fetlocks and teased out the tangles and knots. Then he'd brushed her mane and coat. When they arrived in Hull he took Ellen and the children home, made a fire with some of the wood the Snowden men had collected for them, and drove back to the mill yard.

He was pleased to see that the mare's stall had been cleaned and laid with fresh straw, and the hay bag and feed bucket had

147

been replenished. He topped up her bucket of water and she drank half of it, so he filled it again to last her until the morning. He talked to her as he pottered about, asking her if she'd enjoyed her day in the country, and she gave him a little nudge with her head so that he would stroke her neck. 'I've enjoyed it as well,' he told her, 'and I wish I'd asked your name. If we go out again I'll find it out so we can have a proper chat.'

There was a rug folded over the stall door, so he fastened it over her so that she wouldn't get cold. She'd had a longer journey than she normally had and he didn't want her to catch a chill if she sweated.

'Cheerio then,' he said, as he fastened the bolt on the door. 'I'll have a word wi' you in 'morning.'

'Are you talking to me?' The voice came from outside the stable block.

'No,' Harry said. 'Just to my pal here in 'stall. I was asking her if she'd enjoyed her trip out to 'country.'

A lamp was lifted to head height and he saw the stable lad, Jim Smith. He was grinning. 'What did she say?' he mocked.

'She said it was 'best day she's ever had,' Harry replied as he walked past him. 'Good night. Mek sure you lock up securely.'

The next morning he made a point of thanking Tannerson for the loan of the horse and wagon and said he'd been grateful for the opportunity to go and see his parents. He explained briefly about his mother's condition, but didn't labour the point. Tannerson was his employer, after all, and it was no concern of his.

He was wrong on that score, for Tannerson told him not to hesitate if he should need to visit again. 'If it doesn't interfere with your work, then it's all right with me. And exercise keeps 'hosses in good condition.'

'Aye, it does,' Harry agreed, 'though they need their rest as well if they're working all 'week. I trimmed her fetlocks whilst I had her; gave her a good brush of her coat and mane as well. She's a spanking hoss. What do you call her?'

Tannerson raised his eyebrows. 'Can't say I know,' he admitted. 'Does it matter, do you think?'

148

'Aye, I do,' Harry said. 'She needs to know if we're talking to her or 'other hosses. They all respond in one way or another.'

Tannerson nodded. 'Well, you name her if you like, and 'others as well.' He grinned.

'Righty ho,' Harry agreed. 'She can be Nellie.'

When Ellen came to move the hen back outside to her shelter in the yard she found two eggs in the straw. 'Well,' she said. 'I think you've had a reprieve. You obviously prefer being inside, even though it's not much warmer in 'scullery than outside. But you'll be out of 'wind so mebbe we'll bring you in at night if you're going to pay for your keep.'

She built up a good fire with the wood and dressed the children warmly by it, then scrambled the eggs over it and gave them plenty of bread to eat with them. Her mother had made extra bread for them to bring back as well as several slices of ham and half a dozen eggs. She was thankful too to have Billy's fish and a cabbage and potatoes from her father's vegetable store.

When they'd finished and cleared away, she left the two girls playing with their peg dolls and took Thomas to visit Mrs Johnson upstairs.

Her neighbour called for her to come in when she knocked and Thomas tried to climb into bed with her. Ellen picked him up and scolded him but the old lady shook her head. 'He's full of high spirits, I think.' She patted the blanket. 'I have something to tell you.'

Ellen sat on the edge of the mattress. 'Something good?'

'Yes, I think so.'

'Would you like to come down and sit by our fire?' Ellen asked. 'You can have a cup of coffee whilst you tell me.'

In truth, after her visit home, Ellen realized that though she loved her children dearly, she missed adult company; the days were often long with no one to talk to.

'I would,' Mrs Johnson said. 'Is it all right if I come in my dressing robe? It is so cold to dress in here.'

'Of course. I'll take Thomas down again and then come up to help you.'

149

She asked Sarah and Mary to entertain Thomas for a few minutes and then went up again to help Mrs Johnson. Descending the stairs carefully, she mused that in a few months' time it might be more difficult for her to support her neighbour's weight, slight though it was. If indeed we're still here, she thought. And if we do find another house, what will Mrs Johnson do then?

She settled her by the fire and made them both a hot drink, then sat down opposite her to listen.

CHAPTER TWENTY-THREE

'Whilst you were visiting your family, Ezra came again to talk to me,' Mrs Johnson confided. 'He and Edyta had spoken together, as you know, and she had told him that he must discuss the situation with me.' She gazed into the flames of the fire and Ellen thought that she looked sad. 'We have come to a compromise,' she murmured. 'Ezra now realizes that Edyta will not marry Paul Kline, no matter how suitable he is. She is an independent woman, old enough to choose whom she will marry, or not, as she sees fit. And in spite of my own upbringing, where women obeyed their fathers and husbands, I think she is right. Had their father survived I might not even have been asked for my opinion, but nevertheless I would have given it. Jewish mothers have great influence.'

Ellen gave a little nod. So had hers, and so had she, but she thought that perhaps there were many women in this country, as well as elsewhere, who were controlled by wealth and power. It was not quite the same for poor families, who might be pleased to have a daughter taken off their hands, but either way the woman didn't always have a choice.

'So what is to happen?' she asked. 'Is Edyta going to marry her Karl?'

Mrs Johnson nodded. 'She said she will decide when she has talked to Karl and Ezra together, but I will live with Ezra and his wife. You know they live in Leeds; it is not so far by train and Edyta will be able to visit often.'

151

'Ezra has agreed to this?'

'Yes!' The old lady beamed. 'He says now that he has no objection. Poor boy. He is young and was trying so hard to do right. He was trying to be his father; but his father would not have seen his beloved daughter unhappy or estranged from her mother. It was because of you, my dear,' she said. 'Ezra saw how you and your family embraced us, strangers to this land, and made us welcome; he has seen too that although Karl is a stranger here he also is willing to embrace this new life.'

She gave a huge sigh. 'We must do the same. We cannot hark back to the old life. This is the reason we came here: for a new beginning.'

The next day there were comings and goings upstairs and late afternoon Edyta knocked on Ellen's door. 'May I come in?' she asked. 'Are the children sleeping?'

'No, no, come in. Come in.' She opened the door wider and behind Edyta saw a tall slim man with blond hair, as fair as Harry's was.

'This is Karl Kushner,' Edyta said shyly, and blushed. 'I wanted you to meet.'

'Come in, Mr Kushner,' Ellen said. 'I'm very pleased to meet you.'

He gave a short bow. 'And I you, Mrs Randell.'

'Ellen, please,' she said.

He smiled and Ellen thought how handsome he was. 'Edyta has forgotten to say that I have changed my surname, as she has changed hers. I am now Karl Kidman. I am hoping soon to be a naturalized British citizen. Edyta will be the same when we marry.' He took hold of her hand. 'This is what we wish to tell you, that Edyta has agreed to marry me, and her brother and mother have raised no further objection.' He looked at Edyta tenderly and her usual sharp expression softened. 'But I hope she will keep her given name. I prefer it to Edith.'

'Oh, I'm so pleased for you both.' Ellen was delighted. 'And yes, Edyta is a pretty name.'

Sarah and Mary slipped off the bed where they had been playing with their dolls and stood behind their mother. Mary put the tip of a finger between her lips.

'Say hello, Sarah – Mary,' Ellen said. 'This is Mr Kidman, Miss Johnson's friend.'

Obediently they both said hello, and Mary added confidingly that she had only just come back from her granny's house as she'd had a cough.

Karl Kidman crouched down to their height and said he was very pleased to meet them and asked them what game they were playing. When they brought their peg dolls to show him he seemed very interested, and looked to see how they were made. Ellen caught Edyta's eye and gave her a nod. She had made a good decision.

'I also wanted to tell you that my *Mutter* will be leaving here soon,' Edyta said. 'When Karl and I marry I also will move out of the room upstairs, so perhaps you could rent it as a bedroom?'

When Harry came home that evening she told him what Edyta had said. He asked if she thought it a good idea. 'It could be whilst we look for something else; it will give us more space, but it will mean more rent to pay, and I would dearly love a house with a proper oven.' She sighed. 'It doesn't seem much to ask for, does it?'

In a pan over the fire she had fried up some shredded cabbage and half an onion with small slices of ham and then toasted bread for Harry's supper, but she felt it wasn't enough after a hard day's work.

'What about you?' he asked. 'Have you eaten, Ellen?'

'I ate earlier,' she said, not admitting that she had eaten no more than Thomas.

'Here.' He cut one of the slices of ham in half and handed it to her. 'You're eating for two, don't forget. We don't want you giving birth to a weakling.'

'I won't,' she said. 'I get enough.' But she knew this wasn't strictly true. She was eating plenty of bread, but she knew that since they had come to live in Hull her intake of fresh food was not sufficient to make the child she carried healthy and strong.

*

153

As the weeks moved on, Ellen's thoughts turned to Christmas and how she would cope, with a small fire and little money. At least, she thought, it would be a challenge to occupy her mind, rather than having only a daily walk by the river with the children to relieve the boredom. She had been teaching Sarah and Mary to read, but as their few storybooks were read so frequently she was unsure if they were learning the words or simply remembering them.

Roland Tannerson had told Harry he gave all his employees a fowl or a joint of beef for Christmas, and as the holiday drew nearer he asked for their preferences so that he could put in an order to the butcher. Ellen said that Harry should ask for beef, and she planned to cook it slowly over the fire. She salivated as she thought of what she would cook with it: carrots, of course; onions, parsnips, potatoes and cabbage, which were cheap to buy; and she would make dumplings from flour and lard and chopped suet from the beef to flavour them.

The weekend before Christmas she asked Harry to reach to the top shelf in the scullery and bring down the Christmas pudding that her mother had made, hoping that it hadn't gone mouldy in the damp room. She unfastened the string on the lid of greaseproof paper that Mrs Snowden had carefully wrapped round the top of the bowl and opened it up, putting her nose to it and sniffing.

'I don't know,' she said. 'Does it smell all right? The fruit isn't rancid, is it?'

Harry sniffed at it, and then again. There was certainly a strong aroma. Then he laughed. 'Your ma's been heavy-handed wi' brandy bottle, I reckon.'

Ellen took it from him and breathed the scent in again. She hoped that was what it was, because if it had gone off it would have to be thrown away; she couldn't risk using it.

'It's brandy,' Harry assured her. 'But if I were you, I'd start cooking it straight away, just to be sure.'

'It is cooked,' she said, taking another sniff. 'It just has to be heated through again.' She stood, deliberating. 'If we can keep

154

a low fire burning, I could leave it simmering all night and most of tomorrow, cos if you bring 'beef on Christmas Eve I'll have to start cooking that straight away and there's onny room for one pan on 'fire.'

Her face was a picture of misery as she tried to work out the logistics of cooking a whole Christmas dinner over a small fire. 'And it's Christmas Day on Thursday!'

Harry put his arms round her. 'I swear that one day, Ellen, I'll find you a house with an oven to bake in, a fire to keep you warm and a garden where you can keep your hens and grow food to eat and our children can play.'

'Yes.' She held back a sob for what was missing in their lives, and then silently berated herself as she thought how lucky they were to have each other and the children and a roof over their heads.

On Christmas Eve Anna and her children came to see them, their arms full of brown paper parcels. Although Filip was working quite regularly, they had only a little money to spend once they had bought food and paid rent, but Anna said they were happy. 'Filip has some pipes in the flames.'

Ellen puzzled over this; then she said, 'Irons in the fire? Is that what he means?'

'Ah, yes, I think so. Edyta's brother has been speaking to him about business and how to get it.'

She handed over the parcels. 'We do not celebrate Christmas, as you know, but we have Hanukkah, which is a festival of light, and so we wish to give you presents for your kindness and friendship towards us.'

'Oh, there was no need.' Ellen was touched by the gesture. 'Friendship is for free, but you are very kind to think of us. Is it all right to keep them until tomorrow and we'll open them when Harry is home?'

'Of course!' Anna looked round the room. 'We thought that you would have a tree to place your presents under, as your Queen Victoria does, and as German people do.'

Ellen swallowed. 'We don't have money to buy one. When we lived in 'countryside we used to bring in a small bush or a tree

155

branch to decorate with ribbons and sprigs of green for 'table.' She shook her head; the children perhaps wouldn't remember, so they wouldn't notice the lack of it, but the words brought home to her that this Christmas wouldn't be anything like the last, when all the family got together to celebrate, to go to the Christmas morning service and wish everyone a happy Christmas. 'But not this year.'

'I am sorry,' Anna murmured. 'I hope that next year will be better for you, and you will also have a new baby to love.'

'Yes, indeed we will.' But much as she wanted this infant, she knew that another child also meant extra expense.

Harry came home early; Tannerson's workers had been given extra time off and received a Christmas bonus as well as the meat. Harry, having only been working with the company for a short time, received a smaller bonus than the others, but as he tipped the money on to the table he thanked his lucky stars for the chance that had led him to Tannerson's that very first day.

Ellen drooled over the thick rib of beef. 'How perfect for slow cooking,' she said. 'Did Mr Tannerson know we had no oven for roasting? This is just right for cooking over 'fire.'

'I told him we'd onny a fire. He must have remembered what I'd said.' He pondered over this and thought how very remarkable it was that he had.

Harry told the children a story before bedtime whilst Ellen prepared next day's special meal, cutting the beef into thin slices and adding onions and carrots, with a grating of nutmeg and allspice. She had sent Harry out to the alehouse with a small jug earlier, and now she poured a cup of frothing ale into the dish. He'd bought a small sack of coal with some of his extra money and built up the fire to give the casserole a good start, and when the children had been put to bed he turned down the lamp and sat down by the fire to share the remainder of the ale with Ellen.

'It's mebbe going to be a good Christmas after all,' he murmured. 'We've a good meal to look forward to, at least.'

'And presents to open from 'Boscos,' she said. 'Wasn't that nice of them?'

156

They both lifted their heads when they heard something out-side the front door, and then someone gently tapped on theirs.

Harry went to open it. Edyta and Karl Kidman, whom Harry hadn't yet met, were standing in the small hall.

'Sorry,' Edyta whispered. 'We didn't want to wake the children. Harry, this is Karl.'

'Please come in,' Harry said, shaking hands.

'It is Hanukkah,' Edyta said. 'We have brought presents.'

'It is also Christmas,' Karl added, 'and I have brought some-thing for the children.'

Ellen and Harry were astonished at their generosity. Edyta had brought a gift of honey cake from her and her mother. Karl had brought a bottle of brandy and a small parcel for each of the children.

'There is a small tree outside,' Edyta said. 'Is it yours?'

Ellen and Harry looked at each other and Harry shrugged. But Ellen said, 'Anna called earlier and asked where our Christmas tree was. I said we wouldn't be having one this year.'

'Shall I bring it inside?' Karl asked. 'It must be for you. It was leaning against the door.'

The two men went outside. 'It's a young tree,' Harry said in astonishment. 'Can it really be from the Boscos?'

'As we have in Germany when I was a child,' Karl said, and there was a trace of longing in his voice.

The tree was about four feet tall, and on the topmost stem a white ribbon was tied in a bow, bearing a label with the Boscos' name on it. Harry put his hand over his face; he was deeply touched by the generosity of their new friends, the Boscos and now Edyta and Karl. He had taken an instant liking to him, even after only this first meeting.

They brought it inside; it would fit perfectly near the window, propped inside a bucket. They all tiptoed about, not wanting to wake the children. Ellen bit off lengths of wool and hung the presents on the branches, along with ribbons for the girls' hair and a knitted ball for Thomas; Edyta ran upstairs and brought down coloured ribbon and shreds of white cotton and decorated the branches.

157

'Oh, how lovely,' Ellen exclaimed. 'The children will think it magical in the morning and that Father Christmas has been. All that's missing is an angel for 'top of the tree.'

'Ah!' Karl smiled. 'Wait!' He searched amongst the parcels he and Edyta had brought and pulled one out. He tore open the brown paper and brought out a little wooden doll, with movable legs and arms and a painted face, dressed in white cotton. 'Have you scissors please?'

Ellen took a pair from a drawer and handed them to him, and he sat cross-legged on the floor and fashioned a tiny crown from the brown paper. They all silently watched as he carefully folded each end to fit the doll's head, and then Harry said 'Just a minute' and raked amongst the children's small box of toys and brought out a yellow crayon.

'Perfect!' Karl coloured in the crown, refolded it, and fitted it on the doll's head, and standing up he placed the angel at the top of the tree, securing it with the string from the parcel.

Ellen began to weep, tears running down her face. 'Thank you,' she said. 'Thank you so much.'

Harry too was almost speechless, but he managed to say hoarsely, 'I think we should open the brandy and drink to friendship, to Hanukkah, to Christmas and whatever is to come in the future.'

CHAPTER TWENTY-FOUR

The children were awake early, and as expected were thrilled to see a Christmas tree in the room. Sarah stretched her arms up to reach the angel on top so Harry lifted her and Mary, one in each arm, so they could see it better. Then it was Thomas's turn.

'And see what else there is,' Ellen said, pointing to the parcels, and they forgot the angel in order to see what Father Christmas had brought. The gifts they received were simple: hand-sewn handkerchiefs with their initials embroidered in the corners, woolly socks, mittens and bonnets to keep their ears warm, and as a special treat a sugar mouse each. When they opened the parcels from Edyta and Karl, Mary had been given a small wooden doll with movable legs and arms like the angel, and Thomas a wooden horse and cart with wheels that went round.

As Sarah's doll was on top of the Christmas tree, Harry tied Mary's next to it, but the girls were promised that they could play with them later if they wanted to.

They ate porridge for breakfast with bread and jam; and then Ellen stirred the beef stew and put it back on the fire where it had been simmering all night, the aroma filling the room.

'Shall we go to church and sing a few carols?' Harry suggested. 'It's a nice morning and you can wear your new clothes.'

He and Ellen had agreed that they wouldn't buy each other anything, and would spend what little money they had on the children, but Harry had secretly ordered her a woollen shawl

159

from the wife of one of the men at work who knitted them for only the cost of the wool.

'Oh, but now you're the onny one without a present,' she said, wrapping it about her, and then laughed as she brought out a sugar mouse that she had kept back specially, knowing that he would bring her a gift. 'Edyta's mother sent them,' she whispered to him. 'She said they were traditional Hanukkah gifts.'

She checked the stew again and then they dressed and set off for St Mary's church, an ancient building that had once been in the heart of the rural village of Sculcoates and was now surrounded by timber yards, tanning and glue factories, sugar refineries and a brewery. On the other side of the road was housing built for workers and their families.

They passed a burial ground with ancient leaning gravestones and Ellen thought that she might bring the children another day so that they could run around on the grass; surely no one would object to that as long as they didn't commit any sacrilege.

'We could have gone 'other way towards Charterhouse,' Harry mused, 'but I thought it would be interesting to see how 'village was before industry took over. It was quite separate from Hull, seemingly, but it's now joined up.'

'You can see outlines of how it used to be,' Ellen murmured and pointed towards a stunted, lichen-covered apple tree struggling to survive in a small patch of muddy grass. Nearby, a trail of bramble and ivy climbed over a half demolished brick wall, perhaps once someone's cottage home.

'If we kept on walking we'd eventually come to Beverley Road where there are some big houses where 'toffs live,' Harry commented. 'Or that's what I was told by one of 'men at 'mill. Oh, and 'workhouse too!' He laughed. 'They like to mix folk up in 'district, seemingly, mebbe so nobody gets above themselves. Rich folk can take note of how others have to live, a reminder that anybody can fall.'

'I'd like to take that walk,' Ellen said. 'But mebbe in 'summer when – oh, but . . .' She remembered there was another child due then. So maybe another time.

160

The service was about to start and they slipped into the pews at the back. The church was almost full, and many of the parishioners were very elderly. Ellen wondered if this had been their parish church when they were young.

During the first Christmas hymn, Sarah, who had been looking round, wide-eyed and open-mouthed, pointed a finger towards a stained glass window on which was depicted an angel holding up a light. Ellen smiled and silently nodded and thought how observant the child was, and as she too looked about her she saw the marble font and thought that perhaps this would be where, if heaven blessed them with a safe delivery, they would bring their newborn infant to be baptized.

After the service, the vicar stood by the door and shook hands with everyone, wishing them a happy Christmas. Sarah and Mary were included, but not Thomas, who refused to hold out his hand and put both of them behind his back.

'We've got an angel as well,' Sarah informed the vicar and he nodded benignly. Ellen and Harry were both pleased they had attended the service as they now felt that it really was Christmas Day and they were going to enjoy the rest of it.

Harry lifted Thomas on to his shoulders as they set off on the road home, and as they walked on and the parishioners peeled off in different directions ahead he saw a familiar figure walking in front of them. He called out, 'Hey, Jim, Jim Smith. Happy Christmas!'

It was the stable lad from Tannerson's and he had one hand on the shoulder of another much younger lad. He turned, but didn't make any response until they drew nearer, when he sullenly raised his eyes to look at Harry. His companion glanced at them all, and Mary looked at him and said, 'That boy.'

'Happy Christmas, Jim,' Harry said again. 'Have you been to church?'

'Yeh.'

'Went to get warm,' the other lad said and received a dig in the ribs from Jim's elbow.

'Was your ma pleased with your Christmas box?' Harry asked. He'd seen Roland Tannerson hand Jim a box of groceries and

161

watched the boy take it to his small space in the stable where presumably he kept his own belongings.

'We ain't got a ma,' the younger lad said and got another dig in the ribs.

'Oh, I'm sorry,' Harry said sympathetically. 'So – where are you going for Christmas dinner?' He saw Ellen's eyes swivel anxiously towards him, though she needn't have worried; he hadn't any intention of inviting them to their house, knowing full well that the beef stew wouldn't stretch to feed another two growing lads.

'I've got a place,' Jim growled. 'We manage.'

'Right,' Harry conceded. 'Well, enjoy 'rest of your day. See you tomorrow, 'he added.

Jim nodded but didn't reply and the boys walked on. Harry watched them go until they came to the street next to the graveyard and turned right.

'Who was that?' Ellen said. 'He wasn't very talkative. Poor lads; no mother. What do you think's happened to her?'

'No idea. He never talks. He's Tannerson's stable lad, and he just does what he has to do. He looks after 'hosses. Do you think that's his brother?'

'Bound to be,' Ellen said. 'Younger one said *they* hadn't got a mother. Do you think there's somewhere they can go to eat? I felt as if we should've asked them to come to us, although there might not be enough for two hungry lads. But still!'

'Come on,' Harry urged her. 'You heard him; he said they managed. And Tannerson gave him a box o' groceries; I saw him. They'll probably be all right.'

The beef stew was delicious, and Ellen was pleased to see that if she added more potatoes there would be enough for the next day as well, although for a moment that made her feel guilty again about the two boys. She served the plum pudding with sweet white sauce; she'd been using their milk sparingly, making it last so there was enough left to make the sauce.

'We've still got 'Johnsons' honey cake,' she said in satisfaction. 'We'll eat that at tea time.' I seem to be preoccupied with food, she thought. Perhaps that's because we don't usually have enough, but today we've had a feast and we must be grateful for it.

162

Edyta brought her mother down late afternoon to see the children and the tree; Harry urged her to sit by the fire and she remarked how cosy the room looked with the bright fire and the Christmas tree decorated with fluffy white cotton like snowflakes, and the flickering oil lamp which they had just lit as the sky beyond the window was darkening into dusk.

'You are a true homemaker, Ellen,' she murmured, and then added, 'On Monday I will be leaving to live with my son, and I don't know if I will see you again, my dear.'

'Oh, I'll miss you!' Ellen exclaimed and sincerely meant it. She had found a bond with her elderly neighbour, perhaps because she missed her own mother.

'And I will miss you too,' Mrs Johnson said. 'You have made us very welcome, treating us as friends.'

Ellen crouched beside her and took her thin hand. 'I hope that is what we've become, for you have made a difference to my life too,' she said. 'I was a stranger here as well. Perhaps we could write to each other? I'd like to hear how you get on in Leeds.'

The old lady smiled. 'I would like that.'

Edyta had brought down some firewood and they added more to the fire so there was a blaze; Ellen filled the kettle and prepared to make tea, so Edyta ran upstairs to fetch their coffee and as she came down there was a knock on the front door and when she opened it the Bosco family were on the doorstep, bringing a Polish Hanukkah apple cake.

Everyone crowded into the small room and Filip said heartily, 'We were going to sing you some Christmas songs at the door as people do in England but we don't know any!'

And then there was another knock on the door and Karl was there with a sack of wood over his shoulder, so all the men sat on the floor and Ellen and Edyta made tea and coffee and Anna cut honey cake and apple cake into slices for everyone to share, and as Ellen glanced around the smiling faces and the children playing together on the rug she thought that life really couldn't get much better.

CHAPTER TWENTY-FIVE

Harry was up first the next morning and tiptoed about so as not to wake the children. 'You don't need to get up yet,' he whispered to Ellen. 'I can get what I need for breakfast. Kettle's simmering, so I'll mek a pot o' tea. Can you face a cup, or would you rather have hot water?'

She nodded, putting a fist to her mouth to ward off the nausea that was rising. 'Please,' she managed, swallowing down bile, and swung her legs out of bed as he brought her a cup of hot water.

He pulled a blanket over her legs as she sipped. 'Stay in bed a while longer,' he said. 'It's bitterly cold. Window pane is frozen over, and all 'heat from 'fire is going straight out into 'scullery. Tomorrow, when I finish at dinner time, I'm going out to find us somewhere else to live.'

Ellen gave a wan smile. 'Mek sure there's an oven.'

He kissed the top of her head. 'Essential,' he quipped. 'My wife doesn't ask for jewels or riches, onny an oven to bake her bread!'

She handed him back the cup and slid back into bed. It was early; there was no need to get up. What would she do if she did?

Harry pulled his cap down over his ears and his scarf over his mouth as he left the house. He'd soon get warm with the brisk walk to the mill, and then, if the bargees were ready to discharge the grain, it would be warm work to finish unloading what they hadn't completed on Christmas Eve. In the granary, the bins and

164

grain boxes were almost full to capacity, and so too in the processing mill; the rape seed was ready and waiting to be converted into cattle feed.

He walked through the open gates to the yard and saw that the river was high and the barges were still in place alongside the wharf, but there was no one about; he turned and saw that the mill doors were still shut. He looked up the wooden stairs that led to the office and the door at the top was padlocked. Finally, he glanced towards the stable; those doors were closed too, and he wondered if maybe he'd misunderstood and the workforce didn't come in so early on Boxing Day.

His first thoughts were for the horses and he wandered across to the stable block. When he lifted the latch, letting in a stream of light, he heard a welcome whinnying; Nellie was in the first stall and he stopped to stroke her. He heard a sound and looked up. At the other end of the stable, Jim Smith was hopping about one-legged as he pulled on his boots.

'Morning,' Harry said. 'Where is everybody?'

'Dunno. Slept in, I expect, 'same as me.' He sped past Harry into the yard and raced across to the mill, took a set of iron keys from his pocket, unlocked the large doors and disappeared inside.

Harry watched him, frowning. He remembered his own pride when Roland Tannerson had handed him the keys to the yard; surely such a young lad shouldn't be trusted with keys to the mill, where hundreds of pounds' worth of grain was stored? Then he glanced towards the gates that he'd walked through. Why hadn't they been locked?

Groups of men started to appear, not hurrying but walking casually, and then the foreman, Ellison, sauntered through and was greeted by several of the men.

'Ah, Randell,' he called to Harry. 'Got here in good time, then!'

'Aye, seemingly,' Harry said. 'I didn't realize we came in later on Boxing Day.'

Ellison winked and tapped the side of his nose. 'We don't,' he grinned. 'Your clock must be fast.'

165

Harry cottoned on quickly. 'Tannerson not in today?'

'No, Roland likes to tek an extra day off at Christmas time. Well, he can, can't he? He's the boss; he can mek 'rules.'

Harry nodded. *Roland.* Was Ellison being deliberately familiar by using his employer's first name? He hadn't heard him being called that before; it was always *Mr* Tannerson when the men spoke to him face to face.

'Are we unloading this morning?' he asked. 'There's no sign of 'bargemen yet.'

'Oh, they'll be here, all in good time,' Ellison said. 'We'll unload into 'bins and on to 'second floor so we're ready to start first thing on Monday morning.'

'Oh, not today? Or tomorrow?'

'No, we'll have all on to get 'grain shifted inside today, and there's no point starting on Sat'day. Not on half a day. Don't want to leave 'job half finished, do we?'

'Course we don't,' Harry agreed, not wanting any confrontation with the man, but he had his reservations; he was used to working a full day for a day's pay, and he reckoned that in six hours on a Saturday morning they could have made good progress. 'Well, I'll go and feed 'hosses. Don't know where 'stable lad's got to,' he said, even though he'd seen Jim disappearing through the mill doors in a mighty hurry.

'He'll be skiving off somewhere, I expect,' Ellison said. 'If you see him tell him I want a mashing of tea, and I want it now. Then come back when 'bargemen arrive and we'll get started.'

Harry put up his thumb in agreement, and walked off to the stable to feed the horses and walk them round the yard, for it seemed likely that they wouldn't be working today either and they'd need their exercise. It was as he brought Nellie out first that he saw Jim Smith sauntering from the direction of the mill, and out of the corner of his eye he saw the back of a young lad disappearing out of the front gate.

An hour later the boilers in the engine room were throbbing, the conveyors were running and grain from the barges was heading towards the hoppers, the silo receiving bins and the grain floor. Harry ran his fingers through it as it fell off the conveyor; it

166

felt warm to the touch and he sniffed at it, wondering how long it had been in transit. By the end of the afternoon the barges were unloaded and pulling away from the wharf, the men were checking the machinery, wiping down belts and oiling drive shafts, and in the warehouse some of the younger lads were sweeping up spilt grain with wide-headed brushes.

Harry picked up a brush and swept the yard, putting the fallen grain into a wooden bin. It didn't do to leave grain lying around, for the rats would be on the lookout for it, and although they couldn't be kept out of a grain warehouse entirely, it served to clean up as much as possible.

They were finished by half past four, and as Harry leaned the brush against a wall Ellison said they could go home, that there was no need to stay longer. He had an oil lamp in his hand and was ready to lock and bolt the doors and gates after everyone. 'Smith,' he bellowed. 'Where are you?'

'Here sir.' Jim Smith appeared from the stables. Harry noticed that the boy's manner with Ellison wasn't his usual grumpy one.

'Now then,' Ellison said. 'Am I to lock you in or have you got an engagement wi' a young lady?'

The boy glanced at the wide open gates. Then he gave a weak grin. 'I might have, Mr Ellison. Shall I lock 'gates after you?'

It sounded to Harry as if the exchange was part of a ritual that they had been through before, but he turned away and went to fetch his coat from where he had left it that morning. He glanced back and saw Ellison give Smith a set of keys and padlocks, putting another set in his pocket. As he walked away in the direction of home he was concerned that Jim Smith appeared to live permanently on the mill premises, and that Ellison knew it.

On Saturday morning, the engineers routinely checked the drive belts and machinery whilst other men prepared for cleaning and drying, before the pressing operation started on Monday morning.

They obviously knew what they were doing, and Harry was relieved to see their efficiency. But it was extremely hot inside

167

the mill, so he sought out Ellison. 'There's a smell of heat,' he said. 'There's no chance of firing, is there?'

Ellison stared at him. 'What 'you talking about?'

'It's just that I've known stacks to fire if they're not turned, and grain heaps can combust.'

'Aye, we know about internal combustion; what 'you trying to say, lad?' Ellison had a sneer on his face as much as to ask *What do you know, country boy?* 'We've got ventilation and air ducts. We've been doing this for a long time – some of us.'

Harry gave a shrug. 'All right,' he said. 'Onny asking!' But, he silently considered, familiarity breeds contempt, and although the men working on the machines knew what they were doing, it only needed one careless act to bring disaster and Ellison, flexing his muscles of authority, just might overlook something. They were working with volatile products, and rape seed in particular had a high oil content.

There wasn't a great deal for Harry to do and he asked Ellison if he might take the horses out to give them some exercise. 'I don't know where young Smith is,' he said. 'I was going to ask him if they'd been out over Christmas.'

Ellison looked warily at him. 'He's on another job at 'minute,' he said. 'Know about hosses, do you?'

Harry laughed. 'Yeh, worked wi' them all my life.'

'A farm boy, eh?'

'Hardly a boy,' Harry retaliated. 'Though I was a horse lad when I first started in farming, when I was twelve or thereabouts.'

Ellison appeared to consider. 'Aye, go on then. What'll you do, tek them in turn? There's six of 'em.'

'I'll yoke two of 'older ones together and harness them to one of 'flat-bedded rullies from 'back of 'stable and give them a half hour round 'streets,' he said, and then asked, 'Who generally teks them out at 'weekends?'

'Smith does. Usual drivers don't come in on a Sunday.'

Harry nodded. From what he'd seen so far, young Jim Smith didn't appear to do anything much apart from being at the beck and call of Ellison and some of the other men, who sent him off on errands whenever they needed something.

168

He enjoyed the opportunity of being out of the mill yard, even though it was a bitterly cold day. He'd driven horses every day of his working life when in Holderness, and as a lad had been taught to control the animals by command and rein; he didn't know what system was used in town, but expected that they'd be used to heavy traffic and noise. The first two elderly mares trotted off quite energetically with their empty rully and he took them down to the bottom of Wincomlee and up and down some of the side streets on the way back, using *gee back* for a right turn and *whauve* for left, bringing them to a halt with *whee*, which they understood. He brushed them down on their return, gave them feed and water and filled the hay baskets and they blew down their nostrils at him as he fastened the stall doors and gave them a final pat.

He brought out the next two and did the same with them, and on his return Jim Smith was sitting on an upturned bucket eating a slice of bread.

'Where've you been?' he mumbled. 'Who said you could tek 'em out?'

'I checked wi' Ellison,' Harry said. 'Have you onny just noticed they were missing? They need exercise, you know,' he said, not waiting for an answer. 'Even at weekends.'

Smith pulled a face but went on eating. 'They work all 'week,' he answered, his mouth full of bread. 'I give 'em 'weekend off.'

'They enjoy going out without pulling a heavy load,' Harry told him. 'They need to stretch their muscles just 'same as us.' He led the animals into the stable and repeated the same routine of brushing and feeding as with the others, then brought out Nellie, who, he realized, was fast becoming his favourite.

Jim Smith got up. 'Awright,' he said. 'I'll tek 'other one out. I've nowt else much to do.'

'Good lad,' Harry said. 'Tek him nice and steady. Let him know it's a holiday and not a work day.'

Smith rolled his eyes, but Harry grinned. It wasn't for Jim's benefit but for the horse's.

'What's he called? Does he have a name?' Harry called after the lad.

169

Jim Smith turned his head. 'I don't know!'

'Well, give him one,' Harry shouted. 'How can you give him a command if you don't know his name? You wouldn't like it if you didn't have one.'

He set off again, once more heading in the same direction, but this time going to the far end of the road and coming out in the Witham district. He hesitated for only a moment and then struck out across North Bridge, drove along the edge of the large dock, then headed northwards across the outer edge of the town.

Nellie seemed to want to go the other way and he guessed that would be the way she might routinely take to the railway station with the goods for dispatch, but he called out *gee back* and steered her in the direction he wanted. It wasn't a straight road, there were many smaller streets and clusters of old dwellings to negotiate, but Nellie seemed to know the area and kept trotting on, eventually passing an imposing side-winged building with iron gates which proclaimed it to be the Hull General Infirmary.

A little further along and they turned right on to the road leading to the market town of Beverley, and one of the first buildings he saw was the notable workhouse, which he had recently been told about. The description had been very apt, for it could have been a palace, save for the beggars and ill-clad people standing outside its gates.

It was a delightful tree-lined country road which was in the throes of having splendid villas and private housing built upon it. He mused that if ever his ship came in Ellen would like a house here, but he thought that it wasn't even worth dreaming about. These houses with their balconies looking over their long front gardens were not anywhere near within their means, nor ever likely to be.

Nellie trotted on and they passed the avenue leading to a new park – probably the one the letting agent had mentioned when he first came to Hull, Harry thought – then another with fine houses and trees running down the centre, which he thought would back on to the park; and then they came to a crossroad. To the left was a country road, with *Queen's Road* pointing down it on a wooden signpost; the road on the right, where it seemed that Nellie wanted to turn, bore a sign saying 'Sculcoates', which Harry knew pointed to Church Road where they had celebrated Christmas only two days since, and which would then lead them back to Wincomlee.

The mare kicked up her heels and trotted on at a spanking pace, obviously knowing her way home, and Harry let her be. Turning up his collar, he glanced about him, observing the former village and thinking that this area might also be a decent place to live, even though there was much activity along the riverside with factories and other industrial units in the process of being built.

But Queen's Road, he mused, that's still a country district. Our bairns could fish for tiddlers and sticklebacks in the stream, and there were some cottages there that mebbe . . . well, who knew, there might be one for rent. Ellen would like that; it would feel almost like country but be only a mile or two to walk into town. Yes, he thought. I'll definitely look into that.

CHAPTER TWENTY-SIX

Ellen was nauseous on the Sunday morning, so Harry gave the children their breakfast. Unfortunately, the porridge was burnt because he hadn't stirred it in the pan, and then, having excused them from eating it, he burnt the toast too and tried to cover up the charred parts with jam.

'Oh, you're useless, Dada,' Sarah sighed as she cut off the black bits.

'I know,' he whined in a pathetic voice that made the children laugh, but then Sarah added, her brown eyes wistful, 'I didn't really mean it, Dada. You're not really useless, but you can't cook like Ma can!'

He said he'd take them out for a walk whilst Ellen stayed in bed for another hour. He helped them to dress and then said, 'I know, let's go and visit the Boscos.'

'Yes,' Sarah and Mary cheered, but Thomas said an emphatic 'No!'

'A ride on my shoulders?' Harry wheedled and eventually Thomas was persuaded into his coat and the new Christmas bonnet that covered his ears. A scarf was wound around his neck and they set off, leaving Ellen in bed and feeling guilty for being so.

I'm used to morning sickness, she thought as she snuggled down under the blankets, but this is different and I couldn't describe it if I tried. I really must find a midwife, but who should I ask? Mebbe the baker might know; she seems to know most folk. Plenty of time, of course, but mebbe I should start

172

asking now. Thank goodness it's Sunday and Harry is home. How lucky I am that he's able to look after the children; not all men can, or do.

Harry kept the children out as long as he could, but the Boscos were not in when he knocked, so they walked on as far as the graveyard and the children ran around. Then they came slowly back, walking by the river which was as high as the top of the bank, collecting kindling and watching men and boys fishing. Harry remembered again that he'd forgotten about the fishing rod.

Eventually it became too cold to stay out any longer, so they headed for home. Ellen was up by then and said she felt better for the extra rest and had prepared potatoes and onion to add to what little stew was left over from Christmas Day. She had made soup, though it was not yet ready to eat. The feast they had had was nearly all gone now, and tomorrow she must go out and buy more food, and perhaps a little extra treat with what was left of Harry's bonus.

The day dragged on and the children drew pictures or begged for a story. Harry talked to Ellen about what he had seen when he was out exercising Nellie the previous day, and how they should all go and look down the country road once the better weather came, but he could tell by her lassitude and lack of response that she wasn't really listening.

They ate bread with the soup. There were no eggs from the little hen, so come suppertime Ellen made porridge and toast for the children, and thought miserably that it was exactly the same meal they had had for breakfast. She felt totally inadequate.

'Don't go overdoing things,' Harry said the next morning, as he dropped a kiss on her cheek. 'Come here.' He drew her towards him, and holding her close whispered, 'I love you; now go back to bed. There's no need to get up yet; it's still dark and 'morning's not yet broken. Bairns are fast asleep.' He kissed her again. 'See you tonight.'

'I feel much better,' she lied. 'Don't worry, it's onny 'usual sickness. Another couple of weeks and it'll be gone.'

173

He walked briskly towards the mill. The morning was just about to break. A thin streak of dawn was spreading along the skyline and he thought of how, when he was living in Holderness, he used to watch the dark curtain of pre-dawn slowly lift at break of day, revealing the silver light of a diminishing moon and the promise of a rising golden sun.

By the time the sun is up I'll be inside the mill and will miss it, he mused, but there we are, it can't be helped. There'll be other dawns. Living in Hull was a huge change in their lives, and a life in the country was totally different from one in the town; but we must embrace it, he told himself. There are more prospects here than in rural areas; without permanent work in the country-side, poverty would be claiming them by now.

For the moment he was glad to have been given a toehold in milling, and he was determined to show his worth; and then he thought of Filip Bosco, who had taken such a risk with the lives of his family to come to another country. How daring, how courageous he had been, as had Anna too for having faith in him. Filip had justified that faith, as he must justify the faith Ellen placed in him. In this expanding town work was available, and he must keep his eyes open for all options. One day, he would succeed in something other than simply labouring to put food on the table.

He reached the gates, which were half open, although the mill doors were firmly closed. I'm first here again. Nobody else here. He looked up the office stairs. The door wasn't padlocked; Tannerson must be in. He glanced again at the mill and then up to the top floor. The three opening vents along the top of the wall that had been open when he'd left at midday on Saturday were closed.

He stood for a moment, considering. Could he smell something or was he imagining it? Heat within the waiting grain could have built up if the doors and vents had been closed all Sunday. And although Ellison didn't seem concerned about the possibility of the rape's firing, he was. Impulsively, he ran up the stairs to the office, rapped on the door and opened it.

174

'Sir,' he called, and Tannerson turned from where he was leaning behind a half opened filing drawer with a sheaf of papers in his hand, raising his eyebrows at the interruption. 'Yes?'

'Sorry, sir. I might be barking up 'wrong tree, but aren't 'top vents usually open when 'mill is full o'grain?'

Tannerson looked at him and frowned, and Harry had a sinking feeling that he'd said the wrong thing. After all, he was a newcomer to milling grain, still a raw and inexperienced worker who should do as he was bid and not interfere. Tannerson put down the papers and glanced through the window. 'Yes. Always!' He peered forward and saw what Harry had seen, that the vents were firmly closed. 'What the—'

'I'll get a ladder!' Harry ran down the stairs with Tannerson following swiftly. The wooden ladders were usually stacked vertically against the wall but for some reason they had been laid flat on the ground. They were very long, solid, heavy and awkward to handle; the two men hoisted one and it teetered and swayed as they manoeuvred it upright below the middle louvred wooden frame.

'I'll go up, sir.' Harry was younger than his employer and he thought probably fitter, for Tannerson was of a heavier build, and he was halfway up before the other man could agree or not. Then he cursed himself for not bringing up a hammer or a saw, for the frames were fastened from the inside. He'd have to use his fist, and as he looked below to shout down to Tannerson to fetch a hammer, he saw a figure at the mill doors with a key in the lock and a flickering oil lamp in his hand.

'No!' he bellowed. 'Don't go in!'

Jim Smith didn't hear, or chose not to, and turned the key to open the door. Harry felt and smelt the surge of arid heat rising from the open doors, and before he could take even one step down the ladder the thundering, deafening, explosive *BOOM* blew off the mill roof, doors and vents, and he was propelled off the ladder, across the yard and into the river below.

Ellen hadn't stayed in bed as Harry had urged her to, but had got up to prepare the porridge and was stirring it over the fire when she heard the explosion. The window rattled, the cups hanging from the hooks below the mantelpiece shook and soot came down the chimney, coating the porridge with grime and brick dust and smothering the flames of the fire.

She was becoming used to the thump and throb of machinery echoing around the area, as she was to the pungent smells of industry; it was a constant in the lives of those who lived close by the mills and factories, but now she straightened up and stood, pensive and a little afraid. The sound she had heard wasn't the usual beat of machines starting up for the first shift of the day; this, she thought anxiously, was trouble.

She crossed to the window and drew back the curtain to peer out. A woman had opened the door of the house opposite and was looking down the street; then other women, some still in their nightrobes, opened doors too, and within minutes came the clatter of horses' hooves and the rumble of wagons and carts being driven swiftly towards the source of the blast to offer what help they could.

Ellen felt sick to her bones. It was impossible to judge where the explosion had been. What should she do? Wait for bad news? Would Harry run home to tell her he was safe, or would he be too busy helping others? That would be more likely. If anyone was in trouble, he would be there.

I'll wait, she thought, sitting abruptly on the bed, for what else can I do? I can hardly get the children dressed and take them down there if there's a major fire.

But she couldn't settle; the children were awake now and she dressed them and wiped their faces and hands with a damp flannel, gave them a breakfast of bread and jam and waited for the knock on the door.

It came quickly. It was Edyta and she'd been running.

'Ellen,' she said breathlessly. 'There's been an accident at Tannerson's mill. I was stopped from going past, they are waiting for transport to take people to hospital. The grain fired, someone said, but I don't know what that means.'

Ellen stared at her. She knew that if standing stacks of corn weren't turned regularly the heat built up and could ignite

176

without the aid of carelessly dropped sulphur or phosphorus sticks. Could that happen with grain heaps? Or perhaps the oil had caught fire during the seed-crushing process?

'I should go.' Her voice came out in a strangulated whisper.

'Yes,' Edyta said. 'That is what I thought you would say. That is why I came back. I will look after children. Wrap up warm in case you have to wait.'

Ellen nodded and went to unhook her coat and shawl which were hanging behind the door. 'Your work?' she said. 'You'll miss your shift.'

Edyta waved away the suggestion. 'It does not matter,' she said. 'There are many who will miss their shifts today. People are helping to quell the fire.'

'There's a fire? Of course there is.' She wasn't thinking straight. She was rigid with fear. Someone banged on the outside door, and as Edyta in her haste had left it undone Filip pushed it open and hers as well.

'Come with me,' he said, when he saw Ellen putting on her coat. 'Has Harry gone to work? What time did he go?'

'I – I don't know,' she stammered. 'Early; he's always early.'

'Come then.' He took her arm. 'I will take you. Edyta – can you?'

'Yes,' she answered his unspoken question. 'I stay.'

Filip nodded. 'Anna is coming; she is dressing our children.'

Ellen looked from Filip to Edyta. Does this mean they think the worst? They think that Harry might be injured? She began to shake so much that she couldn't fasten the buttons on her coat.

'Let me do that.' Filip quickly fastened them for her, and then wrapped her shawl around her head and shoulders. 'You must not worry. We go only to find out that Harry is safe. *Tak?* Nothing more.'

With his arm on her shoulder, he led her out, and Thomas set up a screeching wail at her disappearing back. 'It is all right,' Filip told her, guiding her down the outside steps as she looked over her shoulder. 'He must learn that Mama is not always there. He will smile when other children come.'

177

'Yes,' she answered mechanically, and wondered how she had suddenly become so compliant under someone else's guidance.

There were many other women hurrying in front of them, some with young children and babies, and she thought that that could have been her if it hadn't been for Edyta and Filip. How kind they were. She drew in a laboured breath. I know of no one else I could have asked to keep the children safe; I would have had to take them with me to see . . . She took another fearful breath. To see heaven knows what.

They could smell the pungent scent of burning grain and see the plumes of smoke, and the clouds of dust particles drifting down and settling on the ground and on their clothes.

'Did you hear it?' she asked Filip, clinging to his supportive arm. 'The explosion?'

'Yes. I knew it was one of the mills. I have heard that kind of blast before and went out on to the river bank to see where it was coming from. It might not be Tannerson's mill. There are many in the vicinity.'

'Edyta said that it was. On her way – to work. She wasn't – allowed past. I must slow down for a minute, Filip,' she panted. He walked so fast she couldn't keep up. 'I've got a stitch.'

'What?' He looked puzzled. 'You have a stitch?'

She bent over. '*Ow!* Yes, a pain in my side.' She felt as if she couldn't breathe. 'We call it – a stitch.'

'Ah!' He took her arm again. 'I am sorry. I forget you are with child. You must lean on me. Not so far to go now. Not far at all.'

But she felt as if it were taking for ever; the longest journey of her life. But there in front of them was a huge crowd of people; men, women and children, and other men holding hands, making a cordon to keep the crowds at bay.

'They won't let us through,' she said hoarsely and put the edge of her shawl over her mouth lest she should choke on the clogging smoke.

He led her to the edge of the crowd close to a factory wall. 'Wait here,' he said. 'They will let me through.'

And they did. He was head and shoulders taller than anyone else, and with his broad shoulders and dark beard he struck a

178

commanding figure as he strode towards the cordon of men and said a few words and they parted to let him through. In the yard relays of men were throwing buckets of water from the river into the burning mill. He glanced at their blackened faces. Harry wasn't amongst them.

CHAPTER TWENTY-SEVEN

When Filip returned he found Ellen sitting on the ground; she had felt faint and slid down to save herself from falling.

'Come,' he said. 'We must go,' and putting his hands beneath her armpits he lifted her to her feet.

'Harry?' she whispered. 'Is he all right?'

His face was impassive and she could read nothing from it, no message of hope or despair. 'We must go,' he said again. 'He has been taken to hospital. Mr Tannerson will take you in the wagon.'

She grasped at his words; there must be hope then. He wouldn't have been taken to hospital if . . . She couldn't bear to think of the alternative.

He led her to the mill gate, shouldering away anyone in their path. He was used to doing things his own way, she thought vaguely, and in this instance she was glad of it.

A bearded man with his hair singed and his coat in ribbons waited with another man by a horse and wagon. 'Mrs Randell,' he said hoarsely, as if his throat was scorched. He indicated the other man. 'Brown here will take you to the General Infirmary. You might want to stay, I don't know, but Brown will have to come back with the wagon as it's needed. Can you make your way home from there?' He looked up at Filip for an answer, and the tall man nodded.

'H-Harry?' she stammered. 'Wh-what happened? Is he all right?'

Roland Tannerson shook his head. 'I don't know,' he said again. 'He was up a ladder and took the full blast and was thrown into the river; if anything has saved him it was the water that doused the flames. There were two bargemen on the wharf and they went in and pulled him out. I can tell you little else, Mrs Randell. I was knocked unconscious too.'

She saw then that his hands were wrapped in rags and that they trembled as he put them tenderly to his scorched face. 'I'm so sorry,' she whispered. 'I hope there was no loss of life.'

He nodded. 'One I know of, and another in hospital as well as your husband.'

She chose to climb into the back of the wagon while Filip climbed up beside the driver, and sat hunched into a ball with her hands to her head. What will I do without Harry if he . . . No, don't think it. How could he have been blown into the water? It must have been a huge explosion. She leaned forward to catch Filip's attention.

'Will you ask 'driver what happened?' she said. 'What set off 'explosion?'

Filip turned. 'I have asked. He doesn't know. He was late to work and heard the blast from further away. Someone told him the grain had overheated and caught fire.'

'Combustion,' she murmured. And in a closed area; not like in a stack where a fire could be contained or would burn itself out.

The driver seemed to know his way through lines of narrow streets that she had never seen before; workshops and small factories, some newly built on small plots, and countless houses back to back with others so that no light would ever reach through them. Will we ever move now? Will Harry ever be able to work again, if he – if he . . . She couldn't finish her dark thoughts, nor dare to bring forward the dreadful images that were stirring inside her. It was too awful to contemplate a life without him; without her beautiful Harry with his ready smile, his bluest of eyes, his loving nature; there would be no life worth living without him – except that she had their children to consider, children who would need their mother even more if they lost their devoted father.

181

She had an ache in her belly and she put her hands beneath it to protect her unborn child. She felt nauseous and remembered that she hadn't had any breakfast and had been able to give the children only bread and jam.

They passed through many streets of fine tall houses with steps leading up to the front doors, although in between were narrow courts containing cottages facing one another with barely a space between them; also in the area were shops and beer houses, and a fine church, with a porch supported by four pillars. Catholic, she thought vaguely, looking at the embellishments, but there were also Methodist and Baptist chapels, to suit all religions in this expanding town.

'Nearly there,' the driver told them; he had spoken little on the journey. 'I'll have to leave you at 'hospital and get back to 'mill. Will you find your way back?'

Ellen had barely noticed the names of the roads they had driven down, but they seemed now to have arrived almost in the centre of Hull; she said as much to the driver, who shook his head.

'Nah,' he said, as they came to another road where an impressive building stood in front of them. 'If you turned left here and cut through them streets, you'd come to 'proper town where 'docks and 'town hall are. This lot,' he waved the whip back in the direction they had come, 'were built – *mm*, mebbe thirty, forty years ago when 'industry came; so my da said anyway. They've got big plans for Hull.'

'Who have?' Filip asked. He seemed to be having difficulty understanding the driver's accent.

'Corporation,' Brown answered, and pulling across the road he drove through the wide gates of the infirmary to drop them at the imposing door. He then lifted the whip, touched it lightly on the horse's back and pulled out again.

Filip took Ellen by the elbow and led her in through the open door. She began to shake. There was a smell of antiseptic that made her feel sick; nurses in white uniforms were hurrying up a wide stone staircase. A young porter, dressed in navy livery, no more than fourteen or so, came towards them. 'Can I assist you, sir, madam?'

182

His voice was strained, as if it had only just broken and he was memorizing the mantra of what he had to say.

'This is Mrs Randell,' Filip said firmly. 'She has come to visit her husband. He was injured in explosion.'

The porter nodded his head. 'One moment, sir,' he said, and went off to fetch someone. He came back with an older man dressed in similar attire but with a taller hat.

'Mrs Randell,' he said. 'Isaac will take you upstairs to the ward. You must speak to 'surgeon or nurse on duty to ask if your husband is well enough to see you.'

Ellen felt a rush of relief, which was dashed as he continued, 'You'll have had confirmation that Mr Randell is here and has not been taken elsewhere, I assume? There were fatalities, I believe.'

She saw the young porter cast an anxious glance at the older man as he waited for further instruction. He was given a nod and a wave to go upstairs, and said, 'If you'll follow me, Mrs Randell. Sir,' he added to Filip. As they climbed the stairs, he spoke in a low voice. 'I understand that 'fatality was a young lad, ma'am. Not an older man.'

She was grateful to him, but saddened that someone young had died. 'Did you know him?'

'No ma'am, I didn't.'

Of course he wouldn't, she thought. This is a large town, not like the country where everyone knows everyone else and news travels fast. 'Is this your first job of work, Isaac?' she asked, for something to say, anything to take her mind off what might be in front of her.

'It is,' he said proudly. 'This is 'best hospital in Yorkshire. I hope to work my way up to be 'head porter.'

He brought them to the first floor and asked them to wait whilst he went to fetch a nurse.

'Filip,' Ellen whispered. 'I'm keeping you from your work – I'm so sorry.'

He brushed away her apologies. 'It does not matter. I will stay until we know the circumstances.' There was seating against the wall and he insisted that Ellen sat down until Isaac came back.

183

'Someone will be with you shortly, Mrs Randell. I hope all is well,' he said, and headed downstairs again.

It was at least half an hour before anyone came and then a nurse appeared. 'Mrs Randell. Please come through.' She held up her hand when Filip rose too. 'One visitor only for the moment, sir, I'm afraid. If you would kindly wait.'

Filip sat down again and folded his arms across his chest; clearly he didn't like to be given orders. Ellen looked back anxiously and then followed the nurse.

The ward was long, with beds on either side and two tables set in the centre. Most beds had patients in them and Ellen glanced from side to side, looking for Harry. She saw two men in white coats with another nurse beside them, standing by a bed half hidden by a curtain. She began to tremble in anticipation of what she would be told.

One doctor, older than the other, frowned when he saw her. 'Who is this?' he asked the nurse who had brought her.

'Mrs Randell, sir.' The nurse was meek and deferential. 'She asked to see her husband, who has just been brought in.'

'It is not visiting time,' he barked.

The other doctor viewed Ellen more kindly. 'You're anxious to know about your husband?'

'Yes, sir.' Her voice quavered. 'I came straight away after 'explosion. No one knew if Harry was – is – alive or . . .' She couldn't bring herself to state the unthinkable and neither could she glance towards the bed.

He smiled at her. 'He is alive, Mrs Randell,' he said compassionately. 'But he is in shock; he has some burns, and he also inhaled smoke and river water.' His smile faded. 'I'm afraid he will take some time to recover.'

Ellen felt herself crumpling with relief and both the doctor and the two nurses put out their arms to catch her. The junior nurse brought a chair for her.

'I'm sorry,' Ellen said, and bent low. 'I'm with child, and I haven't eaten this morning.'

The older doctor tutted and moved away to the next bed, but the other one raised his eyebrows at the junior nurse. 'A

184

cup of tea with sugar is the best medicine, don't you think, nurse?'

'It is not dinner time, Dr Lucan,' the senior nurse said firmly, 'and neither do we give food or drink to visitors.'

'There are exceptions, Sister,' he said coldly, 'as you are very well aware. And I am not asking you to do it. I will make it myself if you can't spare the staff.'

He ignored her then and, indicating that Ellen should rise, he took the chair and placed it by the bedside for her to sit down. 'Now,' he said. 'Your husband; what is his name?'

'Harry Randell,' she breathed.

He nodded. 'Mr Randell has been given laudanum to help him sleep and recover from the trauma of the accident. I understand that he was thrown from a ladder into the river when the grain exploded?'

She shook her head. She knew no more than he did. Why was Harry on a ladder, she wondered. She turned to look at him. He was covered to his throat by a sheet and his right cheek was hidden under white flannel. Tears flushed her eyes and ran down her face; she wanted to put her arms round him and hold him close, but she knew she couldn't; he must rest and recover. But she put her hand on the bed, to be close to him.

'I happened to be in the vicinity of the mill,' the doctor was saying. 'I heard the explosion. Your husband had just been fished out of the water when I arrived. He is a very lucky man.' He looked at the next bed; the other doctor had moved on. 'We have another patient, a very young man who was also caught in the explosion. Would you know him, by any chance?'

She shook her head. 'Harry hasn't worked there very long. We're new to Hull. The only people we know are immigrants, Polish and Prussian.'

'You're from Holderness?' he asked. 'I can hear your accent.'

'Yes!' she said. 'Are you too, doctor? I was told there was a Holderness doctor living in Hull.'

'Yes, I am,' he said, 'as my wife is too.' He fished in his jacket pocket beneath his white coat and brought out a card. 'Dr

185

Lucan,' he said, handing it to her. 'When you get your husband home, let me know and I'll come to see him.'

He must have seen the doubt on her face. They didn't have money for doctors.

'Please do,' he said. 'There will be no charge for a visit.'

Gratefully, she thanked him and said that she would.

The doctor moved on to other patients and Ellen sat by Harry's side. He was oblivious of her presence. She wanted to lift the sheet to see if his burns were bad, but didn't dare. The young nurse brought her a cup of sweet tea and when she handed it to Ellen she put her finger to her lips. Ellen drank it appreciatively and then thought of Filip waiting outside and knew that they must get back home. It was a long walk and she hoped that Filip would remember the way.

She rose from the seat and put the empty cup and saucer on it, touched her lips with her fingertips and blew a kiss to Harry, and turned away. When he woke, he wouldn't know that she had been to see him. She fished in her pocket for a clean handkerchief and found one that she had used only for wiping away her tears; she felt beneath the sheet where she thought his hands would be and felt his bandaged fingers and put the handkerchief between them.

'I love you, Harry,' she whispered. 'Please get well soon. We want you home again.'

CHAPTER TWENTY-EIGHT

Filip was waiting outside the ward with his eyes closed and his arms still crossed. He opened his eyes and stood up as Ellen approached. 'Is all well?' he asked.

'He's alive.' Her voice was choked. 'Thank you, Filip. Thank you so much for your concern and kindness.'

He shook his head. 'No,' he said. 'You have shared your home with us and given us the hand of friendship. It is we who must thank you; and we will pray that Harry recovers soon.'

Dr Lucan opened the door behind them, nodded to Ellen and glanced at Filip. 'Dr Lucan,' Ellen said for no reason she could think of, 'this is our friend Filip Bosco, who was kind enough to bring me to 'hospital.'

Dr Lucan extended a firm hand to Filip. 'Very considerate of you,' he said. 'I'm sure Mrs Randell appreciates your help. Good day to you both.' He then ran swiftly down the stairs and Ellen, with Filip holding her arm, followed more slowly.

Outside, Filip asked, 'Do you feel able to walk home? We will cut through the streets as the driver say.'

Ellen said yes, but in truth she did not feel at all well and doubted if she could walk so far without taking frequent rests, but she was very conscious that she was taking up Filip's precious time. She saw the doctor climb into a trap drawn by a young pony and give a boy a coin, presumably for looking after it, before pulling away towards the gate, but before he reached it he drew to a halt and waited until they were abreast of him.

187

'Do you have transport home?' he asked.

Ellen shook her head. Filip said, 'No, sir, we have no carriage. We must walk.'

'Where do you live? Is it far?'

'Wincomlee, not far from Tannerson's mill,' Ellen said, hoping that was the area the doctor was travelling towards.

He jumped down from his seat. 'You can't be allowed to walk so far, Mrs Randell. Please, come with me. I'm going back to the mill to see other casualties.'

He helped Ellen into the trap and looked earnestly at her. 'Are you unwell, Mrs Randell? You said you were with child,' he added in a low voice.

'I am,' she whispered, close to tears. 'But I – something isn't right.'

'Very well. Mr Bosco, are you going the same way? Please, let me give you a ride home too.'

'It is good,' Filip said as he climbed in next to Ellen. 'English people are generous. We are lucky to meet.'

Ellen felt very unwell and concentrated hard to keep her mind free of anxieties as Filip and the doctor continued a conversation in which the doctor questioned him about where he had come from and asked if he intended staying in England. She heard Filip say that he and his wife and their children hoped to do so, that he was an engineer and that he wanted to find his family who had also come to England a year ago. His *cowsuns*, she heard him say, which in spite of her increasing discomfort made her give a teary smile as she remembered that Anna had pronounced cousins the same way.

Dr Lucan drove them right to the door of Ellen's house, and when Edyta opened it the doctor seemed astonished to find two other women there and a host of children.

He came inside. 'You don't all live here, surely?'

Ellen collapsed on to one of the beds, explaining that her good friends had looked after her three children whilst she went to find out about Harry.

'I'm so sorry that we've been so long,' she gasped out to Anna and Edyta. 'We've been to 'hospital. Harry was hurt in 'explosion

188

and—' She suddenly gave a great start and drew in her breath. 'Oh! Hah!' She screwed her eyes up tight and bent double. 'Something . . .' She took another breath. 'Doctor?'

'Yes, I'm still here.' Dr Lucan came to her side. 'Do you have another room, a bedroom?'

Ellen began to shake her head, but Edyta broke in. 'You can use my upstairs room.'

The doctor hesitated. 'The stairs?'

'We will take the children upstairs,' Anna interrupted. 'Is that all right, Edyta? Filip, you will help us?'

'Your mother?' Ellen gasped. 'She can't—'

'Gone with my brother this morning,' Edyta said, clasping Ellen's hand. 'She said to give you fond greetings and hoped that your husband is not hurt. Come,' she said to the others. 'There is a fire; the children will be warm.'

Mary and Sarah looked back at their mother with some trepidation, their lips trembling, but obediently they followed Anna and Filip, who were urging the younger children onward, while Edyta ran ahead of them to open her door and then ran down again to be with Ellen.

The doctor took off his jacket and rolled up his sleeves, but when he turned to Ellen she shook her head.

'It's too late, doctor,' she said tearfully, her eyes full of grief. 'I'm bleeding; miscarrying, I think.'

'Cloths then,' Dr Lucan said briskly, 'towels, soap and a bowl of water.'

Edyta nodded nervously as Ellen told her, in short gasps, where to find the things he needed, and when she came back she murmured to him, 'Doctor, I'm a single Jewish woman. I have no experience of childbirth.'

He paused in the act of pressing gently on Ellen's abdomen, and looking up he answered, 'Ah! Then just as well that Mrs Randell and I do. You may turn your back if you wish. I'm sure Mrs Randell won't object.'

'You could refill 'kettle, Edyta.' Ellen let out another wheeze. 'And put it on 'fire to boil. I'll be in sore need of a cup of tea when this is over.' She remembered then that the fire had gone

189

out, smothered by soot and debris, but then she saw that one of her angel friends had relit it and the kettle was merrily steaming.

She sobbed after the doctor had left, having held back her tears and heartache. He'd said that he would call again in a day or two, but that she must send for him if she needed him urgently. Two catastrophes in the space of one morning. She was sure her miscarriage was associated with the shock of the explosion and the worry of whether Harry had been caught in it.

Dr Lucan had been very considerate. He'd said how sorry he was and that she mustn't worry about not conceiving again, for she was a healthy young woman. 'You might have miscarried without the shock you have experienced,' he had told her. 'You have had three children in quick succession; your body hasn't had time to fully recover from three pregnancies. For the present, you must take care and build up your strength.' He had picked up on her anxiety over Harry, for he had added, 'Your husband will come home, Mrs Randell, be assured of that.' Then, thoughtfully, he said, 'Is it imperative that you live so close to your husband's work?'

She'd shaken her head. 'No,' she murmured. 'This room was all that Harry could find when he first came looking for employment. He'd lost his farming work; his employer had died and 'new man had different ideas which didn't include Harry; and 'rent here was all we could afford.'

Tears had run down her face and she'd brushed them away with her fingertips. 'He was going to look for somewhere else in 'new year, but now . . .' Now what will we do, she had thought. How long will it be before we find somewhere else?

The doctor had asked if they'd be prepared to live a little further out of town. 'Somewhere not quite so near to the industry, where Mr Randell might possibly have further to walk to work?'

'We're used to walking, doctor. How else would we get about?' She'd given a watery smile. As a Holderness man he ought to have known, she thought, except of course he might always have had the use of a horse and carriage. 'Harry occasionally borrowed a wagon when he was on 'farm, and if I wanted to go to

190

Withernsea I'd sometimes catch 'carrier, but apart from that we walked. What other option was there for folk like us?' She'd said it without a trace of envy or rancour; that was just the way it was.

'I'll ask about,' he said. 'I often hear what's happening and who's moving on where.'

She had felt slightly heartened by his words even though she wondered whether Harry would be able to go back to the same kind of work; but surely, she thought, the doctor of all people would know about the state of his injuries and their effect on his prospects for employment. After he had left, Anna and Edyta had insisted that she remain in bed for the rest of the day and not worry about anything for the time being. Anna would stay and entertain the children upstairs in Edyta's room and Edyta would go back to work for the afternoon shift.

She slept for an hour and felt a little refreshed when she woke. She could hear the children's voices upstairs and wondered what she would have done without her friends. Family and friendship are so important, she thought later; Anna had fed all the children, having sent Filip out for bread and eggs, and before they left she had prepared Ellen's three for bed and said she would come back the next morning. Edyta had come home from work and stayed with her until the children's bedtime, when she had given them and Ellen cocoa before going up to her own room to sleep.

Ellen lay quietly in the flickering firelight and realized that she must write home to tell Harry's family about his accident. I'll drop a postcard to Billy and ask Edyta to post it. He'll tell Harry's father and sisters, but maybe not his mother; I don't want to upset her, seeing as she's not well. Unsteadily she put her feet to the floor, and holding on to chairs and table she crossed the floor and took a postcard and pencil from the table drawer.

She told Billy as much as she could in the few words she could fit on the postcard about Harry's accident and her own miscarriage, assuring him that Harry would improve in time, as she would too. She also told him about the support she had had from their friends, for she didn't want their families to be anxious about them, but simply to be aware of what had happened.

191

A reply came back from her mother within a few days, saying she was sorry to hear of their tragedies and hoped they would soon recover, and then imparting the news that Lizzie's husband Albert had died. *Our Lizzie is bearing up with fortitude,* she wrote, *and his funeral is later in the week. It seems that our families are having a difficult time, but we will overcome it with strength and courage.*

In spite of her sorrow for her sister, Ellen couldn't help but think warmly of her mother's words; she was so resolute and strong and always full of determination. I must try to be the same, to follow my mother and not give in because of misfortune.

Although Anna had called each day to see her, Ellen was still wearing her dressing gown and hadn't been out for a week, although she had insisted that the children should wash and dress each day, and if the fire was hot enough had sliced bread to make toast for their breakfast. Now, with her mother in mind, using hot water from the kettle, she washed and dressed, brushed her hair and rebraided it, and was pleased she had done so when a little later someone knocked on the outer door.

It was Roland Tannerson. His horse and trap stood outside on the road with a boy holding the reins. He lifted his hat and Ellen saw that his hands were still wrapped in bandages. 'Might I come in, Mrs Randell?'

Ellen began to shake, her former strong resolutions melting away. She nodded and opened the door wider and he exclaimed, 'I'm not the bearer of bad news, Mrs Randell, please don't think that! I'm calling as a matter of courtesy.'

'Please come in, sir.' She beckoned him in and saw his swift glance around the room before his gaze settled on the children, who were sitting on the beds. Sarah and Mary were playing with the dolls that Karl had made them for Christmas, and Thomas had his wooden train. They all looked up at him but didn't speak.

'Won't you take a seat, Mr Tannerson?' Ellen indicated one of the chairs by the fire.

'Thank you.' He sat down. 'I don't want to disturb you, Mrs Randell, but I wanted to be sure that you were managing all right

192

whilst your husband was in hospital.' He shook his head. 'A bad business; a tragedy.'

'I believe that one of your employees died,' she said softly. 'I'm so sorry.'

'No.' He shook his head. 'Not an employee. It was a child.' He cleared his throat. 'At least . . .' He gave another shake of his head. 'We don't yet know who he was. He shouldn't have been there, at any rate, and I don't know why he was in the mill.'

Ellen's face drained of colour. 'A child?' she whispered. 'But – surely you don't employ children?'

'I do not,' he said sharply. 'The cotton mills do, in spite of the Factory Act. But I don't.' He looked at her directly and his words were abrupt. 'I worked in a cotton mill when I was a child. I know what it's like and I won't allow it in my mill!'

So he's 'same as us, she thought. He's hauled himself up into a position of a mill owner from – what? Who knows what he's been through, and now isn't the time to ask, even if one could.

'Well,' she said at last. 'Most folk I know worked when we were not much more than children. I left school and worked in service when I was young, but working wi' machinery at that age must surely be wrong.'

'It is wrong,' he agreed, but his tone was softer. 'There are laws that say machinery must be fenced off to avoid injury, but not all employers follow those rules, and that is why . . .' He paused for a moment and then went on, 'That's why I do my best to ensure my employees are safe and also why I take out insurance in case anyone is injured due to no fault of their own. Your husband comes under that category; he was trying to stop a perceived fire risk.'

'Really?' she breathed. It was the sort of thing Harry would do, she thought, and maybe he took a personal risk to do it.

'So, don't worry that Harry will lose his job. He'll get some money whilst he's recuperating, but there'll have to be an inquiry first and that might take some time. There are inspectors all over it. ' He sighed. 'Mill isn't working, of course, and will have to be rebuilt.'

'There's a young man in 'bed next to Harry,' she said. 'I think he's one of your men.'

193

He nodded. 'So he is. I'm going to visit 'hospital later today and hope to talk to him. You can come with me if you wish?'

She would dearly have loved to do so, but who would look after the children? She couldn't take them with her. She explained this to Mr Tannerson, who understood at once.

'But would you take a letter to Harry?' she asked. 'Would you mind?'

'I don't mind at all,' he said. 'He'll be pleased to hear that you're coping.'

'Thank you. And, Mr Tannerson, if he asks how I am, please would you say that I'm perfectly well.'

He stood up. 'And are you?'

She hesitated. 'More or less,' she murmured, not wanting the children to hear. 'I've lost 'child I was carrying, but I don't want Harry to know that. I don't want him to worry. I just want him to get better and come home.'

'Of course you do,' he sympathized, 'but you must also take care of yourself.' He glanced again at the children and commented, 'Your children are very well behaved.'

'They are.' She smiled, and putting out her hand she said to them, 'Come and say hello to Mr Tannerson.'

The two girls slid off the bed and first Sarah and then Mary shyly said 'Hello' and then dipped a knee to him, whilst Thomas hid his face in a pillow.

Tannerson gave a wide smile and said hello back, and Ellen asked, 'Do you have any family, Mr Tannerson?'

She saw a momentary blink of his eyelids, and his lips parted and then closed. Then he said briefly, 'Sadly no; my late wife and I were not so fortunate,' which led Ellen to believe that it might be a sensitive subject. When he had gone, her letter to Harry in his jacket pocket, it occurred to her that he must be the son in the family business of R. Tannerson and Son. But if his father had been a mill owner, why did he work in a cotton mill as a child?

194

CHAPTER TWENTY-NINE

Two weekends later, at midday on the Saturday, Ellen opened the front door to find her brother Billy and sister Lizzie on the doorstep. Both were laden with parcels and baskets and the same old horse and wagon was tied up outside.

An image flashed across Ellen's mind of a young boy standing watching them unpack the wagon when they'd first come here. She hadn't seen him since – except, had she . . .? The memory faded as Lizzie dropped what she was carrying and held out her arms.

The sisters hugged tightly, Ellen murmuring, 'I'm so sorry about Albert; heartbroken for you,' and wept whilst Billy went into her room to put down his parcels and came back for Lizzie's. When everything was inside he returned to put his arms around both of them.

'Come on now,' he said in a tight voice. 'This is no way for 'Snowden girls to behave.' He gave a slight tug on Ellen's plait and patted Lizzie's shoulder and they both drew away and dried their tears, and Lizzie exclaimed at Sarah and Mary who were looking anxiously at them and Thomas whose mouth was puckered up ready to wail.

'I'm crying with happiness at seeing you all again.' She gathered them up in her arms. 'It's such a long time since I last saw you.'

'You saw me a lot when I came to stay at Granny Snowden's,' Mary told her.

195

Lizzie put a finger to her mouth and made a pretence of trying to remember, and then exclaimed, 'Oh, so I did! Silly me!'

'But you haven't seen me or Thomas for ages,' Sarah said, 'cos we didn't stay long when we came to collect Mary.'

Ellen, watching her sister chatting to the girls, felt sad for her, for she clearly loved children. She wondered what Lizzie would do now that she was widowed. She would have to find work again; Albert had been a farm labourer and Ellen doubted that he would have left her any money to live on.

Billy unpacked a cooked chicken, a knuckle end of bacon that Ellen could cook over the fire, a bag of potatoes and a large swede. Other parcels yielded bread, biscuits, an apple pie, a fruit cake and more vegetables.

Ellen's eyes began to prickle again as she gazed at her mother's gifts and thought that she couldn't have any chickens left when she kept giving them away, unless perhaps she was exchanging or bartering with a neighbour, which country folk tended to do. 'She's too good,' she began, but couldn't continue.

'You know how she likes cooking and baking,' Billy said, 'and now that there's onny me and Da at home she doesn't need to bake so often. But Harry's ma has been coming over; Meg brings her and Mrs Randell scrubs 'taties and carrots for dinner, and prepares scone mixture and suchlike, and they both have a grand natter together about 'old days.'

'Ma's a hero,' Lizzie butted in. 'I don't know how I'd have managed without her these last few weeks.'

'Listen, our Ellen,' Billy interrupted. 'I want to go and visit Harry so that I can give everybody news of how he is. But I have to go now, cos I've to tek 'hoss and wagon back tonight, so do you want to come wi' me?'

'Ellen should go; I'll stay with 'bairns,' Lizzie said, and looked up at her sister. 'And I can stay longer if you want me to. I've no reason to dash home.' Her voice cracked. 'I'd like to.'

'Oh, yes, *please*!' Ellen was delighted. Edyta and Anna had been unfailingly caring and helpful, but she was conscious of taking them away from their usual commitments; also, if Lizzie stayed, she could visit Harry more often.

196

She quickly put on her coat, shawl and boots, whilst Lizzie made chicken sandwiches and thrust them at her for her and Billy to eat as they drove, and said she'd feed the children. Ellen asked them to give her a kiss for their dada who wasn't very well but would be coming home soon, and then she was climbing into the wagon with Billy grasping the reins and asking her if she knew which way to go.

'Not sure,' she confessed. 'I've onny been once and I was in no fit state to take any notice.'

He shook the reins and turned the horse and wagon about, and set off. 'I've an idea where it is,' he said, and shortly afterwards he turned right and cut down the many narrow streets around Wincomlee.

Ellen agreed that this was the right direction. 'It's more or less 'same way we came back last time. We go down Francis Street and we should pass a church and 'infirmary is straight on.'

And it was; within half an hour they were driving through the hospital gates. Billy tied the horse securely to a metal fence in the courtyard and took Ellen's elbow to shepherd her through the door, where as luck would have it they were greeted by Isaac, the young porter. He remembered Ellen.

'Good afternoon, Mrs Randell.' He touched his forehead courteously. 'Nice to see you again. I saw that Mr Randell was out of bed yesterday.'

'Was he?' She was immediately brightened by the news. 'Can we go up? Is it visiting time? This is my brother come from out of town to visit him.'

'How do you do, sir?' Isaac touched his forehead again and then glanced up at the clock on the wall. 'Yes,' he said softly. 'Near enough.' He gave her a wink. 'Blame me if anybody says owt.'

Billy smiled at Ellen as they made their way up the steps. 'You've made a conquest there, Ellen.'

She raised her eyebrows at him as they approached the ward doors. Just as they were wondering whether they should go in, the doors swung open and Dr Lucan came out. He too recognized Ellen, and asked solicitously how she was, saying he hoped she hadn't walked.

197

'I feel much better, thank you, doctor,' she said. 'And thank you for your concern.' She indicated Billy. 'My brother has come over from Holderness this morning and brought me in 'wagon, otherwise I wouldn't have been able to come. How is my husband? Is he any better?'

'Much,' he said, 'though still sleepy and under the influence of medication. But come in,' he added, opening the door again and ushering them inside, 'you can see for yourself,' and he walked the length of the ward with them to the bed where Harry was lying propped up against the pillows with his eyes closed.

Billy brought Ellen a chair to sit on and Dr Lucan bent over Harry and said softly, 'Mr Randell, here's another tonic for you.'

Harry gave a slight groan. 'I've just tekken some, doctor. It's not time for more.' He blinked to open his bloodshot eyes. 'I'm really tired.'

'This tonic will wake you up,' the doctor said. 'Come on now, where's that Holderness spirit?'

Harry shifted on his pillow. 'Wh-what? How do . . .' He blinked again and opened his eyes wider, and as his vision cleared he saw Ellen on the chair, with Billy standing behind her. 'I'm dreaming,' he muttered.

Dr Lucan smiled at Ellen. 'I'll leave you to waken him.' Turning to Billy, he said, 'If anyone questions you about being here out of visiting hours, tell them I said you can be here for half an hour.'

Billy grinned. 'Thanks, doctor. I will.'

'Will you also tell Mrs Randell that I've had words with the mill owner and there's something to discuss. I'll try to call in and see her on Monday.'

Harry was holding Ellen's hand with his bandaged fingers. 'It's you,' he was murmuring. 'I've been having nightmares, and just now I thought I was dreaming. Do you remember when I met you, Ellen?' He closed his eyes again. 'You were just a schoolgirl and I waited till you were grown.'

Ellen smiled. She had left school on the occasion he meant, and clearly he'd forgotten, and she didn't bother to remind him.

'There was a song.' His words were slurred. 'It was about you. Irish, I think.'

Billy laughed. 'I didn't know I had any Irish sisters!'

'He's under 'influence of something,' she murmured, and chuckled. 'I bet he won't remember that we've visited after we've gone.'

Harry opened his eyes again. 'You came to see me, didn't you? I found your handkerchief when I woke up. I told Jim' – he indicated the next bed, whose occupant had his back to them – 'that you'd been and I don't think he remembered anything. He didn't answer me, anyway. He's in a bad way, poor lad. Got burned in a fire. Is that why I'm here?'

'Yes,' Ellen said. 'Don't you remember?'

'Keeps coming back,' he murmured. 'Falling off a ladder. I was on 'top of a barn, I think. That was a stupid thing to do, wasn't it? I've climbed many a ladder but never fallen off one. Is that you, Billy? Were you there? Did you see what happened?'

Billy approached the bed and shook his head. 'No, I didn't. I was away on another job. Heard about it, though. You were knocked off 'ladder. Luckily you fell into 'water so you didn't break any bones.'

Harry looked at his hands. 'But I'm bandaged and my hands are sore – I mean, really sore – and my chest is too.'

'That's why you're in hospital,' Ellen told him quietly. 'It's so you don't try to do things before you're healed. But you'll soon be home again,' she added. 'Children are looking forward to seeing you.'

He gazed at her. 'You've never left them on their own, Ellen?'

'Of course not. Someone is looking after them.' She didn't say who; to mention her sister's name would bring up another set of questions, and Harry was definitely confused, or perhaps, she thought, still concussed.

As they set off for home a little later, she wondered how long Harry would stay in the hospital, and also what it was that the doctor and Mr Tannerson wanted to discuss with her.

'What am I going to do, Billy?' she asked her brother. 'Harry's not going to be fit for work so I'll have to; we have to buy food, and if we don't pay 'rent we'll be turned out. But how can I leave 'children? Mr Tannerson said that Harry would get his job back and be paid something whilst he's off, but he mentioned something about an inquiry first, and it could be weeks, or months even, before 'mill can be in production again.'

'Well, first off, you'll have to sit down and work out your options. Harry can't work, that's true, but that means he'll be at home and can keep an eye on 'bairns whilst you're out. Mebbe you could do a few hours cleaning, early morning; or washing?'

She nodded. 'I sometimes helped with 'washing when I worked for Mrs Hodges – when they were short-handed in 'summer, you know. Mebbe I could do that once Harry is home, as you say. But where? Nobody near where we live could afford to have somebody in to do their washing!' She thought for a few moments. 'Harry said there were some big houses on 'road to Beverley.'

He drew in the reins. 'Did he? Well, tell you what. Let's cut back and see if we can find them. If we head north' – he lifted the whip – 'which is that way yonder we should be able to find 'road. I've got an hour before setting off back home, and it shouldn't tek us that long.'

'Workhouse!' she exclaimed. 'Sculcoates workhouse is on 'Beverley road, that's what Harry said. He said it was like a palace, so we could ask anybody and they'd be able to direct us.'

Billy grinned. 'You had me worried for a minute, Ellen. I thought you were going to book us in!'

'No,' she said determinedly. 'Never! Not while I've got breath in my body.'

They passed the workhouse and discovered many substantial houses on Beverley Road that would need staff to clean them and she mused over the possibilities; she would write several notes offering her services on a daily basis as a general maid or a washerwoman and describing her experience, which she worried about as she'd only been with Mrs Hodges for three years before she married. For references she would ask Mr Tannerson and Dr Lucan if she could give their names, and she was sure that Mrs Hodges wouldn't mind in the least: if, in

200

fact, anyone asked her when there were two eminent gentlemen much nearer at hand as alternatives.

Walking there and back again, she decided, would be possible, for she would be fit again by the time Harry came home from hospital. Spring would soon be here, and she convinced herself that the only difference from working for Mrs Hodges would be walking past factories and mills and noisy foundries rather than through meadowland, with the sound of the sea in her ears.

CHAPTER THIRTY

'How are you, Mrs Randell?'

True to his promise, Dr Lucan came to see her two days later. Lizzie had taken the children upstairs; Edyta had told Ellen she could use her room if ever there was the need. She kept the fire in all night and topped it up with coal and wood in the morning before leaving for work, and Ellen always added more during the day so that Edyta came home to a warm room.

Ellen had asked her when she would be married and she'd said, 'Soon. I want my mother to feel settled with Ezra first. Karl says that she could live with us, but I'm afraid it would make difficulties with Ezra again, and at the moment everyone is trying to be cooperative. For the sake of *Mutter*,' she had added.

'I'm quite well, I think, thank you, doctor,' Ellen answered now, buttoning up her blouse, for he had listened to her chest with his stethoscope, and taken her pulse. 'But very sad about losing the baby; though given our difficult circumstances . . .' She left the rest unsaid, not wanting to admit that with another small child life would have been even more difficult.

'And your sister is staying with you just now?'

'Yes. Her husband died recently and being with 'children seems to be helping her.'

'It's good to have family,' he said, as he packed away his instruments. 'Has Mr Tannerson been to see you yet?'

'No.' She shook her head. 'Not recently, but I expect he has a lot to think about with 'mill and everything.'

'Indeed he has; the building is gutted. A miracle more people were not hurt.'

'The child who was killed,' she said softly. 'Does his family know about him, or anyone know why he was there?'

Dr Lucan was thoughtful. 'Tannerson is hoping that the boy who was injured can throw some light on the matter. The one in the bed next to your husband's,' he added. 'But he can't be questioned just yet.'

'Has he family?' she asked. 'Does anyone visit him?'

He shook his head. 'Not to my knowledge.'

'Poor boy,' she murmured. 'No one to hold his hand.'

He gazed at her. 'Would you do that for him?'

'Of course,' she said instantly. 'I'll be sure to do so when I next visit Harry. If my sister stays all week and will stay with the children perhaps I'll walk there one fine day. I think I'm strong enough now.'

He stood up to leave. 'You probably are, but it's quite a long way from here.'

'Not for me.' She smiled. 'I'm thinking that I'll apply for work on Beverley Road when Harry comes home and that's a couple of miles further.'

'Doing what?'

'Housekeeping or washing. I was in service when I was a girl.'

'I see.' The doctor looked at her for a moment, and then said abruptly, 'I was hoping to see Tannerson today. I know of a small house that's to let. I think it might suit you. It's near enough for your husband to walk to work once he's fit enough, and until he is it would be handy for you to work on Beverley Road, if that's really what you intend.'

She gazed at him, her lips parted, as if considering how best to give him the obvious response. 'Somebody has to work, Dr Lucan,' she said. 'How else will we manage until Harry is fit again? And a house? A whole house? That would be a miracle, but how could we pay for it on 'wages of a skivvy?'

His forehead creased, and then he said earnestly, 'That's what I was going to ask Tannerson.'

*

203

The thought of having a whole house dominated her thoughts all day, and she discussed the subject with Lizzie.

'What I'd originally thought,' she said, 'was that when Harry comes home from hospital I'd try for work doing washing or cleaning jobs in those big houses on 'Beverley road. I'd go early morning, leaving 'children with Harry, and they'd all stay in bed until I came home to give them breakfast.'

'What sort o' time are you thinking of?' Lizzie asked.

'When I was working for Mrs Hodges, 'washerwoman used to be there for five in a morning and left at about seven,' Ellen told her, 'so if I did 'same, I could be home by eight o'clock easily, as I'd soon find short cuts through nearby streets.'

'You'd be worn out.' Lizzie had never liked early mornings.

'What is it Ma says? Needs must if 'devil drives, or something like that.' Ellen laughed.

'I've never understood what that meant.' Lizzie shook her head. 'And I've always had difficulty getting up in a morning.' She was silent for a moment. 'I could stay for a bit longer, if you like?'

Ellen considered. It was nice to have Lizzie here, but it was another mouth to feed, and besides . . . 'We're in one room, Lizzie. We have to eat and sleep in here; it wouldn't do, would it? Not with Harry here as well.'

Lizzie's face crumpled. 'Ah, no, of course it wouldn't.' She began to weep. 'I'm so lonely at home, Ellen; and I'll have to leave 'cottage in any case. I've no means to pay 'rent. I know I have to work, but what can I do? Will anybody tek me on as a widow? Most of 'employment goes to girls just out of school. I'm twenty-five! I wish I'd been born a man. I could have done so much more.'

Ellen commiserated with her sister. Right now she seemed to be rudderless, not able to cope with the loss of her husband, but Ellen knew that she was bright and intelligent; she had been good at her schooling and could have been a nursery maid or even a governess with training, but her marriage to Albert had put paid to that. Ellen had often thought that he had held back her potential, for he always had to come first, and Lizzie had forever been at his beck and call.

204

'I thought I'd walk down to Tannerson's mill,' she said. 'If Mr Tannerson is there I'll ask him when Harry will be due any money, and . . .' she paused, 'I wonder . . .'

'What?' Lizzie asked.

Ellen ran her tongue around her lips. 'Harry took some of 'horses out over Christmas time. Just to give them some exercise, you know, and I was thinking that if 'mill isn't running I'd ask Mr Tannerson if I might do that. There was one mare that Harry took a fancy to; she took us to Holderness when we went to collect Mary. He named her Nellie, and if Mr Tannerson's agreeable I could tek her by way of 'infirmary and go to see Harry.'

'Oh!' Lizzie drew in a breath. 'Would you dare do that?'

'What? Drive to 'infirmary?'

'No, I know you can do that. Ask Mr Tannerson.'

Ellen stared at her sister. Lizzie had never been afraid to stand up to anyone. She had lost her spirit since marrying Albert. 'Of course I would,' she protested. 'I know he's Harry's employer, but he's still onny a man at 'end of the day, so why shouldn't I? I can onny ask!'

Lizzie said that she would go with her and the children would benefit from some much-needed exercise; she was going to say 'and fresh air', but thought better of it. This was not the countryside, after all.

As they walked towards the mill, Ellen spotted Anna and the children coming out of the baker's and called to her. 'I was coming to see you,' Anna called back. 'Are you feeling better?'

Ellen crossed the road and put her arms about her. 'I am,' she said, and introduced her to Lizzie.

'Edyta told me that your sister was staying with you; it is why I haven't visited. I didn't want to intrude. She said that you seemed a little better. It is good to have family with you, is it not?'

'Family and friends.' Ellen smiled. 'I'm blessed to have both,' and Anna squeezed her hand.

Ellen told Anna that she was on her way to see Mr Tannerson, to which Anna replied that Filip was with him also; he had gone to discuss working there once the new machinery had arrived.

205

'Oh!' Ellen said on a breath. 'So perhaps it won't be long before the mill reopens. There'll be work again.'

'Yes,' said Anna. 'For everyone. Filip has some *leetle* work, you know, but he needs more bigger jobs for – erm – comfort, do you say?'

'Consistency?' said Ellen; 'Security?' Lizzie added.

'Security,' Ellen agreed. 'The kind of regular work that we all need to go to every morning, so that we can earn an honest living to put bread on 'table and food in our children's mouths.'

They went their separate ways, agreeing that they would meet the next day at Anna's house. Lizzie told Ellen that she would buy fresh bread and cheese tomorrow to take with them, as she had a little money with her. Ellen told her that Anna would want to prepare her own food for religious reasons, to which Lizzie responded in astonishment that she had never met anyone who did such a thing.

'Well, there you have it, Lizzie,' Ellen replied, pleased to think that she knew more than her older sister. 'When you come to live in a place like Hull, you learn all kinds of things that you never knew before.'

The mill gates were closed but not locked and Ellen pushed them open, suggesting that Lizzie wait in the yard with the children whilst she went up the steps to the office.

She could hear voices from inside and tentatively knocked. 'Yes?' a voice called, and she opened the door a crack.

'It's Mrs Randell, Mr Tannerson,' she said, and although she had told Lizzie that it was all right to speak to him she was anxious; anxious that perhaps there wouldn't be any money due yet and that there wouldn't be any of the promised work when Harry was well enough.

She heard the scraping of chair legs on the wooden floor and Tannerson's voice calling for her to come in, and found on entering that Filip was still with him.

'I'm so sorry to interrupt,' she murmured. 'I'll come another day.'

206

'No, come in, please,' Tannerson said. 'Take a seat. You are looking rather better than when I last saw you.'

'I'm feeling much better, thank you, sir.' She sat down on the chair and smiled up at Filip, who had got to his feet. He bent towards her and kissed her cheek.

'I don't wish to break up a meeting, Mr Tannerson,' she said. 'But I was wondering if there had been any developments since we last spoke.'

'I intended to visit you later today, Mrs Randell,' Tannerson told her. 'But let me conclude my business with Mr Bosco.' He turned to Filip. 'I like to think this should work to the benefit of both of us. Shall we have another meeting, say the day after tomorrow, to sort out the paperwork?' He looked down at the open diary on his desk. 'Ten o'clock?'

'Excellent!' Filip said, and Ellen was sure she heard a suppressed exhilaration in his voice. He turned to Ellen. 'I will wait for you outside, Ellen, and walk home with you.'

She thanked him and said the children were in the yard with her sister. Filip turned again to Tannerson and, putting his hand to his chest, said 'Thank you, sir,' before he left.

'A reliable sort of fellow, would you say, Mrs Randell?' Tannerson asked her. 'I understand you know him and his wife quite well.'

'I do, sir,' Ellen said. 'We've become firm friends, out of adversity I suppose we could say, in spite of 'short time we've known each other. We were all in need of friendship.'

He nodded. 'Well said.' He cleared his throat. 'You are, I'm sure, worried about your husband's future prospects?'

She nodded nervously.

'And I'm waiting for insurance details to come through and my lawyer to sort out the compensation and everyone seems to be taking their time; although,' he added thoughtfully, 'I must admit there's a great deal to consider, as everyone agrees that the mill needs completely rebuilding and all the machinery has to be replaced.'

Ellen drew in a deep breath. It sounded as though a lot of work had to be done before the mill could begin to operate again. Whatever would they do for money until then? She would definitely have to find work, and they could say goodbye to the possibility of the small house that Dr Lucan had mentioned. She swallowed hard, but couldn't prevent tears from trickling down her cheeks.

'You're upset, Mrs Randell?' Tannerson gave a little frown. 'Is it something I've said? I told you that your husband will have work again; you have my promise on that.'

Ellen swept the tears away with her fingertips. 'Yes,' she said croakily. 'You did, sir, and I'm grateful. We'll both be grateful, it's just – it's just that—' A sob escaped involuntarily. 'I don't know how we'll manage until then. The parish – I don't know if they'll allow us any relief as we haven't lived in Hull for very long – I think there's a minimum time before a claim can be made.'

He leaned forward and clasped his hands together. 'Mrs Randell. It won't come to that. Your husband is due to receive compensation for his injuries. Everything is in hand, it's just taking time.' He stood up and went to a metal box on top of a cabinet. 'I'm sorry,' he said, opening the box with a key that he took from his pocket. 'I should have thought before. I've had so much on my mind. I'll give you something on account, just to tide you over. Five shillings?' he asked, turning to her. 'That'll buy food and pay your rent. Only pay the usual,' he warned. 'Don't pay any extra, as you'll never get it back if by chance you should move house.'

He fished about in the desk drawer for an envelope and put the coins inside and handed it to her. 'I'll make a note that it's on account of what is to come, and I'll try to come and see you tomorrow.'

208

CHAPTER THIRTY-ONE

Ellen hurried down the steps to where her sister and the children and Filip were waiting.

'You've been crying,' Lizzie said, eyeing her keenly, and Sarah came and put her hand in her mother's.

'Is everything all right, Ellen?' Filip asked. 'Harry is not to lose his job? If so I will speak for him to Mr Tannerson!'

'No, no,' she said shakily, and put her other hand to her nose and sniffled. 'He's been very kind. He assured me that Harry will go back to work and he's – he's given me some money to tide us over until 'compensation comes through. He'd said there'd be some money while Harry was recovering, but I didn't know – didn't think there'd be compensation! I was only hoping that Harry would get his job back.'

Tears ran down her cheeks again, but she saw the children were watching her and gave a rather watery smile. 'I'm crying because I'm so relieved. I thought we'd have to apply for parish relief and thought how ashamed I'd be, and anyway, I was doubtful we'd get it.'

'I don't understand,' Filip said, with a puzzled frown. 'What is this relief?'

'It's given by 'local parish,' Lizzie explained. 'And most folk only apply when they're at rock bottom. They're sometimes given milk and bread if there are any children, and sometimes money for 'rent. It's demeaning.' Her mouth curled. 'But not as bad as going into 'workhouse, I suppose. I'd sooner jump into 'river as do that.'

209

'No!' Filip said. 'Never!' He pushed open the gate to let them out, then closed it behind him. 'It is a sin to take a life. There is always hope. But this relief is perhaps the same as we were given when we first arrived here, I think. We were very grateful for it.'

'Folk get desperate sometimes, Lizzie,' Ellen said, and thought that her sister must have been through a very difficult time to say such a thing. 'Oh!' She suddenly remembered what she was going to say to Mr Tannerson. 'I forgot to ask if I might exercise Mr Tannerson's horses.' She sighed. 'Never mind. I'll ask him tomorrow when he calls.'

'He comes tomorrow?' Filip said. 'Why is that?'

Ellen shook her head. 'I don't know,' she said. 'Dr Lucan mentioned he had something to discuss.'

'You've been singled out, Ellen,' Lizzie said comfortingly. 'Things are looking up.'

Anna and the children met them again on the way back to Ellen's room; Filip told them that Tannerson had asked him questions about putting in a new crushing plant. Filip had shown him plans of other systems that he had worked on in his home country and Tannerson was sufficiently impressed to suggest that they might agree on a contract, asking him if he would be willing to discuss the proposal with other engineers and mechanics, in which case he would put him at the head of a proposed new system.

Filip was ecstatic to think that at last he would be in worthwhile employment. He picked up Thomas and lifted him on to his shoulders, and then Aron scrambled up his father's back like a young monkey, and clung on to Thomas while Filip carried the two of them.

'One day soon I will have my own company,' he crowed. 'I will employ men. Everyone will want my services!'

He began to sing in a language that the English women didn't understand, but Anna began to hum too; Filip's voice was a deep bass and he began to dance sidesteps in time to the song, making his fingers move as if he were playing an accordion, much to the children's delight. The women laughed, and then another familiar voice broke in from behind them: '*Hej, Polski.*' Dozens of women were appearing from the direction of the cotton mill and one of them was Edyta, who joined in the melody, putting her hands on her hips and following Filip in the dance.

'Why are you all leaving work?' Ellen asked her.

'Two looms have broken down, so we have been told to go home; there is no more work for us today. They will pay us for today,' Edyta added, 'but not tomorrow and not until they have fixed them.'

Filip stopped singing. 'Why?'

Edyta shrugged and shook her head. 'I don't know. I think they have to pay us once we've started the shift.'

'But why have the looms broken?' he asked, bending his knees to slide the boys down to the ground.

She shrugged again, lifting her hands and shoulders. 'How do I know? No one tells us anything. They only say *go home.*'

Filip ushered the boys towards their mothers. 'God is good!' he pronounced. 'Today is a lucky day,' and he began to run back in the direction of the cotton mill.

They all stood and watched him, including the other women who had been told to go home, and Edyta nodded. 'I will believe that it is,' she murmured, 'if he can repair the looms and we can all go back to work tomorrow.'

'Come,' Anna said. 'I have brought sweet cake and coffee. Do you have tea, Ellen? We will celebrate in your house.'

'Yes.' Ellen smiled happily, though her eyes overflowed with tears. It seemed as if things really were going to be better, but life wouldn't be complete until Harry came home.

When Ellen and Lizzie climbed into bed that night they discussed the possible connection between Mr Tannerson and Dr Lucan, and the house that Dr Lucan had said might be available.

'Wouldn't it be an answer to our prayers?' Ellen said, adding, 'If only we can afford it.' She sighed, her earlier euphoria fading. 'I won't get my hopes up just yet, because it might be out of reach. I don't think Dr Lucan knows what it's like to live in poverty; not knowing where the next meal is coming from or how to pay 'rent man when there's no money left in your purse.

But with the five shillings that Mr Tannerson's given me we can manage a bit longer.'

'You can have all I've got, Ellen,' Lizzie told her. 'It's not much; Albert never had a large wage and when he was ill there was no money coming in at all, and I had to use what little I'd saved. Without Ma baking bread and bringing eggs, I don't know what we'd have done. I never told Albert, for he would have said it was charity.'

'Ma wouldn't have thought of it like that,' Ellen consoled her. 'We have to help each other. If we should get this other house, and there are two bedrooms, you can stay if you'd like to. Harry won't mind. You'd have to work, though. We couldn't afford to keep you.'

'I know,' Lizzie nodded. 'I've been thinking about that and wondering what I could do. Mebbe I could work at 'cotton mill like Edyta. Will she leave when she gets married? I could mebbe have her job if she does.'

Ellen sighed. Her sister had always had big ideas. 'Edyta's a foreman, Lizzie.' She giggled suddenly. 'Fore*woman*, I suppose. Anyway, you couldn't do her work, and besides, you don't like getting up early.'

Lizzie slid down under the blanket next to Ellen. 'I don't. I could mebbe start at eight,' she mused. 'But I'd prefer nine. That's what I'll look for, Ellen, a job that starts at nine. Or even better, I'll look out for a rich husband, even though it's too soon yet after Albert.'

Ellen was shocked that her sister could even think of such a thing. She'd never want to marry again if Harry – well, she wouldn't even contemplate such an awful possibility, but when she glanced at Lizzie to admonish her she saw she had a gleam in her eyes and her mouth was twitching and realized she was joking. She stuck her elbow in Lizzie's ribs and said, 'Naughty girl!' and they both began to giggle like the schoolgirls they had once been at the impossibility of such a fantasy.

Roland Tannerson arrived at half past eight the following morning as the children were finishing their porridge. Ellen had

212

been up at six, and going into the scullery to fill the kettle had discovered that the little hen who had so obligingly provided them with eggs had expired during the night. She'd picked her up and stroked her soft feathers. So be it, she'd thought. She did well to survive so long, but I can't consider cooking her. The children thought of her as a pet.

She'd put the hen carefully into a brown paper bag which had previously held bread, put on her coat, shawl and boots and stepped outside into the yard, where she unlocked the gate and carried the parcel down the muddy slope to where a single wizened, gnarled and leafless tree grew near the river bank. An unexpected thin skin of ice lay on the water, but it hadn't deterred two fishermen who stood on the opposite bank with their rods and lines.

She'd placed the parcel carefully under the tree, murmuring, 'Thank you, little hen,' knowing that the creature might save another from starvation, and walked back up the slope, the puddles soaking into her boots. She felt the soles of her stockinged feet become damp and thought that she must find some cardboard to pack inside her boots; repairing them was not an option even though she now had money in her purse. That was spoken for: rent, food and coal for the fire were the essential priorities.

'I'm sorry I'm so early, Mrs Randell,' Tannerson said when she opened the front door to him. 'But I thought I'd call before going to the mill. I've so much paperwork to sort out that I might forget at the end of the day.'

She invited him to take a seat by the fire and asked him if he would like a cup of tea or coffee. He asked for coffee, which she was pleased about as Anna had left some behind yesterday and that would save her precious tea. The room was tidy. Lizzie had made the beds and she and the children were sitting on one of them; she was reading them a story and up to now no one had missed the little hen.

She introduced him to Lizzie and said that she was staying with her at present to look after the children so that she could visit Harry.

213

Tannerson looked about him. 'It's very homely, Mrs Randell,' he said. 'How many rooms do you have?'

She gazed at him; of course he wouldn't know. 'Just this one, sir.' She pointed to the empty doorway. 'We've a scullery with a sink and an inside tap for water, which is a blessing. And we've a copper outside in 'yard for doing a big wash, but it's still too cold to use it just yet, and besides, we've to save our coal and wood to heat this fire, so I go to 'wash house when I can.' Which isn't as often as I'd like for it's all extra money to pay out, she thought.

'And you've – what . . .' he glanced round, 'a stove of some kind for cooking?'

'No,' she said. 'I cook on the fire.' The kettle was simmering, and she lifted it off with a cloth and poured water into the jug that contained Anna's coffee grounds.

'Ah!' he exclaimed. 'Yes, now I recall that Harry did tell me.' He frowned, looking into the flames in the grate. 'And you're saying this is where you cooked your Christmas dinner?'

Lizzie looked up from the storybook and her mouth shaped a round O as if she too had only just thought about it. When she had arrived they had eaten the cooked chicken that Billy had brought and had had chicken broth each day since.

'Yes,' Ellen said matter of factly. 'Fire draws well so there's heat for cooking, though it's a slow process; and I can boil 'kettle for bathing or mekkin' hot drinks, though not both at 'same time. And it keeps us warm. I think that there are people worse off than us. We're lucky that Harry found work when he did and we can pay 'rent.'

Tannerson nodded and lowered his voice. 'It might surprise you to know that I do understand. I was born in Ireland and when I was a young child I worked in a cotton mill, but I was sacked when I grew older for it was cheaper for the mill owners to employ younger children. Then my family moved to a country district where my father had relatives and he thought there'd be work for us. There wasn't. Many people were leaving Ireland to travel to England or America to escape starvation. You'll perhaps have heard of the potato famine? The Great Famine it was called in Ireland, when the only food available to the masses was

214

green potatoes? But the potatoes were diseased and the blight was poisonous and a million people died of starvation. '

Ellen shook her head; she hadn't, but Lizzie piped up. 'Yes, I've heard of it.'

'Well, that was when I decided to leave,' he said, including her in the conversation. 'It was 'best part of twenty years ago; my two brothers and I had struggled to find work and I was a young man eager to see the world and earn a better living. My father cursed the English and said the trouble we were in was their fault and to some extent he was right; but when my sister died in childbirth and I told him I was leaving to come to England to find work, he cursed me too and said he never wanted to see my face again.'

He stopped as if he'd said too much. 'And – did you ever go back?' Ellen asked quietly.

'No, I did not,' he replied. 'When I found work I sent money home to my brothers, but then Dada discovered it and sent it back, saying they didn't need my dirty English money.'

'I'm so sorry,' Ellen said softly. 'I hope you found happiness eventually?'

'Sure I did.' He smiled, and she heard the soft lilt of his accent coming through. 'I did anything I could to earn a crust and eventually went to work at Tannerson's mill *and* met the lovely woman who became my wife.'

Ellen gazed at him. She could imagine him as a charmer when he was a young man. Though his hair had streaks of grey, it was predominantly black and curly and his eyes were a greeny blue. He would have broken a few hearts, she thought. And yet, she wondered, how had he become a mill owner and why was he visiting her today?

215

CHAPTER THIRTY-TWO

Tannerson drank his coffee slowly; he didn't seem to be in a hurry to leave even though he'd said he had paperwork to attend to. He spoke generally about the mill and said he was meeting surveyors the next day who would study whether the mill building was safe to use again or if it should be pulled down and rebuilt.

'Fortunately I've taken out insurance. At the beginning I could ill afford to pay the premiums,' he gave a gentle shake of his head, 'but my wife insisted. She was a most astute woman; took after her father. I'm so glad that I did.'

'Was her father a businessman?' Ellen asked.

He looked up as if in surprise. 'Indeed he was. He it was that began the company in the first place. He was the original Tannerson and he gave me my first proper job of work in England; when I asked for his daughter's hand in marriage a few years later, he welcomed me with open arms into the family and said I was the son he'd always wanted.' He gave a grin. 'When he died and left the business jointly to his daughter and me I changed my name to Tannerson and became the *Son* in the business.' He nodded blithely. 'You know, Mrs Randell, I haven't spoken of this in years, but you have such a way of drawing out people's confidences.'

Ellen was astonished to hear this. She had hardly said a word.

'My wife was a majority shareholder, so of course when she too died everything fell on my shoulders. She was very good with the administration, whereas I am not. I'm a practical man, good

216

with my hands and ideas.' He laughed. 'The Irish never leaves you, you know. I'm a proper Murphy, happy with a spade over my shoulder.'

He took another sip of coffee, then pushed his cup and saucer to one side and looked at her seriously. 'But I must stop rambling on and explain why I came here today. It was Dr Lucan's idea. I don't know whether you are acquainted with his wife?' When Ellen shook her head, he went on, 'She's a lovely woman, from country stock; has great business acumen even though she is still quite young. She runs both a successful hotel in Hull and several other properties, and has put her name to a very worthwhile project of renting these properties at reasonable rates to those who through no fault of their own have fallen on difficult times.'

'And how are you involved, Mr Tannerson?' Ellen still didn't understand where the conversation was going.

'I've, erm, put some money into the project.' He seemed reluctant to say more, but added, 'When your husband was injured, I told Dr Lucan that he and your family had only been in Hull for a few months, having come from the country to look for work, and were having difficulties. I said that I would recommend you as tenants. He in turn then told his wife.'

'I see,' she said cautiously. 'It isn't . . . erm, it's not charity, is it?'

'Certainly not,' he said firmly. 'Whoever takes on one of the properties must pay the rent and keep it in good order, although any major work, like roof repairs and so on, will be attended to by the company.'

Ellen looked at him. Was there a catch? Could they afford the rent? He seemed like an honest man, but how could she possibly tell? Not all businessmen were, or so she'd heard, for she didn't know any others. Would she have to ask Harry first before committing them to moving elsewhere?

'It seems too good to be true, Mr Tannerson,' she murmured.

He smiled as he perched his bowler on his head at a jaunty angle. 'It does, doesn't it?' he agreed. 'But I assure you it is not. I'll take you to look at it, if you'd like to?'

217

Ellen turned to Lizzie, who was listening avidly and nodding her head at the suggestion. 'Well,' she said, turning back to him, 'I suppose . . .'

'You've nothing to lose, Mrs Randell,' he said in a kindly tone. 'If you don't like it, you can refuse.' His eyes sparkled. 'But I'd place a bet that you won't. This afternoon?'

'What about your paperwork?'

'Pah!' he said. 'It can wait an hour or two.'

They'd reached the outside door when Lizzie, suddenly galvanized into action, jumped off the bed and followed them.

'Mr Tannerson!' she said. 'I couldn't help but hear what you were saying to my sister and of course I'll treat all you said as confidential, but I was thinking – well, I'm considering coming to live in Hull. I'm recently widowed and need to find work. I'm not as good as Ellen with practical household matters, but I have a head for figures; I was always top of 'class at school and I'm an excellent organizer. I looked after 'household bills for my husband and kept us out of debt.'

She drew in a breath. 'Unfortunately, I doubt that many businesses would take on a woman as an employee unless it's to clean or wash floors, but from what you said you were thankful to have your wife in 'role of administrator.' She swallowed. 'If you would ever consider employing a female clerk or office manager, I'd like to apply.'

He stared at her for a second and then closed the front door and took off his hat again. 'You're quite serious?' he said.

Lizzie nodded. 'Yes, sir.'

'Mm. Well, come and see me in the morning at my office. Say nine thirty? Whilst nothing's happening at the mill I'm going in later than usual.'

'You said you had surveyors coming in tomorrow, sir,' Lizzie reminded him.

'Ah! Yes, so I did.' He scratched his short beard. 'Nine o'clock then. We'll have a chat and maybe you can take some notes whilst the surveyors are there, for I'm apt to forget the detail. Will that be all right?'

'Thank you, sir.' Lizzie dipped her knee. 'Perfectly.'

'Good. A very successful morning. And,' he added, 'you don't need to curtsy to me, Mrs . . . ?'

'Robson. Very well, Mr Tannerson.' Lizzie kept her back tall and straight. 'Thank you. I'll see you in 'morning. Nine o'clock sharp.'

Ellen and Lizzie both said goodbye and involuntarily dipped their knees. He raised his eyebrows and gave them an enigmatic glance, said, 'Until this afternoon, then, ladies,' touched his hat and went out to climb into the trap.

Ellen closed the door, barely looking at Lizzie, who had clamped her hand across her mouth, her eyes wild. It wasn't until they were safely in their room and Mr Tannerson had driven away that they each gave an excited shriek, startling the children, and putting their arms round each other swung round and jumped for joy, just as they used to do when they were girls.

'I can't believe I just did that,' Lizzie screeched.

'I can't believe you did either,' Ellen squealed. 'A house,' she said breathlessly.

'A clerk to a businessman,' Lizzie gasped. 'An office manager!'

The children slipped off the bed and grabbed the women's skirts, and they all swung round and round in a jubilant and exuberant circle.

Ellen put on her outdoor clothes and boots. 'I'm going out to buy food; bread, vegetables and eggs.' She lowered her voice; the children still hadn't noticed the little hen had gone and she hadn't intended to mention eggs. She drew Lizzie into the scullery and pointed to the empty space where the box used to be, and put her finger to her lips. 'Not a word,' she breathed. 'We'll scrub 'veg and put them over 'fire to cook whilst I go with Mr Tannerson. I wonder if he'll go past 'hospital on 'way back? I haven't got my bearings yet. But if he does I'll ask him to drop me off to see Harry and then I'll walk home.'

She gave a deep sigh, and her thoughts turned into words and came tumbling out. 'I really hope this house is all right. He didn't say where it was, did he? And I suppose we can onny look

219

at it from 'outside. He won't carry a key. What's Harry going to think?'

'He'll think he's got a wife who can think for herself,' Lizzie advised her. 'And how thrilled he'll be to get out of hospital and go home to a whole house and not just one room. I hope you like it, Ellen, cos if you don't I'll have to find a room of my own when Harry comes home – that's if Mr Tannerson offers me this position.' She thought for a moment. 'Has Edyta gone in to work this morning?'

'I think so. I heard her coming downstairs first thing, so Filip must have managed to mend the looms. She hasn't come back, anyway. Why?'

'I wondered if I could share her room, mebbe, until she marries; just thinking ahead, you know.' She fiddled with her hair. 'Will you put my hair into a bun in 'morning when I go to Mr Tannerson's? And can I borrow your best brown dress? It'll look smarter than this navy skirt and blouse for an interview.'

'Course you can,' Ellen told her, 'but I'd planned to wear it today when I go with him.'

'He'll not notice,' Lizzie said nonchalantly. 'Men don't.'

Ellen gave a wry smile. Harry would, she thought.

Tannerson arrived at one o'clock; he helped Ellen into the trap and handed her a blanket to wrap over her knees before he clicked his tongue to the pony and they set off. How considerate, she thought; there was a cold and gusty east wind.

'I thought you might like to visit your husband after we've looked at the house,' Tannerson called over his shoulder. They were travelling in the direction of Sculcoates. 'It's in Queen's Road; Mrs Lucan's brother will be there with the key so you can go inside. He looks after the management of the properties.'

'Thank you very much,' Ellen called back. 'I'm so grateful. Will I . . . erm, will I have to make 'decision today?'

'Mm, don't know. Is there a reason why you shouldn't?'

'I – I wondered if Harry would have to sign 'agreement?'

He half turned to catch a glimpse of her. 'Can you not do that?'

220

'Oh, yes,' she said quickly. 'I have a good hand. I just wondered if it would be permissible.'

'Don't see why not,' he said cheerfully. 'Mrs Lucan manages the property. If she has any objection I'm sure she'll let you know.'

It's a very strange situation, Ellen thought as they trotted along, passing so much industry that she wondered if eventually housing would cease to exist in this area, but she also conjectured on the mysterious Mrs Lucan; how had she made her fortune to be able to afford property? Mr Tannerson had mentioned she ran an hotel. She must have been left it in her father's will, Ellen decided, but on the other hand, why wasn't it left to her brother? That was the usual state of affairs when there was money and property, as far as she knew. Mr Oswald, Harry's previous employer, had left everything to his wife and daughters, but then, she reasoned, that was because he hadn't any sons.

They were coming up to a crossroad and Tannerson called to her that this was the road to Beverley and she must visit the ancient market town at some time; he crossed over it into a narrower country road which had a stream flowing along it on one side and on the other a cluster of old cottages with small front gardens. Further along the road were fenced-off plots of land and she proffered the remark that there must be house building planned.

'Big ideas for the area,' Tannerson agreed. 'The corporation is inspecting plans for the development of this space; this and the Newland area further along will be a high class development to complement the new park.'

'There's to be a park?' Ellen exclaimed.

'There is already a park,' he told her. 'The land was given to the people of Hull by Zachariah Pearson, a philanthropist and benefactor of the town. It's the people's park, free for everyone to enter. Lots of fresh air and walks in the gardens that are presently being laid out, with places for children to play. It will be a very desirable area in which to live.'

'Is this where Dr Lucan and his wife will live?' she asked, thinking that she could perhaps work for them, though it might be a long time before any buildings were finished.

221

'That I don't know,' he said, and drew up outside the cottages. 'They live in a villa on Beverley Road at present, which is why he looks after patients in the Sculcoates and Wincomlee district.'

But can't earn any money from them, she thought as she stepped down from the trap. I can't believe that anyone living in that area has any.

The cottage was the first on the left in a close of eight houses built of brick, stone and boulder, all facing each other. The two end houses that she could see had small casement windows on the ground and upper floors on the side walls facing the road which would bring in extra light, and a larger window to the front.

She wanted to shout in sheer elation as they walked up the path through the small front garden. A bedraggled honeysuckle valiantly showing emerging green leaves clung to the fence, as did small bushes; she recognized daphne, with its purple winter blossom on the bare wood. Hydrangea with fragile dried heads of flowers and several roses on one side were all in need of pruning and attention; on the other side was an apple tree with withered fruit hanging from the branches, and small plots of potatoes, onions and other vegetables which hadn't been tended in quite some time. It won't take long to put in order, she thought. It's just a small patch to turn over, nowhere near as large as our garden in Holderness.

The door opened as they approached and a dark-haired young man of about seventeen stood inside.

'Good afternoon, Mr Tannerson sir,' he said politely. 'Mrs Randell? Nice to meet you.'

'Mrs Harry Randell,' Tannerson introduced her. 'This is Henry Thorpe, Mrs Lucan's brother.'

'How do you do?' Ellen smiled at the young man as he invited her in.

'These are old cottages, it's only fair to say, Mrs Randell,' he told her. 'We think they were once farm buildings, but that's only an assumption, and we've upgraded them to be fit for habitation.'

There was a lobby, too small to be called a hall, just a place to wipe your boots, which led into a parlour with a planked floor where a low fire burned in the hearth; a bow window with a deep

222

sill faced across to the other cottages. A door led to a kitchen with a cooking range, a deep stone sink and a staircase door leading upstairs to the bedrooms.

There wasn't any furniture, which was a pity, she thought, clasping her hands to her face, because she wanted to sit in a chair and cry. She hoped with all her heart that they might become the tenants of this lovely little house.

Mr Tannerson and Henry Thorpe looked at her anxiously. 'Is it not up to your expectations, Mrs Randell?' Tannerson began.

'Oh, no . . . I mean yes,' she stammered. 'It's so much more. So much better than I expected.'

'Oh, that's a relief.' Henry Thorpe blew out his cheeks. 'This is 'first time I've ever shown anyone round and I thought I'd made a hash of it.'

'May I look upstairs?' she asked, and Henry eagerly opened the staircase door and ushered her up the narrow steps, begging her to take care on the dog-legged curve at the top which led straight into the main bedroom, where there were two windows the same as downstairs, a small fire grate, and a door leading to another smaller bedroom with a tiny one not much bigger than a store cupboard off that.

'Oh,' she breathed. 'It's perfect, Mr Tannerson, Mr Thorpe.'

'Call me Henry,' the young man said. 'Do you like it?'

'It's perfect,' she said again. 'I feel as if I've come home.'

CHAPTER THIRTY-THREE

Tannerson turned the horse and trap along the Beverley road back in the direction of Hull, and Ellen told him that she and her brother had driven along it when they had visited Harry. 'I'll walk next time if 'weather's clement,' she said. 'I think I know how to cut across from 'hospital to Wincomlee, though mebbe' – her voice softened at the prospect – 'once Harry's feeling better he might soon be allowed home.' Then her mood suddenly changed. 'Mr Tannerson,' she exclaimed, 'I don't know who's paying for Harry's stay in hospital.'

He kept his eyes straight in front. 'Your husband, and indeed Jim Smith, were admitted as emergencies after an accident, so there won't be a payment due.' He glanced at her. 'But I should warn you that it is highly unlikely that he will be allowed home just yet. If you were assuming that your husband would be in a fit state to make the decision about moving house, Mrs Randell, I fear you were mistaken. This is something you must decide.'

'What about 'rent? Mr Thorpe didn't say how much it would be.'

'He didn't, did he? So assuming it's the same as you are paying at present, how will you pay it?'

She did a quick calculation based on the money she had been given in advance by Mr Tannerson himself. 'If it's 'same as 'rent we're paying now, I can pay it for another month. After that I'll have to earn some, but it's 'children,' she said, almost talking

224

to herself as she thought it through. 'I can't leave them alone. If my sister gets work' – she didn't say *with you* – 'she'll pay her share and we'll manage till Harry comes home; then they'll stay with him whilst I go to work until he's fit again. I've planned it out already.' She lifted a guileless gaze to him. 'It's putting it into practice that's the problem.'

It was the older porter who greeted them at the door. He seemed to know Mr Tannerson, as he greeted him by name before he ushered them upstairs to wait outside the ward door. Tannerson told the nurse he was visiting Jim Smith and went in first, and then Ellen was called.

One side of Harry's face was still covered by a thin dressing but both hands were outside the sheets, although loosely dressed with bandages. He seemed relieved to see her and she leaned over and kissed his forehead. Her eyes filled with tears. 'You look so much better.' Relief cracked her voice.

'Aye, it's not so painful now,' he said hoarsely. 'Got a cough, though.' He cast a glance at the empty bed next to him where Tannerson was sitting waiting with his back to them. 'Jim's gone for a cool bath,' he said in a low voice. 'He's had one most days. He got caught by 'full blast so they're cooling him down and getting rid of dead skin. Is that Tannerson waiting?'

'Yes,' she whispered back. 'He brought me.'

'Did he?' Harry was astonished. 'That's good of him. I think Jim's going to be here for a long time. I heard one of 'nurses saying that he'd have died of his burns if somebody hadn't drenched him with water.'

'Oh.' Ellen was horrified. 'How lucky that someone thought to do that. And falling into 'river was what saved you, so I was told.'

'It's onny just coming back to me,' Harry said vaguely. 'I couldn't remember owt about it to begin with, then . . . well, I think there was onny me and Tannerson there at first . . . and then I seem to recall seeing Jim . . . he was opening 'mill doors . . .'

'When will you be able to come home, Harry?' she interrupted anxiously. 'Are you well enough?'

225

His face clouded. 'I don't know. I don't know how we're going to manage in that one room, Ellen. I need dressings changing regularly, and baths too. I've had several since I've been in here and it's so soothing. Teks pain away, you know.'

She wanted to hold his hands, but couldn't because of the bandages. He needed more time in hospital, she could tell. She decided not to tell him about the cottage. She'd find out about the rent: why hadn't Henry Thorpe told her how much it would be? He must have forgotten.

But I'm going to have it, she determined. One way or another it's going to be ours. I'll ask Mr Tannerson if he'll lend me a horse and wagon to move our bits of furniture and I won't tell Harry until we've moved in and then he can come home and sit in 'parlour and look out of the window or by 'fireside until he's well enough to work again.

The very thought of it filled her with such pleasurable anticipation that she felt suddenly uplifted, and Harry looked at her and said, 'What?'

'I didn't say anything.'

'I know you, Ellen Randell.' Harry put his head back against the thin pillow. 'You're planning summat.' He gave a deep sigh. 'I can tell.' Ellen heard an unfamiliar sound and realized he was trying to hum with his dry throat the refrain he said was hers. As she hovered between laughter and tears, Jim Smith was brought back to his bed swathed in towels and thin bath sheets, and he cried out when he was eased gently back on to the mattress. Harry turned his head away. He couldn't bear to see the boy in pain, but even when the nurses had finished giving him medication and covered him with clean sheets they could still hear him crying for his mother and 'Benny'.

Tannerson got up from his chair and came to stand by Harry's bedside. He was obviously upset, and covered his mouth with his hand. 'He's called that name before,' he muttered. 'I think it's the boy who died.'

The nurses put a canvas screen round Jim's bed and moved away. Ellen waited a moment and then, getting up from her seat, moved the screen slightly and went to stand by his side.

226

'Sh-sh-shh,' she said softly. 'It's all right. Benny's resting.' Tenderly, with the lightest of touches, she placed her fingers on the back of Jim's neck where there were no burns and gently stroked him. 'He's quite safe, onny sleeping.'

'Ma!' he whimpered, his eyes wide open but not seeing her. 'Ma! Is that you?'

'Yes,' she murmured. 'I'm here.'

'Ma, it's hurting.' His voice dropped, sounding not quite so desperate, and Ellen guessed that the medication was starting to take effect. 'Did I kill Benny?'

'No,' she breathed. 'Of course not; you're dreaming, Jimmy. Be my own brave boy.'

'Jimmy,' he whispered, his words slurred. 'You allus called me Jimmy, didn't you, Ma?'

She stroked his neck again. 'I did,' she said. 'What else would I call my lovely boy?'

'I love you, Ma.' He closed his eyes. 'I miss you. Benny said . . .'

'I love you too. Hush, now,' she coaxed. 'Go to sleep. Everything will be all right by 'morning.'

He took a shallow breath and dropped into a deep sleep; she kept her fingers on his young skin for a moment longer and then drew away, and turned to see Tannerson with a nurse behind him, watching her.

She swallowed. 'He's sleeping,' she said unnecessarily, and was troubled to see tears in both Tannerson's and the nurse's eyes.

They moved away to let her through and she sat by Harry's bed without speaking. Then silently she began to cry, her shoulders shaking with sobs, and no one spoke a word.

Tannerson drove her home. For most of the way he didn't interrupt her silence by talking, but when they were almost there he began to tell her Jim's story.

'Jim Smith came asking for work a couple of years ago. I think he'd done the rounds of most of the mills and factories and been turned away from all of them. He was barely twelve but said he was fifteen. Just a little scrap, he was. He'd left the workhouse

227

after his mother died. He would have been set to work anyway when he reached twelve, but he told me he wanted to make his own way so that his mother would have been proud of him had she lived.'

He gave a little grunt. 'I took him on because he reminded me of my youngest sister; she was nearest to me in our family and died of tuberculosis when she was twelve. He had the same dark hair and blue eyes, and had a vulnerable expression about him, just as she had.' He sighed. 'Anyway, I told him he could look after the horses until he was old enough to start work in the mill.

'And then about a year later this other lad turned up, and Jim asked if I'd give him a job too, because he hadn't got anybody either and they'd been like brothers when they were in the workhouse. I said no, because he was far too young to work for me, maybe eight or nine, and besides, he seemed a shrewd little fellow and I thought he might get into mischief. Turned out I was right on that score, because although he went back to the workhouse he would turn up from time to time and nag Jim to ask me to give him work, and I always said no.'

'Was he the boy who died?' Ellen whispered the question, and Tannerson nodded.

'I don't know if Jim let him into the mill or if he found his way in by himself, but he was there that night. It was bitterly cold, if you remember, and someone had closed the vents from the inside; that was why the heat in the grain had built up until it only needed a spark from Jim's lamp to explode.' He shook his head and took a deep breath. 'Poor lads.'

'No use blaming yourself, Mr Tannerson,' Ellen said, for she could hear the regret in his voice. 'Benny must have crept inside to keep warm, or mebbe Jim had left the doors unlocked for him.'

'I think so.' He pulled up outside Ellen's house. 'But it's a terrible indictment on society when a child has to choose between living in a workhouse or on the streets.'

'It is,' she said softly. 'But you saved one child at least; you can't save them all.'

'And you brought that child comfort,' he answered. 'For a child is what Jim still is, and heaven only knows what's in front of him now. He'll probably be sent to the workhouse hospital, for he won't be able to live a normal life again.'

Ellen, feeling sad, nodded and climbed down from the trap. She thanked Tannerson warmly for taking her to see the cottage, and Harry, and went into the house.

The following morning Ellen helped Lizzie button up her own brown dress, and then brushed her hair and pinned it up in a neat twist; Lizzie had curly hair and a few wisps fell across her forehead.

'There, you look lovely,' Ellen said generously. 'The dress suits you; you look very businesslike. I'd give it to you if I had another but I haven't, so I can't.'

Lizzie gave her a smacking kiss on her cheek. 'I'll buy you a new one when I get my first wage packet.'

Ellen laughed. 'No you won't,' she said. 'You'll pay 'rent first. That's 'first priority. Off you go, don't be late. Good luck,' she added.

It's what we all need, she thought as she gave the children their breakfast and made herself another cup of tea. She wondered about Jim Smith and whether he would survive; if he did he would be badly scarred, that was for sure. Suddenly she recalled the boy who had been with him on Christmas Day, the one who had said that they hadn't got a mother: Benny, who had died in the fire. And what was it that Mary had said that day? She searched back in her mind. *That boy*, she remembered. What had she meant?

She cleared away the breakfast dishes and washed them in the sink with the remaining hot water from the kettle, which she refilled and put back on the fire to heat again before going to the window to draw back the curtains to let in some light.

Instantly she remembered. He had been leaning on the wall the day they arrived, watching them unpack the wagon, and had asked them . . . what?

229

Sarah came and stood beside her and stared out of the window too. 'That boy,' she piped. 'He said he wouldn't play with lasses. Why wouldn't he? We know how to play boys' games.'

'I don't know.' Ellen was startled. How did Sarah guess what she was thinking? 'But he's gone away now.'

Sarah turned away from the window. 'Yes, I know,' she said sadly. 'And we would have played with him.'

CHAPTER THIRTY-FOUR

Tannerson was concluding a discussion with Henry Thorpe when through the office window, placed strategically opposite his desk so that he had a full view of the yard below, he saw Mrs Robson enter the mill gates and head towards the office stairs.

'So if you'll tell Mrs Lucan that I'll highly recommend Mr and Mrs Randell as tenants, Henry, but not a word to them that the rent is a special rate, as Mrs Randell in particular will think it charity. In fact, if she should ask, tell her it's a kind of peppercorn rent; a ground rent if you will. She'll understand that, being a countrywoman.'

'Very well,' Henry said. 'She seemed a good sort. And I'm to tell my sister that you'll guarantee them?'

'I will. It's the least I can do; and,' he added as he heard feet on the steps, 'send the paperwork to my home address marked private and confidential, will you? I'm taking on a new administrator in the office and this is an entirely separate matter.'

Henry Thorpe touched his forehead with his fingertip as someone knocked on the door. 'Very good, sir. Thank you. Goodbye.'

He opened the door to Lizzie. Tannerson stood up to greet her, lifting his hand in farewell to Henry as he asked her to come in.

'Right on time, Mrs Robson,' he said approvingly. He asked her to take a seat and then viewed his cluttered desk, which was strewn with papers, files and notebooks. 'As you will see, I am not the tidiest of men. Do you think you can take all of this in hand?'

231

Lizzie looked dispassionately at the desk, at the wooden cabinets with their open and overflowing drawers, at the dishevelled piles of books and documents on the shelves, and then at the stacked boxes on the floor, filled with she knew not what, and turned to him. Then she smiled. 'I can't wait to get started,' she said.

The rent agent called and Ellen paid him for the current week and the following week in advance, so that she would know exactly how much money she would have left to pay for the new house if she was told they could have it. She began to sort out the bedding and wrapped it in an old sheet, then put her spare crockery into a cardboard box along with knives and forks, only keeping out enough basics to use for the present.

It was as she was doing this that Mary asked where the little hen was. 'She died,' Ellen said. 'It was her time.'

'Oh!' Mary said, and Sarah gazed at her mother.

'I'm going to tell you a secret.' Ellen lowered her voice to distract them and Thomas looked up too. 'We're going to live in another house.'

The three children all stared at her. 'What about Dada?' the girls said simultaneously, with Sarah adding, 'He won't know where to find us!'

Mary's mouth trembled and Sarah shook her head. 'I'll wait here for him,' she said, crossing her arms to show there would be no argument about it.

Ellen's heart swelled with love for them. 'What I thought we'd do,' she whispered conspiratorially, 'we'll move whilst he's still in hospital and get everything ready for him; then, when he's ready to come home, we'll go and fetch him and he'll say *Why are we going this way? This isn't 'way to go home!'*

She hadn't worked out the logistics of getting Harry to the new house, but she would think of that later, just as she would think of how to pay the rent.

The children all clapped their hands in glee, including Thomas, who didn't really understand what she meant.

'It'll be a proper secret surprise,' Sarah said. 'So we mustn't tell him.'

232

'No, we won't. And we'll ask him to guess where we're going,' Mary added.

'Yes, and I'll tell him,' Thomas piped up. 'It'll be a *big* surprise. What is a surprise? Is it cake?'

Ellen picked him up and hugged him. Her toddler was growing up. 'It might be cake,' she said, laughing, and put him down as someone knocked on the front door.

It was Anna with her children. 'I came to tell you that Filip is going to a meeting for Mr Tannerson and he is borrowing his, erm, how you say, small cart? And he say he will take you to hospital on the way if you can walk home.'

'Today?' Ellen said. 'But I can't take 'children with me.'

'This I know; that is why I come. I am not working every day now Filip has some work. He hope to get soon – I don't know the word, but money in front? I will – no, I *have* come to take children back with me. We will make cake,' she told the children and they all said, 'Yes!'

'It's a surprise!' Thomas cheered and jumped up and down. 'For me!'

'Come then, get your coats,' Anna said, 'and we will go now.'

'Thank you,' Ellen said gratefully. 'I was hoping to visit Harry when Lizzie gets back. She's gone to see Mr Tannerson. She's hoping he'll give her a job too. In the office.'

'Oh!' Anna said. 'He is very good man. He gives us all work.'

'He is,' Ellen agreed. 'Anna – he took me to see a cottage yesterday; we can have it if we can afford 'rent. I'm hoping to find out how much it will be later today, but I'm not telling Harry in case it doesn't happen.' She clasped her hands together. 'It'll be the answer to our prayers. Harry will be able to rest and recover and I'll be able to work whilst he stays with 'children until he's ready to go back to 'mill.'

Anna nodded. 'When mill is built again. I hear from Filip that Edyta's man, Karl, hopes to do work there too. He is excellent carpenter. He has been working at Flax and Cotton Mill. Filip saw him when he went to repair loom. I think when he has plenty of work he and Edyta will marry soon. That will be good, yes?'

233

Ellen fastened the buttons on Thomas's coat and tied his bootlaces. 'Yes,' she agreed. 'Things are looking up.' She saw Anna's puzzled frown. 'Getting better,' she explained. For some, she considered, as her thoughts flew to young Jim, but not for all.

'Ah!' Anna said. 'Yes, we are looking up. No longer looking down in gutter.'

Lizzie arrived back at midday full of excitement and longing to tell Ellen about her interview, but Filip arrived at the same time. Ellen had to put on her coat and leave immediately, but not before Lizzie told her that she was starting work the next morning.

Another slice of good luck, Ellen thought as they bowled through the back streets in the direction of Albion Street, where Filip was meeting surveyors who would be working on the plans for the mill. 'I think they will say pull down old one,' Filip said. 'It is almost a ruin. It will be quicker to build new than repair old. Ellen, tell me. Can I ask you? Is my English good enough?'

'It's excellent. You have learned so much in such a short time.'

'But there are some words I don't know,' he said. 'For example, what do I say to Tannerson for – can I have some money first before I begin work?'

Anna had mentioned the same thing this morning, Ellen recalled. 'If someone is giving you work that'll take a long time to prepare or complete – perhaps weeks or months – you can ask for an *advance,* or part of the price you've agreed on, rather than have to wait until 'work is finished. I think that can be done, although I have no experience of it.'

'Ah, of course! In *advance*, yes, to come first. I understand. That is good. Thank you, Ellen. You are a good friend.'

She smiled, and said, 'I hope so, Filip, but I know nothing about business. I only know how to look after 'money in my purse.'

He drew up outside one of the houses in Albion Street which had a brass plaque at the side of the door, above a short flight of stone steps.

234

'Nice house,' she commented, her gaze travelling from the basement area past the elegant windows to the rooftop. 'Very nice. It must cost a great deal of money to have a house like this.'

'I think so.' His gaze followed hers. 'I think we do the wrong kind of work to afford this, Ellen.'

She laughed and laid the blanket aside. 'I think you're right. Thank you for bringing me, Filip. The infirmary is onny five minutes' walk from here, and I can find my way home again.'

'Good,' he said, jumping from his seat to come and help her down. 'You won't get lost? For I don't know how long I will be.'

Telling him not to worry, she set off for the bottom of Albion Street, where she saw the hospital gates on the opposite side of the road.

The older porter greeted her again and said she was a little early for visiting, but she should go upstairs and sit and wait until she was told she could enter the ward.

Dutifully she did as she was bid and sat with her hands folded in her lap. She felt her eyes closing and must have been on the point of falling asleep, for she jumped when she felt a tap on her shoulder and opened her eyes to see the young nurse who had been present when she had spoken to Jim Smith.

'It's Mrs Randell, isn't it?' the nurse said softly.

'Yes, it is.' Ellen got to her feet. 'I'm so sorry,' she said. 'I was miles away.'

'You've come to see your husband?' The nurse cast a glance about her.

'Yes, is that all right? The porter said—'

'It's perfectly all right. Mrs Randell, could I ask a favour of you? I shouldn't really, and I might get into trouble, but I don't care.'

She's very young, Ellen thought. I'm surprised they take anyone so young; perhaps she started as a ward maid. 'What is it?' she asked.

'The boy, Jim Smith . . . you know him?'

'Not really. But I know he was injured in 'same accident as my husband.'

235

The nurse gave a series of quick nods as if she knew that. 'He's very unwell,' she said quietly. 'I don't like to think of him being alone, but I have to go off duty now and my replacement won't get to him immediately . . .' Her words trailed away but Ellen understood immediately what she was saying.

'Oh, no,' she whispered. 'May I go to him?'

'Would you? Please. He settled so quickly when you were here last time. Your husband is asleep.'

Ellen patted her arm, and pushed open the ward doors and walked quickly down to where a screen concealed Jim's bed. She glanced at Harry and saw that he was indeed fast asleep and breathing easily.

She slipped off her coat and folded it into a pad, then drew a chair nearer to the boy's bed, placed the coat on it and sat down. The bandages had been removed from Jim's face and hands and she could see that his injuries were very severe. He must have taken the full force of the explosion and she wondered how he had survived at all.

She slipped one hand beneath his, her fingertips gently touching his palm; the skin on his hands and arms was blackened and blistered and she guessed that he had put his arms up to defend himself from the blast. She felt a slight movement on her hand, and with the gentlest touch she stroked his palm.

'Hello, Jimmy,' she whispered. 'My lovely boy. I'm here to see you again. How are you today?'

'Better, Ma.' His voice was so low she could hardly hear the words. But then he went on quite lucidly. 'I told Benny you'd been to see me. He asked if he . . . if he . . .' He stopped; either he had forgotten what he was going to say or he hadn't the breath for it.

'You should tell him I might see him one day,' Ellen faltered; she was so choked she could hardly say what she wanted to tell him.

'I will . . . when I see him.' He sighed, the breath catching in his throat. 'I'm going to sleep now,' he whispered on a breath. 'I'm very tired. Will you stay . . . until . . . like you used to?'

236

'I'll stay until you fall asleep, just like I used to when you were a little bairn,' she murmured.

She heard a slight sound behind her and put up her free hand to stop whoever it was. 'Hush now, Jimmy. You're quite safe; there's nothing to harm you. Sleep well, my lovely boy.'

CHAPTER THIRTY-FIVE

He'd gone. Ellen stood silently by the bed, unable to cry; there was only relief that the boy was at rest. No more pain, no embittered future or hiding in shadows because of his shattered face and body.

Someone touched her elbow and she slowly turned. Matron, by her dress, Ellen thought: a dark navy long-sleeved high-necked gown and a white muslin cap.

They gazed at each other for a second until the matron moved forward to cover Jim with a sheet. She held out her hand to Ellen and led her back through the screen into the ward and towards another chair.

'I'm so sorry that you were alone at his passing,' Matron said quietly. 'Are you a distant relative, or a friend? I understood he had no close family.'

Ellen shook her head. She could barely trust herself to speak. 'Neither. I know little about him,' she answered in a small, tight voice. 'His employer, Mr Tannerson, will know more.' She took a quavering breath. 'He was injured in 'same accident as my husband' – she gestured to where Harry was beginning to stir – 'and I understood that he was an orphan; that's why I sat with him.'

'That was a great kindness,' Matron observed.

Ellen stared straight ahead. 'He thought I was his mother,' she whispered. 'I hope it brought him comfort.'

'Ah!' A look of understanding showed on Matron's face. 'That was indeed a special kindness.' She paused. 'Would you like a cup of tea, Mrs . . .?'

238

'Randell,' Ellen murmured. 'Yes, I would, please.'

Matron touched her briefly on the shoulder. 'I'll have one sent to you; and to Mr Randell too. He'll be upset about the boy under the circumstances.'

Ellen nodded. He would. 'Thank you, Matron,' she said, and her voice was wobbly. 'Thank you very much.'

Harry seemed surprised to see her when she went to his bedside, and put up his arms to bring her close and kiss her cheek. 'I didn't expect to see you again so soon.'

'Filip brought me.' She pulled up a chair and sat down and hoped that the tea would have sugar in it; she felt decidedly shaky. 'He was going to a meeting for Mr Tannerson and he'd lent him a trap.'

'Who lent who a trap?'

'Mr Tannerson lent Filip a trap so that he could go to 'meeting.' She sought to clear her head. 'It was a discussion about 'plans for 'mill, so he, Filip, said he'd drop me off. He's onny across 'road in Albion Street. I'll have to walk back, though, cos he doesn't know how long he'll be.'

Harry gazed at her. 'Are you tired, Ellen? You look worn out. You're overdoing things, aren't you? You don't need to come traipsing over here to see me, you know; I'm going to be all right now, so don't worry yourself. I think I'll be allowed out afore long.'

He glanced to the next bed where he could hear the murmur of voices behind the screen. 'Not so sure about young Jim,' he whispered. 'He's not doing well.'

Ellen placed her hands on the bed and Harry put his over them. The bandages had been removed and the skin had pink and white patches, and dark leathery ones too. How could she tell him that a young life had been lost, or even imagine the life he might have had if he'd lived?

'Harry,' she said simply, 'I'm sorry to tell you that Jim died not five minutes since. He's at peace now.'

After a moment, Harry's lips formed a question. 'Was he alone? I'd have sat with him.'

'He wasn't alone, Harry. He was with his mother, and I think probably Benny was there too.'

239

Another question was formed, but he couldn't speak and his eyes brimmed with tears. 'You were there?' he said huskily.

'Yes,' she answered softly. 'I think he was content.'

'I love you, Ellen,' he murmured. 'I can't tell you how much.'

She leaned forward and kissed his forehead, murmuring that she loved him too, and then there was really nothing more to say, except that the children had sent big kisses and hoped he'd soon be back home with them.

A ward nurse came with cups of tea for them both and carefully manoeuvred the screen round Jim's bed across to shield them instead, saying brightly that they could chat in private, but both knew that they were being protected from what was happening in the ward beyond.

When Ellen stood up to leave, explaining that she would have to get back because Anna was looking after the children, she suddenly said, 'Don't let them give him a pauper's funeral, Harry. Ask them to speak to Mr Tannerson first. There's 'graveyard near St Mary's, remember, where we saw him and Benny on Christmas Day? We could lay flowers on 'grave.'

She saw a smile on his lips and he nodded. 'I'll tell them, my darling wife,' he whispered, and he reached out to touch the chestnut braid he loved so much.

When she left his bedside there was an empty space where Jim's bed had been, and she saw that it had been moved to the bottom end of the ward and stripped down to the metal rails and springs.

Mr Tannerson's trap was still parked outside the building in Albion Street and the horse tied to a lamppost so she walked on to the top of the street, coming towards Mason Street where there were terraces of fine houses with courts, alleyways and arches built in between them, and other houses set close to one another with narrow paths dividing them. A public house standing on a corner appeared to be thriving.

She crossed over to look at the terraces and saw that they were not quite as grand as they appeared to be from a distance, and the courts set between the rows were dark and squalid,

240

with steps leading down into undrained areas which looked wet underfoot.

She turned on to another road, hoping she was going in the right direction, and came to a busy street full of shops with boxes of potatoes, root vegetables and greens stacked outside their doors. A plaque set high above one of the buildings informed her this was Charles Street.

She stopped outside one shop and bought a bunch of carrots and a string of onions; the grocer put them into a paper bag and touched his cap when she paid for them. Further along she bought a small meat pie from a baker as the smell was tantalizing; she was very hungry, not having eaten since an early breakfast, and she ate it as she walked, knowing that there would be no one here who knew her and might make a comment on her eating food outside in such an improper manner.

She crossed another road and made another turn into Charterhouse Lane, which she thought Harry had mentioned at some point in regard to an ancient church or possibly a school; she could see towering chimneys and the tops of mills and allowed herself a small smile of triumph as she arrived in Wincomlee.

By the time she reached the house, the sky was darkening and rain threatening, but Lizzie had lit the lamp and the fire was burning bright, and she'd set the vegetables to cook over it. They were simmering nicely and giving off a savoury aroma, enticing Ellen's taste buds and increasing her sense of hunger.

'Have you had anything to eat, Lizzie?' she asked.

Lizzie nodded. 'I bought a savoury pie on 'way back from Tannerson's,' she said. 'But I'm sorry to say I ate it all.'

Ellen gave a small laugh. 'Well, I did 'same,' she said. 'What extravagant women we are. I caught 'smell of meat pie in a baker's shop and decided I deserved a treat.'

'Why?' Lizzie asked, sitting in the easy chair and spreading out her feet towards the fire. 'What made you think you'd earned a meat pie? Is Harry coming home soon? And why are you so late?'

241

Ellen took off her coat and sat down to remove her boots and rub her red and tender toes. 'He thinks so,' she murmured. 'He looks much better. And I'm late back because I've walked and I think I might have come a long way round.'

She sighed, and put her fingers to her forehead, stretching the skin and smoothing her eyelids.

'What's up, Ellen?' Lizzie asked perceptively. 'You're upset over something.'

Ellen nodded, but didn't look up at her sister, knowing that the floodgates were about to open. Lizzie waited; she knew her younger sister wasn't one to make a fuss over a petty concern.

'The boy who was in hospital with Harry, Jim; you didn't know him, and neither did I,' she murmured. 'I onny ever saw him once. He worked at Tannerson's mill: ran errands, did odd jobs and exercised 'horses, I think. He died today, just after I got to 'hospital.'

'Oh!' An exhalation of breath escaped Lizzie's lips. 'Just a boy, you say? Was anyone with him?'

Ellen nodded and the tears began, two small streams leaking unbidden and slowly tracing their paths down her cheeks. 'A young nurse told me as I sat waiting to go on to 'ward. You can't go in without permission, you see. She was going off duty, she said, and . . . well, she must have known Jim was near 'end and she didn't want him to be on his own, cos 'nurse tekking her place might have – missed him.'

'Why did she ask you?' Lizzie said softly. 'How did she know that you'd be able to . . .'

'I'd sat with him last time I was there,' Ellen said in a rush, as if to get the explanation out as soon as possible. 'He thought I was his mother.' Her voice caught in a sob. 'And she'd heard me. So that's what I did.'

She lifted her eyes to her sister, though she could barely see her through the veil of tears. 'I pretended I was his mother. Did I do wrong, Lizzie? I onny wanted to bring him comfort; to let him know he wasn't on his own. He hadn't anyone, you see. He was an orphan, and his onny friend, Benny, another young lad from 'workhouse, was inside 'mill when it fired.'

242

She took a handkerchief from her skirt pocket and blew her nose. 'It wasn't a difficult thing to do. I'd have felt far worse if he'd gone off on his own with no one to hold his hand, poor lad, so I just told him what I thought he'd want to know, what any mother would want her child to know.' She swallowed. 'That he was loved and safe, and that I'd stay with him until he fell asleep, just as I used to when he was onny a bairn.'

She sniffed, and saw that Lizzie had tears running down her face too. Tears were healthy, she thought. Tears proved that you were mortal, that you had warmth and feeling and love in your veins. She wiped her streaming nose. 'So that's why I decided I deserved a penny meat pie, and hang the expense.'

Lizzie blinked away her tears. 'Well, Ellen,' she muttered, 'I've absolutely no excuse at all to offer for buying a pie and eating every crumb of it. I must be 'most selfish and extravagant creature anybody might have 'misfortune to meet.'

The sisters gave watery smiles. Standing up simultaneously, they put their arms around each other, to comfort and endure.

243

CHAPTER THIRTY-SIX

Ellen was preparing food for the evening meal. She and the children had been out walking; it had been a lovely bright morning, and although the odours of the tanning and glue factories had overridden any scents of spring in St Mary's graveyard, there were traces of what was to come. The hidden snowdrops were just beginning to fade, the tips of their petals turning brown, but sweet violets, lesser celandine and golden aconites turned their faces up to the sky, and pale clusters of primroses nestled beneath hedges, with early shoots of pussy willow promising that winter was almost over.

The children had played hide and seek round some of the old tombstones while Ellen watched them carefully to make sure they didn't damage anything, and when Thomas valiantly tried to climb a tall monolith she had lifted him down. There were newer graves too, and she had explained to the children that these were places where people were put to rest after they had died.

Sarah and Mary were both quiet for a few minutes whilst Thomas ran about collecting dead leaves and patting them into piles.

'We should have brought our little hen and made her a grave,' Mary said, and Sarah added a question: where had she been put to rest?

Ellen cleared her throat. 'I put her near 'river bank,' she parried, and lamely said, 'I thought she'd be happy there with 'other creatures.'

'Like ducks and gulls and water voles and things?' Sarah asked, and Ellen, still feeling sad over Jim, couldn't bring herself to explain the reality. What am I doing, a born and bred countrywoman who should know better, feeding my children myths instead of truth?

She was thinking of this as she put the pan of vegetables on to the fire and placed the guard round it, for she couldn't risk Thomas leaning over to have a look in the pan. She gave a jump when someone knocked on the outer door. The children raced to the window to see who it was, and Sarah turned to her mother and said, 'It's a lady and she's in a little trap with such a pretty pony. I'm going to have one like that when I'm big.'

Ellen couldn't think who it might be; she took off her apron and straightened her cap and went into the hall, with the children following her. It was indeed a lady, modestly dressed, but better turned out than anyone she knew. She dipped her knee out of force of habit. 'Good day, ma'am', she said.

'Good day to you. Is it Mrs Randell?' The visitor, older than herself, perhaps in her early thirties, held the pony on a long rein. 'I'm Bella Lucan, Dr Lucan's wife.' She smiled in such a friendly way that Ellen smiled back.

'Won't you come in, Mrs Lucan? The pony will be quite safe tied to 'lamppost.' As she spoke, she saw again an image of Benny, and wondered when he would be at peace.

'Thank you, I will. I wanted to be sure that you were in before I tied him. He's a young pony and rather frisky.'

'He's lovely.' Ellen stepped down to help her. 'What's his name?'

'We call him Young Bonny. My husband used to have a horse called Bonny when he was a young man, so it was a sentimental choice.'

She laughed as she spoke, and Ellen thought how alike she and her brother Henry Thorpe were. She followed Ellen inside, and although Ellen initially felt embarrassed over bringing her into their single room with its unmistakable aroma of soup, Mrs Lucan seemed to be quite at ease as she said hello to the children and asked their names.

245

'I have four children,' she said to Ellen, 'though much older than yours,' and she cast a humorous glance at Thomas, who was showing off by turning tipple tail on the floor. 'Boys can be a handful, can't they?'

She sat down by the fire as Ellen bid her, commented on the delicious smell coming from the pan, and putting her head to one side said, 'I can detect a Holderness accent, I think? It's like mine used to be before I came to live in Hull.'

'Really?' Ellen was astonished. 'Dr Lucan did mention you were from Holderness too, but I can't hear a trace of an accent.'

'I've lost it, I think,' Mrs Lucan answered. 'Probably because I became an innkeeper and mixed with many different people. But it's still there sometimes; I don't try to hide it.'

Ellen warmed to her and sat down in the chair opposite. 'Would you like a cup of tea, Mrs Lucan? I have to warn you that it could take some time for 'kettle to boil as this fire is my onny means of cooking.'

'Oh!' It was Mrs Lucan's turn to be astonished. 'No, I won't, thank you. However do you manage? You must be very organized.'

'I've had to be,' Ellen admitted. 'I had no option. This was 'onny place we could afford when we came.'

'And why did you come?'

'My husband – Harry – lost his job on a farm. His employer died and 'new landowner wanted to do things differently and had no place for him.'

'That must have been really hard for both of you. Being lifted out from all you'd known.' She wore a serious look. 'I remember how I felt when my mother said we were moving to Hull. She was born here, you see, and wanted to come back after my father died.' Then her face lit up with a beam and Ellen thought how lovely she was and how Dr Lucan must have fallen in love with her the very day they'd met. 'But it was 'best thing that could have happened to us – to me and my brothers and sister.'

She leaned forward. 'I do hope that your fortune changes soon, Mrs Randell. My husband said that your husband is in

246

hospital following the mill explosion – but that's all he did say,' she hastened to add. 'He doesn't discuss his patients.'

'That's all right,' Ellen assured her. 'I'm hoping that Harry will be home again before long.'

'And have you given any thought to renting the cottage that my brother showed you?' She clasped her hands together. 'I do hope you decide to take it. It's so important that we have someone living in it who'll treat it as their home.' She glanced at the children. 'The garden can soon be made nice again. The previous tenant, a widow, wasn't able to give it the care it needed, but it would be a safe place for the children to play.'

Ellen hesitated; now that the moment had come she was no longer sure it was a decision she could make on her own. She and Harry had always discussed matters together before, but he was in a hospital bed with no means at present of looking at the cottage. She explained this to Mrs Lucan.

'I do understand,' the doctor's wife said quietly. 'But there are times in a woman's life when we have to decide one way or the other, and whether we choose the right way or the wrong one is a chance we have to take. I know that for myself.'

She began to smooth on her gloves in preparation for leaving and Ellen felt a sudden panic; she desperately wanted the cottage and she was sure that Harry would love it once he had seen it.

'The rent, Mrs Lucan? Is it – will it be more than we can afford?' She told her how much they were paying for this room.

Mrs Lucan's eyebrows rose. 'That is disgraceful,' she said. 'I'll report it. I know who the owner is. Our cottage is the same rent, and yet it has so much more to offer.' She leaned forward. 'Let me explain. We can let the properties we own at a moderate rate because of a trust fund we put in place when we first bought them. The rent is not intended to be used for profit, but for maintenance of the properties and . . .' She paused. 'Well, it is not charity, but a form of goodwill towards those who have fallen on difficult times through no fault of their own, in the hope that they can get back on their feet and recover.'

247

Ellen stared and swallowed as her thoughts raced. We've fallen on difficult times; it wasn't our fault that Mr Oswald died and someone else took over the farm and didn't want Harry; nor that the grain should explode and burn out the mill and put Harry in hospital. Besides, not only were these things nothing to do with Harry, they were certainly nothing to do with the children; they and I have been caught up in them through no fault of our own. So why should we refuse a helping hand? She felt a sudden lightening of spirit.

She gave a great beam of pleasure. 'We'll take it, Mrs Lucan,' she declared. 'It's exactly 'chance we need. When can we move in?'

The move was arranged for a week the next Saturday, and in the meantime Mrs Lucan said that the garden would be tidied up and she'd send someone in to make sure the cottage was clean. Ellen was astonished that she would go to so much trouble.

'It's no trouble at all, Mrs Randell,' Mrs Lucan said. 'You'll have enough to do to move your furniture and keep an eye on the children without having to think of scrubbing floors or cleaning windows.'

'My sister will be staying with us for 'time being,' Ellen told her. 'I hope that's all right? She's just started working in Mr Tannerson's office.'

'Oh, was that your sister? I called to see him before coming to you. Well done her for applying to work with him. I was so pleased to see a woman behind the desk, although I don't know why I should be. Mrs Rose of the Rose Down oil company kept a firm hand on business, so I understand, as did Mrs Tannerson for many years, though I didn't know either of them.'

'Lizzie has a good head for figures,' Ellen said proudly. 'And she's very efficient.'

'Is she a single woman?'

'Recently widowed. That's why she was able to come and help me after Harry's accident. We – well, we'll have to make some arrangement when we move to Queen's Road. It might be too far for her to walk to Tannerson's mill.'

248

'Perhaps she'd take lodgings nearer to Wincomlee?'

Ellen considered. It was nothing to do with Mrs Lucan, but on the other hand ... 'I was thinking that if I can get work, washing, or a scullery maid, early in a morning, Lizzie would be there to watch over 'children until I get back and then she'd go off to work. At least, that was how I'd planned it until Harry returns home. Then we'll have to think again.'

'Good gracious! And you said your sister was organized.' Mrs Lucan gave a sympathetic shake of her head. 'You'll be exhausted.'

'Perhaps I will be,' Ellen agreed. 'But whenever there's some difficulty to get over, my mother always says *Needs must when 'devil drives.* And I'm inclined to agree with her.'

Mrs Lucan nodded and rose to her feet. 'Brave ladies,' she said, and held out her hand. 'I'm so very pleased to have met you.'

CHAPTER THIRTY-SEVEN

When Anna heard they were moving to Queen's Road, she immediately said that they would help with the move. 'I will help you pack your belongings,' she said, 'and Filip will borrow a cart – a wagon. He will ask Mr Tannerson.'

'I was going to ask him myself,' Ellen said. 'Or at least ask Lizzie to ask him if I could.'

It turned out that Lizzie had already asked him, and also if she could have the Saturday morning off so that she could help Ellen pack. It would seem, Ellen thought when Tannerson asked Lizzie if he might help in any other way, that there would be more people packing than their few belongings warranted.

'Your sister seems to gather people about her,' Tannerson said, perching himself on a corner of the desk which Lizzie appeared to have taken over, leaving him superfluous.

Lizzie nodded as she stacked a sheaf of papers together and tied a length of black ribbon round them. 'These are not going to be needed, Mr Tannerson, so I'll put them in a file on 'top shelf. Yes, she does.'

She put her fist beneath her chin. 'I think it's because she's caring, and thoughtful too. She doesn't like to think that people are having difficulties. She was like that when she was onny young. Did you know she sat with 'boy who died?'

Tannerson lowered his head. 'You mean Jim Smith? I knew he'd died, yes. The matron at the hospital told me, and Harry said that your sister had asked if he could be buried in St Mary's

250

churchyard. It will be up to the vicar, of course, when the inquiry is over.'

'I meant did you know about Ellen sitting with him until 'very end?'

Tannerson's lips parted. 'No. I didn't. I didn't know she knew him.'

Lizzie shook her head. 'She didn't,' she said, and handed him a letter that she had opened only that morning. 'This is to say that 'deceased, Jim Smith, may now be removed from 'mortuary and taken for burial.'

He took it, and after glancing at the contents he held her gaze for a few seconds before getting up from the desk and unhooking his outdoor coat and hat from the coat stand. 'I'm just slipping out,' he said, putting the letter into his pocket. 'If anyone wants me I'll be back this afternoon.'

She nodded and rose from the desk to cross to the shelf where she intended to file the unwanted papers. Catching sight of Tannerson in the yard below, she watched from the window as he went into the stable block, coming out a few minutes later leading a black roan, which he hitched to a trap and drove off through the gates. Her gaze wandered over the yard, noting the buildings that had been undamaged in the fire, until she saw a shadow by the entrance. A man was standing there, half hidden by the wall. He was looking in the direction Tannerson had driven and she saw how he bent forward as if to watch his progress.

She took a step back out of sight when she saw him turn and head towards the office stairs. Who was he, and why didn't he speak to Tannerson if that had been his intention? She heard his booted feet as he ran up the stairs and she swiftly stepped to the side of a filing cabinet where she was hidden from the door.

The door handle moved slowly, as if being tested, and was then pulled down so that the door clicked open. He was no one she had seen before, not an engineer or insurance official; more a working man by his garb. He crossed to the desk and leaned over it, and then, as if becoming more confident,

251

moved to the other side where he sat in her chair and opened a drawer.

'May I assist you?' she asked in a calm and confident voice, quite unlike the way she was feeling, but she had the satisfaction of seeing him gasp in alarm as he jumped up.

'I'm – I'm looking for Tann – erm – Mr Tannerson.' His face flushed.

'You won't find him inside my desk,' she said coldly. 'What else did you want? We don't keep money on the premises.'

'I'm not a thief! I work here, or I did until 'fire.'

'Did you? What's your name? I have a full list of employees.' She opened the top drawer of the cabinet, not taking her eyes from him, and drew out a random sheet of paper.

She saw indecision on his face, as if he were weighing up whether to give his name or simply make a run for it; she rather hoped it would be the latter, for she could describe him perfectly.

'Who are you, anyway?' he asked boldly. 'I might ask why you're in Mr Tannerson's office when he's not!'

She crossed her arms and stared at him. 'I have 'advantage of knowing where he is and when he'll be back; whereas you, whoever you are, only saw him drive away as you were skulking by the gates and don't know where he's gone or for how long.' She chanced a glance out of the window and allowed an uplift of her lips.

She turned back to him. 'For your information, if indeed you did formerly work for Mr Tannerson, you'll be pleased to know that our paths will cross again. I run this office now; you'll answer to me in 'matter of timekeeping, and I pay out 'wages. Another matter of possible interest to you: we'll be starting with a clean slate, so to speak, once 'mill is up and running again, and I will be handling 'interviews of potential workers.'

This last was a lie, for it hadn't been discussed, but she could spot a shirker a mile off and knew there was one right here. She glanced down at the paper in her hand. 'What did you say your name was?'

He didn't stop to tell her but swore at her in fulsome and fruitful language on his way out of the door, which didn't upset

252

her at all, though she found the sheet of paper in her hand was shaking when she sat down.

She was calmer by the time Tannerson returned. She had found a half bottle of whisky in one of the cupboards and filled a chipped cup with water from the tap in the yard, hoping it was drinkable and trusting that the whisky would kill off any infections if it wasn't. Then she had returned to the office and poured herself a generous splash, which she drank with the bread and cheese that she'd brought to work with her.

Tannerson wrinkled his nose when he entered the office, and as she hadn't removed the cup from the desk there was no point in prevaricating, so she told him what had happened, describing the man who had entered the office exactly: his thick grey hair and slightly bent long nose, and more remarkably his eyes, one brown, one blue.

'Ellison! To a T,' he exclaimed. 'He's my foreman. I've trusted him!'

Lizzie looked askance at him. 'Well, you might want to think again about doing so in future, unless there was something in your desk drawer that belonged to him?'

'Nothing!' he said, anger in his voice. 'And why was he here? He knows there's no work at present and I've given him and the other workers money to make up for loss of earnings.'

'He was watching by the gate and saw you leave,' she told him. 'He came up 'office steps after you'd gone. I saw him from the window, Mr Tannerson. There's a good view over 'yard.'

He gave a sudden grin. 'I know there is. I placed the desk there deliberately.'

She gave a grim laugh. 'Thoughtful indeed,' she agreed. 'But if I'm to keep this desk it needs to be moved slightly nearer, as I'm a few inches shorter than you are and I was standing by the window when I saw him. And by the way, he might not come back unless he really is brass-necked.' She wondered if he understood the local term for shameless, but he did, so she went on. 'Because I told him that I'd be vetting a new workforce when 'milling begins again.'

253

He looked at her and she saw admiration in his eyes. 'Mm,' he said. 'You remind me of my late wife. She was fearless too.'

He told her that he'd been to see the vicar of St Mary's regarding the funerals of Jim Smith and the young boy whose name he thought was Benny. 'They maybe could be buried together, though I might have to visit the workhouse to ask if they know anything more about him. He can't be buried if we're not even sure of his name.'

Lizzie gazed at him; he must be a decent sort of man to take the trouble to do that for an unknown child; especially, she thought, as it seemed likely that the young lad had climbed up and closed all the vents in the mill so that he could keep warm, thus inadvertently probably causing the disaster.

'Poor little lad,' Tannerson muttered. 'A short life, but not a merry one. It makes you wonder why he was alone except for Jim Smith . . . and to die in such a way.'

He looked very downcast and Lizzie guessed that he was sorry that such a tragedy had happened on his premises, so she said gently, 'It would have been quick, you know. He wouldn't have known much.'

He nodded. Then he suddenly straightened his shoulders. 'Have you much else to do, Mrs Robson? Because if you haven't I suggest we lock up the office – securely,' he added, 'and go to a nearby hostelry where they cook a very good meat pie.'

She closed the file she had been working on and stood up, saying, 'There's nothing that can't wait until tomorrow, Mr Tannerson, and I'll come in early to do it. And would it be beyond 'bounds of etiquette for you to call me Lizzie in private? I'm recently widowed, it's true, but in 'district where I'm from widows have to carry on with their everyday lives and can't hide away with their sorrow, as I believe some in society do; life is short, as we've discovered.' She licked her lips. 'And I could devour a meat pie with no trouble at all.'

He laughed, his mood lifting. He took her coat down from the peg and helped her on with it. 'Right then, Lizzie. Let's go, and when we've eaten we can discuss the organizing of a new work force, as you suggest. Then perhaps we can talk about the matter of compensation to the men for loss of earnings.'

'Very good sir,' Lizzie leaned across her desk and picked up her notebook and pencil and put them in her bag. 'I'm ready when you are.'

CHAPTER THIRTY-EIGHT

Lizzie had felt a sense of freedom since coming to Hull. Her mother had suggested that she come to assist Ellen after the mill fire, hoping that the need to support her sister might pull her out of the melancholia that had overwhelmed her since her husband's death.

But I'm a fraud and no one knows it, Lizzie thought as she walked back to Ellen's house after eating a good dinner with Roland Tannerson. I need to talk it out, she decided, and although Ellen has worries of her own, I know she'll listen; and that's all I need, a good listener.

She didn't want anything to eat, she told Ellen, even though the vegetable soup smelled good; she was always astounded at how Ellen could rustle up something nourishing in one pan on a small fire. Ellen was full of the news of Mrs Lucan's calling again to discuss the cottage; she sang her praises and told Lizzie she'd said they could definitely move in at the end of the following week.

'She says they'll make sure that 'cottage is fit for us to move into. My goodness – if she'd seen this place when we first came, before Billy arrived with a pot of paint and a paint brush! But she said she understood, for it had been 'same for her family when they first moved to Hull and took over an old inn.'

'Not a toff, then?' Lizzie said. 'Did she marry money?'

'Don't know.' Ellen shook her head. 'But I'd guess there's a story there.'

256

Lizzie waited to talk until the children had gone to sleep. Sarah was the last to drop off, spending her time staring at the ceiling, drawing attention to the cracks which she said made pictures and then talking softly to herself.

'She's ready for school,' Ellen murmured. 'Perhaps I'll find somewhere after we move.'

Lizzie nodded. 'Yes, I'd say she was ready. She's a bright little girl.' She half rose to her feet. 'Shall I make 'tea?'

'I'll do it,' Ellen forestalled her. 'You've been at work all day.'

Lizzie gave a small grimace. 'It's hardly working wi' a team o' plough horses or harvesting,' she said. 'I've had an easy kind of day, though rather a strange one, especially this morning.' Whilst Ellen made the tea, she told her about Tannerson's going to see the vicar about the boys' funeral, about Ellison's sudden appearance in the office and Tannerson's subsequent anger, culminating in going to a hostelry for midday dinner.

'It was whilst I was in 'hostelry that I suddenly felt guilty.' She stared into the fire, dry-eyed. 'I should have been wearing widow's weeds, weeping and tearing my hair, and even though I said to Tannerson that in 'countryside widows had to get on with their lives and couldn't sit about in mourning but must work to keep a roof over their heads, it was a lie.'

'What was a lie?' Ellen asked, handing her a cup of hot tea, knowing in her heart that if it had been Harry who had died in the mill fire she wouldn't have ever recovered from grief.

Lizzie turned to her. 'All of it! I haven't mourned Albert. I'm sorry that he died, but I never should have married him in 'first place,' she said bluntly. 'I realized that in 'first week of our marriage. He wanted somebody to clean 'house, cook his dinner and warm his bed. He didn't require anything else, certainly not conversation. He might as well have stayed at home wi' his ma, cos she could have provided all of those things and put a hot brick in his bed instead of a wife.'

'But if you'd kept 'babby you were expecting,' Ellen whispered. 'That would have made a difference, wouldn't it?'

'Yes.' Lizzie's voice was low and she glanced frankly at her sister. 'It would have tied me to him even tighter. But I didn't keep it, did I?'

257

Ellen briefly closed her eyes and opened them to see Lizzie still gazing at her. She didn't need to hear more; she could guess the rest. There was always someone who would help a young woman out of an unwanted pregnancy, but usually it would be an unmarried one.

'If I'd known.' Lizzie sipped her tea and turned back to stare into the fire. 'If I'd known that he'd be took ill with influenza and not recover, well – I'm really sorry about Albert's death, and it's a regret that I don't have a child, and perhaps I might have behaved differently; but on 'other hand I now have my freedom, and that, Ellen, is why I'm now full of guilt, for I love my new job. I'm asked my opinion by my boss, and this morning I saw off an intruder with 'tip of my sharp tongue; and that's not how' – her tone of voice changed as if she were choking – 'that's not how women are supposed to behave.'

'I suppose women are meant to conform, but our ma always said we should think for ourselves and never be browbeaten,' Ellen murmured in appeasement. 'She asked me on my wedding morning if I was sure about marriage, and told me that I was very young to decide on such an important lifetime event; that it wasn't onny about being starry-eyed over a handsome young fellow, and that there was still time to change my mind.'

'Ah, yes, but we all knew about Harry and how he'd waited for you. Albert was an incomer to 'village, wasn't he? We knew very little about him.' Lizzie pursed her lips. 'And I wanted my independence, and thought if I was wed with a husband I'd have it.' She shook her head. 'I was wrong. I could only do what Albert wanted us to do and not have an opinion, and it wasn't enough. I wasn't stretched; I was meant to be passive and compliant.'

Ellen smiled wistfully at her. 'Well, you've got your freedom now, haven't you? There's no one to say nay to you. You can mek your own decisions about your life, Lizzie.' She raised an eyebrow and added, 'Perhaps for decency's sake you won't do anything too outrageous for 'next six months or so and damage your family's reputation!' Then she reached across and took hold of her sister's hand and said softly, 'You've always been a loving and caring person, Lizzie, and you will be again, but right now you're

258

feeling low and mebbe you think you've made some faulty judgements in the past, but it doesn't mean they'll impede you. You are grieving, no matter what you might think, and you cared for Albert when he was sick, and you'd have done it lovingly.'

Lizzie's voice trembled as she spoke. 'I did 'best I could for him. I wanted him to get well,' and she squeezed Ellen's hand as she began to weep, saying, 'When did my little sister become so wise?'

Ellen walked to the hospital the next day, first taking the children to Anna then cutting through narrow streets, feeling much surer of her sense of direction. She arrived in half an hour, well before visiting time. It was the young porter who greeted her this time, and he said he'd seen her husband out of bed when he went into the ward on an errand.

'I reckon he'll be out of here very soon,' he said cheerfully. 'You'll be pleased to have him back home again.'

'Oh, I will,' Ellen agreed, 'and so will our children, for they keep asking about their dada.'

He told her to go upstairs and wait to see Sister. As it happened, Dr Lucan was leaving the ward as she reached the top of the staircase. She hesitated about approaching him, but he saw her and came to speak to her.

'Good news, Mrs Randell,' he greeted her. 'Your husband is almost ready for home, but I haven't told him so; I thought you could tell him yourself. Does he know about the new house yet?'

'No,' she said, in almost a whisper. 'It's a surprise. I'm going to borrow a cart if I can, and take him there after we've moved in.'

'We'll release him the following day, then.' He began writing in a notebook. 'I must tell you that he won't feel well after leaving here. He'll be stiff and achy and his burned skin will itch, but I'll give him something for that, and being at home again will help his recovery, from the shock as well as the burns, which thank goodness are not as bad as they could have been. Falling into the water saved his life, even though he might have drowned but for the bargemen being there.'

'And the fact that you were nearby,' she said.

259

'That too, I suppose. I'm pleased that I was. Good day to you, Mrs Randell. You can go on the ward now. Good luck with your move to the cottage.'

She watched him run down the stairs and hail the porter and thought that although he was friendly he was also very professional, as if he put on a different coat when dealing with patients or their families.

Harry was sitting in a chair by the side of his bed and attempted to get up when he saw her, but she gently pushed him back down. 'I said not to come, didn't I?' he said as she bent towards him and he kissed her cheek. 'But I'm glad that you did. Where are the children?'

'With Anna,' she said. 'What a blessing we met them when we did, for we can always help each other out.' She pulled up another chair so that they could sit close to each other. The ward was quiet, with only a few patients in the beds.

'You've become good friends,' he said. 'Who would have thought it possible? We'd never have known so many people of different cultures if we'd stayed in Holderness. Polish and Prussian Jews, an Irish employer. Tannerson came 'other day. He told me that Lizzie has started working for him in his office.'

'She has, and loves it. She's very organized; she had a fright, though, with an intruder.' She told him of Ellison going into Tannerson's office as it had been told to her.

'I've never trusted him since I first met him,' Harry told her. 'He was an idle beggar and had some scheme going wi' young Jim, but I can't remember what it was. Something to do with 'keys for 'mill doors and the gate.'

'Mebbe 'explosion wiped out your memory of it?' Ellen suggested. 'Don't think about it now. You must rest and get well.'

'Don't know how I'll do that, living as we do,' he said dejectedly. 'We must find somewhere else soon, Ellen. We'll be crowded in one small room, especially if Lizzie is staying as well. Just as soon as I'm up on my feet I'll start looking for somewhere else. Tannerson says I'll have a job once 'mill is built, but how long is that going to tek?'

260

She almost told him about the cottage but knew he would then worry about her handling the move on her own, so she decided not to and instead said mysteriously, 'I'm mekkin' plans, Harry; talking to people, asking around, you know, so try not to worry.'

She didn't stay long, telling him that Anna was going to work at the baker's when she got back and she would take her turn to look after all the children.

'If any one of us had any money, you could set up a baker's shop between you.' Harry managed a smile. 'Then Filip and I could live in 'lap of luxury and not have to work at all.'

'But neither of you would like that,' she said, bending to kiss him.

'We wouldn't,' he agreed, and whispered in her ear, 'I can't wait to get home and into my own bed wi' you right next to me, Ellen.' Then he blinked. 'Where does Lizzie sleep?'

Her eyes were merry. 'In bed wi' me, just as we used to when we were bairns.'

And then she saw the real Harry, the one who could share a joke and often had a merry quip on his lips, who until now had disappeared into the misery of a hospital bed.

'In our bed?' he asked huskily. 'Yours and mine?' and when she solemnly nodded his eyes widened and he said quickly, 'Bags I sleep in 'middle.' And with a rush of relief she knew that her loving husband was on the mend.

CHAPTER THIRTY-NINE

Tannerson asked Lizzie if her sister had much furniture to move.

'Two beds, a table and bench, and two chairs. Then there's bedding and pots and pans and suchlike,' she said. 'It'll all fit into one wagon.'

'I'll bring one round early on Saturday morning and give her a hand,' he said. 'It's the least I can do.'

'She'd appreciate it, Mr Tannerson,' she said, not telling him that Filip Bosco had already offered, and wondering why he often said something was the least he could do. Did he feel guilty that Harry had almost died and was in a hospital bed not earning a wage? Harry, she was sure, didn't hold his employer responsible but considered that an unfortunate series of events had culminated in the explosion. But there again, she pondered, perhaps in the eyes of the law Tannerson was responsible: he should have made sure that all reasonable precautions were in place or put someone in charge to do that.

Ellison, she mused. If he was the foreman, shouldn't he be accountable? She decided to ask the question.

'Sir.' She lifted her head from a file. 'I was wondering about Ellison. Was he in overall charge of 'working arrangements in the mill, as well as of the men?'

'He was.' Tannerson was standing with his back to her, looking out of the office window. He turned to face her. 'Oddly enough, I was just thinking about him, and wondering what he was looking for in the desk.'

262

'Money, I'd have thought,' Lizzie suggested. 'Or did he have a contract with you saying what his job entailed?'

Tannerson shifted uneasily. 'He did, but whether it would stand up in law is debatable, and in any case I'm not looking for someone to blame. Ultimately it was my responsibility, and the death of those two lads lies heavily on my conscience.'

Lizzie gave a slight nod. That's what she'd thought. 'You left Ellison in charge, though, didn't you? He was the one who unlocked 'gates and opened up the mill in a morning?'

'He was, except on that particular morning he was late and didn't arrive until after the explosion. I was earlier than usual, because there was a suppliers' contract I needed to look at; the gates were unlocked and half open when I arrived. Harry Randell was the first man in and he came up to the office to warn me about the vents being closed.' He frowned. 'At least – I thought he was the first, but he can't have been.' He stood engrossed in thought. 'Who unlocked the gates? It didn't occur to me at the time. Somebody must have already been here when I arrived, but who? Ellison was the only one with a set of keys.'

After a moment he said slowly, 'It must have been Jim Smith. He had the keys, for he opened the mill doors; Harry Randell saw him from the top of the ladder and shouted to him to stop, but it was too late. So who gave them to him?'

He turned as he heard boots on the outside steps and someone rapped on the door. He called 'Come in', and Kirkwood, one of the mill workers, looked straight at the desk and appeared surprised at seeing a woman there, before seeing Tannerson by the window.

'Mr Tannerson, sir.' He gave a half laugh. 'Thought I'd got to 'wrong place for a minute.' He touched his forehead to Lizzie.

'This is my secretary and office manager, Mrs Robson,' Tannerson told him. 'This is Kirkwood, one of the regular mill workers,' he said to Lizzie, and turned again to Kirkwood. 'You might be just the fellow to solve a conundrum.'

'I will if I can,' Kirkwood said. 'I just came along to ask if there's any news about what's happening about 'mill, cos,' he hesitated,

263

'well, I need to look for more work. And I wondered how young Jim and Harry Randell are getting on.'

Lizzie looked up at Tannerson and then at Kirkwood. Of course, no one would know; how would they without enquiring? Ellison hadn't asked when he came unannounced.

Tannerson took a deep breath. 'Randell is recovering well and will be out of hospital soon, but I'm sorry to say that Jim Smith has died. He was too badly injured to make a recovery.'

'No!' Kirkwood exclaimed. 'Aw, that's terrible! Terrible. Poor lad.' He was silent for a moment, rubbing his hand across his face. 'Did he have any family? Cos I'll organize a whip-round among 'men, for funeral, you know?'

When Tannerson shook his head and said there was no family, Kirkwood muttered, 'That shouldn't surprise me, I suppose, when he and his pal practically lived on 'premises.'

'How do you mean, lived on the premises?' Tannerson asked. 'And which *pal*?'

Kirkwood opened and closed his mouth. 'Erm, I thought you were privy to it, sir. Ellison told Jim that he'd clear it wi' you when he first asked, oh, ages ago, a year at least. He slept at 'back of 'stable block, wi' hosses,' he added unnecessarily. 'I suppose 'young lad stopped with him. I used to see him go out of 'gates in a morning; though come to think of it, he'd always gone afore you got in.'

Tannerson folded his arms across his chest. 'It's odd to think of what was going on here without my knowledge. So Jim Smith had a set of keys to lock up at night and unlock in a morning? Did he always lock the mill doors, or did Ellison do that?'

Kirkwood was beginning to look uncomfortable. 'I – erm, I couldn't be sure. Summertime when nights were light I think it might have been Ellison, but in winter when we all wanted to get off home after our shift it was probably Smith.'

'And the other lad?' Tannerson asked.

Kirkwood shook his head. 'Don't know, sir. He used to come and go. I think he onny came to see Jim; he was just a bairn. Mebbe nine or ten, about 'same as one of my lads. He allus seemed to be at a loose end. I thought he was Jim's brother

264

when he first started coming, but seemingly he wasn't. I think they met in 'workhouse. So where is he? I suppose he cleared off after 'fire, did he?' Then he added, 'Does he know about Jim? Has he been to ask about him? He might have been his onny friend.'

Tannerson put his hands to his forehead and pressed hard, emitting a deep sigh. 'Depending on what you choose to believe, Kirkwood, it would be nice to think they are having great sport together in some other place, but I can't answer that question; I can only tell you that a young boy's body was found in the mill after the fire and we can only assume that it was Jim Smith's friend.'

'Benny.' Lizzie, who had been sitting quietly listening, finished the sentence for him. 'We don't yet know his other name. But we hope that the vicar will agree to bury them together.'

Kirkwood's face was grey and he backed away to the door. 'Excuse me, please,' he said. 'I need some air.'

Tannerson followed him out and found him sitting on the top step. He sat down next to him. 'It's bad news, isn't it? If I'd been aware of what was happening, things would have been different. Both lads are on my conscience; I was slack with discipline, leaving it to others, trusting them to uphold my standards.'

Kirkwood blew his nose. 'I was on 'point of saying summat several times,' he admitted. 'It didn't seem right that such a young lad had responsibility for 'whole building, but Ellison – not that I'm blaming him, he allus said he had your ear. There was no use arguing wi' him, in any case,' he said bitterly.

'Things are going to change,' Tannerson told him, 'so I hope you can hold on, maybe get temporary work for the time being? I'm waiting for confirmation from the insurance company and then from the corporation that I can start rebuilding. Plans are being drawn up with engineers, draughtsmen and builders, so once we have everything in place we should be almost ready to start. I'll need a foreman,' he added. 'Ellison won't be coming back.' He glanced at Kirkwood. 'You've been here a long time.'

265

'Aye, since time of 'first Mr Tannerson and his daughter, your late wife. I was onny a lad back then; it was my first job after school. A job for life, I thought.'

'Well, so it can be.' Tannerson stood up, and Kirkwood did too. 'I'm pleased we've had this discussion, Kirkwood. I feel more positive than I did. I confess I've been knocked sideways by this tragedy.'

He put out his hand to Kirkwood, who shook it and then said, 'And you've got someone to deal wi' paperwork and mundane stuff.' He nodded up the steps towards the office. 'I remember your wife, sir; nowt much got past her, did it? Mrs – Robson, did you say?' He grinned. 'These women, they're made of strong stuff. You'd want 'em with you, not against you.'

'My thoughts exactly,' Tannerson agreed. 'Call back in about a week, Kirkwood, and there might be more to tell you. Then perhaps we can organize a meeting with the men who want to come back.'

'I can do that, sir,' Kirkwood said eagerly. 'I know where they all are; those who are reliable and those who are not.'

'Set up a meeting with Mrs Robson then,' Tannerson agreed. 'Her favourite passion is lists!'

Kirkwood ran down the steps and across the yard; Tannerson watched him. The man had a spring in his step that he'd never noticed before. Then he turned and walked back into the office. 'I think I have a plan,' he announced.

Lizzie folded her arms and sat back in her chair. 'So have I,' she said. 'Mine's a good one. I hope yours is too.'

Tannerson pulled out his own chair and placed it opposite her. 'Right you are then, Mrs Robson. Let's hear yours first.'

266

CHAPTER FORTY

Ellen had kept in constant touch with Billy and their mother and also with Harry's sisters, Meg and Polly, who quite naturally were concerned about Harry. She had told Billy in confidence that they were about to move house but urged him not to tell Harry yet as it was to be a surprise.

Quite coincidentally he arrived on the Saturday morning when she was in the midst of packing the bedding into a clean and washed flour sack that Mrs Brownlee, the baker, had given her. There had been no one else in the shop when Ellen had gone in and she'd told Ellen that although she was pleased that they were moving to a better house than the one they had at present, she would miss seeing her as well as her custom.

'You introduced Anna to me,' she had said, 'and she's been a godsend.'

'It was Anna who brought me to you in 'first place,' Ellen told her, 'but she couldn't have asked you for work then because of 'children. We've all benefited from our meeting by helping each other.'

The baker had looked at her; her face was sprinkled with flour. 'It's a circle within a circle, isn't it? That's what I believe, anyway. You create a circle with your family or friends inside it – it's a kind of protection, I suppose – then you meet someone like-minded and draw them into that circle and they create another within it and so on. Some say that it's perfection and that God is in the centre. But it depends what you believe. I think it means complete friendship.'

267

She had seen Ellen's astonishment at her lucid explanation and rubbed her hands together until a cloud of flour floated from them. 'I used to be a teacher,' she'd explained. 'Science and mathematics. Then I met my husband and he taught me to bake, so here I am. A baker of bread. A provider of the staff of life.'

Ellen was thinking of her as she packed, and how remarkable people were, with talents you'd never guess at, when Billy knocked on the front door. Sarah ran to open it, thinking it was Filip or Anna, and Ellen heard her excited shriek of 'Uncle Billy' and then Mary and Thomas dashed to greet him too.

'Oh, Billy,' she said. 'I never expected you today. It's moving day! I was going to write again, but what with one thing and another—'

'Shall I go away again?' he said with a pretence of misery.

'No!' she said. 'Of course not, but I can't even offer you a cup o' tea. Fire's out, as you see.'

She pointed to the cold grey ash in the grate and got to her feet. 'Oh, it's always good to see you, Billy.' She put her arms round him to give him a hug and saw the children standing looking at someone behind the door.

'You've brought somebody with you,' she said. 'Is it Ma? Or Meg?'

'Nope.' He grinned. 'Ma's busy and so is Meg with her brood; did I tell you she's had another lad?'

'No, you didn't! Are they both all right? So who's come with you? Polly, come to see Harry?' She peered round the door and saw a complete stranger, a young and comely woman, with fair hair and smiling blue eyes.

'This is Florence,' Billy murmured and Ellen turned to look at him in astonishment. Never to her knowledge had her brother ever brought a young woman home to meet his family. He was, they had always thought, a confirmed bachelor.

'Come in, Florence.' She smiled at the young woman, whom she guessed to be about her own age. 'I'm Ellen. You've caught us at an awkward time, I'm afraid, but it's very nice to meet you.'

She cast a surreptitious glance at Billy; whatever was he thinking of, bringing a young woman all this way from Holderness on her own?

'You needn't worry about me, Mrs Randell,' the girl said; she'd quite obviously caught the look of censure that Ellen had given her brother. 'My ma and da know I'm here wi' Billy and that he's come to see his sister and brother-in-law.' She gave a huge smile. 'My da's already threatened what he'll do to him if he does anything amiss. But I can do as I like,' she added. 'I'm of age.'

Billy gave a whimsical grin as he glanced at them both. 'I wanted Florence to meet my littlest sister, and maybe Lizzie too; where is she?'

'She'll be here before long. Did you know she's working? She's office manager to Mr Tannerson and she's had to go in this morning for an hour; something important that she said she had to do.'

Billy didn't know and expressed surprise. 'I'm pleased to hear it,' he said. 'She'd got very morose after Albert died. Anyway, 'reason I came was to visit Harry and I thought you'd like to come along, but clearly not.'

'Don't tell him we're moving, will you, Billy?' she reminded him. 'I'm fetching him home tomorrow in any case and it's going to be a big surprise. I've told 'children and they can't wait to see him. Anna's made a cake for him; she works for a baker who lets her use her oven.'

'Oh, my, Ellen!' Billy gave her another squeeze. 'Things are looking up at last. So where is this new cottage? Mebbe we could have a look at it on 'way to hospital.'

'You can,' she agreed, 'except it's not new, except to us. It's a very old one.' She told him where to find it. 'It's not quite country,' she explained. 'Not as we'd know it. But you can see that it has been at one time, and it leads on towards a park though I haven't seen it yet. It'll be somewhere for 'bairns to play when summer comes.'

'We'll get off then,' he said. 'Don't want to hold you up, unless there's owt I can do?'

269

'Oh, wait and see Lizzie,' she begged. 'She'll be so disappointed if she misses you.'

He pondered for only a minute and then nodded. 'She'll not be coming back to Holderness then, not if she's got a permanent job?'

Ellen heard a rattle outside and pointed to the window. 'That might be her now with Mr Tannerson.'

'What? He brings her home from work!'

'Not usually,' she laughed. 'But today he will. He knows it's a special day and that I want everything to be just right for Harry.'

'How will Harry feel, not being here to help?' Billy asked astutely.

Ellen's face froze; it was something she had worried about. 'It's just, well, he has to recover from the accident, Billy.' She pressed her lips together. 'He's being allowed out, but he has to mend; he couldn't go back to work even if there was any to go back to. I'm planning on getting a job once he's home and he can keep an eye on 'children while I'm out. As will Lizzie. She's coming with us.'

'Harry won't be able to chase after 'bairns,' he said in concern. 'He won't have 'energy.'

'They'll still be in bed,' she said, 'and I'll be home afore anybody's awake.'

'What kind of work will you do, Mrs Randell?' Florence asked curiously. 'Night shift? I didn't think women did that.'

Ellen explained her plans.

There came another rap on the front door. It was Lizzie and Mr Tannerson. Ellen introduced Mr Tannerson to Billy and Florence, and Lizzie raised her eyebrows at her brother as she said hello to Florence. Suddenly the room was full: Edyta came in with Karl, having taken the morning off, and within minutes Filip, Anna and their children arrived.

'You've a lot of friends, Mrs Randell,' Florence commented.

Ellen gave a teary smile. She was beginning to fill up with emotion. 'I have. I'm so very lucky.'

Filip and Billy started to lift the beds out of the room and put them in the wagon Filip had brought; Tannerson took the sack

270

of bedding and the box of crockery and cutlery and the rag rug and packed them in his trap, and Ellen called after Lizzie not to forget the kettle and the window curtain. The children gathered up their few toys and in half an hour everything was stowed away.

Ellen gave Edyta the keys to give to the rent agent and Edyta said she was going to ask him if she could move in. 'Move in now,' Filip suggested. 'We can bring your furniture down. The rent man won't care; he is a villain anyway.'

Edyta looked at Karl, who grinned and said why not, so they set about dismantling her bed and bringing it downstairs. Billy carried her chair, pans, kettle and cutlery, Lizzie put back the curtain she had just taken down from Ellen's window, and within fifteen minutes Edyta had a new home and Karl began to build a fire in the grate.

'At least I know it's clean,' she said. 'Unlike our room when my *Mutter* and I moved in.' Sotto voce, she said to Ellen, 'I can't tell you how much I've longed for my own privy instead of having to share with half a dozen others.'

'I'm so sorry,' Ellen murmured. 'I never thought. You could have shared ours,' but then thought that proud Edyta would never have asked, and in similar circumstances neither would she. The necessity for such indignity should not be permitted, she considered.

Edyta waved them off, saying she would come the next day to see Harry; Lizzie went with Tannerson in the trap, Karl set off next in his carpenter's cart with last-minute items, all six children climbed into Filip's wagon with Anna, and Ellen travelled with Billy and Florence in the Holderness cart. Billy said they might as well come to see the cottage now and visit Harry on the way home.

'What is it with our Lizzie and Tannerson?' Billy asked as they drove. 'And why is he being so helpful? Most unusual for an employer, isn't it?'

'He's a good man,' Ellen said. 'I think he feels guilty over the fire at 'mill. Two young lads died, and he has them and Harry on his conscience. Some things had been going on that he wasn't aware of and I believe he's blaming himself. He wasn't unscathed,

271

either. He has some burns on his hands that he generally keeps covered. I think he must have tried to put out 'flames on young Jim. He was bandaged when I first saw him after 'explosion.'

'Mm. And Lizzie?'

'What? What about her?' She cast a glance at him. 'She's fortunate to get such a position, isn't she? But he's used to working with women. His late wife ran his office previously.'

'Ah!' he said, and changed the subject.

It won't feel like home at the cottage until Harry's there, Ellen thought, waving back at Thomas who was waving to her from the tail end of the wagon in front. They were all travelling in convoy, with Tannerson and Lizzie leading the way towards what was once the village of Sculcoates.

'It's been ruined, hasn't it?' Florence said, looking at the industry along the river side. 'It must have been a pretty hamlet once.'

'Aye, but with no work for 'inhabitants,' Billy reminded her. 'That's why 'workhouses were built, to care for those who couldn't care for themselves, and at least there are now places where men can work and earn a wage; there's industry here to feed folk and their animals, and houses to live in, even though some of them are dire, but that's 'fault of 'landlords for not keeping them in good order.'

Their conversation went over Ellen's head as she looked towards the river in the gaps between factory buildings and caught bright glimpses of water with the sun glistening on it, and once a lone willow tree with the slightest hint of pale greening on its tips trailing a slender branch towards the water. That tree will endure, she thought, in spite of the commerce around it. It has life growing within its core and it will survive, just as we will.

Outside the cottage Ellen saw Lizzie and Mr Tannerson waiting, along with Karl in his cart and the Boscos with Thomas clamouring to get out of the wagon but being held in check by Filip. Mr Tannerson got down from the driving seat, plucked up Thomas and came towards her, holding a set of keys.

'Here you are, Mrs Randell.' He put Thomas down to stand by his mother's skirts, and handed over the keys with a flourish.

272

'I happened to see the Lucans this morning and offered to bring the keys to you. Welcome to your new home. I hope you'll all be happy here. I'm sure that you will be once Harry comes home.'

Ellen felt choked and could barely speak to thank him for his efforts to help them. 'Harry will want to say 'same,' she said. 'He'll be very grateful.'

'Can we go inside, please?' Sarah piped up, and Mary joined in and then Thomas, saying, 'Yes, please. We want to look inside.'

Everyone followed Ellen and the children; she opened the door wide and the girls rushed in. 'But where are the stairs?' Mary asked and Ellen laughed and opened the staircase door. Mary squealed and said it was just like Granny's house in Holmpton and she and Sarah dashed up the stairs to look.

Ellen turned with a big smile on her face and saw Filip and Karl bringing in the iron bedsteads and hoped they'd get them upstairs. Tannerson carried in a basket of logs and kindling, Billy brought in the two chairs and placed them opposite each other by the fireplace, where miraculously a fire was burning. Ellen had a question on her lips as she looked at Tannerson, who shook his head and shrugged his shoulders as if to say he knew nothing about it.

She heard Mary upstairs telling Filip and Karl that their bed should go in the big bedroom. 'This is 'one Sarah and me have chosen,' she heard her carol, 'not 'middle one.'

'I don't think so,' Filip boomed, 'but we'll hear what Mama has to say, shall we?'

Mary clattered downstairs. 'Ma, Mr Filip says we have to go in 'middle room and we want to go in 'biggest one cos there's Sarah and me and Thomas.'

'And what about when Dada comes home?' Ellen said gently. 'Where will he sleep? You know what I said about him having to rest after being in hospital?'

Mary stared up at her with her mouth half open, then about-turned and ran upstairs again. 'Sarah,' she called. 'We have to have that lovely room in 'middle cos Dada needs 'big one so's he can get better. Aunt Lizzie'll have to sleep in 'littlest one because there's onny her.'

273

CHAPTER FORTY-ONE

Billy and Florence left to visit the hospital, being sworn to secrecy about the move. There was little left to do. The furniture was in, the beds were made, clean cupboards with oiled lining paper on the shelves were filled with crockery, and in the kitchen sink was a jug containing spring flowers, narcissi and primroses and small branches of dark green butcher's broom still wearing waxy red berries.

'Butcher's broom,' Ellen said softly. 'I haven't seen that since leaving Holderness. We had a shrub growing at 'bottom of our garden. These must be from Mrs Lucan. She was a countrywoman.'

She carried the jug into the parlour, placed it in the middle of the table on her chenille cloth, and turned to everyone. 'I can't thank you enough. I'm so very grateful.' She took a breath. 'There's just one person missing and I wish, oh, how I wish that Harry could be here.'

Everyone nodded or murmured in agreement, and Tannerson put his head back and pursed his mouth as if thinking. 'Well,' he mused. 'It's not late.' He paused. 'Let me think. You'd want the children with you – yes of course you would; so if you took the trap, Filip, to take your family home I'll drive the wagon with Mrs Randell and the children to the hospital. I'm sure we can arrange for Harry to be discharged tonight, and then we'll bring him home.'

'I'll make a simple supper, shall I, Ellen?' Lizzie asked, and Anna said, 'There's more cake in the tin.'

'Oh!' Ellen's voice was wobbly. 'Could we?' She turned to the children. 'Would you like to come with me and fetch Dada home?'

All the children cheered, including the Boscos, so coats and bonnets were put back on and blankets picked up for the journey back; Ellen said goodbye and thank you to Anna and Filip and kissed them and their children, and then did the same to Karl, and they all said, 'See you tomorrow.'

'I'm dizzy with excitement,' Ellen said to her sister, who helped her on with her coat and put a shawl round her shoulders and gently kissed her cheek. Then she handed her Harry's clean clothing, for his own shirt and trousers had been thrown away, and an extra blanket. 'Thank you, Lizzie,' Ellen said. 'I would have forgotten.'

'It's all worked out well,' Lizzie told her. 'And don't worry about a thing, just enjoy being with your lovely Harry. I'll put 'supper things on 'table and entertain 'bairns when you come back, so you don't have to do anything. Off you go, and let Roland do the talking. He has a way wi' words, being Irish!'

Roland, is it? When did it switch from Mr Tannerson to Roland, Ellen wondered as she climbed up next to Tannerson and settled Thomas on her knee, not trusting him with the girls at the back. Sarah and Mary wrapped themselves up in their blankets as if they were going on a long journey.

The Beverley road was busy with people walking home from work, horse carriages and hand carts, and families were streaming out of the avenue that led to the public park, which Tannerson told them was called Pearson's Park.

'I thought it was somewhere at 'top of Queen's Road,' Ellen said. 'I've got it wrong.'

'No, you haven't,' Tannerson told her. 'There are two entrances. This is the main one; did you notice the arch and gates leading in? The second is at the other end, where it's still mainly grassland; Newland, it's called, and it'll be built on eventually, but that will take years and years.'

What a lot he knows, Ellen thought. He has his ear to the ground all right.

275

'I wanted to tell you about the boys' funeral,' he went on. 'Finally we have permission for them to be buried together. I'll speak to the vicar and arrange a simple service. Kirkwood and some of the men who knew Jim will want to come, and I wondered . . .'

'Yes, I would too, but not Harry.' She made the decision for him. 'It would depress him, I'm sure, and I want him well. He won't notice if I say I have to slip out on an errand.'

'It won't be yet,' he said. 'I'll let you know.'

At the hospital, visitors were leaving the premises and Ellen hoped they were not too late to be admitted. Tannerson parked the wagon and went inside and once again worked his magic, for he came back ten minutes later. 'You can go in now, Mrs Randell. Tell anyone who says you can't that Matron has given permission. We'll come to the doors in ten minutes to meet you.'

Thomas began to wail to go with her when Ellen walked away, but Tannerson put his fingers to his lips and whispered, 'No crying, or we'll be sent home without your dada.' The little girls hushed Thomas and told him that their father would be out in a moment and they must look out for him and give him a cheer. When the time had lapsed, Tannerson lifted them down and put Thomas on his shoulders so that he had a good view and they walked to the doors to wait.

Ellen ran silently up the stairs and pushed open the ward doors. A nurse looked up as if she was about to say that visiting was over until she recognized Ellen. 'We haven't told your husband that he can leave yet,' she said quietly. 'He's had his brother to see him, and that's cheered him up.'

'*My* brother,' Ellen told her. 'Harry's best friend. Can he come home now?'

'He can,' the nurse agreed. 'He'll have to rest and be careful that he doesn't knock his burned skin, but once he's home he'll soon recover.'

Ellen walked to the bed. Harry had his back to her and was talking to another patient in the next bed, who raised his head from his pillow when he saw Ellen. 'A young lady to see you, Harry; some fellers have all the luck.'

276

Harry turned slowly as if his body was unbendable and carefully rose to his feet. 'My wife,' he told the other patient. 'Ellen! It's late. However did you get in?'

'I have influential friends,' she murmured, and held up his coat, shirt and trousers. 'How would you like to come home?'

He dressed slowly, sitting on the bed to put on his trousers and shirt and carefully putting first one arm into a coat sleeve and then the other. Ellen buttoned him up and said, 'Say goodbye to your friend in 'next bed.'

'Am I really going home at last?' He kissed the top of her head and sighed. 'I thought 'day would never come. Cheerio, Greg,' he said croakily to his neighbour. 'Hope all goes well wi' you.'

'You too, Harry,' the man said. 'Tek care now.'

Harry nodded and took Ellen's arm, but before they left he called his thanks to the nurse. 'Say thank you from me to everybody, won't you?' She nodded a goodbye.

'Careful down 'stairs,' Ellen told him. 'Take hold of 'banister rail.'

'I don't remember coming in,' he muttered, taking the stairs slowly and looking about him. 'None of this. Who brought me?'

'I don't know,' she admitted. 'But Dr Lucan was near 'mill when you were pulled out of 'river.'

'I don't remember what happened,' he said, pausing at the bottom of the staircase. 'It's really strange.'

'Well, you mustn't worry about it,' Ellen told him. 'It's nature's way of healing. We don't want to think of it right now. All we want is to get you home.'

'Where are the bairns? Who've you left them with?'

'Erm, let me think.' She led him across the wide hall. 'I know I left them somewhere; now where was it?'

Isaac opened the doors for them and touched his forehead as they went through and Ellen smiled at him, mouthing *thank you*, and said, 'Oh, yes, now I remember! Here they are!'

The children standing outside cheered at Mr Tannerson's prompting and tears streamed down Harry's face as the mill owner lifted the children one by one to give their father a kiss to save him from bending.

277

As they walked slowly across to the wagon, Tannerson suggested to Ellen, 'I'll sit in the back with the children if you can take the reins, then Harry can sit up next to you. Are you able to do that? The mare's a steady drive.'

She was about to say yes when Harry said, 'I can drive. I know this horse. We're friends, aren't we, Nellie?' He stroked the satiny nose and she snickered and blew at him.

Ellen was doubtful, worrying about the strain on Harry's hands and back, but he insisted, 'I've got to get back to normal some time and there's no time like 'present.'

'Just halfway, then,' Ellen said, 'then I'll take over.' She wanted to make the left turn towards Queen's Road and Harry didn't know about that. 'Turn left out of 'hospital gates,' she told him as Tannerson helped him up.

'We can go straight across,' he told her. 'Down to 'bottom of Albion Street. I thought you knew that way.'

'I do,' she said, 'but I want to show you something. And just look at the sky!' She pointed up to divert him. 'It's almost, but not quite, as good as a Holderness one.'

'You're right,' Harry agreed, turning left as she directed; the sky in the west was suffused with blue, red and gold. 'It's just that 'buildings get in 'way.'

'We've got a surprise,' Thomas said from behind Harry's ear as he stood in the back with Tannerson holding on to his coat. 'But you don't know what it is, Dada, and we do!'

'Don't tell him,' Sarah said. She put her hand over Thomas's mouth and he promptly tried to bite her.

'It's a surprise!' he shouted again, having fortunately forgotten what the surprise was.

They continued along Prospect Street and Ellen asked Harry to turn up Beverley Road and Harry noticed that the mare was heading that way in any case. 'We've been this way before, haven't we, Nellie?' he said, and the mare pricked up her ears at his voice and snickered again. 'Does Nellie know about this surprise?' he asked Thomas, who was leaning into him, and Ellen thought he already sounded brighter than when they had left the hospital.

278

But a little further along he drew the horse to a halt and took a breath. 'You're right and I'm wrong, Ellen,' he admitted. 'I'm not ready yet. Will you tek over, or mebbe you could, Mr Tannerson?'

'I'm quite happy in the back with my young friends,' Tannerson said. 'We're enjoying the scenery, isn't that so, ladies?' He gave the girls a big wink. 'Shall we let your mama drive?'

'Yes!' they chorused and Ellen climbed over Harry to take the reins as he shuffled into her seat.

'You need to go right here,' Harry pointed out as they reached the crossroads. 'Nellie knows 'way from here,' and he frowned as Ellen seemed not to have heard him. 'I really would like to go home, such as it is.'

'Nearly there,' she assured him, and the children started to giggle and whisper. 'Why don't you close your eyes for a minute?'

'I'll close my eyes when I'm in bed,' he said. 'Ellen, where in heaven's name are we going? I'm not ready for a tour.'

'Home!' Mary couldn't contain herself any longer, and Sarah repeated, 'Home, home, home!' Then Thomas joined in until all three children were laughing and shouting and Tannerson put his fingers to his lips once more to quieten them.

Ellen drew up outside the cottage. The curtains were open and through them they saw the dim light of a lamp and the flickering glow of firelight.

'Home,' she said quietly, hoping that her decision had been the right one. 'This is where you wanted to be, isn't it, Harry? A place where 'children could play safely and we could have a separate bedroom.'

'And a kitchen with an oven?' he asked, turning towards her.

She nodded, and smiled. 'I knew you wanted that more than anything.' Her voice cracked as she spoke. 'Shall we go inside and have a look? I'm sure that 'kettle will be on 'boil and supper waiting on 'table.'

He grasped her hand. 'Have we come into money, Ellen? Because if we haven't, how can we afford this?'

Tannerson had climbed out of the back to lift the children down, and now he said, 'It's a long story, Harry, and will keep

279

until later. Sufficient to say you are not in debt. Shall we go inside, for it's a long way off summer when we can sit in the garden and chat, and I'm fairly sure there'll be a good fire burning in the hearth.'

He came round to the passenger side and put out his arm for Harry to lean on as he stepped down. 'Is this your doing, Mr Tannerson?' Harry asked, good-mannered as always.

'Not at all,' Tannerson said. 'Blame your lovely wife entirely.'

Ellen also offered Harry her arm but he shook his head, and understanding he wanted no mollycoddling she followed the children to the door, which was opened by Lizzie.

'How good to see you, Harry,' Lizzie said, standing aside to let him pass, and then she slipped out into the lobby, supposedly to speak to Tannerson but in fact to let Harry take in his first impression of their new home. She heard his gasp and his incredulous questions and then the excited chatter of the children as they rushed about showing him various special things.

'Are they going to be happy here, do you think, Lizzie?' Tannerson murmured, gazing at her.

She nodded and smiled. 'Wouldn't anyone be?'

280

CHAPTER FORTY-TWO

Harry's recovery was going to take time, the doctor had said, but Ellen was relieved that he was delighted with her decision to move house. Gradually he took a longer walk on his own each day, testing out his strength and ability and regaining confidence, for whilst in hospital he had often doubted that he'd ever be useful again. He walked the short distance to the top of Queen's Road towards the green fields of Newland, and sometimes if he felt strong enough he would walk a little way towards the western entrance of the park, though he never went in. That was a pleasure waiting for a time when Ellen and the children would come too.

On the day they brought him home he had thought he must be dreaming. It was such a luxury to sit in the parlour by a warm fire and to hear Ellen talking to Lizzie in the kitchen and the children chattering as they played upstairs in their bedroom.

That night, when Ellen slipped into bed beside him and gently kissed him, he knew he was recovering. He drew her close, running his fingers over her smooth skin from her throat to her silky thighs, and then remembered. 'The baby,' he whispered. 'Were we not expecting a child?'

'We were,' she said softly. 'But it was not to be. Dr Lucan brought me home after visiting you that first day you were in hospital and I began to miscarry. I don't know what I'd have done if he hadn't been there.' She tenderly kissed his lips. 'We will have another,' she murmured. 'But not just yet.'

As she had already determined that she would, Ellen found work on three mornings a week in the villas on Beverley Road. She helped with the washing for a large family on a Monday, and on Tuesdays and Thursdays she scrubbed floors and front steps of two others. She had asked a local grocer if she might put a note in his window advertising her services and he'd agreed. His was a busy shop, selling flour, sugar, butter, lard and general commodities as well as vegetables; she often saw a queue of women outside when she returned home from her chores at seven o'clock in a morning, having started at five.

She called in one day when there were not so many waiting and asked for bread; she had been tired the night before and hadn't set any dough to prove, and she thought she would buy instead of making.

'Sorry, missis, I don't keep fresh bread, not since my wife died some years ago. She was a fine baker and we've two ovens going a-beggin' for want of someone to fire them up. There's a woman down in Wincomlee who bakes good bread, but maybe it's too far for you to walk?'

'I know her,' she told him, 'and she's an excellent breadmaker. But I have an oven in 'house I'm in now and I can make my own.' She sighed. 'I didn't set any to rise last night, and I'm so tired this morning I don't think I can face it.' She gave a half laugh. 'But I will. I'll make soda bread, that's quick and easy.'

'I see you walking down the road sometimes,' he said. 'You're an early riser. Do you work locally?'

She nodded. 'My husband isn't well,' she confessed. 'He had an accident at 'mill and I'm working to earn some money until he's able to go back.'

She was intrigued by his accent and asked him if he was a Hull man. 'No,' he said. 'I'm Australian. Came to England thirty years ago when I was a young man, going walkabout, you know, like the Aborigines.' He grinned. 'Only came here for a visit to try and trace my ancestors; I met my wife and married her and here I am still.'

'I don't know what *walkabout* means,' she confessed. 'Is it like when we say *up sticks*, and it means to go off somewhere new?'

282

'That's about it,' he said. 'I always intended going back but somehow I never did. Got a nice little business going here, although it's lonely sometimes without my wife, and I can't leave her all alone in that pretty cemetery, can I?'

'No, you can't,' she agreed. 'And your old country wouldn't be 'same as you remember it in any case, would it?'

He shook his head and gave a rueful laugh. 'It wouldn't, you're right, but the weather would still be warmer than it is here, that I do know!'

'Did you find out about your ancestors or where they lived, Mr Foster?' she asked him, having seen his name – M. W. Foster – on the board above the shop window.

'I found out where they had lived in Hull – it was a poor place, so I guess they'd had a hard time making ends meet – but then the trail went cold; it seemed they'd left to live elsewhere. It was disappointing, but then I gave up; I was trying to run a business and then Maggie took ill so it didn't seem important anymore.' He sighed. 'It would have been good if I'd found some living folk who'd come from the same roots, you know, but it wasn't meant to be.'

'I suppose not.' He seemed sad, and she was sorry that she'd brought up some unhappy memories by her question. 'Not meant to be,' she said gently, 'but a pity nevertheless.'

Mr Tannerson sent a message with Lizzie to say the boys' funeral had been arranged and he would collect Ellen from the end of Queen's Road so she wouldn't have to tell Harry where she was going. She put a dark shawl in her bag to slip over her head once she reached St Mary's church.

As they drove the short distance, Tannerson told her that his enquiry at the workhouse had revealed that the boy Benny Dent had been born there. His mother had died at his birth, and he had spent the whole of his short life there until Jim Smith had befriended him and they had become as close as brothers. When Jim had left to work in the mill, Benny had run away.

He also told her that at the inquest he had been repri-manded for allowing unsuitable persons to supervise access

283

to a dangerous environment and had been heavily fined. Kirkwood and some of the other men had spoken up in his defence, saying that he had always been a good and considerate employer, and offering the suggestion that the fault might lie elsewhere.

'But ultimately it was my fault,' he said regretfully, 'and I accept that. The death of those boys will be always on my conscience; I left someone in charge who was totally unfitted for a position of trust.'

Ellen remained silent until they reached the church. She saw the small group of people waiting by the gates; she assumed they were Jim's fellow workers and so they were, Tannerson told her, together with representatives of the workhouse who remembered both boys and had come to pay their respects.

Inside, Tannerson shed a tear, as did she, when they saw the small coffin containing the remains of the two boys. *That boy*, she recalled Mary saying, and she knew that young Benny was the same boy she had seen watching them from the street on the day they had moved in.

Poor lad, she thought, blowing her nose as tears ran down her face; he must have been looking for friendship and companionship all his life, and he had been given it by his friend Jim. She gave a deep shuddering sigh. She was glad that she had been able to give Jim Smith at least a little comfort by telling him they would soon be together.

The small crowd of mourners followed the coffin, carried on the shoulders of Tannerson, Kirkwood and two of his co-workers, to the graveyard where Ellen had taken her children to play, and she thought that she would now think of it as a place where Jim and Benny were safely watched over by the residents of the older graves.

She told Harry about it a few days later, when she could think about it without weeping, and he said he wished he could have been there.

'It's very sad,' she said, 'and we all have regrets. I think of Christmas Day, when we could have invited them to eat with us, and I was worried that 'food wouldn't stretch to feed two more.'

Harry shook his head, 'And I said that Jim had been given food by Tannerson and that they'd manage. We could all have done more if onny we'd known 'circumstances.' He sighed. 'We've had our eyes opened, Ellen. We must look to our friends and neighbours more closely in future.'

The weather was improving; everywhere Ellen looked as she tramped to work in a morning, she saw clumps of narcissi holding their golden trumpets up to the sky. The trees were greening, and here on the road to Beverley the oily odour drifting from the mills and factories was not as keen as it had been in the industrial area of Wincomlee.

Anna and the children called to see them one afternoon to tell them that they too were moving again and coming to a small terraced house off Beverley Road. It wasn't far away from Queen's Road so they would see each other more often. 'It is Jewish welfare board who do this for us; they help us find house. Filip goes to synagogue in Posterngate near where we got off ship, and he is assisted to find more work also. And, 'she said excitedly, 'we have letter from Filip's *cowsuns*.' Ellen and Harry both smiled; her accent was so endearing. 'They are coming on train from Leeds. Edyta's brother, Ezra, he make inquiries through his people and found them. Abraham and his brother Daniel are – erm, *shnayders*? In English is – tailors,' she remembered triumphantly. 'Filip is very happy.'

'We're so pleased, Anna,' Harry said, and Ellen agreed. 'It will be comforting to have family nearby, but I hope you don't leave us and go to live in Leeds.'

'No!' Anna said. 'It is good here and we have your friendship; Filip he is happy to have work and soon they will be starting to build mill.'

'Will they?' Harry asked anxiously, hoping that he would be fit in time, but also wondering if he would ever be capable of hard physical work; he was still in some pain, although his burn scars were healing.

'Mr Tannerson say that he will have news for us all soon. So this is why we move now, and I shall have house with oven like

285

yours to make my bread, Ellen. But it will be too far for me to work for Mrs Brownlee. I cannot leave children.'

Ellen nodded vaguely. Something was bubbling in her mind, but it wasn't formulated yet; she must leave the idea on the back burner until Harry was back at work again.

Anna called to the children, who were playing outside in the garden; the gate was securely locked, but both women knew that Jakub was almost big enough to be able to climb over the fence, which was what he was trying to do now, and what he did, Aron and Thomas would follow.

'They need to go to school soon, I think,' Anna said. 'That is the next step.'

When Anna had left, Harry said he was going to take a walk. He wanted to test himself to see how fit he really was. He set off with a normal stride until he was out of sight of the cottage and then tried a faster pace, just to see if he could. His breath quickened and he started to run, just a short distance at first before he had to slow down, then faster again, and then he turned back towards home. He walked by the grassy narrow drain and saw bubbling frogspawn and the whooshing tails of tadpoles, and stopped when he saw the dark head of a frog in the midst of it.

The sight of it lifted his spirits and reminded him of his childhood, when he and Billy would look in a pond or a ditch and count the number of frogs they saw. I'd like to see him again, he mused as he walked on. He came to see me in hospital and brought a young lady with him. First time I've ever seen him with a girl. I wonder what will become of his travel plans now?

As he approached their cottage he saw Lizzie walking towards him from the main road. She gave him a wave. She was still working full time for Mr Tannerson in spite of the mill's not being in production, and he knew that Ellen was pleased to have her contribution towards the rent. Lizzie had told them that she was constantly taking notes regarding the plans for the new mill when Tannerson had meetings with other mill owners, who were proving very helpful with advice in spite of being competitors.

Harry held the gate open for her and in an extravagant gesture ushered her in before him. 'After you, Mrs Robson,' he said, and she graciously bent her head and replied, 'You look very well today, Harry.'

'I feel well,' he told her, opening the front door for her. 'I think I'm almost ready to go back to work, except there's no work for me just yet, is there?'

'I've brought a letter for you from Mr Tannerson. Perhaps that'll tell you. I've posted others, too.'

Harry took the envelope from her and felt a flurry of tension. Would he still be wanted? He was the newest employee at the mill. Some of the men had been working there for years. True, he had been injured in the explosion, but that didn't mean that Tannerson had to take him on again if he wasn't up to it.

He didn't read the letter immediately. Ellen had a meal ready and waiting, and as soon as Lizzie had washed her hands and changed out of her work clothes – she was still borrowing Ellen's brown dress, and Ellen thought that she could probably say goodbye to it – they were sitting down to eat.

'Elbows off 'table please, Thomas,' Ellen said as she dished up a cottage pie, still marvelling that she could cook a nourishing yet cheap meal in her own oven at last.

'I was just saying that Harry looks well today,' Lizzie commented. 'I think he's on the mend at last.'

'Hope so.' Harry forked up some mince and mashed potato, but before beginning to eat he added, 'It's about time I was back at work. Mebbe I could find a temporary job until 'mill is built. I don't like to think that Ellen's having to get up so early in a morning to pay 'rent.'

'Needs must—' both women began, and then laughed. Sarah looked up from her plate.

'When 'devil drives,' she finished for them.

'It's what Gran says,' Mary added. She had gravy on her chin. 'I don't know what it means.'

'I'll explain one day,' Ellen said, wiping her younger daughter's chin with a clean rag.

'When you've read Ro— Mr Tannerson's letter, you'll have some idea of 'plans for 'mill. It might seem that nothing's been happening but he's been talking to various people, and Filip

287

Bosco has been very helpful in discussing 'equipment. He says we should scrap the old machines and begin again.'

'Can Mr Tannerson afford to do that?' Ellen asked.

'If 'insurance company agree, and they have in principle. In confidence, there's a meeting with 'insurers tomorrow and Filip will put forward his suggestions and show how 'running costs will be less in 'long run.'

Once they'd finished their meal and the children had gone upstairs to play before bedtime, Harry opened the letter and read an invitation to attend a preliminary meeting to discuss the formation of a new company under the name of Tannerson and Partner.

'I don't understand.' He looked up. 'Why has Tannerson sent this to me? I've no money to put into a company!'

'He hasn't asked you for any,' Lizzie said bluntly, 'but he'd like to hear your ideas on how it should be run.'

'How would I know?' he objected, his confidence still at a low ebb. 'I'm a farmhand.'

'You ran Ozzie's farm, didn't you?' Ellen said.

'Aye, true, I did.' He paused and considered. 'Well, I suppose, yes, it comes to 'same thing, whatever kind of business it is. It has to be efficient or it fails. When I went to Tannerson's I thought it was being run too casually, which is dangerous when there's moving machinery.'

Ellen nodded. Tannerson had admitted as much.

'So there you are then, Harry,' Lizzie observed. 'You do know, and that's why he's asked you. He doesn't want businessmen on 'committee who look at figures on a balance sheet, he wants working men who understand 'needs of other reliable working men if a company is to be run efficiently. He has a role for you, but I can't say what it is. So will you come?'

Harry glanced at Ellen, who gave him a nod of approval. 'Lizzie's family, Harry; we know we can trust her.'

'Course we can. I've no doubts about Lizzie,' he agreed. 'It's about myself where 'doubts lie.' He gave a lopsided grin. 'But with two such women on my side, how can I fail?'

CHAPTER FORTY-THREE

When Anna next visited Ellen it was to tell her that they were moving in two days' time. 'Will you take care of children, Ellen?' she asked. 'There are people Filip knows from synagogue who will help us move, but I can trust you with children.'

'Of course,' Ellen said swiftly. 'You know I'll be glad to. You have helped me so often.' She gave Anna a hug. 'I'm so pleased that we met when we did and became friends, and glad too that our lives are improving at last.'

'I am also,' Anna said. 'I told Mrs Brownlee that we are moving and she was sad, but I say it is too far to come. I must find something else to bring in a little money, but I did enjoy baking bread for her.'

'I enjoy it too,' Ellen agreed. 'It seems important, doesn't it?' She hesitated for a moment. 'I've had an idea, but I'll ponder on it some more and then ask you what you think. Has Filip received a letter from Mr Tannerson?' she asked, changing the subject.

'Yes, he has.' Anna was animated. 'He is very excited about opportunity for him. It is great – erm, I don't know the English word. It is important for him to show his – erm – for people to understand what he can do.'

'Reputation? Prestige?' Ellen asked. 'Are those 'words you're looking for?'

'*Prestiż*, yes. That is the word I think. It is the same, yes?'

289

'It seems so.' Ellen agreed. 'Harry is curious about the meeting. He can't wait to get back to work, but I'm being careful with money as I expect 'new mill will take a long time.'

'I don't think so,' Anna said. 'Not the building of it.' She shrugged. 'The machinery perhaps, I don't know. Mr Tannerson and Filip have been talking to a company called Rose who build these presses.' She put her hand to her mouth. 'Oh, perhaps I shouldn't speak of it. I am sorry, my tongue it runs away with me.'

'Don't worry,' Ellen assured her. 'I won't discuss it. The meeting is at the end of 'week in any case, so then we'll all know what's happening.'

When Anna brought the children on their moving day, it was gloriously sunny and Harry suggested that they should all walk to the park. Ellen packed a picnic of bread and cheese and home-baked scones and they walked along the back road, which was quieter than the Beverley road with its carriages, wagons and hand carts.

They entered through the gates and passed the park keeper's lodge. Seeing the keeper, Harry asked the ticket price. To his delight they were told it was free and they could stay as long as they wished until closing time.

The children ran on to the grass, running round in huge circles, for it had been a long time since any of them had had the freedom to do so. Then they walked by the lake where swans serenely swam; they admired the fine tree planting, though Harry and Ellen noticed that several large trees had reacted badly to a previous drought, and Ellen pointed out to Sarah and Mary the gardens that were laid out with fresh spring flowers.

They let them run for half an hour while Harry and Ellen walked slowly, hand in hand as they used to when they had first met, but keeping a close watch on the children, especially the boys. Mary ran back, followed by Sarah, to ask if they were allowed to pick the flowers. 'Sarah says we can't,' she pouted, 'and I wanted to take some home and put them in a jug.'

Her mother shook her head. 'Suppose all of 'children who come here picked the flowers,' she said. 'How would the gardens look then?'

290

Mary gave it some thought, and then said slowly, 'There wouldn't be any left to look at?'

'There wouldn't be, would there? There would onny be bare earth.'

Mary nodded. 'Ah, until someone else scattered some seeds and waited for them to grow.'

'That's right, so no one else would have 'pleasure of seeing their lovely colours for a long time. Anything else?'

Sarah looked about her. 'Erm, the bees and butterflies wouldn't be able to collect any nectar and they'd die of hunger.'

'Oh,' Mary said. 'Oh, no! I'll never pick another flower. Ever!' she said emphatically.

Ellen glanced round. 'I have an idea,' she said. 'Let's sit down and have our picnic and then we'll make daisy chains, cos I can see daisies, and as there are so many and they grow wild on the grass we can pick those before the gardener comes along with his cutter and cuts off their heads.'

Mary ran off to chase everyone up and Ellen smiled at Harry, who had parked himself on the grass and started to pick the daisies, slitting the green stalk with his thumbnail and sliding another stalk through it.

'I can remember my sisters teaching me to do this when I was just a nipper,' he said, 'and then I taught Meg and Polly. It seems like a long time since we saw our families, doesn't it? We've had some ups and downs since we came to live in Hull.'

'We have,' she agreed, 'but things are getting better. We've got a lovely little house and you're on 'mend now and will soon be back at work. I can cook proper dinners in my oven and 'children are happy. Life is just about perfect.'

They enjoyed their picnic and made their daisy chains and all of them, including Harry and the boys, walked home with garlands of daisies in their hair, with Mary and Zophia each clutching a bunch of wilting dandelions.

'What a lovely afternoon it's been.' Ellen took hold of Harry's hand again as they walked. 'We must do it again before you go back to work. The children are growing so fast, and we

291

must mek good use of this time, before they leave childhood behind.'

The meeting was held in Tannerson's office. Lizzie's desk was moved further back, leaving just enough room for her to sit behind it and make notes. Kirkwood and Filip brought up a wooden bench for themselves and Harry, and Tannerson had his own chair which he placed at the side of Lizzie's desk.

When they were all settled, Lizzie provided them with note-paper and pencils so that they could jot down any questions or ideas that occurred to them; then Tannerson stood up and thanked them for coming to the inaugural meeting regarding the restructuring of Tannerson and Partner.

'This is only an informal gathering,' he began, 'but I would like to think that the people here today might be at the core of such meetings in the future. Harry Randell already knows Filip Bosco, but Jack Kirkwood doesn't.' The two men bent forward to acknowledge each other.

'The work to begin clearing the site will begin next week, and the faster it is done the sooner we can make a start on building at least the shell of the new structure; a poster will go up on the gates from tomorrow asking for reliable labourers. The rubble and waste will be sold and used for the extension of Victoria Dock and the resiting and extension of railway lines, and the price received will go towards the new mill. This is an exciting time in England's history of industry, and although we have been beset by disaster I hope we can turn our adversity into great success.

'I've been consulting with engineer Bosco, who has been conferring with others on the suitability of various new hydraulic presses, with the possibility of purchasing these machines from Rose Down and company who will build them according to our specification; you will know, Kirkwood, that they are a long-standing and well-thought-of company.'

Kirkwood nodded in response and Tannerson went on. 'If all goes to plan as I hope it will, there will be many changes within the company; too much was left to chance previously, and familiarity bred contempt.'

292

Harry breathed in and out; he had known it for months.

'Which possibly led to fatalities in the workplace,' Tannerson went on. 'However, I do not choose to parcel out blame. As owner of this company the responsibility rests with me entirely.'

Kirkwood shifted on the bench as if he were about to say something, but then changed his mind.

'Filip Bosco is an independent engineer, but if he is in agreement I will discuss a contract with him and he will fit and subsequently arrange a regular servicing of the new machinery, by him or some other company that he would recommend.'

Harry now heard Filip draw in a breath; this obviously was what he had been hoping for. It would be a good foundation on which to build.

'Jack Kirkwood has been with this company since the days of the original Tannerson and his daughter, my late wife, who like Mr Rose's daughter ran their company efficiently and profitably. I'd like to offer you, Kirkwood, the position of foreman; you know the work and the processes, and I'd give you the opportunity of choosing the men who you think would enhance the company without fear or favour.'

Harry glanced at Kirkwood. He barely knew him, but he seemed to grow in stature at Tannerson's words.

'Mrs Robson has proved to be a most efficient secretary with a keen head for procedure, and she has agreed to continue in the post.'

Harry saw the flush on Lizzie's cheeks and wondered if she was being offered more than Tannerson was saying here.

'I had also invited the carpenter Karl Kidman to the meeting, but he declined my proposal as he is about to launch his own company. However, he will be pleased to offer his services if they should be required, as I'm sure they will be.

'And finally, because I think he has a good sensible head on his shoulders, I would like to make Harry Randell, if he is willing to take on the responsibility, manager and buyer. He is the newest employee in the company and as yet is not fully conversant with the inner workings of the hydraulic

293

seed-pressing industry; nevertheless, he knows about grain and seed, having grown up and worked with it all his life, and he was the first to notice that we might have a problem with combustion before the disastrous fire.' Tannerson gave a slight nod in Harry's direction before continuing. 'He perhaps didn't realize that I had also noticed that he is efficient and organized. If you're willing to take this position, Randell, I will ask a neighbouring company to initiate you into the practical industry of seed-crushing and pressing without any cost to them, before our new company begins production.'

Harry swallowed; it was more than he could possibly have dreamed of, and it meant that he could start almost immediately to watch and learn with another company. He cast a glance at Lizzie, who turned her head and slowly closed one eye.

'Just one more item before we finish this meeting, for there will be others, but I would like to put it to you that I'd be grateful if you would be willing to form a working committee, so that once the new company is in production we can discuss any problems or future opportunities. Mrs Robson has agreed to be committee secretary and will take your notes and suggestions to be discussed at a later date.'

A local grocer brought in a box containing plates of beef, ham and cheese and warm bread rolls and Lizzie made coffee on a paraffin stove set safely in the corner of the room, and as the men ate they talked informally yet decisively and eagerly about such things as hydraulic cylinders, compressive forces, steam engines, pumps, pistons and pipes; Filip seemed totally fired up, answering all of Kirkwood's enthusiastic questions as to what type of machinery he would be recommending.

When the discussion rolled to an end and notes had been made on questions to be asked or referred to, Kirkwood stood up to speak. 'I'd like to thank you, Mr Tannerson, for this opportunity, not only for myself but on behalf of other men who have previously worked for this company who would like to come back; aye, and some new ones too. There were many men thrown out

294

of work when Kingston Cotton Mill closed and it's a chance for them and this company to prove that we're more than capable of future success.'

He seemed choked up with emotion, but went on, 'If you're willing, sir, I'd like to begin wi' three teams of men working in different areas and put a capable and responsible team leader at 'head of each of them. I'll mek a plan and discuss it with Mr Randell once we're closer to being up and running.'

Tannerson thanked him for his support, and told them that at the next meeting they would make the formal arrangements to form a working committee. 'I'd like to assure you all that there will be no financial input required from any of you, but the prospect of future bonuses for those of you working full time will be considered at a later date. Thank you, gentlemen – and lady.' He turned to Lizzie, who smiled. 'I appreciate your time today.'

Filip offered Harry a lift to Queen's Road as he was heading that way. He had bought a second-hand trap and an old mare which he was stabling near his house. 'You must come to us for supper now that we are in our new home, and bring children too. I will tell Anna that is what we will do.'

Harry smiled and thanked him. Filip obviously hadn't yet been told that their wives had already arranged an early evening supper at the new house. They were to share in the making of food and Anna had said she would ask Filip to collect them. That's how it works, he mused. Men think that they're in charge, but then we find that what we propose has already been agreed.

Look at Lizzie, he thought. A matter of weeks working for Tannerson and she's coming up with new ideas. He was quite convinced that it was she who had suggested a team of suitable men who could help Tannerson build up his company once more, rather than struggle on his own; and as for his own position, it would be perfect for him, especially until he got his full health and strength back.

But there was something else. Ellen was up to something. She had been trying out different types of flour when she made their

295

bread, white, dark, wheat, rye and oat, and asking him and the children what they thought of the taste and texture. Some they liked; others, like the dark flour containing bran which she said was cheaper, they didn't. Then she had said that there was something she wanted to discuss with him, Anna and Filip when they went to look at the Boscos' new house.

CHAPTER FORTY-FOUR

On the morning of Mr Tannerson's meeting, Ellen had walked home from her work on Beverley Road, seen that there was no queue at the grocer's shop, and decided to call in and have a word with Mr Foster. He was standing at the top of a pair of wooden steps restocking shelves. He looked down as the doorbell clanged and turned to step down.

'No hurry, Mr Foster,' Ellen said, 'though I'll have a small bag of bicarbonate of soda whilst you're up there, please.'

She noticed that he had the lightweight produce on the top shelves and the heavier goods at the bottom. At the front of the counter were sacks of potatoes and other root vegetables and boxes of broken biscuits with reduced tickets on them.

He brought down a tin from a lower shelf, scooped out a portion of the powder, weighed it, and poured it into a paper bag. 'There you are, Mrs Randell. Can I get anything else for you?'

She was pleased that he had remembered her name; it was important to customers, she thought. 'As a matter of fact, I wanted to ask you something,' she said.

'Not a loan, is it?' She saw he wasn't serious by the twinkle in his eyes, but he glanced significantly at the notice on the wall behind him, and she followed his gaze. *Sorry, No Credit.*

She laughed. 'No. *Neither a lender nor a borrower be.* My ma and da taught us that.'

297

'Mine too. Comes from Shakespeare, so I understand. Not that we had much to lend in any case, but neither did we borrow. So what was it you wanted to ask, m'dear?'

'You said you had ovens at 'back of your shop that weren't in use.'

'Not since my wife died,' he said, leaning his elbows on the counter. 'I'm no baker, and nobody's ever asked me if they could use them.'

'But if you were asked – if I and a friend asked you – how would you feel about it? Would you mind anybody else using them?'

'Why, no,' he said. 'There's no sentiment attached to a piece of cast iron that's taking up a great deal of space. In fact, if I'd had the time and energy I might have dismantled it and sold it for scrap.'

'There's just one, then?' she asked. 'I thought you'd said two?'

The doorbell clanged again and he looked up as someone came in. 'G'morning, Mrs Harris. How are you today?' He turned to Ellen. 'Take a look if you wish. Be careful you don't fall over anything back there. I've never had the heart to clear up, though I should.'

Ellen went through the narrow doorway and saw a steep staircase which, she guessed, would lead to his living quarters; in front of her was another door which opened into a dark and dusty room. A pair of old curtains shut out any light from the window behind them and she pulled them back, causing a scattering of dust but illuminating the contents of the room.

Filling all the space against the furthest wall, as Mr Foster had said, was a massive cast-iron cooking range with two ovens, one at each end, a door in the middle which she opened and saw was the fireplace for feeding in the coal, and a tall chimney above it going up through the ceiling. On top of the range was a long hot plate with a kettle perched on it as if about to boil.

'Oh!' She put her hand to her chest. She had never seen such a thing in her life. An army could have been fed from this cooking appliance. Attached to the range above the hot plate was a pierced metal shelf with tarnished copper pans set upon it.

298

She turned as she heard Mr Foster come in. 'Bit of a mess in here, I'm afraid. Don't know what my wife would think.'

'Oh, it wouldn't tek long to clear up, Mr Foster,' Ellen said, 'and it's such a waste not to use it. Where does 'chimney go?'

'There's a little box room above here with a fireplace, and then the main chimney stack.' He looked at her. 'So what would a young woman like you want with this old thing?'

'I'd bake bread. At least my friend and I would; she bakes better bread than I do. We could set up a business together if you'd be willing to sell it through your shop.

'Would you buy your flour from me?'

'We could probably buy it cheaper from 'flour mills, but I'm sure we could come to some arrangement.'

He put his head to one side and nodded. 'I quite like the idea of selling bread again,' he said. 'Folks used to smell it and come in, and then they'd buy other things too to spread on it, jam and marmalade and such, those who didn't make it.'

'I haven't made jam or marmalade since I came to live in Hull,' she told him, 'though I did when we were in 'country. Everybody did. But not everybody has a fruit garden or a cooking range either. It will still work, won't it? The range, I mean.'

'It would want cleaning, and the chimney might want sweeping, but yes, I think so.'

'My friend's husband is an engineer; he could check it to see if it's workable.' She felt a rush of enthusiasm. 'Could I – would you be willing, that is, for me to bring Anna to have a look at it?'

He looked at her and smiled. 'What work did you say you do at present?' he asked.

She pointed up the road towards the villas. 'I help with washing on a Monday and on two other days I scrub 'steps or scullery floors; I'll do anything I'm asked to as long as I'm home in time to see to 'children. My sister is staying with us at present so she washes and dresses them when they wake, and when I get home I prepare breakfast for them and my husband; I think I told you he'd been in hospital, but he's much better now.'

'You'd still have to get up very early to make bread,' he said.

299

'I know,' she said, 'but we could prove it 'night before. Isn't that what your wife did?'

'Come to think of it, that's right, she did.' His face broke into a grin. 'She'd be thrilled to think someone was using her precious range.' He wiped his eyes. 'She really would.'

'So could I bring Anna to look at it? And how much would you charge us to rent it, Mr Foster, and for selling 'bread? Neither of us has much money coming in yet, but we're hoping that Harry will be back at work soon, and her husband has got work already. He's very clever. They're Polish,' she added, 'and they haven't lived here for very long.'

It was quite a lot to explain, especially about the Boscos, but it needed to be said. Some people were prejudiced against foreigners.

'Well, shall we wait until your friend has seen it?' he suggested kindly. 'She might not like the idea. And maybe her husband would like to take a look at it too, as you say? It's a few years since it was in use. And I'd need to consider the scheme carefully too.'

'Oh, of course!' I'm getting carried away with the notion of it, she chastised herself; but it seems such a worthwhile venture and we must do something to bring money in until the men are able to. But then she began to have doubts. How would they finance a bakery? They'd need money for coal for one thing; then flour, baking bowls and accoutrements, for hers wouldn't do and she knew that Anna wouldn't have any either.

Oh, it's pie in the sky, she thought as she trudged home; I'm such a dreamer, and now I'm late and Lizzie will be worrying where I've got to. I won't mention it to Harry yet. He's got enough on his mind, wondering what this special meeting will mean for him.

As she walked along Queen's Road, she saw two ladies walking arm in arm towards her; she recognized them from the house at the end of her terrace. They hadn't yet spoken, though they had both politely nodded when they had seen her in the front garden. She had been outside telling Harry where she wanted carrot seed sowing on the tiny vegetable plot. All the old vegetation had been cleared before they moved in and the soil was ready for planting. It was too late for most seed, but she knew that carrots would survive, and in an old rusted bucket he had already planted a few green potatoes that had begun shooting and couldn't now be eaten. Waste not, want not, she'd said. She'd thought of what Mr Tannerson had said about poor people eating the green potatoes in Ireland and the tragedy that had ensued from it and told Harry about it.

The ladies were coming nearer. She thought they were probably sisters for they were very alike, both of slim build with fair skin and hair that was tucked neatly under prim bonnets, and she determined to speak to them. She said good morning and commented on the weather, to which they both murmured something, and then they chorused 'Good day to you' and moved on.

A few yards further on, she turned and saw them turning right on to Beverley Road. One of them turned her head slightly and looked back towards her.

Ah, well, she mused, not everyone wants to talk, but I've broken the ice. Maybe they'll speak another day. She wondered where they were going and if they had an occupation, for it was still early; and she tried to imagine what had brought them here to Mrs Lucan's property. Had they been subjected to difficulties too?'

Lizzie was putting on her coat as Ellen went in. 'Kettle's on 'boil,' she said, adjusting the scarf round her neck and putting on a velour hat. 'Harry's given 'children their porridge, but Thomas says he wants toast as well.'

'Thank you, Lizzie,' Ellen said gratefully.

'No, thank *you*, Ellen.' Lizzie plonked a kiss on her sister's cheek. 'My liberator.'

'What?' Ellen laughed. 'What does that mean?'

Lizzie tapped the side of her nose. 'You'll see.'

She called goodbye to the children and to Harry, saying she would see him at the office later, and went to the door. 'Must dash or I'll miss my lift and have to walk.' Mr Tannerson always waited for her in his trap at the top of Sculcoates Lane on the other side of the Beverley road.

301

Ellen followed her to the front door. 'It's a special day today, isn't it, Lizzie? Do you think everything will turn out the way we want it to?'

Lizzie turned and smiled at her. 'Don't worry, Ellen,' she told her. 'It will.'

CHAPTER FORTY-FIVE

Filip came to collect them to take them to their house and they all squashed into his trap; Lizzie too, as she had also been invited. Ellen was disturbed when he said it was too far for Harry to walk between the two houses at present, as she thought that if that were the case it would also be too far for Anna to walk to the proposed bakery. We've to think of the children; how can we possibly do this? She had previously thought they could take it in turns to have the children on different days; prove the dough in an evening and bake the following morning. It's not going to work, she thought miserably, and I really want it to.

The rooms in the house the Boscos were renting were in Margaret Street, off the Beverley road; it was a pleasant street, with only a few houses as yet but plans for future development, according to Filip. 'But it doesn't matter,' he said jovially. 'When I make my fortune we will move to a whole house and not just have a few rooms.'

He's very ambitious, Ellen thought, but there's nothing wrong with that; he's willing to work hard for what he wants, as we all are.

He and Harry, who was sitting at the front with him, were discussing the plans for Tannerson's, and Ellen could tell that Lizzie was listening to what they were saying, although she didn't comment.

'Lizzie,' Ellen said, trying to speak so quietly that only Lizzie could hear her over the chatter of the children and the rumble

303

of the wheels on the rough road. 'I keep meaning to ask; Harry said that Tannerson and Son's company name is to be changed to Tannerson and Partner.'

Lizzie nodded. 'So it is.'

'So has the partner's name been announced yet?'

Lizzie paused and then looked steadily at Ellen. 'Not yet it hasn't,' she responded. 'It will be. But not yet. It's too soon.'

Ellen held her gaze for a further few seconds before looking away. It had been a significant pause that Lizzie had chosen not to break, and Ellen allowed herself a little smile: her sister was shrewd and wise and imaginative; what better partner could Mr Tannerson need?

Anna was thrilled with her new house. They had the whole of the ground floor and the yard at the back, though they had to share the privy with their upstairs neighbour, who had access from the back of the property via a wooden outside staircase. She had an oven in her kitchen, and a scullery with a wash boiler set into a corner with a grate for a fire beneath it for wash days. They had only a small patch of garden at the front, but she said she didn't mind about that for she had lived all her life in a city and didn't know about growing things.

Ellen had brought fresh bread and coffee, Harry had brought a flagon of cider and Anna had made delicious chicken soup with dumplings. Edyta and Karl dropped in too and said they could only stay for an hour as Karl had some work to finish for a customer. Edyta looked more relaxed than they'd seen her for a while, and said they were planning their wedding. Afterwards they would live in Karl's present house until they found something more suitable.

When they had eaten and the children were playing board games, the conversation came round to the proposed new company. Harry said he thought he might walk to the mill on the coming Saturday and help to organize the bands of men who were bringing down the building. He was keen to get back to something like normality.

'Are you fit for that, Harry?' Lizzie asked. 'I'm sure that Mr Tannerson would appreciate your help and would collect you to

304

save you the walk. I'll be going in too on Saturday morning, but he won't expect you yet.'

'I won't go in once they start the demolition,' he said. His voice was still husky from the smoke of the fire. 'There'll be a lot of dust then; you might not want to be there either.'

'I won't,' she said. 'Mr Tannerson said I can use his home office if I prefer. It's in Jarratt Street, not far from Wincomlee, so I might do that.'

Her cheeks had a slight flush as she spoke, but she thought that only Ellen might notice.

Ellen, however, had other things on her mind. Hoping that bringing up the topic of the bakery might initiate practical ideas that she hadn't thought of herself, she said, 'Could I change the subject to one that I've been considering, which might interest Anna? Although, Anna, it might not be so convenient now that you've moved.'

She told them about Mr Foster and his shop and the cooking range in the back room and her idea of starting a bakery to try to earn a living until Harry was back working full time.

Harry took hold of her hand. 'Ellen, I'm so sorry that you've even had to think of such a thing. I feel as if I've failed you for a second time. Bringing you away from all you'd ever known in Holderness and now . . .' He shrugged despondently, words failing him.

'Harry, don't! Don't blame yourself. When have I ever complained about coming to Hull? We've met wonderful friends, we have a dear little house, the children are happy.' Emotion made her throat close up and her words were teary, and Harry frowned. 'What happened at 'mill wasn't your doing. Besides, things are changing for the good.'

She glanced round at everyone and then back to Harry. 'We've all had troubles in our lives and I think we, you and I, have been luckier than most, but 'thing is . . .' She sniffed. 'Thing is, I'd like to do this. I'm a good bread-maker, and if Mr Foster decides that we can rent his range I believe a success can be made of it. Everybody needs bread.'

'Oh, Ellen!' Anna said. 'That is such a wonderful idea, and I would have done this also with you. But,' she glanced at Filip, 'now I can't.'

305

'I realize that; it's totally impractical.' Ellen shook her head. 'It's too far to walk with 'children and one of us would always have to stay with them.'

Anna clasped her hands together. 'No!' Then she reached out to grasp Filip's extended hand and held it. 'No, that is not reason. Reason is that Filip and I make baby. An English baby!' she whispered, and tears glistened on her cheeks. 'Born in freedom.'

On the way home, with Filip driving and Harry beside him, Lizzie, with Mary on her knee while Ellen held Thomas and Sarah was squashed in between, turned to Ellen and said, 'I think you've had a brilliant idea, Ellen, and you should ask Filip to look at Mr Foster's cooking range.'

'I don't see how I can manage it,' Ellen objected. 'I can't take 'bairns with me. Can you imagine letting Thomas run amok whilst I'm baking in hot ovens! And,' she went on, half laughing, half miserable to her core, 'he'd be poking his fingers in 'dough!'

'You're a scamp, aren't you, Thomas?' Lizzie tickled her nephew's round belly as he curled up on his mother's knee. 'But it's going to be at least six months before the new mill is built so Harry can look after them when you're not there. He won't have to go in every day to 'other company that Roland mentioned, just mebbe for a few hours a couple of days each week, and you could get a young girl to mind them whilst he's out.'

Then she added flatly, 'You don't have to have them tied to your apron strings all of 'time, you know. You need your independence, as do they; they must learn that you have a life too and cope without you. It'll make them stronger.'

Ellen was lost for words. Lizzie made it sound so easy. 'I don't know any young girls,' she said weakly.

Lizzie looked at her. 'There's one living at 'cottage right opposite. I've seen her twice when I've been coming back from work.'

'Have you?' Ellen was astonished. Apart from the two sisters who lived at the bottom of the terrace, she hadn't seen anyone

306

else. When she went out in a morning and when she arrived back, most of the windows had their curtains closed.

'Yes,' Lizzie said. 'She's generally looking out of 'window as if she's waiting for someone.'

Filip drew up outside the terrace and he and Harry came to hand the family down from the back of the trap. Harry took a sleeping Thomas from Ellen and gave her his hand. She turned to Filip and asked diffidently, 'Would it be much of a bother for you to take a look at the ovens, Filip? Then if they're in too bad a state I can forget about it.'

'I will of course look at it for you,' he said. 'And you do not have to forget about it, Ellen, if it is what you want to do. Anna would have wanted to help you, but,' he gave a happy grin, 'soon we have four children.'

True to his word, he went to look at the range the very next day, and told Mr Foster that apart from surface cleaning and having the chimney swept, it was in excellent condition. 'It will make good bread,' he said. 'And keep your house upstairs warm.'

'It will,' Mr Foster agreed, rubbing his chin. 'At least, it always did. Well, we'll see if the little lady still wants it.'

Ellen told him of her predicament. How Anna couldn't come after all and how she would need to find someone to look after the children. He then suggested that she might look for someone to help her, not with the baking but with the washing up of the utensils and crockery.

'I've an errand lad,' he said. 'He delivers groceries locally, and he's got a sister who keeps asking me if I need an assistant in the shop. I don't have enough trade to warrant taking on anyone else, but she might be willing to come and help you.'

Ellen drew in a breath. Was this all getting out of hand? It made sense, but ... 'I don't think I could afford to pay anybody, Mr Foster,' she said. 'Whole point of doing this is to raise some much-needed money for essentials.'

'Yes, I realize that,' he said. 'Maybe when you're run off your feet by demand, then we could think of it, eh? I'll get the chimney swept anyway, and we'll go from there as soon as you've found somebody to help with the children.'

Harry had been contrite and apologetic whilst at the Bosco's and that night, when Lizzie had gone up to bed, he murmured, 'I feel I've let you down, Ellen. I swore to protect you and I feel I've failed.'

'How have you failed, Harry?' She put her arms round him. 'Nothing was your fault.' She realized that he still hadn't got over the shock of the accident, was still feeling insecure and probably doubtful of getting truly well again. 'But now you have this chance of creating a better life for us all. There's an opportunity of making 'kind of livelihood we never would have dreamed of.'

'I know,' he said. 'But it hasn't sunk in. The accident knocked me back, Ellen. I keep wondering if there was anything I could have done to prevent it.'

'If you're thinking that, Harry,' she murmured, 'how must Mr Tannerson be feeling?'

He was feeling very low, Lizzie knew. Although she had known him for such a short time, she felt she was as well acquainted with him as anyone, through spending most of their working days together. She hadn't known him before the accident, of course, but she had seen occasional glimpses of his former personality when he forgot momentarily about the disaster that had fallen not only on him, but on the men who had worked diligently and conscientiously for the company for many years; the company that had fallen into his lap because of his marriage to the daughter of the original Tannerson.

He had shown respect for her organizational abilities and original thinking, but she had noticed recently that he sometimes looked at her in a different way, not just as a secretary or note-taker but as if he were interested in other things about her; asking questions about her marriage to Albert and how long ago he had died. She had told him on their first meeting that she had been recently widowed, but now he was asking more specifically. But why?

She thought he would be easy prey for a man hunter because he was vulnerable; his confidence had been shattered by the realization that he had let things slide, that he had become

308

overwhelmed because he had no one to whom he could turn for advice and assistance, as he had once turned to his wife, a strong woman by all accounts.

He was down in the yard now, talking to someone about the demolition work, and she got up from her desk to look out of the window. She didn't want to become only a partner, although a partnership was in the offing; he had said as much. She wanted more than that. Her life with Albert had been boring and predictable. One day was much like the last and would be the same as the next, and she had known when she married him that she didn't love him; she doubted that he had loved her. For some reason they had both wanted to change their lives but had found, too late, that they had made the wrong choice.

Now she wanted a challenge in her life, but she also wanted love, and she didn't know if it was possible to have both. She needed a strong man to match her sometimes cynical personality, to make her want to show her softer side; she had one, she knew that, but she kept it hidden from everyone, except perhaps from Ellen, who was more perceptive than most.

I'm as mixed up as he is, she thought, as she saw him turn and look up at the office. I don't want to be simply a shoulder to lean on whilst he is putting himself back together, only to be discarded when he has recovered. On the other hand, does he feel more than he is presently saying?

She turned back to her desk and threw her notebook across it. 'It's such a pain being a woman sometimes,' she said aloud. 'Look at Ellen, holding back on something she wants to do, telling herself that she only wants to do it to help the family finances, when it isn't true; in her heart, she wants to do it for herself, just to prove that she can.'

309

CHAPTER FORTY-SIX

It was true, there was a young girl living opposite. Ellen hadn't seen her or her mother before simply because she hadn't been looking, which isn't at all like me, she thought. Generally I'm aware of people around me. I've become wrapped up in my new house, looking after the children and Harry, and my domestic work.

Every morning on arriving home she changed from her work clothes into her house ones, and after having her own breakfast she started the household chores. She loved her cottage and kept it tidy, and this and cooking and baking in her new kitchen range kept her occupied. If it was a fine day, she and Harry took the children for a walk.

The following morning when she arrived home she made a point of sitting at the window with a cup of tea, noticing who was about and where they lived. And there she was: the young girl in the cottage opposite, opening the curtains and windows upstairs and down.

A boy, perhaps fifteen or sixteen, opened the front door and came out. He wore a black jacket and trousers, with the corner of a white handkerchief jutting from his pocket. His brown hair was slicked back from his wide forehead and his eyes stared straight in front of him as he came through the front gate and closed it carefully behind him. He carried a bowler hat, which Ellen thought strange for someone so young, and placed it carefully on his head.

She watched him walk straight-backed past their window until he reached the road, when he turned left and out of sight from his home, and then, oddest of all, he threw the bowler up in the air and gave a jump, kicking his heels as he caught it.

Ellen laughed out loud and Sarah came to find out why she was laughing. 'I've just seen a young man throwing his hat in the air,' she said. 'It looked so funny.'

'That was Robbie,' Sarah said. 'Julia's brother. He does it every morning.'

Ellen turned to Sarah; the child was very perceptive. 'Who is Julia?' she asked.

'She lives there.' Sarah pointed to the cottage opposite. 'She's a grown-up girl, older than us. The house with the little cat. Her mother won't let her bring her in, cos she's having babies and might make a mess. I said we'd have one of them when she gets them and that you wouldn't mind.'

'Oh, and how do you know about this? Have you spoken to Julia?'

Sarah nodded, and then Mary came to join in the conversation. 'We talk to her when her mama goes out in an afternoon. We stay inside our garden,' Mary added quickly, as they'd had instructions not to go out of the gate, ever, unless one of their parents was with them. 'The day she told us about the baby cats you were in 'kitchen and Dada was asleep in 'chair. And Thomas was as well, on his knee.'

'Kittens,' Ellen said automatically. 'Baby cats are called kittens. I see. And where is Robbie going when he throws his hat in the air?'

'To work,' Sarah said.

'In a h'office,' Mary added, not to be outdone. 'But he doesn't like it. It's just that his mama says he has to, cos his dada who's gone to heaven used to work there and said he had to.'

Well, my goodness, Ellen thought. Such a lot of information from my observant children. I must look out for Julia. 'Is she nice?' she asked. 'Julia?'

'She's very nice,' Sarah said solemnly. 'We asked her if she'd like to come in and play wi' us, but she said better not as she

311

hadn't been invited. We said we'd invite her but she said it had to be a grown-up person.'

'Well, next time you see her you may ask her again, and then come and ask me or Dada.' She smiled. 'Would you like that?'

'Yes, please,' they chorused.

'You were right, Lizzie,' Ellen said later when her sister arrived home. 'There is a young girl living opposite, I haven't met her yet, but Sarah and Mary have. She's called Julia, apparently, and lives with her mother and brother Robbie who works in an office and doesn't like it. Oh, and their cat is having kittens and 'girls have put in an order for one.'

'Really?' Lizzie laughed. 'There you are, then. Out of the mouths of babes – you might have found your perfect person for looking after them.'

Ellen nodded. 'I'll still need money to start up, though – I'm not putting obstacles in the way,' she said hastily. 'I mean it. Wood and coal have to be paid for – and flour and lard.'

Lizzie sighed. 'Why don't you use your cleaning money strictly for those things, and pay 'rent out of Harry's wages?' She held up a letter addressed to Harry. 'Insurers have given an indication of 'compensation. Where is he?'

Ellen's eyes glowed. 'He's gone up to Mr Foster's to look at 'range. He hasn't seen it yet and 'other night I told him how much I'd like to do this if we can manage. So he's gone to introduce himself and tek a look at it. I have to have his support, Lizzie, otherwise there's no point in going ahead.'

'I'd like to have a look at it too, Ellen,' Lizzie observed. Slightly hesitantly, she added, 'And although strictly I shouldn't say so, you will be able to afford it.'

Ellen ran her tongue around her lips, which seemed to have suddenly gone dry. 'If what you might be hinting is that we could manage without me setting this up after all—'

Lizzie's expression was impassive. 'The mill will probably take at least six months to build and I don't know how long to fit and set up machinery and equipment; it's not within my knowledge. But you might be looking at twelve months all told.'

312

'I could have made a ton of bread in that time,' Ellen pointed out.

Lizzie nodded. 'And scones and cakes on 'residual heat?'

'Yes!' Ellen whooped. 'Those too.'

'You thought that all you wanted was a house with an oven to cook your family meals!'

'I did,' she agreed. 'I do, and I've got it; but it's all right to want something else as well, isn't it?'

'Of course it is.' Lizzie opened her arms wide. 'Come here and give your sister a big hug. I'm so proud of you, Ellen.'

'I haven't done anything yet.' Ellen's voice was muffled on Lizzie's shoulder.

Lizzie held her at arms' length. 'But you will, Ellen, you will.'

When Harry returned from seeing the grocer he had a big grin on his face. 'Incredible,' he said. 'It's an ancient cooker but an extremely well made piece of ironwork. Bill Foster's really keen on seeing it working again. Sweep's coming early tomorrow morning, and what's more – did he show you 'coal shed, Ellen?'

She was reeling, not only from Harry's response but from the fact that the grocer had set her proposal in motion by arranging the sweep so swiftly. Perhaps in case she changed her mind? She shook her head in answer to Harry's question; she hadn't been out at the back of the shop.

'Well, there's this massive brick-built coal shed in 'back yard next to 'privy,' he said, 'and there's a couple of tons of coal in there; apparently they'd just had a delivery when his wife became ill and he's hardly used any since as he doesn't make a fire in his rooms until late afternoon. So he said 'coal might as well be used and as soon as 'sweep's been he'll make a small fire under 'ovens to test them out!'

Ellen's mouth dropped open. 'But nothing's been settled, not 'price he's going to charge for renting 'range or how much bread he'll sell for us, or anything.'

'Mebbe you'll both need a couple of weeks to work out a plan, Ellen,' Lizzie suggested. 'He'll have some thoughts about it from

313

when his wife was alive: how much demand there was and how fast you can turn the bread out. You could do a trial run.'

Ellen thought of how flustered Mrs Brownlee had been the first time she went into her bakery shop, but she was baking and selling single-handed until Anna stepped in to help her. I'll only be baking, she thought, and I'll do the bulk of it early; I won't have to sell it over the counter. Mr Foster will do that.

Harry slipped his arms round her. He seemed quite animated. 'You're so clever to come up with the idea. I admit I was uneasy about it to begin with and I thought it would be too difficult to organize, but now – well, it's just tremendous, Ellen, and I'll be able to help with 'children until I'm back at work full time.'

Over his shoulder Ellen saw Lizzie raise her eyebrows, and the expression on her face shouted *What did I say?*

'And did Bill Foster tell you about 'reason he came to this area from Australia,' Harry asked.

'Erm, yes.' Ellen's mind was in a whirl as she mentally began to plan the project. 'His forebears came from somewhere round here,' she said vaguely. 'Somewhere in Hull, he said.'

'Aye,' he said. 'That was a generation before, but somehow they finished up in Holderness and Foster's great-grandfather – I think that's what he said – upped sticks from there and emigrated to Australia. Are you listening to what I'm saying, Ellen? Lizzie, are you? What was your ma's name before she wed your da?'

Harry's gaze swept Ellen's expression of bewilderment and then Lizzie's of dawning enlightenment.

'Foster,' she cried. 'We're related!'

The next morning Ellen traipsed sleepily down Queen's Road towards Beverley Road to begin her morning chores. She could see a sweep's brush above the chimney tops and as she turned the corner she saw it was over Bill Foster's shuttered shop and was immediately enlivened. It was happening. Neither she nor Harry had slept well; Harry had opened the letter that Lizzie had brought home and after reading the contents was completely speechless and handed it over to Ellen instead.

314

'What does it mean?' she whispered after reading it, and looked at Lizzie, who shook her head. It was not for discussion with her, she was saying, except she remarked to Harry, 'Don't forget it has to last you until you're back at work and earning again.' She smiled. They were not spendthrifts, and it would last them for a long time. It would put them firmly on their feet. This was not to replace lost earnings; those would still be paid. Tannerson had promised. This was compensation for Harry's injuries and some scars that would stay with him for life.

So many things were rushing through Ellen's head during the night and she tossed about so much that she was glad to get up, get dressed and make herself tea and toast before leaving the house. Harry slept on, completely exhausted but free at last of worry for their immediate future.

She was early and therefore earlier finishing her work; she gave in her notice, explaining that family circumstances prohibited her from continuing, and walking back along the road she saw smoke coming from the chimney above the shop. The door opened and Bill Foster came out carrying a trestle table, then brought out crates of produce to arrange in front of the window before returning inside again and bringing out sacks of vegetables.

She crossed the road and walked towards him. 'Good morning, Mr Foster,' she called. 'I see you have a good fire going this morning.'

He put down another sack. 'G'morning, Mrs Randell.' He grinned. 'Yes, I'm trying out a small fire and it's burning well. The ovens are getting hot already.'

'May I have a look? And as we seem to be related, would you care to call me Ellen?'

He put his hands on his hips. 'Now isn't that a coincidence? But yes, come along in, Ellen, and you can see the ovens for yourself.'

'It's my mother who was a Foster,' she explained as she followed him inside. 'She's a Snowden now, but she has brothers who are Fosters, and *my* brother is named Billy, 'same as you!'

315

'Well, isn't that the oddest thing.' He went on talking as he led her through the shop. 'I'm Mark William,' he disclosed, 'though I've always been known as Bill Foster. And come to think of it, one of my nieces is called Ellen. Now,' he said, his arms outstretched to show her the gleaming range, 'isn't she the loveliest thing?'

Ellen agreed. The range had been scrubbed and polished, and probably black leaded, she thought, for it gleamed as if it had been buffed and burnished, and the formerly tarnished copper pans now shone so brightly that she was sure she could have seen her reflection in them.

'I even boiled the billy on the hob this morning,' he told her. 'I scrubbed it out first and threw out the first lot of water, then boiled it again and made a pot of tea. Perfect. Saved me lighting my little oil stove.'

'It's wonderful,' she said. 'I'm so excited. I can't wait to start the first batch of bread.'

'Well, whenever you want,' he said. 'I'll leave it fired up today and then let the fire out until you're ready to give it a try. If you'll excuse me now, my early customers will be along soon and I need to get set up, but stay as long as you like. I found some earthenware pancheons in a cupboard, by the way,' he added. 'There are some cream ones and some that are red on the outside and cream on the inside. You'll know what their use is, I expect, but I've washed them and put them in a cupboard, which I've also washed out, as you'll see. I've been pretty busy.' He laughed, and Ellen thought he'd probably enjoyed bringing out all his wife's baking utensils and giving them a purpose again.

'One type is for mixing and kneading,' she said. 'And the other will be for proving.'

'Well, if you say so, Ellen.' He lifted a finger and hurried away into the shop, and she warmed to him for the effort he had made.

She had a look around. Everything in the cupboards had been scrubbed clean and stacked tidily, the floor had been swept and washed, the wooden table in the centre of the room had been scrubbed almost white and the ovens were belting out heat; she took off her shawl and folded it up to make a pad for her hand

316

and carefully opened one of the oven doors. It was just right for baking bread. She bent down to close up the vents beneath the ovens and stop the fire drawing so much, and made a quick decision.

She went back into the shop, where he was setting up the counter, putting out boxes of sweets and jars of barley sugar. 'Is it all right if I come back?' she asked, her heart thumping in excitement. 'I'm going to make some soda bread. Just to try it out. It doesn't need to rise or prove; I can mix it and put it straight into 'oven.'

'Right you are,' he said cheerfully. 'Just as you please.'

CHAPTER FORTY-SEVEN

A customer came into the shop just as Ellen was bringing out the first batch of soda bread and placing it on a wire rack on the table; the smell of baking was drifting through.

'Can I smell bread, Mr Foster?' the woman asked. 'Are you baking again?'

'We're trying out the ovens, Mrs Sharp, with a view to possibly baking bread again.'

'Put my name down for a regular order if you do, please. I can't bake like I used to,' Mrs Sharp replied. 'My hands are racked with rheumatism. I don't suppose I could try some now?'

'I'll ask,' he said, grinning, and went through to the back to ask the question.

Ellen beamed with delight. She thought that the soda bread was just right, light and fluffy on the inside and a golden crust with a cross scored on top. 'She can certainly try it,' she said, 'and give her opinion. Tell her that it won't keep. It needs to be eaten today.'

He smacked his lips. 'I'm sure that won't be difficult. It smells superb! Will there be enough for me to try?' he asked, and she laughed and said there would be.

'Why don't you go through and introduce yourself?' he suggested. 'Customers do like to know who's baking for them.'

So she dusted her hands of flour and went through to make herself known to her first customer and put the loaf in a paper bag, with her compliments.

318

'Why, you're just a slip of a girl,' Mrs Sharp exclaimed. 'Your mother must have taught you to bake.'

'She did,' Ellen said. 'But I've been baking since I was twelve. I'm also 'mother to three children, so I'm not a girl any more.'

Mrs Sharp put her nose to the bag and breathed in the aroma. 'Delicious,' she declared. 'You've been well taught. Mr Foster, I'd better have an extra pack of butter,' she told him. 'And a wedge of cheese. I'm feeling quite hungry.'

And so it began. Bill Foster was delighted with the response; he'd enjoyed a slice of soda bread and butter with a wedge of cheese too, just like Mrs Sharp. Ellen came back in the evening to mix white bread and brown and set them to prove, and next morning after baking she cut a few slices from each and Bill Foster put them out on the counter covered by muslin and invited his customers to try them. The comeback was encouraging, and every day that week she tried out different types of flour until customers were flocking to the door.

Anna came to look and brought some Polish recipes for Ellen to try using rye flour and caraway seed, and another sweetened with honey. 'For English taste,' she suggested, 'perhaps mix with wheat.'

Lizzie came to see the range and made suggestions for a working arrangement with Bill Foster, who was so easy-going he would have agreed to anything that brought customers to his shop. But most of all, Ellen was pleased that Harry was delighted with her success.

'I could mebbe retire and never work again,' he joked. 'My industrious wife can keep me in 'lap of luxury.'

She knew he was joking, of course, and within a month he was invited to join the company Tannerson had approached, who were going to acquaint him with the more complex aspects of seed-crushing and milling. He was ready, he told her. He felt much fitter now, and although he would always have scars they were mostly on his chest and under his arms, as he'd been thrown backwards off the ladder and the river water had doused his burning clothes within seconds.

He was an apt student and asked many questions about the technical side of the hydraulic conveying operation; about the grain and the risks and hazards of working with highly combustible products in an enclosed space, a subject he had been aware of only in the context of working in open fields during hay making or when harvesting corn.

'Venting seems to be the most important part of indoor procedure,' he said to Tannerson in his weekly meeting with him. 'As we know to our cost, closing them can be dangerous, especially where there's a lot of dust; and I've learned too that an old mill of brick and stone like Tannerson's contains any explosion within the building and so creates a fire, but if the cap and upper walls are of thinner material they will blow if there's a heat build-up, thus saving the rest of the building and possibly lives as well.'

'Write a report, will you, Harry?' Tannerson suggested. 'Any information is valuable.'

Ellen had obtained permission from Julia Brown's mother for her daughter to come and play with the children a few times a week, and once Ellen knew the girl was trustworthy and sensible she asked Mrs Brown if she would allow her to look after them occasionally whilst she was at the bakery and Harry at the mill. Mrs Brown hummed and hawed and said that Julia was 'delicate', and she wasn't sure if she could manage to control three children.

At thirteen Julia was a strapping girl, and she had already told Ellen that as she assisted her mother with chores around the house and helped her brother with his studies in an evening, she hadn't been able to work out how it was that she came to be considered delicate when she was never ill.

By judicious enquiry, Ellen discovered that it was the late Mr Brown who had laid down the rules. His son Robbie had been enrolled as a junior clerk where Mr Brown had been employed since he too was a young man. Perhaps, Harry suggested to Ellen, Mr Brown senior had been disappointed that he was still only a clerk after thirty years, and thought that his son might have more success.

320

'You could be right,' Ellen declared, 'and it seems that Mrs Brown is still obeying his directions whereas what Robbie would really like is to be an engineer and get his hands greasy with machine oil. Do you think that Filip might like an apprentice?'

As for Julia, her father had decreed that she must stay at home and be a genteel companion to her mother rather than start to earn a living and bring in much-needed funds, which is why they had been offered the cottage on his death two years before. She was much too hearty to be genteel, Ellen thought, and as she was jolly and willing to play children's games would be a perfect companion for the children.

Mrs Brown agreed to allow Julia to come on two afternoons, and since it meant that she didn't have to rush home from her assignation with a long-time male friend, it worked perfectly. Soon Julia was coming every day, receiving a small wage that made her feel worthwhile.

'I must write to Ma,' Ellen commented to Lizzie one Sunday. 'She must wonder what we're up to. Perhaps Billy will bring her and we can show her 'bakery.'

Lizzie nodded. 'I was thinking 'same, and I'll show her where I work. Or at least where I will work when 'mill is built.'

Work had started. The old mill had been demolished, the waste disposed of, and the site was in the process of being prepared for the new building. Lizzie was still working in Tannerson's home office. Ellen had wondered what she had to do when there was no production at present, but Lizzie said there was plenty of note-taking, not only from Mr Tannerson but the engineers too. She confessed to being a martinet for recording notes on every little thing that had been discussed or agreed to.

'Mr Tannerson must bless 'day that you started working for him,' Ellen commented. 'He must wonder how he ever managed without you.'

There was such a long and silent pause that Ellen looked up and saw a small smile on her sister's face. 'He does,' Lizzie murmured, and turned to face her.

Ellen waited; Lizzie could be so annoying sometimes. She never blurted out spontaneous thoughts, but always seemed to

321

be weighing up what reactions there might be to what she was about to say.

'Lizzie?' she exclaimed. 'Is it something momentous?'

Lizzie heaved out a breath. 'I rather think it might be, and I don't know whether I should defy convention and say yes now, or wait for a more appropriate time.'

Ellen's lips parted. 'Would it hurt anyone if you defied convention?'

Lizzie gazed up at the ceiling as if debating on the shape of it and listening to the chatter of Sarah and Mary upstairs in the bedroom. Her gaze then drifted outside to where Thomas was helping his father in the garden and holding up his muddy hands to show him. 'No, I don't think so,' she said. 'Not anybody who matters, anyway.'

Ellen sat back in her chair and picked up her knitting. She was making a white jacket and bonnet for Anna's expected baby. I'm not going to ask, she decided. She can confide in me in her own good time.

After a few minutes, Lizzie cleared her throat. 'Aren't you going to ask me?'

Ellen began another row. 'What?' she said. 'What am I supposed to ask you if I don't know what it is I'm expected to say? You were speaking of defying convention. What's that supposed to mean? Which convention?'

'The convention of not remarrying before finishing the allotted mourning time considered proper for widows.'

'Since when have you ever considered that personal matters are anything to do with anybody else?' Suddenly, Ellen dropped her work. '*What?* Lizzie!'

She jumped to her feet, scattering wool and needles, and put out her arms. 'Oh, Lizzie! Has he asked you? Mr Tannerson – oh, should I start calling him Roland?'

She pulled Lizzie out of her chair and hugged her. 'Oh, *dearest* sister. I am so pleased, thrilled, delighted for you.' She kissed her cheek and hugged her again. 'Are you happy?'

Lizzie put her head back and laughed. 'I rather think I am!'

322

CHAPTER FORTY-EIGHT

Harry, being careful with finances, bought an old trap with his compensation money and asked Karl Kidman if he would make it serviceable for him, which he did; he then asked Roland Tannerson if he would let him have the use of Nellie, and in return he'd exercise the other horses every evening. Tannerson was feeding them himself, but no one was exercising them regularly. There was a field at the top of Queen's Road, just off Mucky Peg Lane, and Harry had enquired if he might be allowed to graze a docile old mare on it. There was a shack there too where she could shelter and room enough to secure the trap.

'Look at you,' Ellen wryly joked one day when he arrived back from his session at the other mill. 'Proper gentleman of means.'

'With my second-hand cart and old nag I certainly am.' He laughed. 'I've had such an interesting day, Ellen. We've talked about ductwork and valves and prevention of dust explosions; and aerating grain heaps to prevent self-heating . . .'

'Which you knew already!' Ellen interrupted.

'I did,' he agreed. 'But out in 'fields you can smell it and see 'smoke rising. It's quite different in a factory environment.'

'I'm so glad that you're happy.' She gave him a gentle squeeze. 'Who'd have thought that something good would come out of such a terrible disaster?'

'I know,' he said seriously. 'Those poor young lads. I think about them every day, Ellen, and I was wondering – well, it's not up to me. I'm onny an employee after all, but . . .'

323

'What?' She was about to set the table for their meal, but she stopped what she was doing. 'Say it!'

'Well, you know 'other day when you said about Filip offering that young Robbie an apprenticeship? I know you were onny joking, but it set me thinking, and – Ellen, do you think that Roland Tannerson would consider offering an apprenticeship to a young lad from 'workhouse in 'name of the two lads who died?'

Ellen's eyes were moist as she stood with the tablecloth in her hands. 'Oh, Harry,' she breathed. 'That's 'nicest thought anybody could have. It'd be a memorial to them, wouldn't it?'

And not only that, she thought, but it might ease the lingering guilt that still plagued not only Harry, but Roland Tannerson too, and probably some of the men who had known Jim Smith and had not cared enough to worry that there was another boy in a place where he shouldn't have been. 'You'll ask him, won't you?'

Harry saw the profound relief in Roland Tannerson's expression when he made the suggestion: a palpable deliverance from guilt and an assurance that he could make amends. 'What—' Tannerson swallowed. 'What a magnificent idea, Harry.'

He put his hand to his chin as he thought about it. 'It could be set up as a regular apprenticeship – the Smith and Dent apprenticeship scheme.' His voice trembled as he spoke, and Lizzie, who was back at her own desk, looked up at the two men who were so obviously emotionally affected.

'I'll look into it, shall I?' she said softly. 'I'll write and make an appointment for you to meet 'workhouse governors.'

Tannerson nodded. 'Please, Lizzie. If you will. For both of us,' he added hoarsely. 'Harry too. It's his idea.' He put out his hand to shake Harry's. 'We're going to make a good team.'

When Harry left the office he offered Lizzie a ride home but she said she still had odds and ends to finish off. The office had been cleaned and painted, Karl Kidman had made and fitted new cupboards and drawers exactly as Lizzie had specified, and she was organizing a new filing system.

Karl had told her that he and Edyta had booked the register office for their wedding ceremony with only her mother, her brother and his wife present, but there would be a party afterwards in a local hotel when all their friends would be invited.

She said she was very happy for him, but didn't mention her own forthcoming marriage. So far she had only told Ellen and Harry and had yet to tell her parents that Roland Tannerson had proposed and been accepted. Seeing his response to a suggestion that might put it in his power to improve someone else's life, she knew without a doubt that here was a man with love in his heart who could undoubtedly love her too, and he'd vowed that he would.

'Billy's coming tomorrow,' Ellen said, excited as a schoolgirl when Harry arrived home, 'and he's bringing my ma and da, and Florence too. I think it must be serious, Harry; I've never known him court a young woman for so long. As soon as he thought they had their eyes on marriage, he always backed away.'

Harry knew that that was because of Billy's plan to emigrate to Canada, but he'd never told Ellen, because somehow he'd thought that Billy wouldn't carry the plan through. He was convinced that Billy wouldn't want to leave his family. But he's in a dead end job, he'd thought; he'll never improve his position in the work he's doing. Harry hadn't realized either just how many opportunities there were, until he'd been forced into a position where he had to open his eyes to other prospects.

They all came the next day, Billy having borrowed the wagon again, and Ellen's father, who hadn't seen the previous room in Wincomlee, exclaimed in astonishment at the pretty cottage and its situation.

'Why, it's almost 'country, but not quite,' her mother agreed, 'and close enough to 'town. An agreeable walk on a nice day, I should think. Billy showed us round some of it on 'way here; we saw two fine churches and what looked like a good market. I do like a good market,' she said, putting her head into the kitchen and nodding her approval. 'Now then, Harry,' she went

325

on, looking him over critically, 'Have you got over that spot of bother? Back at work now, are you?'

'Part time, Ma Snowden.' He grinned, without going into detail, and knowing she would show no outward compassion even though thinking of him kindly. 'Got a living to earn, you know.'

'Quite right.' Sitting down, she folded her arms and said, 'Now then, our Ellen, and you, Lizzie, what's this I'm hearing? One a baker lass, and one a secker-tery?'

'I'll make 'tea, Ma,' Lizzie said, nervous of her mother's response. Her father would no doubt nod off in a chair whilst his womenfolk were talking. 'Ellen will tell you what she's been doing.'

The children sat cross-legged on the floor looking at their grandmother, the two girls with their arms folded and Thomas staring up at her. They knew they would come under scrutiny too and so were on their best behaviour, hoping that there might be a treat in store.

'I'd like you to come and see it, Ma,' Ellen told her when she'd finished explaining about the bakery. 'I told Bill Foster you were coming and he said he'd like to meet you.'

Ma Snowden nodded her head. 'I suppose we could fit him in afore we return home, couldn't we, Mr Snowden?' She raised her voice to include her husband and stop him from falling asleep.

'Aye, I expect so,' he grunted and sat up straighter. 'If you say so. I expect you'd be right,' he added, and Ellen smiled, knowing that he hadn't heard a word.

Lizzie brought in a tray of tea and her mother looked her up and down. 'I'm pleased to see you mekkin' yourself useful, our Lizzie. Now you sit here next to me and tell me what you will while Ellen pours 'tea.'

Ellen and Lizzie both pressed their lips together to hide their laughter. Their mother expected all her daughters from the eldest to the youngest to be stoic young women under any circumstances, but she alone could treat them as children who would benefit from her advice; and they reluctantly acknowledged, though not within her hearing, that she was generally right.

326

She looked at Lizzie now, weighing her up critically. 'You've got a brighter look in your eyes, Lizzie. Hull seems to suit you.'

'I've got an interesting job, Ma, and I'm respected for what I do.'

'Aye, well, you allus had a brain; you just didn't get 'chance to use it afore. You're working in 'office where Harry works – or will work when it's built – as I understand it from your letters?'

Lizzie swallowed. 'That's right.' She wondered how her parents would take the news of her marriage so soon after Albert's death. Or how her mother would, at least; her father always treated his daughters fondly, even if he grumbled at having more daughters than sons.

'I work with the owner,' she said, 'Roland Tannerson, as I've mentioned. There are going to be a lot of changes when 'mill is up and running; a new company set up, new management, with Harry included in that, and 'workforce will be represented too, as they'll be affected in their everyday working lives.'

Mrs Snowden gave a little frown. 'What? An employer taking into account his workers' suggestions, d'you mean?'

'Yes,' she said. 'They're going to have a working committee.'

'Never heard o' such a thing!' She folded her arms and sat up straight. 'I'd like to meet a man o' business wi' thought for his employees. He's done all right by you, hasn't he, Harry?'

Harry answered that he had, giving Lizzie the chance to glance at Ellen, who nodded furiously as if to say there'd never be a better opportunity than this one.

'You'll be able to meet him, Ma, and you too, Da.' She'd noticed that her father was now listening intently. 'He's going to call in' – she glanced at the clock on the wall – 'in about half an hour.'

'Call in? Call in here?' Her mother looked about her and her glance fell on the children. She gazed at them and then took a sip of tea. Keeping her eyes on them, she said, 'I think there's more to this than what's been said. What do you think?'

Sarah and Mary nodded solemnly, and Thomas got up and stood in front of her. 'I know,' he whispered.

'Do you?' His grandmother looked at him. 'And is it a secret?'

He nodded, pressing his lips together.

'And you do know, don't you, that if someone tells you a secret you've never to tell *anyone* what it is? Regardless of who's asking?'

Thomas nodded again, and said, 'That's why I'm not going to tell you.' He leaned towards her and in a breathy whisper that they could all hear said, 'But I think it's *cake* and it's in your basket in 'kitchen.'

Ma Snowden tapped her mouth with her finger conspiratorially, then turned to Lizzie and said, 'I don't suppose he's coming to discuss business matters wi' us, Lizzie, and as you're of an age and experience to do as you wish, I gather that he's coming as a matter of courtesy to your parents rather than for our approval.'

Lizzie wondered how on earth her mother could have guessed, when her own regular letters gave nothing away except details of her daily work. But she knew, all right; she could tell from the knowing glance that took them all in: Harry's grin, Ellen's happy smile, and her own – what? What signals was she giving that said that the man who had asked her to marry him was coming to meet her parents, who when she said there was no need had replied that there was every need, and what's more he wanted to; he already knew Ellen and Harry and the children, had met Billy and Florence. One unknown only, her mother and father, and then she realized why.

His own father had denied him, his sisters and brothers were lost to him, he had no children from his former marriage, which he had told her was in name only because that was how his wife, older than him, had wanted it; he was ready now to embrace her family and their own.

'Come here, then, Lizzie,' her mother said softly. 'Come here and give your ma a kiss.'

She bent and kissed her mother on the cheek, and then did the same to her father, and as she straightened up she saw through the window that Roland, earlier than he'd said, was walking up the path towards them.

328

CHAPTER FORTY-NINE

Lizzie welcomed Roland at the door and murmured, 'It's going to be all right. Ma has guessed already that there's something in the wind. I think she's pleased, and Da will be, that's for sure.'

'I'll put on the Irish charm,' he said softly, and followed her into the parlour.

Lizzie's father was totally unprepared when Roland said he hoped he would be welcomed into the family when he and Lizzie were married, but her mother eyed him up and down and then floored him by saying that she hoped he'd treat Lizzie amiably, and although she didn't mention the late Albert, her meaning was clear.

'Our Lizzie will be an asset to you,' she told him. 'I hope you realize that? She's got a sensible head on her shoulders as well as a loving one and deserves someone good in her life, just 'same as her sisters and *eldest* brother have.'

She glanced critically at Billy during this remark; he was perched on the wide windowsill with Florence sitting next to him as they had run out of chairs. Billy cleared his throat and said, 'All right, if it's confession time, Florence and I have something to say too. You might have guessed that Florence is going to stay in my life; she's agreed to marry me, and that's summat I never really expected to happen.'

He clasped her hand, and added, 'Neither did I expect that she'd agree to 'plans I've had in my head for a lot o' years, and she's coming wi' me to Canada.'

329

There was a sudden gasp from both his parents, but like the stoic people they were they didn't oppose the announcement. Mr Snowden got to his feet and first shook hands with Roland Tannerson and then proffered a chaste kiss on Florence's cheek; then Billy stood up and bent to kiss his mother, giving her a hug, and moved away to allow Roland to take her hand and murmur that he would guard Lizzie with his love and his life. This must have had the right effect, for she suddenly had a mote in her eye and had to fish in her bag for a handkerchief to remove it.

Ellen decided that now was the time to make more tea and coffee and put out the cold meats, cheese and warm bread that she had made in her home oven, along with a fruit loaf, plain and fruit scones, and butter and jam for everyone to help themselves. They had almost finished when Filip and Anna and the children arrived as arranged, to meet Mr and Mrs Snowden.

'By, tha's a big lad!' Mr Snowden proclaimed as Filip towered over him to shake his hand, and Filip looked about for someone to translate for him.

Roland obliged in his strongest Irish accent. 'Well now, he said you're a big feller to be sure,' which left him even more confused, but he burst out into a great guffaw which set everyone else laughing.

When they had all finished eating and drinking, Ellen saw Billy glance at the clock; they had yet to show her mother and father the bakery. Billy would be wanting to move off home soon, although now that the days were longer there wasn't quite the urgency that came in the winter months.

They came up with a compromise. Billy would drive his parents, Florence, Ellen and Anna to see the bakery, and then after waving them goodbye Ellen and Anna would walk back to the house where the rest of them waited.

The children lined up as their grandmother told them to, and Zophia, Jakub and Aron joined them too whilst she fished in her cavernous bag for paper bags full of sweets: barley drops, fudge, chocolate truffles and treacle toffee.

'I'll know to make twice as many next time I come,' she said as they waved goodbye and climbed into the wagon, 'and I see there'll be another mouth to feed.' She glanced at Anna's thickening waist line and smiled. 'But that one won't be eating sweets for a while.'

Just as Filip hadn't understood Ellen's father, neither did Anna fully understand Mrs Snowden's Holderness accent, but she nodded as if she did and patted her midriff. 'I will have English baby when I see you again, yes? If it is boy we will call him Albert and if a girl she will be Rose Victoria, like English rose and Queen Victoria.'

They pulled up outside Bill Foster's shop, which was closed today, being a Sunday, and Ellen went to the door to rap on it. She looked up to the upstairs window and Bill Foster appeared, waved, and disappeared again. They waited a moment and presently the door was unlocked and opened.

'Mr Foster – Bill,' Ellen said. 'Should I not have a key to your yard, and then I wouldn't disturb you?' It was the first time she had seen him without his beige overall covering his clothes, and over his cord trousers he wore a pale blue wool jumper which suited his sandy hair.

She introduced him to her mother and father, Billy and Florence and he put out his hand to each of them in turn.

'Mrs Snowden and Mr Snowden? G'day to you both. Won't you come along in? Brother Billy? How are you, mate, and is this your young lady? Nice to meet you, miss.'

Ellen's father had kept his eyes on Bill Foster since he'd shaken his hand, and during a pause in the conversation in the bakery kitchen he put his hand on his wife's shoulder and whispered, 'I don't know what you think, Sarah, but yon chap is 'very spit of your brother George.'

'He is.' Mrs Snowden's voice was husky. 'I saw 'likeness straight away. He could be him come back to 'land of 'living.'

She brought out her handkerchief again and blew her nose. 'My eldest brother,' she explained, 'and a family name.'

Bill Foster seemed rooted to the spot. 'If that's not the oddest thing, I don't know what is. I have a brother George too,

331

the liveliest feller you'd ever meet. He's a good deal younger than me, always in scrapes, but always comes up smiling! We'll have a chat about it some time, shall we, about our beginnings? I reckon it's not that far back in our heritage to trace to the start, or at least as far as we know.' He gave a great beaming smile. 'It's good to know I've got my own folks living here in England as well as in Australia, and I reckon that you might like to see the place in Hull where the first William Foster, a whaling man, lived with his family. I managed to track him down when I first came to England; I found a few folk who had heard of him and his family.'

Ellen had never seen her mother so moved as she was now; she always kept her emotions under control, and although she showed an interest in Ellen's plans and expressed astonishment at the massive range, her daughter saw that she constantly glanced at Bill Foster and it was as if she were seeing her late brother again.

'You must go to see this place in Hull, Ellen, you and your bairns,' her mother told her, 'and you must tek Lizzie, and see where it all began, and put down roots again.'

'Don't expect much,' Bill was anxious to convey. 'I was shocked when I saw it. I reckon he must have been as poor as a bandicoot for his family to live there, but then he survived right enough, to leave so many descendants.'

'Holderness air saved them,' Mrs Snowden asserted. 'There's nowt like it. You must come, Cousin Bill,' she said, and again there was a catch in her voice, 'and meet 'rest of our family. We have eight daughters, not just 'two that you've met, another son as well as Billy, and there's other members of my family too.'

'Better pack a large trunk when you come,' Ellen's father grunted. 'It'll tek some time to meet 'em all.'

Ellen and Bill Foster had come to an amicable arrangement regarding the bakery and the making and selling of the bread, and both were benefiting for customers were increasing in droves. Ellen had agreed to take an assistant, the sister of the

332

errand lad, to wash up the bakery utensils, scrub down the baking table and wash the floor every day after she had finished baking, which eased her load, for her priority was always to be home in time to be with the children and take over from Julia, who looked after them so well.

Occasionally Ellen helped out in the shop, serving the customers, and Bill often referred to her as his niece if anyone ever asked if they were related.

Lizzie and Roland were planning their wedding and both had agreed that they would marry in the ancient church of St Mary's in Sculcoates in October: Roland in particular was pleased with the choice of church as he said that whenever he passed it he'd be able to think of a happier time rather than the sad memory of the boys' funeral.

'It's such a time for weddings,' Ellen remarked to Harry. 'Edyta and Karl have arranged for theirs to take place in September and I'm *so* delighted that her brother has agreed to attend the ceremony and bring their mother too. I hope she'll come to 'party afterwards so that I can see her again. I'd become very fond of her.'

'I know that you did,' Harry acknowledged. 'I'm sure she'll be there if her health permits, but what about Lizzie and Roland's wedding? Will all of 'Holderness relatives come? I know your sisters will want to be here; they'll be curious about Roland.'

'They'll not all be able to come, but Lizzie says that Roland is in charge of 'arrangements and he's going to book a room in an hotel for 'party afterwards; someone he knows, he said, and I wondered if it might be Mrs Lucan's place, but I didn't like to ask. I can't believe that Lizzie's allowing him to do everything; she'll have a hand in it somewhere. Sarah and Mary are so excited since Lizzie said they can be flower girls,' she told him, and added, 'and I'll have all on to do the baking.'

'No,' he said. 'You don't need to. Roland is arranging 'food for reception, he told me so.'

'Oh!' Ellen seemed disappointed. 'I was looking forward to doing it.'

333

'No!' he said again. 'You're going to relax and enjoy it and not worry about whether or not you've made enough bread and cakes for everybody.'

She laughed. 'You're right,' she agreed. 'I am going to enjoy it. The last wedding we went to was ours, and that was 'best one ever!'

Harry put his arms about her and swung her gently round in their small parlour. 'It was,' he whispered, and nibbled her ear. 'And I got 'best girl ever! What a lot has happened in such a short time, Ellen.' He looked tenderly down at her. 'Three lovely children, 'best gift anyone could give a man – and oh, this last year! How lucky we've been to emerge from such a harsh beginning to our life in Hull.'

'But we've survived, Harry,' she said softly. 'We've come out of 'bad times and into 'good.'

'You realize, don't you, that we'll have to leave this cottage one day? Once we're properly on our feet and I'm earning a salary?'

'Yes,' she said, a little sadly, 'and I'll miss it. It's been a haven for us; but one day, though not just yet, I hope, there'll be someone else deserving of a chance of a sound roof over their heads, just as we were, and then we'll move on. But we're more secure now and we'll find somewhere else where we'll be able to thrive.'

'Lizzie,' Ellen said one Sunday afternoon. The sisters were alone, as Harry had taken the children to the park. 'You're going to be busy soon, planning your wedding and honeymoon, and Roland said he wanted you to enjoy a quiet time before the mill starts production.'

Lizzie nodded. 'The mill is going up much faster than he anticipated. They'll have the roof on before Christmas and they can start fitting the machinery in 'new year. Filip is hoping that Anna will have her baby before then and then he won't have to worry that she's on her own whilst he's busy with 'installation.'

'I'll stay with her,' Ellen said, determined that she would fit in visits to her friend in spite of the bakery work. 'Sarah and Mary will be starting school after Christmas, so I'll have some time.

334

Julia says she'll still look after Thomas, and Aron too if Anna wants her to.'

'So – what were you going to say?'

'I was going to ask if you'd like to come into town next Sunday. Bill Foster said he'd take us to look at where William Foster lived if we didn't want to wait for Ma and Da to come; they're dependent on Billy to bring them and he's busy at 'minute. He and Florence will be getting wed too before they leave. I can hardly bear to think of him going so far,' she added. 'Do you think he'll ever come back?'

Lizzie lazily stretched her arms above her head. 'Maybe his great-grandchildren will come,' she said. 'Like Bill Foster did.'

Ellen shook her head. 'I like everyone close by,' she said.

Lizzie raised her eyebrows. 'You left, didn't you?'

'That's different,' Ellen sighed. 'Not 'same at all. But anyway, will you?'

Lizzie yawned. 'What?'

'Come with us to see 'Foster house?'

'Yes, course I will, you goose.'

Ellen came and sat down next to Lizzie. 'I'll miss you when you leave here, Lizzie.'

'I know,' Lizzie said, and put her arm round her sister. 'Best thing I ever did was come and live with you and Harry and your bairns. It made me realize what I was missing.' She laughed. 'And look what I found, an exciting opportunity to use my brain, and a handsome loving man waiting for me.'

Ellen gave her a squeeze. 'I'm so happy for you, Lizzie, and Roland has been good for us all.'

The following Sunday, Ellen drove Nellie, Lizzie sat beside Ellen and Sarah, Mary and Thomas sat in the back of the trap whilst Harry and Bill Foster walked into town. When they drove along the cobbled road that ran alongside Junction Dock Thomas called enthusiastically for them to look at all the ships; then they made a turn down a narrow street which brought them into Market Place, where they waited for Harry and Bill to catch up and give them further directions.

335

'There's so much to see, Lizzie,' Ellen said breathlessly. 'Look at that lovely church. This must be where Ma said it looked as though there was a good market. Do you think they sell bread? I could have a stall here.'

'I thought I was supposed to be the one with ambition,' Lizzie said wryly. 'Slowly, slowly, little sister, take your time; Harry's going to be earning a good living before long.'

'I'm not thinking of 'money, Lizzie. It's hard being without it, but I'm enjoying what I do; the aroma of bread rising and 'wholesome smell when it's fresh out of 'oven. It's the staff of life, an age-old occupation, and I like being part of its creation, I suppose.'

'Come on, you chump,' Lizzie teased. 'Here's Harry and our uncle Bill.'

They stabled Nellie and the cart in an inn yard and booked a table in the hostelry to eat dinner later. Then they set off walking towards the area where Bill said the house stood in one of the old courts.

They could smell fruit, flowers and vegetables even before they reached a long street which had warehouses on either side where empty wooden crates were stacked outside the premises. 'It'll be very busy early in a morning,' Lizzie remarked, and Bill said it was, and that he came twice a week to buy the vegetables he sold in his shop.

'Now then,' he mumbled, looking about him. 'Where's this place I'm looking for? Blanket Row, it was called.'

Sarah was holding her mother's hand, and suddenly gripped it so hard that Ellen jumped.

'What is it, Sarah? Does something hurt?'

Sarah didn't answer but shook her hand free and pulled away, her feet scurrying.

'Sarah, come back,' Ellen called, but the little girl didn't turn.

Ellen quickened her pace to catch up with her and then almost crashed into her as Sarah suddenly stopped by a narrow alley, Martin's Alley, which was wedged between two warehouses.

'This is it,' she faltered. 'It's down here.'

Bill Foster turned and looked at Harry. 'So it is,' he said. 'How did she know? I remember now, I came to it from the back of these buildings and cut through. There are lots of these little alleyways running through, and some of the houses – if you can call them such – are not fit to live in.'

They peered down; there was no drain, only a gutter, which was blocked with mud. It wasn't a court, as Ellen was expecting, but an alley with a wider entrance at the other end. 'Surely no one lives down here now?' she said to herself, not expecting an answer.

Sarah slid her hand back into her mother's. 'They did,' she said in a low whisper. Her eyes were huge and her face pale. 'Once they did.'

CHAPTER FIFTY

'Sarah.' Ellen gently shook her daughter's hand. 'How do you know this is 'place we're looking for?'

'I don't know,' Sarah whispered. 'It's somewhere at 'bottom of this alley. I just know. It was the man, Will, who lived there, but not the little girl called Sarah.'

'Did somebody tell you?' Harry bent down to face her. 'Mebbe Gran Snowden?'

She nodded. 'Mebbe, but she's never been. Gran'd never been to Hull before she came to see us.'

'We'll go down and tek a look,' Harry said, 'and never mind the mud.' He told Thomas to jump on his back, knowing he'd splash about in it otherwise.

'Will you come, Lizzie?' Ellen said, holding her hand out to Mary, who was hanging back.

'It's dark,' Mary objected.

Lizzie took her other hand. 'Let's be brave together,' she said.

'I don't remember it being as bad as this,' Bill said as he brought up the rear. 'But it's some years since I was here.'

They reached the other end, which led into another narrow court and then another alley. This had a wider entrance but narrowed into a thin strip with six houses, three on each side of an opening just wide enough to walk through. At the other end they found themselves in a wider street called Blanket Row.

Ellen looked back and called to Sarah, who was standing looking at one of the houses. 'This one,' she said softly. 'This is it.'

338

Bill Foster was staring back at the alley. 'Look,' he said, pointing up to the top of the wall. 'Wyke Entry. This is the one all right.' He looked at Sarah. 'Second sight, we call it. Aborigines have it, and so did one of my aunties. It's a gift. Sarah should cherish it.'

Ellen held out her hand to bring Sarah to her and Mary said, 'Sarah always knows when something's going to happen, don't you, Sarah?'

Sarah nodded, and when Ellen put her arm around her she leaned into her. It's a gift, Bill Foster had said, so the gift had come down the family line from somewhere. She looked down the dark alleyway and she believed what Sarah and Bill had said, that this had once been the home of her ancestors before they moved to Holderness.

I hope they had a good and fulfilling life, she thought, pondering on the many branches of the family that must be scattered in all directions. We have come back to our roots, she thought, sure they would stay in this welcoming town. And, she realized with a flash of understanding, we have come home.

ENDING

In September Edyta and Karl were married in a quiet ceremony and had a merry celebration party afterwards where Ellen was able to meet up with Mrs Johnson, who was looking fit and well, and told her that she was pleased to see her daughter so happy.

In October came Lizzie and Roland's wedding, a dignified service as they had both been married and widowed before, and Lizzie took flowers from her bouquet to lay on the resting place of two boys in the peaceful graveyard.

The wedding reception, as Ellen had guessed, was held in Mrs Lucan's hotel, the Maritime, where the bride and groom were staying overnight before catching a train to Liverpool and then a ship to Ireland, where they would visit the fine city of Dublin before moving on to the country district where Roland had been banished from his family. His father must be long gone from this earth, he'd told Lizzie, but he lived in hope that perhaps there might be at least one brother alive and ready to welcome him.

And there was; Lizzie sent a postcard to say they were visiting County Mayo and had found not just one brother but two, both fishermen making their living from the wild and plentiful waters of the Atlantic who had greeted Roland with wide open arms.

Christmas Day was spent in the warm and cosy cottage, and whilst snow fell gently down outside their windows Ellen and Harry and their children, Lizzie and Roland and Bill Foster, spent a happy day consuming a golden goose provided by

Roland, vegetables from Bill and a Christmas pudding cooked by Ellen some weeks before.

On Boxing Day, they invited some of their neighbours to visit them: Julia and her brother and her mother too; and the two sisters who proved to be not shy at all as Ellen had thought, but very merry and entertaining in spite of being almost penniless.

And then there was Anna's baby. Filip hammered on the cottage door at five in the morning during the first week of the new year to say they had God's gift of a daughter; they welcomed him in and this giant of a man broke down in tears and said how happy they were and kissed both Ellen and Harry on each cheek and hugged all the sleepy children that he had wakened.

In the first week of March, as the first green buds began to show on the stalwart trees alongside the river bank, the opening of the new mill took place. On the first day of production workers and their families crowded outside the gates while dignitaries from the corporation waited in the mill yard with some of the other mill owners who although competitors had been willing to give a helping hand during the disastrous explosion. At ten o'clock exactly, Kirkwood appeared at the mill doors with Tannerson, Lizzie and Harry by his side, and with a look of pride gave the thumbs up to Tannerson. The rumble and reverberation of conveyors beginning to roll echoed from the mill, and a rousing cheer was heard down the length of Wincomlee.

The sign was high at the top of the factory wall. *Tannerson and Partner* was painted in clean white letters on the red brick; they'd brought the children to witness this momentous day and Harry pointed out the sign to them. He put his arm round Ellen's shoulders. 'One day,' he murmured, 'there'll be an *s* at the end of *Partner.*'

Ellen looked at him curiously. 'Lizzie is the partner,' she said.

'Aye, but Tannerson has said, and Lizzie agreed, that one day they'll need others on 'board of directors. Not yet – it's too soon, and too much has happened in such a short time to make any decisions – but this is going to be a successful growing company,

341

and who knows what or who might be coming next? Lizzie might produce a board of directors of their own. But in 'meantime . . .'

Ellen smiled and they all held hands as they went to collect their new trap, a larger one than the other, which was just as well, she thought, for they would soon be needing extra space. Harry glanced at her; he'd said that he always knew when she had a secret to tell him, and she guessed that he was gleaning the news now. Sarah wasn't the only one with second sight. 'Let's go home, Harry. Tomorrow is another day,'

What was it, she thought as they bowled back to the cottage, that someone had once said about circles? That we gather together the people we care about and encircle them, our family in one, our forebears in another, and our friends in the next. They're conjoined, timeless and infinite, and bound together, and there we have it, she thought. A circle within a circle, without an end.

ACKNOWLEDGEMENTS

When incorporating local history into my novels it is essential to bring in authenticity in order to capture the essential elements of the once living past. I have found throughout my writing career that local historians and those with an interest in social history have been more than willing to furnish information on their particular subject, and I therefore give my sincere thanks to:

Paul Gibson www.paul-gibson.com for permission to use details from his website of the past industries in the Wincomlee and Sculcoates district.

Dan F. Tunnicliffe and John Netherwood for details of Mrs Christiana Rose who was one of the few women, and probably the first, to be involved in the seed-crushing oil industry in Hull and who with her partners founded what subsequently became Rose, Downs and Thompson Ltd.

Marian Shaw on Pearson Park from her book *Zachariah Pearson: Man of Hull* (The Grimsay Press, 196 Rose Street, Edinburgh).

John R. Key for driving me through Sculcoates and Wincomlee districts to 'set a place' in my mind, where I visited the old St Mary's graveyard and knew I had to incorporate it into the novel.

The sketches and drawings of F. S. Smith's *Images of Victorian Hull* are always inspirational in creating a scene from what is now long gone from this vibrant city, and I can heartily recommend them for anyone with an interest in local history. Enquiries to the Hull History Centre www.hullhistorycentre.org.uk/home.aspx

Finally, but not least, I give my appreciative thanks to the Transworld publishing team both past and present who, over the last twenty-five years since 1993 when my first novel *The Hungry Tide* won the Catherine Cookson Prize and propelled me into a much-enjoyed writing career, have shown their support and encouragement.

Larry Finlay, MD, the late Diane Pearson, Linda Evans, Vivien Thompson production editor and Nancy Webber peerless copy editor with their keen and discerning eyes deserve a special mention, as does my present invaluable editor Francesca Best. There are many more unsung team members, editorial assistants, proof-readers, design staff, publicity and marketing, et al, who ensure the books are ready for our readers. I thank you all.

AUTHOR'S NOTE

Twenty-five years ago in September 1993 the most exciting event ever to happen to me was when I was awarded the Catherine Cookson Fiction prize, presented in honour of author Catherine Cookson's long career as a storyteller.

As a storyteller myself and now with a long career of my own behind me, with many regular readers who tell me they have read all of my books, I thought that with my latest book *A Place to Call Home* I would put out a teasing challenge to my regular readers by including some of the characters or characters' names from previous novels in the latest story. I hope my newer readers, after reading *A Place to Call Home*, might be curious or interested enough to find out who these characters were and what role they played in previous novels. Fun!

That's what reading should be: entertaining, stimulating, informative and a chance to travel to another point in history, another place in the world, and to meet people who are not real in the flesh, but who can live on in our hearts. And we can have all of this without leaving our armchairs.

Val

ABOUT THE AUTHOR

Since winning the Catherine Cookson Prize for Fiction for her first novel, *The Hungry Tide*, **Val Wood** has published twenty-three novels and become one of the most popular authors in the UK.

Born in the mining town of Castleford, Val came to East Yorkshire as a child and has lived in Hull and rural Holderness where many of her novels are set. She now lives in the market town of Beverley.

When she is not writing, Val is busy promoting libraries and supporting many charities. In 2017 she was awarded an honorary doctorate by the University of Hull for service and dedication to literature.

Find out more about Val Wood's novels by visiting her website: www.valeriewood.co.uk